sad strains of a gay waltz

sad strains
of a gay waltz

A NOVEL

IRENE DISCHE

METROPOLITAN BOOKS • HENRY HOLT AND COMPANY • NEW YORK

Metropolitan Books
Henry Holt and Company, Inc.
Publishers since 1866
115 West 18th Street
New York, New York 10011

Metropolitan Books™ is an imprint of
Henry Holt and Company, Inc.

Library of Congress Cataloging-in-Publication Data
Dische, Irene.
[Fremdes Gefühl.   English]
Sad strains of a gay waltz : a novel / Irene Dische. — 1st
American ed.
p.   cm.
ISBN 0-8050-5357-3 (alk. paper)
I. Title.
PT 2664.1725 F 7413   1997
833—dc21   97-9992   CIP

Henry Holt books are available for special promotions and
premiums. For details contact: Director, Special Markets.

First American Edition 1997

Designed by Iris Weinstein

Printed in the United States of America
All first editions are printed on acid-free paper. ∞

10   9   8   7   6   5   4   3   2   1

CONTENTS

waltz 3

PART ONE

chapter 1
Marcia maestosa: Benedikt's family, its history and his
place in it, leading up to his current predicament 7

chapter 2
Lightly, nervously: Benedikt falls into the hands of a
psychiatrist 18

chapter 3
Not always the same tempo, and not as sweet as others
like it: Benedikt's love life was not conventional, really 29

chapter 4
Speed it up: certain events occur which have no obvious
relationship to each other, being attached by an invisible
but as yet slack bond called the Future 36

chapter 5
Hurrying on: Benedikt has his future predicted by various
acquaintances. Opinions are divided 43

chapter 6
Seriously now: Benedikt thinks his plan for survival has
backfired, and perhaps it has, but perhaps it hasn't   54

chapter 7
Picking up speed: the fact that the Russian mother exists
quickly begins to affect Benedikt. Can he get rid of her
again?   66

chapter 8
Long-lasting sweetness: Benedikt dreams about his
homeland   75

chapter 9
Resolutely: fate has its way with Benedikt. He objects,
but cannot find words or actions to oppose it   81

chapter 10
Presto!: Benedikt makes a fast decision. He retreats   88

PART TWO

chapter 11
Without regret: Benedikt returns home   97

chapter 12
Dragging: some changes in Benedikt's life are inevitable,
some unpredictable   116

chapter 13
Interruption of a silence: Valerie giggles twice while
stillness regales the Countess with memories   129

chapter 14
Gravely, majestically: Benedikt takes part in a family
ceremony   135

chapter 15
Volubly: Benedikt expresses some ideas about child-
rearing. This makes Marja nervous   148

chapter 16
Wild steps: the wedding guests and the newlyweds take
certain liberties   156

chapter 17
Wilder still: the liberties that certain humans take affect
the animal kingdom   169

chapter 18
The maternal heart, fluctuating   177

chapter 19
Upwards and downwards   187

chapter 20
For the advanced only: slowly, but with overtones and
undertones. After the party is over the aftermath begins   195

PART THREE

chapter 21
Powerfully: Valerie develops. But Marja grabs all the
attention   203

chapter 22
Keine Ruh in Tag und Nacht: Einstein's ghost is fed up with
being asked for advice. Nevertheless, he gives some   217

chapter 23
Allegro assai: fear   220

chapter 24
Binding: Benedikt and Marja re-enact the pietà. Einstein
is watching. He is not impressed   227

chapter 25
Smoothly: love begets confessions and all kinds of
nastiness   233

chapter 26
Slow rocking: Benedikt sets forth his plan to get rid of
Marja   242

chapter 27
Frantic: Isabella sets all sorts of cogs into motion, without
realizing it   254

chapter 28
Forced: a climax, but rather different from the
planned one   263

PART FOUR

chapter 29
Hesitantly: Benedikt makes some decisions. He visits his
sister and finds his relationship to her changed   269

chapter 30
Singing pain: Benedikt returns to Berlin and tries to
forget his loss by finding another child   274

chapter 31
An aria: with great expressiveness, including a pinch of
irony: Benedikt searches his body for the source of
emotions   279

chapter 32
At the tempo fate designates: Benedikt, his friends, and
his acquaintances prove once more that if novelty repeats
itself again and again, turning over like the ingredients of
a soup cooking in a pot, then the soup in the pot must
be oblivion, and this proves that novelty is oblivion   285

chapter 33
Minuet   303

Any strong emotion is like a tone of music: it makes memories along the entire range of one's history resonate. No tone exists by itself; there are no pure emotions. And these memories carry other emotions, including hope, disappointment, and rage, so that the feeling of love in an adult is always a violent chord.

—EINSTEIN'S GHOST

sad strains of a gay waltz

His sister had cooked him some soup but he planned not to eat. She said, 'Sure, oh, you'll eat, since I've gone to such trouble, you'll eat. You can die when you're finished.'

He did as she ordered; why not? All morning he'd sat on the sofa, and after the soup he went back, as if food only fattened the shame that he felt for a physical need. But his sister was quicker this time. In spite of his height he was frailer than she. She could push him away.

'I was hoping you'd tell me a story or two, about numbers that never existed—then they appeared, that sort of thing. You can die when you're finished.'

He did as she ordered; why not? He stood at his desk with his back turned to her and explained his ideas while she lay on his sofa, spreading her toes in a fit of enjoyment, admiring her brother, who loathed admiration, she knew. When he saw her expression he headed for bed.

She pleaded, 'Oh please, let me love you, it's fun. Like adoring a stone. You might try it yourself, admiring someone—a child might be good. You'd be able to die with your feelings informed, you'd know what you missed.'

He couldn't escape her, a satellite orbiting him, and he cried, 'We must leave, for God's sake!'

He cheered up at the airport. He waved and he smiled. On the bus going home, he sat at the window, a hard frosty shoulder, and wished for a change. That same afternoon he drafted an ad for the personal page:

UNMARRIED MAN WITH TERMINAL DISEASE
SEEKS CHILD, PREFERABLY TODDLER,
FOR PURPOSES OF ADOPTION.

He sat on the sofa, and waited a while till a rush of good humour, which some would call hope, overwhelmed him. He enjoyed the short walk to the mailbox. Why not? Well, why not? His limp had a bounce in it, turning his usual shuffle into a dance.

part one

CHAPTER 1

*Marcia maestosa: Benedikt's family, its history and his place in it,
leading up to his current predicament*

The sick man called himself 'Herr Waller,' and this was, in its brevity—'Herr,' 'Waller'—a statement about his family. He belonged to a minority, a besieged population, a people who claim and feel kinship even though they live scattered all over the globe, a singular weed that does not crossbreed easily. They remain united by their certainty that they are special, even the poorest feel this and strive to practise their traditions. Periodically robbed as a group of their social standing, individuals have nevertheless often filled important positions in society. Their surnames give them away, as does their appearance, their behaviour, their odd relationship to money, and the fact that they can unfailingly pick each other out in public places. The sick man belonged to the aristocracy.

From the first time he consorted with other children, on his first day at school, he detested his full name, Benedikt August Anton Cecil August Count Waller von Wallerstein. He blushed just remembering the extra bits, like a shabby fringe, and refused to sign his schoolwork.

His teachers, weak with confused envy, tweaked him. 'But aren't you proud of your family?'

The word 'family' made him wince. There was not much left, anyhow, in the way of living examples. His parents had died before his memory could grasp them, during a marital quarrel that accelerated into a car crash. The two survivors, brother and sister, were raised by visitors, cranky staff, and a grandmother hastily summoned from a gambling hall in Lindau. She enjoyed losing in small sums, not in large ones; it was her only son.

She had given up her apartment next to the casino, returned home to the uncomfortable fourteenth-century castle a few miles inland from the lake, in Biederstein. She was going to mourn, she announced in a voice so soft it peaked at a whisper, in bed, where she kept her social register. She had a bedroom made up for her behind double doors that opened into the huge front hall.

A few years passed. She no longer mentioned her loss but she stayed supine; she had become a resident of the sheets. There she worried about her health, searched the Bible and astrology guides for tips and the social register for hard facts, used up time, sucked chocolates, dictated invitations to everyone she knew, whispered orders to the nurses, secretaries, chauffeurs, children, saved up the hours to use them again, whetting her temper on her will to live. She consulted the register to determine in which of twenty guest rooms a visitor belonged and what kind of flowers they deserved; she was less successful dictating the seasons, which she followed through the upper panes of her bedroom window, wet weather enraging her because humidity made the gossamer pages of her old books stick together. She was thought to pray but no one was certain, just as no one had ever seen her eat, although her use of the bedpan was a matter much discussed by the nurses. In the evenings, the servants heaved and scraped open the double doors of her bedroom and the sound, painful to the dog's ears, prompted the howling that came to signal dinnertime. She presided over meals from her bed, the long table positioned with one end in front of her doors. Although she always stayed in exactly the same place, her principal method of intimidation was the ambush. She sat up in bed, pulled the folds of her cheeks into a bunch at her ears, and asked visitors whether she should have her face lifted. She once reared up from a prone position to slap an American woman for comparing the Schwarzwald to the Catskills. The visitors served her need to ridicule. After they left, she summoned the children, asked for their impressions. Snorting at their slight powers of observation, she showed them what they had missed by imitating the guests, most ferociously those who had, in her mind, warranted the best treatment. After her performance she watched from the pillows, waiting until her grandchildren's laughter turned warm and hilarious. Suddenly, she snapped at them for laughing about their betters. They retreated, cowed, wishing her dead. Benedikt loved only his sister, who had been with him at the moment of impact and with whom he bicycled every morning through the arches and the gates, past the deer and the dogs, over the bridge, down the lane, downhill, to the village school. He began by despising his grandmother and went on to hate the staff at home, the teachers, and finally, and most vehemently, his peers.

Sadistic fantasies preoccupied the boy. After school, he trudged up the narrow stairs—even as a child he had a slow, cautious gait—to his bare round room in one of the towers. He pulled the white muslin curtain over the tiny window, opened a wooden chest filled with coloured notebooks, selected one, then a pencil from his desk, and lay down on his bed, a hard historical object he shared with innumerable ancestors, and began to draw. He always drew the same thing: stick figures battling each other with swords, spears, truncheons, whips. He held the pencil in his fist and pressed so hard that the point pierced through the paper. He clamped his tongue between his teeth, and sometimes he had blood on his lips afterwards. Apart from this hobby, he was the gentlest of creatures. At school he never quarrelled; he declined to take sides. No amount of teasing or even hurting could make him fight back, but he did not run away, either. Having a strong sense of honour, he turned the other cheek. He perplexed his uncles, refusing to join them on hunts, and never set foot inside the castle chapel because the crucifix threw him into a turmoil of aversion. The stateliness of his step was simply a precaution to avoid crushing insects. His family nickname became Lämmchen, Little Lamb.

When he reached his teens, he stopped drawing fighting

men, and instead of notebooks he bought newspapers. Now he was riveted by the social injustices depicted in the news and gradually began to see them at home; he became a socialist. His convictions drifted along the muddy banks of the Left, finding them too slippery to get a foothold there. He spent his small allowance on various causes. He could not say no. He was incapable of uttering the word. He gave his money to whoever asked for it, willing to share what he did not need in the first place, as his appetite for money or creature comforts was minimal. Nor did he crave success or applause, and he took his talents for granted; nature had been generous with him.

Benedikt Waller grew into a handsome young man. He was tall and regular as a cupboard, his hair golden, his eyes wide and blue without being ingenuous, because they did not convey any warmth, so there was something rather noble about him. He was not proud of his looks, because he cared so little about others that he did not care either what others might think of him. Yet he thought a great deal about beauty. His libido had dropped anchor there; he loved higher mathematics and all forms of technical achievement. Fairness as a kind of symmetry became his reason for preferring a Communist state and condemning the German past, or disliking the thought that he was a German at all.

At fifteen, he spent money on himself for the first time, buying a telescope from an American mail-order catalogue. He set this up in the highest tower, beneath the skylight of the so-called *Angst* room, where the young, the female, and the weak of his ancestors could hide if the castle was under attack and where later relatives had built the tower clock, a huge machine that pounded the time through the whole house. With his telescope perched next to the dark grinding clockworks, he discovered the simplicity and grandeur of the universe. Perfection, he concluded, was never to be found in living things. And finally, he admitted to himself: living things were ugly, no perfection there at all. Breathing was hideous: a form of constantly taking, it made noise, especially at night. His grandmother's snores made century-old walls wobble.

Nature, he concluded, was an experiment of grotesque complexity doomed to failure. Evolution cramming molecules in ever-crazier configurations created one Frankenstein after the next, with a kind of wanton fallibility. A good example was the pettiness of inventing two sexes, only to complicate matters, after a single one had proven perfectly viable. But no one ever questioned it. Instead, they waxed sentimental. Everyone pondered the sense or fairness of disease but not of reproduction, a time-consuming pursuit that obsessed all moving beings and resulted in pregnancy, with its danger of explosion. And without any critical reflection they took the countryside to be attractive. Benedikt shuddered beneath the trees because they were so selfish, unmoving, uncommunicative, flailing in every breeze, grasping for sunlight. He dreaded the hysterical colours of spring and the unintelligence of grass. And yet, living things loved Benedikt, Count Waller von Wallerstein. Dogs preferred him, ancient forgetful relatives always remembered his birthday, the children appointed him their favourite uncle and flocked to him. Benedikt was never unkind to them: their friendliness puzzled him, and he waited patiently for them to turn away.

The estate included a forest and a hops plantation. The rituals of rural family life made going outdoors necessary and emphasized all aspects of life itself, with pompous baptisms and funerals and an endless roster of unfamiliar people all liable to visit on account of a mutual relative several centuries back. He didn't listen when the family talked about the family. He sulked, remembering that recently his fine old family had not even had the distinction of co-operating with other fine old families in opposing Hitler; his father had been a high-ranking fan with a secure desk job. No one felt embarrassed about this. They were forever chafing about the unfairness of the Nuremberg trials, where the judges had failed to take into account the defendant's virtues. What an outstanding hunter his father had been, for example. One recalled a buck he had levelled with one shot from a distance of two hundred metres.

'What do you say to that, Benedikt?' an uncle once asked. 'Isn't that inspiring?'

Benedikt shrugged his shoulders.

'My grandson seems to carry every dead beast on his conscience,' his grandmother commented from the bed.

'Oh dear; but why, how, since when?' rustled the aunts.

'Ah, the reasons,' complained the old Countess. 'I find psychological explanations so boring. Racial ones are amusing— that's probably why they're considered wicked! But it's a fact— Benedikt's bad conscience is simply typical of us. We always felt responsible for everyone and everything.'

'That's the whole point of hunting: responsibility. To keep down the population of animals who would otherwise die horribly from overcrowding,' bayed the uncles.

And then the Countess said, 'See, you're a perfect specimen of a Waller von Wallerstein, Lämmchen.'

Benedikt, heckled out of his silence, spoke up. Staring down at his plate, he recited the family history, beginning with the crusader who sacked Bethlehem in 1295, followed by a dynasty of self-righteous knights, an imperial debt collector rewarded with the first 500 hectares of forest after taking on an archbishop's army, and on and on through the centuries. There were few off generations, the relations' distinguished participation in every war led to a steady accumulation of land and wealth which they consolidated through marriage and theft.

'And my father . . .' He flushed with shame.

His grandmother smiled and asked him, 'Would you care to be related to someone else?'

He didn't answer but he thought: Einstein.

Everyone stared at the mute, flushed teenager. He'd grow sensible in time, he was certainly a beautiful boy. He could be a knight, his aunt said later, no pimples at all.

As Benedikt grew up he took less and less notice of people. Even his relationship with Einstein was a professional one. For a while he conversed with him daily, spending his afternoons in the chapel he used to avoid, where, after lighting a candle, he could chat quietly with his mentor. He kept his eyes away from the most morbid Christian paraphernalia and concentrated: he pictured Einstein without a body, a shadow smelling of cosmic wind, who spoke with Benedikt's voice.

One day his little sister had followed him there and sat in a back pew observing him.

'Why did you light a candle?' She grabbed his sleeve on the way out. He shook her off. 'Why!' she pressed him. 'To whom!' She always prevailed, an energetic, freckle-faced girl on the prowl for simple pleasures. She laughed at him straight out when he told her.

'You can't talk to dead people, Benedikt. And why should you want to? Imagine if the dead really went straight from earth to heaven, exactly as they are at the end, and you could visit them there as if heaven was some sort of old-age home. Then it would be overrun with the sick, bad-tempered, and senile. Einstein was ancient when he died.' She relished talking sternly to him, and that he always listened to her and never to anyone else.

Benedikt's fury at nature had cooled, hardened into indifference. He lost all interest in socialism after he realized he didn't like the idea of being ruled by the working class. He wanted to learn everything that Einstein had known, in order to continue on where the prophet had left off. He worked so hard at his studies that he forgot his body entirely. Sometimes grogginess overcame him and he realized he hadn't slept for two nights. He skipped several grades at school and took his high-school exams at sixteen.

When he received his results a few months later, he asked for an audience with his grandmother. He stood at the foot of her bed, looked along the covered Colossus of her body into her sly eyes that spun with second thoughts, and told her that she consisted of protons, neutrons, and electrons, no different from any stick or stone. And she wouldn't last that way. Only the laws of physics, he said, survive.

With a smile of condescension she accepted his decision to study physics at a university instead of taking over the business of running the estate. She sat up a bit higher in bed, the chocolates spilling everywhere when he came to say goodbye. He glanced up at her window before climbing into a taxi and saw her standing there, enormous, unsteady, framed by the fortress of generations before and after him. It transpired later, in the walled city where he felt at home, that there would be no more generations after, because he, the last in the line, was unable to make love to a woman.

Intensely happy and intensely miserable families have one thing in common: the children, as the only witnesses, become especially close. The sick man was just one year older than Dolly. The resemblance between them was striking, but their temperaments were opposite: Dolly was outgoing, socially skilful, and not as intelligent. She was nevertheless inordinately attached to her brother. She also tried to free herself from their family, moving to Lindau, where she became a secretary, but it seemed to her that she had even greater problems freeing herself from her brother. At twenty she had never had a boyfriend, because no one compared to him. She was matter-of-fact about it: she wrote him a letter and complained. He wrote back to her: he was twenty-one already, and there was no woman that interested him. He was open to the suggestion that he might be in love with Dolly. The two met a few miles across the German border in Switzerland, drove south into the mountains, to a village which Nietzsche had visited with his sister. After a romantic walk taken at Dolly's insistence, they checked into a hotel as Herr and Frau Waller from Wallerstein in Germany.

The manager, a hard-eyed woman tired of the humanity that checked in just to hammer around on the beds, treated them with respect, because this lot was married. She had a fright at the size of Benedikt's suitcase and alerted the staff to the possibility of theft from the bathroom and minibar. But Benedikt's suitcase was full of books he intended to study that evening, as well as a dictionary in case he needed to explain something to his sister. While he read, Dolly watched television or phoned her friends and every so often the bellboy burst in to check on the minibar. He reported the earnest features of the young couple, the tomes about physics. Didn't physics have something to do with explosives? While the pair were dining, the manager reported their names to the police. It was 1970. The couple ordered as if their minds were on other things, corroborated the waiter, although she, at least, ate with enjoyment. He might just as well have been eating at McDonald's. After dinner, they returned to their room and Benedikt told Dolly about unexplained sources of light in the universe. When he asked her to look something up in his science dictionary, she absentmindedly leafed through the telephone book, realizing her mistake during his awed silence.

'Never mind,' he said. 'Don't feel bad, for heaven's sake,' he pleaded.

She cheered up, just as the police were establishing that there were no Wallers in the only Wallerstein they could find on the south-German map. They didn't trust Germans anyway. The police hurried to the hotel. Count and Countess passed the night with Swiss officials quizzing them about democracy. They spent their remaining emotions on the fear that their grandmother might find out. She did not: the police in Biederstein vouched for them.

Dolly returned to Lindau and married an older man who ranked with her in the social register. She became dowdier with each pregnancy. Periodically, she came to Berlin to see him. Benedikt looked at her and concluded that he did not like women for aesthetic reasons; this perception did not preoccupy him, it surprised him a bit, but only because any information about himself came as a surprise. He sometimes had a shock catching a glimpse of himself in a mirror and realizing he had an exterior; he identified himself literally with his work and not with the laurels or with the income that it earned, either. He soon acquired the habit of turning his body ninety degrees away from people during conversations, conversing with them in profile in order to minimize contact. After his graduation *summa cum laude* in mathematical physics, he had accepted a job at an institute and lived so unobtrusively that time practically overlooked him. He was unnaturally youthful, his skin smooth, his hair thick and blond as he approached his forties.

Dolly's marriage had been the last event to affect his heart. The day he received the wedding invitation he had gone to the local supermarket, marched with his modest purchases to the cash register, and taken a good look at the cashier. She was as familiar to him as the white paper bag that wrapped his rolls, yet he would not have recognized her outside the shop. He saw that she was young and didn't wear a wedding ring. For the first time he realized that she had a personality. There was no one behind him in line, and the store was nearly empty.

As he was paying, he mumbled, 'Would you like to go see a film with me tonight?'

Her eyes registered surprise. She replied in a friendly tone, 'No, thank you.'

'Ring the doorbell after work,' he said, handing her his card, 'if you change your mind. I haven't been to the movies since I was a child.'

This seemed to arouse her sympathy. 'Oh, in that case,' she murmured, 'all right. After all, we've known each other for years.'

That evening he sat shoulder to shoulder with her during a comedy that apparently amused her, for every so often she screeched and her body shook like a train on a bad track. Afterwards he thanked her and said goodbye in the lobby of the movie house. He did not ask her where she lived. He saw her the next morning and established with surprise that he remembered her name, Gabi, and the sound of her laugh. It felt odd handing over his money to her. For the next few months, he could not pay for his rolls without chatting about the weather. Then one day he forgot to chat with her, and again the next. The following year she changed her hairstyle several times, also the colour, and her face became unfamiliar to him again. He did not recognize her when he passed her out of uniform on the street, and after a few more years, he had forgotten her name.

And this lack of change lulled him into ignoring his situation. His illness came as a shock, rubbed his nose in the hard fact that he was alive. He found it hugely embarrassing.

CHAPTER 2

Lightly, nervously: Benedikt falls into the hands of a psychiatrist

The instructions on the plastic, gold-embossed card read:

> Plumb your memory. Find the setbacks and embar-
> rassments. Prepare to discuss at least one but no more
> than three per session.

The professor of psychiatry reached over her desk and handed the card to her new patient. He sat sideways on the seat and did not respond to her formal smile. While he studied the card, she jotted down her impressions of Waller, Benedikt: 'Patient plasters over his considerable anxiety with calmness. Refuses eye contact.' She was an expert on the psychosomatic component of this disease, she expected she'd find his cracks. He dared to turn his face in her direction, kept his eyes on her paper, deciphering her comments backwards over the foreign territory of her desk, although her print was tiny, stingy. It amazed him that she should write about him; he didn't mind, either, it was her prerogative.

'I'm here to help you,' she said. 'Your illness is personally yours, you have a reason for getting sick, and the sooner we find out why, the sooner you'll recover.' She reached into her tweed-jacket pocket and pulled out a pack of cigarettes, then dropped it back in again. Her hand stayed there, caressing the pack.

'Don't believe all the hogwashers who say this illness is in-curable. Scientists are a lousy lot: they believe in facts rather his small modern bachelor flat in the centre of West Berlin and into a lifestyle, expecting to follow it forever. He announced this to his sister, Dolly, the first time she suggested his life was emotionally drab: repetitive.

'Those who claim to be bored by life are not bored by repetitions, don't you believe them.'

She was one of his most reliable repetitions herself. Twice a year she came to see him, once for his nameday in the early summer, to make sure he had a birthday cake with candles, and once a few days before Christmas, to make sure he had a Christmas tree. It was an old family tradition not to celebrate his birthday because he had had the misfortune to be born on Christmas Eve. ('You're a typical Capricorn with Scorpio ascendant,' she complained, 'a loner.') He was lethargic about throwing away what she had brought and inevitably when she arrived for Christmas she had to dispose of the stony birthday-cake remains, and her first act on his nameday was to lug the skeleton of the Christmas tree downstairs to the trash. The year before she had given him a potted pine, which required almost no attention, but it withered quickly, doused by his dislike, and then last Christmas when he was already ill she brought him a green polyethylene tree with gold tinsel and chains of flickering candle-shaped lightbulbs. She had placed it on the table next to his sofa, 'where the normal keep their knickknacks.'

The tree didn't bother him, and occasionally he even turned on the lights for a few minutes, remembering how his sister had looked standing next to it in her stocking feet, towering over him as he sat on the sofa, her mouth wide open, singing 'Lo, how a Rose ere blooming.' She longed to arouse his sentimentality, which she named proof of humanity. She felt guilty about his poor emotional reflexes, and she suffered a sense of responsibility for his life that she never had with her children. Before leaving him alone with what she considered her contributions—the tree, the knickknacks, and, somehow, his illness—she had bought a turtle, a little female—'the females are more intelligent'—which

than the truth. You can recover. If you want to. Not everyor
really wants to. Do you?'

He was caught daydreaming about a solitron, his pet child
bit of theoretical matter always on its own.

The red plastic chair shook with him as he nodded his he
and took a guess: 'Yes.'

'If it helps you to organize your thoughts, then write do
what you want to discuss with me in here.' She had to let gc
the cigarettes while she selected one of several coloured nc
books. She gave aggressive patients red covers, hysterical c
yellow. This system helped her to remember each individ
After deliberating she handed Waller, Benedikt, a blue noteb
blue for what she called 'depressive-repressor.' The notebook
familiar to him. It was the same kind he had used as a child
had naturally selected, as an adult, for his scientific speculat

'I'll see you next week,' she said, her sudden trained dis
est shooing him out the door. Her right hand trembled sh
his, her left hand was fumbling for the cigarettes, a lighte

The psychiatrist's office was a dimly lit nook along the
dor that had become familiar to Benedikt after several mor
being an outpatient. Before his illness he had viewed c
with the repugnance a vegetarian feels for a butcher. N
accepted their impersonal and powerful attention. He c
show his appreciation; they took it for granted, anyway. A
he presided over his new household of pills but found it
and a distraction to root around in his memory for setb
could not identify. He had volunteered for the university
in psychiatric treatment of the terminally ill because h
asked to and was too polite to say no.

'I'm sorry, I don't know what you mean,' he told th
sor. 'I don't have setbacks.'

'So your life is only pleasant?!'

'My life,' he said, 'is repetitive, and therefore pleasa
understand what convention has against the word "a
answered.

At thirty, he had settled with five boxes of note!

came in transparent plastic housing. This home had a lagoon, which the owner had to keep filled with tap water, and an island with a green plastic palm tree in the middle, where the owner had to scatter the dark, ashlike turtle food.

'Have to, have to,' grumbled Benedikt. 'The weak always emit imperatives.'

Dora, Countess of Sieseby, nicknamed Dolly, placed the turtle house beneath her brother's Christmas tree and instructed him how to care for it.

'It'll fit into your routine perfectly.'

The turtle, like all other living things, seemed reassured by Benedikt's presence. It began swimming around and around the lagoon and then dragged itself up on the island, where it basked.

'I'm not changing my routine to accommodate a reptile,' protested Benedikt.

'You will,' she said.

'It sounds,' said the psychiatrist, several months later, 'more like a ritual than a routine. You don't mind, do you, if a student sits in on our sessions?' She didn't introduce the young woman who had already taken a red plastic bucket seat. They sat in a triangle now. Somehow, people accumulated around Benedikt no matter how much he disliked company.

'You can identify someone as much by their routine as by their appearance,' he told the expert on the disease, whom he viewed as his sister's henchman, and the anonymous young woman who had joined them. 'And it doesn't change over time, it changes less than a face does.'

At midnight one can identify him like this:

A being lying in the darkness on his back, breathing lightly in his sleep as the slender, the abstemious do, his hands crossed on his stomach, his legs straight, in plain cotton pyjamas. The room on the first floor is not entirely dark, because the blinds are pulled up. The flashing neon sign of a private bar called Club Madamn across the street rhythmically splashes the word 'damn' in bright blue on his pale face that has neither laugh lines at the corners of the eyes nor frown lines on the wide forehead. He does not sleep more than five hours a night, and soon he will stir, waking up because his bowels tell him to.

He responds, eager as a windup doll, and heads for the bathroom. There he deals with his body, relieving and washing it in the darkness, shaves electrically with his eyes closed, and then, choosing from a selection of almost identical suits lined up in a small wardrobe, dresses, crouching to run shoe polish over his shoes. He makes his bed, tidies up without cleaning up; between his sister's visits the dust grows high in the corners. He finds his way through the living room, where he straightens a collection of notebooks stacked along several rows of bookshelves and removes one secreted at the back of the shelf, behind the others.

He retires with this to his sofa. He turns on a small light, opens the notebook, and sitting rigidly, one hand on his knee, he leafs through illustrations clipped from fashion advertisements showing male models. His interest is perfunctory; he is tempting himself, but he does not find the material tempting. Soon he moves a few metres along to the narrow corridor of a kitchen.

He makes himself instant coffee and toast, which he consumes standing up, along with a handful of pills. In the living room, he takes a soup ladle swinging from the fake Christmas tree, scoops up the turtle, hangs the ladle with turtle back up on a branch while he changes the water in the lagoon, and scatters a bit of turtle food. Then he spoons the creature out onto the island. The turtle panics every morning when she sees the ladle approaching, and pulls her parts under her armoured back, so that she has the size and weight and coolness of a five-mark piece. She huddles inside her shell until she feels the thud of her owner's retreating footsteps. She slides her head out and begins her day.

Benedikt has gone to his desk, with its view of the empty balcony, and pulled the blinds down. His desk is made of a slaughtered tree, and he doesn't want a ray of sunlight there, wakening its appetite or competing with the computer. His new Scandinavian office chair has a shin pad in front so that he kneels all morning. He has no peculiar mannerisms at his workplace. His hand does not tug at his earlobes, scrotum, nor does his mouth nurse a cigarette. He knows how to sit still.

The next hours pass as eventfully as the night: he reads until noon, when he walks over to the Institute to check up on his colleague, Dr Graf, who is tying up the last odds and ends of his solitron calculations for him. Once a week he makes a detour to the clinic, puts himself in the hands of the doctors, before proceeding to the Institute.

Dr Waller eats lunch by himself in the cafeteria and then works at his laboratory desk, so that mornings and afternoons bear a certain resemblance. Of course there are interruptions: he might have a guest, a scientist come to see him about a scientific problem, a staff member with a question. He notes their presence, not their personalities, and, forced into communication, uses simple formulas of conversation. Thus he has a reputation for being rude, even mean. But when the secretaries collect money to throw an office party or buy a present, Dr Waller empties his wallet, without listening for a 'thank you.'

Leaving the Institute in the afternoon, Waller attends to errands, and in the evening he takes a ritual walk from his apartment, one kilometre along a congested boulevard, to the train station and back. Then he eats a sandwich standing up in his kitchen, works at his desk until just before midnight, when he retires, and immediately falls asleep.

This routine does not bear any adverbial decoration. Only Sunday passes a bit differently: on Sunday afternoon he visits Dr Anhalt, the head of his institute. Dr Anhalt also loves repetition: if he reads a name more than three times in the newspaper, he tries to guarantee the acquaintance by summoning the holder of this name to his Sunday gathering. Benedikt reserves the occasion for communication. He finds talking to others very boring; it is his form of self-flagellation. He chats about his work and even musters a kind of formal interest in what some have to say, although many are not scientists. Artists and writers with a weakness for the university attend, alongside university professors with a weakness for artists; by dinnertime everyone's teeth are purple from red wine.

'Is not the love of fame also a love of repetition?' Dr Waller asked the psychiatrist, after finishing with this description of himself.

Illness had poked its fingers into his routine, but it did not tear. For one month he followed the regimen of the hospitalized. The doctors studied the solar system from a different vantage point: they saw it inside their patients, the planets of the organs, the sun of the brain. Benedikt found this the most deluded of all perspectives. He left the hospital determined less to get well—he did not yet accept that he was ill—than to avoid another stay there. He had scarcely been missed at the Institute, where his presence was not required, or at Dr Anhalt's Sunday salon because a four-week absence bore the rhythm of a vacation. No one realized that, since the onset of his illness, his brain was no longer working well. He still sat at his desk, but all he did there was reread his old scientific papers in order of publication. By the time he admitted this to the psychiatrist, he was already on his fifth reading. The expert on the disease found Waller's account interesting. She could write a paper about him. Her student's pen scratched wildly on a pad.

She sent the patient home with an assignment: 'I would like you to describe one incident from your past, Herr Waller, where you felt human.'

He went home. He laid the blue notebook on his desk, where it was indistinguishable from his research manuals. Finally he opened it and wrote on the first line:

$$A = 0$$

That was something he could discuss with a stranger. He wanted her to understand the beauty of this simple ambition, that A, meaning his health, should equal zero, meaning, in this case, equilibrium. At his next session, there was yet another student present, and Benedikt found himself sitting in a circle. The room was stuffy.

'If you don't want someone listening in, that's no problem,' they can leave at once,' offered the psychiatrist.

'Students,' he mumbled, 'no problem,' and handed her his equation.

At once, she scolded him. 'For me, zero is no candy left in the box—it shows me your negative attitude towards yourself. Please. The next time I see you, you'll have written a few lines about your living, breathing self.'

The word 'self' set his teeth on edge.

Embarrassment is one of the most enduring of the emotions, with a terrible, needling rhythm. Grief heals; hate, like love, fades over time; but when touched by memory old embarrassments throb like fresh wounds. The psychiatrist was convinced that these hidden sores seeped and disseminated disease. The household remedy—distraction, or applying a huge poultice of pride—had at best a cosmetic effect, and was more likely to hinder treatment.

The psychiatrist pressed on. 'Or you can examine your embarrassment, come to terms with it, understand it. Then you'll accept it. Even be proud of it, because it's yours.'

This appeal fell on the barren ground of his vanity.

Having reached what he considered the climax of his routine, the Sunday exception, Benedikt lost his patience. He did not want to hurt the expert's feelings, since she was so fascinated by him, but he balked. What he found really embarrassing could not be entrusted to his lips: group activity. And he considered a group one person more than solitude: anything done in unison struck him as undignified, including walking, singing, cheering, eating, and sleeping. He did not take comfort in the collective experience of illness, as did the more sociable patients. And while others took a certain delight in being ill because it attracted attention, he felt embarrassed by any reference to himself at all; when blood was taken and the nurse advised him to close his eyes, he refused. He was ashamed of closing his eyes in public.

'Go back!' insisted the psychiatrist. 'Early memories! We have work to do there!' Two more students had joined them, and everything he said was echoed by the scribble of pencils.

'I am so embarrassed,' he admitted, 'about Auschwitz.'

'All Germans are. That's why we can't forget it. Were we ashamed, it wouldn't be on our minds today, making us itch inside. My point too. But . . .' said the expert, and then sighed, exhaling her discouragement.

Two weeks later he was back at the hospital, having his eyes checked, his blood drawn, his stool analysed, his brain scanned. He remembered his assignment as he reached the smoked glass of the Therapy Room, and saw the five-headed shadow waiting for him. He pulled the notebook out of his briefcase and wrote in his heavy simple print, 'The praying mouse . . .'

'Now that's something,' said the psychiatrist. Her facial expressions wafted slightly in a cross-breeze of guilt and pride at having elicited a reaction from the patient. 'Tell me,' she sighed, 'about the mouse praying!'

The circle looked at him hopefully, their pencils poised. He did not want to disappoint them. So he described a telephone call that had taken place six months earlier, the last day of a period of time in which he was healthy. He had come down with a cold, and his sister had called to see how he was. She heard at once that his cold had not improved.

'Doesn't matter,' he said, 'I made a deal with my body—it has a right to a day in bed, and then I have a right to my peace and quiet again. I'll stay in bed tomorrow.'

He had just finished writing up his findings on solitrons after three years of investigation. He had served his own curiosity with the humility and endurance of a good soldier. But then its authority over him weakened; he had reached the limits of his own speculations, where no more questions occurred to him. Writing up his theory for public consumption was a final let-

down. He did not care what the others would say, did not sub-
scribe to the theories that really preoccupy scientists, about
envious colleagues trying to hamper publication. He spent most
of his working day with the computer, but he didn't view this as
a companion either, as others did. He admired the computer's
capabilities because it proved the poverty of his own. Information travelled much faster electronically than via the communication nature had foreseen, with its clumsy reliance on speech and
hearing. He had told his sister about that, how he would send his
manuscript, called 'Observations on the Collision Behaviour of
Solitrons,' directly from his computer to *Annals of Physics*, a prestigious journal in the United States. Within seconds, his prose
would be transferred to another computer, quicker in fact than
the human eye could read it.

'Oh my,' Dolly said, 'and you know, prayer is also a quick
form of communication. Well, I'll say a little prayer for you that
the paper gets accepted.'

'Prayer!' he had sputtered. 'For acceptance! Don't bother! It's
not necessary.'

She continued, 'Even animals pray. Yesterday I saw a mouse
pray. If mice pray, why shouldn't people?'

'I see,' he said, turning on his computer. 'Well, well.' He
reread his article on the screen as she talked.

'I went up to the third-floor bathroom. And I heard something rattling around in the bathtub. It was a mouse. And when
the mouse saw me, he knew he was in terrible trouble. He sat up
on his hind legs and clasped his front paws together, and prayed
that God would save him.'

He listened to her, against his better judgement. She was
waiting for some sign from him that he was interested. He refused her. She cleared her throat, as she always did when his
silence unnerved her, and he took pity and said, 'Well, then
what?'

'I filled the bath up with hot water. Can't have a mouse
running all over the house, can I?' she replied.

He had ended the conversation, afraid that he would offend

her. That night he woke up because he could hardly breathe, as if the hot water that had drowned the mouse were rising in his lungs. The expert was not idle. She recognized explosions in a calendar. The night that Benedikt's body broke with his routine was the late autumn night when the Germans tore down the wall between East and West that apparently divided them. The psychiatrist was inclined to view this as a parting of ways, the nation recovering just when the individual succumbed. But the patient maintained that swelling up was as dangerous a symptom as slimming down. Moral malnutrition had produced this calamity. The German reunion was a hunger oedema.

One of the students listening in on the therapy session stopped scribbling. 'Oh, bullshit!' he said.

Then they all looked up, one after the other, from their pads and stared at him. The expert lowered her gaze, allowing the students their hostility. The patient excused himself.

He did not return to the hospital. When his prescriptions for drugs ran out, he did not renew them. He abandoned his daily routine. He holed up on his sofa, sitting sideways with his feet drawn up to his chin, and waited, waited for nothing in particular. But before long his sister came, wrinkling her nose as she entered his flat. Dolly squeezed in next to Benedikt's limp body on the sofa, commented that the turtle looked depressed and smelled neglected, and reminded him that it was the feast of St Benedikt. He was forty-one. He had, as yet, no plan for salvation.

CHAPTER 3

Not always the same tempo, and not as sweet as others like it:
Benedikt's love life was not conventional, really

The experts on the disease were not entirely off track when
they suspected that Benedikt had on occasion harboured
sentimental feelings for his own gender, but this is an exaggera-
tion. He had quite enjoyed sex, as a pleasant, localized sensation,
a kind of anaesthesia of the groin. He did not appreciate that it
made him lose his breath, but then, with a bit of training, it no
longer made him lose his breath. He had shared this pleasure
reluctantly. He was so easily dismayed by the smell and warmth
of others that he avoided standing close to them and often kept
his eyes averted during conversations for fear of noticing a physical characteristic that might disgust him.

He had lost his virginity by accident, to a man who admired
him for his talent, and perhaps even loved him for his curious
character, but Benedikt could not bear the scorching of intimacy
and unintentionally treated him badly, treated him as an incomplete replication of himself. His name was also Benedikt, Benedikt Schmidt, and they had a certain physical resemblance which
belied their differences. Benedikt Schmidt was a high-school
teacher, the success story in a family of Schwabian florists and
housewives. Despite the professional heights he had attained, his
heart remained vulnerable. His emotions were like knives, he was
constantly nicking himself on them, and it scarcely helped that
he kept them wrapped up in a pride as delicate as tissue paper.
He did not tolerate suspense, avoided it, kept his eyes closed in

the movies and read the endings of novels first, was crazed by the uncertainties of infatuation. Benedikt Schmidt had met Dr Waller while giving his high-school students a tour of the physics institute. He was only twenty-five but socially mature. He already had a wife and baby; his feelings for women were unromantic, practical, and constant. He only lost his head over men, and in particular over men who were more talented than he. As he had little ability to judge for himself what constituted talent, he had to base his admiration on reputation: Benedikt Waller had been called 'brilliant' by a national news magazine. Benedikt Schmidt pursued him with the sensitivity for the object of his infatuation that a truck might feel for the road. He bounced but did not slow down to think when, after pressing Benedikt to stop calling him Herr Schmidt, Benedikt had agreed to call him just 'Schmidt.' Dr Waller, for his part, pretended it all wasn't happening, even as one thing led to another, from the forgetfulness and anaesthesia of sex through recovery, and then the bother of conversation.

Afterwards, Schmidt was tender, gentle, demonstrative; Benedikt bore it stoically, but he wasn't having Schmidt's head on his shoulder all night long. He didn't want to be impolite, but he did not want to get squashed, either. He shook Schmidt off, asked him whether he wouldn't be more comfortable sleeping in his own bed at home.

Schmidt worshipped Dr Waller's idiosyncrasies and slept on the sofa. He was a decade younger than the mathematician and this made him both sure and unsure of himself. The next morning, he noted his lover's readiness to accept suggestions on the question of social form. He said: After one has spent a night together, one breakfasts on one's balcony. Benedikt had never used his balcony before. It was a bare, filthy place with a view of the small central street and the sleazy bar opposite. Schmidt was enthusiastic. He would plant tomatoes or wild wine in the sunny corner and a clematis in the shade; the mathematician would learn the pleasures of sitting in the sun, sharing a newspaper with a lover, drinking espresso—Benedikt needed an espresso machine. Had he ever been to Florence? Schmidt's wife took care of their balcony; she had told him about the wild wine and the clematis; she had introduced him to espresso and Campari and dragged off the family to Tuscany; like many Germans she preferred Italy.

The mathematician evaded the teacher's suggestions. He longed to sit alone and think. The evening was wearing away in his memory. Yesterday he had been a virgin, today he was not; had Benedikt Waller bothered to reflect on the difference between these two states, he would have found its reputation exaggerated. Nevertheless, he gave in to Schmidt's certainty that they should breakfast together on the balcony. He could not reject the younger man's efforts, dragging table and chairs outside, fixing the croissants and coffee, after running downstairs, the keys in his pocket like a talisman. It was a Sunday, his family was spending the weekend with a relative. He was a free man.

Schmidt should have been warned by Dr Waller's current research project. The mathematician was studying the solitron, a particle that is by definition always on its own. Dr Waller's theory was that when one solitron collided with another, each particle remained unaffected. He had spent the past years banging solitrons against each other on the computer, until he had infinite rolls of paper showing the following drama: the solitrons approached each other, collided, separated. During the collision, spikes formed. But short of this, nothing happened. They emerged from the collision with their curves intact, not a millimetre changed. Schmidt knew about Dr Waller's project, but he didn't take it personally. His mistake.

The morning after their first night together, they had remained in their underwear at Schmidt's urging. Benedikt had noticed the spring sun and recognized their place in it: two young men with pleasant faces, blue eyes, short blond hair, and well-made bodies. The younger one was more muscular by nature and training, although a bit pudgy, his features thicker, while the older man was thinner, taller, his face composed with a geometer's tool and seldom altered by expressions. Their moods were entirely different; while Schmidt revelled in the sweetness of possessing the man he so admired, the mathematician seemed engrossed in an article he was reading, making notations in the margins. His eyes had a dull sheen of concentration. Nevertheless, the impression these two men would have made on strangers and indeed on themselves was of compatibility.

Schmidt read the newspaper and noted the fragrance of his coffee. Suddenly, Dr Waller picked up his pen, held it to his companion's belly, where two folds of fat formed, pressed the pen between them and said, 'Look, Schmidt, you can hold a pen with your stomach.'

An hour later, Benedikt Waller had said goodbye to Benedikt Schmidt without asking for his phone number. When Schmidt called, he seemed surprised, but quite willing to see him again. Schmidt sent him presents for his apartment—a handsome coffee spoon, a tablecloth—and wrote him long letters about his feelings, about life, that Waller never answered. He could not remember Schmidt's profession or his age. Nothing about Schmidt seemed to make a lasting impression on him; even his appearance seemed unfamiliar and therefore irritating.

On their second morning together, he regarded Benedikt Schmidt's hands and said, 'Your fingers are like sausages.'

This combination of indifference and criticism exploded like shrapnel everywhere in the schoolteacher's pride, before he could summon the strength to hate Benedikt Waller. He wrote him a last letter, itemizing all his presents, asking him to throw them away and destroy all of his letters. In fact, Waller had disposed of the letters within minutes of receiving and skimming them.

Schmidt retreated to his wife and infant trying to feel smug that he didn't live alone, that he had a family. He stayed in touch with Benedikt, phoning him, behaving like a friend, waiting for the moment when he might prove to him that he was the happier of the two, confounded that Benedikt could be so utterly indifferent to his happiness. All the more did Schmidt strive to prove it. But Benedikt Waller did not know what pleasure pettiness can bring. He accepted Schmidt's invitation to become a godfather when a new baby came along, forgot to show up for the baptism, was forgiven by the father but not the mother (a sports teacher who enjoyed resentment), remained noncommittally cheerful, accepted friendliness without complaint, if it didn't last too long. He didn't mention to Schmidt that other men sometimes—occasionally—stayed with him, always tall blond men who approached him, usually younger men, who had somehow fallen short of a goal in their careers. He kept this from Schmidt because he didn't consider it interesting. He only told him about his illness in order to get rid of him one afternoon when Schmidt, sore with mixed feelings for Benedikt, came for a visit and did something unforgivable.

Several months into Benedikt's illness, Schmidt had rung the doorbell in a state of excitement. 'I was just passing by and saw a bird hanging from your balcony!' he said.

An obvious ploy but Benedikt had no choice but to let him in. At once, Schmidt rushed to the balcony door, Benedikt following him to see what he would do next. Schmidt had not invented it: a pigeon had somehow got tangled in a piece of wire hanging from the roof. The pigeon flapped his wings but could only swing like a pendulum because the wire was hooked into the feathers on his back. Schmidt went back inside, grabbed a pair of scissors from his host's desk, and cut through the wire. 'Free again!' he called. The bird had no time to right itself. Like a plane stalled at a low altitude, it plummeted to the ground. It lay on its back, its legs twitching.

Schmidt's triumph paled. 'Oh well,' he said, 'I tried. That's what counts, morally speaking.' He stood there, waiting for Benedikt to invite him to stay for a while.

Benedikt left him there, rushed outside to the victim. Passersby stopped and stared, walked on, were replaced by others. The pigeon made feeble efforts to turn over. Benedikt felt responsible; after all, the bird had ended up on his balcony, where his friend Schmidt had misjudged the problem and sent him to his death. Benedikt did not care for the pigeon, but he knew how to behave and looked around for a weapon to put the creature out of its misery. He went to the street hawker on the corner selling different-sized fragments of the now defunct Berlin Wall as souvenirs and bought the largest piece. Returning with this, he hurled it downwards with all his strength onto the bird's head.

He went back upstairs—later, he would blame his limp on that act, and it was true, his limp set in as he reached his living room and found Schmidt still there, sitting on his sofa. 'Where did you go?' Schmidt complained.

Benedikt replied, 'I have to work now. I lost a lot of time because of that pigeon.' And then, as Schmidt did not disappear instantly, Benedikt told him about his illness. He thought it would terrify Schmidt and then dispel him for good. Benedikt did not anticipate the feelings that a sensitive heart, prone to infatuation and envy, would suffer at hearing of a friend's misfortune. (After an initial panic, to be sure. But then, Schmidt had a test that proved he was still healthy. Besides, he felt that he wasn't the type to become ill.)

Nor did Benedikt know that Schmidt, who dreamt of going into analysis, was anxious to know what it was like to grieve. In his family no one had ever died, all his siblings were well, and his grandparents were still alive. So the real climax to the drama of Benedikt's illness was, for Schmidt, his own reaction to it. And since he hated suspense, he preferred finding out the ending of this particular story, at the expense of having it occur early.

When Dr Waller no longer answered the telephone, Schmidt came and knocked on the door, went home, huddled beside his wife and children, measured his sadness, called again. Nothing. In the absence of information, Benedikt died in ten different places, at his desk, in the hospital, even while walking along the street, but his last words were always directed to Schmidt: 'My happiest moments were with you' or 'Why didn't I take advantage of your friendship?' or just 'Schmidt . . .' The next day, when Schmidt imagined the Waller relatives would be cleaning out the little apartment, he called again. Benedikt's sister picked up the phone and told him Benedikt was not getting up off the sofa but there was no need to worry as long as she was there with him. The caller could start to worry next week when she left again. Schmidt began to worry again punctually and placed a call. No answer. A sweet sadness tinged with relief overcame him.

He could not have imagined that Benedikt was limping to the mailbox, clutching the ad he had written for the personal column, 'seeks child,' which he was inexperienced enough to have signed with his name and address. Schmidt could not foresee that, as he was trying to ring him again, Benedikt was just making an unplanned visit to the clinic, where he insisted on a blood test because he wanted to prove that he felt better. A few hours later, as Schmidt tried again, Benedikt was wandering around a toy shop that specialized in 'natural' materials. The children all looked rather dull and bored. Their mothers, in contrast, seemed to be suffering from a horrifying kind of alertness. At a nearby department store, the children rioting among the plastic toys still showed all their vital signs, but Benedikt's visit was perfunctory. He had established at once that children did not interest him intellectually. He wanted one of his own, an offspring. Nothing more. He headed home. Schmidt was fetching his daughter from kindergarten just as Benedikt crossed the threshold of his front door, heading for the sofa, where he holed up for the rest of the afternoon with a smile on his face.

CHAPTER *4*

Speed it up: certain events occur which have no obvious relationship to each other, being attached by an invisible but as yet slack bond called the Future

On that same bubbling hot morning in June that Benedikt placed an advertisement in the paper, an event with no obvious relevance to Benedikt Waller took place at the far eastern end of what was then still East Berlin. A man easily recognized by the cloth and cut of his clothes as a resident of the 'West,' a German in his mid-thirties accompanied by his nine-year-old daughter, entered a shoebox-shaped building at the entrance to a compound of smaller boxes, all fenced off from the surrounding rural landscape by a high concrete wall. No official signs identified this institution, and a friendly atmosphere welcomed the visitors: an affable policeman behind bullet-proof glass at a reception desk in the lobby buzzed them through a heavy door leading to a neon-lit hall that was clean but not disinfected, and they were free to continue on their own. The girl registered the sound of children playing nearby and the unpleasantly heavy fall of her father's footsteps on the linoleum floor; she understood that he had changed his weekend sneakers for a pair of lace-up shoes because this visit required serious dress. Holding her hand for reassurance, he led her to an office, where they enjoyed an enthusiastic 'Hello, again!' from the administrator.

'Do you have any pianists?' asked the visitor. 'I'm looking for someone who can give my daughter Saskia piano lessons.' The chubby blond girl smiled wearily, the way she had learned, corners of her mouth up, lips together—eye participation was not required.

Her father, Herr Weltecke, had been there the week before looking for a seamstress who could sew dresses for Frau Weltecke, who wore only hard-to-find, extra-large sizes. He paid four marks an hour for menial help, which was twice the per diem paid by the city to the residents of this compound.

The administrator knew that his charges were as a rule more energetic than the population outside, and he did everything in his power to keep them occupied. They were immigrants from all over the world who had applied for asylum, and his main duty was to immobilize these people—he always referred to them as 'fellowmen,' Sri Lankan fellowmen, Russian fellowmen, and so on—while other bureaucrats figured out what to do with them. The administrator did not realize that a good half of his clients had already earned themselves into top-income brackets with black-market activities. Still, many did not participate, hampered by intellectual interests.

The administrator viewed Herr Weltecke as a godsend. The German from the well-to-do part of town was also having new fitted shelves built, and his wife, who could no longer bend down comfortably, had domestic help three times a week. The administrator had a pianist for him, too, just the thing, in fact, a Russian woman, a Frau Golubka. He had recently forbidden her to practise on the house upright because her playing was so unusually loud, and after all, the piano was reserved for holiday entertainment. He had been forced to lock the room where it was kept, but he saw no reason why the little girl couldn't have lessons there. Herr Weltecke was impatient to meet the pianist but no one could say where she might be—the tenants were allowed to move around the city freely.

Herr Weltecke and his very well-behaved Saskia had to wait until lunch. They passed the time in the cafeteria reading old magazines until the smell of soup and foreigners made them look up. A central table had been laid with plastic plates brimming with a thick soup, and the Welteckes saw the administrator fight-ing his way through an excited mob at the table. A woman followed him whom Herr Weltecke, with his accumulated expe-rience, would have called typically Russian-looking: stubby, firm, with cropped dark hair worn in a helmet around rosy cheeks, high cheekbones, and bad teeth, awful, brown, broken-off teeth. Behind her came a large bony man holding a plate that slopped soup on the floor at each footstep. Saskia spotted the child of perhaps seven years holding onto this man from the back, pulling his sweater out of shape. She wouldn't have been allowed to do that.

'Here's the pianist I told you about,' the administrator said. 'Frau Golubka knows a bit of German. And I've explained the situation to her. She's interested in teaching.'

'My daughter,' said Herr Weltecke, holding his child by the shoulders. 'Piano.' He wiggled his fingers in the air, then poked the woman gently on the arm. 'You teach . . .' He patted Sas-kia's head, 'her?'

'I would pay her ten East marks an hour,' said Herr Weltecke to the administrator, 'but I have to come all the way out here, and time is money. I own a restaurant. I need to be there. So let's make it six East marks. That's about two West marks at the cur-rent official exchange rate. Can you explain it to her?'

At this point the tall Russian man caught up with Frau Golubka from behind, tugged at her sleeve until she turned around. They exchanged a smattering of what sounded like hos-tilities, so it was a safe guess that they were husband and wife, which made him Herr Golub.

Herr Golub's hand began to tremble and the soup splattered on the ground at her feet. Frau Golubka hopped away, position-ing herself with her small back to his huge torso, so that Herr Golub had to stay behind her while she resumed her conversa-tion with the administrator and his guests, accepting Herr Weltecke's generous offer in such good German that the admin-istrator felt uneasy, looked at his watch, then at his shoes. Behind him, Herr Golub's expression turned fierce. He made snorting noises through his nose and talked angrily to the child, who had wisely taken refuge from the cascading hot soup by squeezing between his father's legs. Frau Golubka was smiling at her new pupil. The girl smiled back, while the Russian man muttered sentences packed around the explosives 'Nyet, nyet.' His wife ignored him; she volunteered to skip lunch in order to begin the lessons right away.

The administrator pointed Herr Golub and his child back to the lunch table, before walking the German pupil, her father, and her new teacher down the long hall to an assembly room. A white upright stood in a corner, its lid pasted over with paper bunny rabbits.

The administrator said, 'This is certainly a good start, Frau Golub. Very hopeful.'

The Russian woman was just sitting down on the piano bench with her pupil. She remarked, 'The price of hope is at an all-time low—anyone can have it, but it's worthless.'

The administrator stared and withdrew. Herr Weltecke was preoccupied. Now that he had what he wanted, he began to envy the immigrants out there with their soup and no long drive ahead of them before they could lie down for a short nap and then off to the restaurant again. The administrator called, 'Good luck,' closed the door, and Frau Golubka, without giving the child another glance, began to amuse herself playing very loudly, her fingers moving with astounding velocity. The administrator poked his head back through the door again and glared.

Frau Golubka turned to Saskia. 'Your turn,' she said.

The child had learned 'Für Elise' from her best friend. She played quickly when she could, and when she couldn't, she played slowly.

Within several miles of this scene, Benedikt Waller had arisen from his sofa and approached his desk. He sat down and remembered a theoretical project he had once entertained. During his weeks in the hospital his brain had taken him on a strange journey, without the usual restraints imposed by the owner. With his body plugged into a battery of electrical machines, his mind had worked out a model theory computing the effect on the earth if huge chunks of space matter were somehow dragged into the atmosphere. By the time the patient was weaned from his life-support system, he had come up with a theory that if part of the moon (what earthly use was it anyway?) were removed by nuclear explosion and subsequently sunk into the oceans, one could raise the temperature in certain places on earth with such precision that one would free the colder nations from their heating systems. The patient was not yet aware of his dependencies. For example, the girl and her teacher studying 'Für Elise' would have a lasting effect on him and his illness, but their existence did not even occur to him. He felt no twinge of fate. He was toying with the variables, weight and temperature and weather models, and Saskia Weltecke and her Russian teacher were playing Beethoven.

A few hours later, the following events occurred, all attached to each other as if by an invisible but as yet slack cord:

The piano student and her father entered their semi-detached house in a middle-class neighbourhood, and their ways parted, one headed for the kitten, the other for the kitchen. With his head deep in the refrigerator, Herr Weltecke suddenly felt resentment like a bad smell in his brain. He had paid the Russian woman too much. After all, he had waited almost two hours for her.

'Oh, dammit,' he said, bent double in the fridge, 'I won't be able to enjoy the rest of the day because of her.'

He had experience. The awareness that he had been duped would needle him during his afternoon nap, throttle his appetite for a snack, and wrestle with him all night. Herr Weltecke decided to drive back out and renegotiate the teaching salary. She was from the East. Why shouldn't geography be something worth penalizing? They did it in England, where northerners earned less than southerners, and in Italy, where southerners earned less than northerners. If his daughter learned well, then

he would pay the teacher. She would earn royalty fees, a nego-
tiable sum per piece . . .

. . . at the same time, Frau Golubka had a fight with Herr
Golub on the hot barren street in front of their home about why
they had left the Soviet Union. This argument was not open to
the non-Russian-speaking public but the word 'Royal!' kept
pounding the East Berlin sky. Royal, in Russian, means piano.
Their demeanour adhered to the international norm for bickering
couples . . .

. . . meanwhile, Dr Waller, devout at his desk, remembered
his idea of sinking the moon into the oceans and shuddered,
because it did not deal with hypotheticals at all. He did not want
to rule his environment, oh no. It occurred to him that he was
like a king in a chess game. The game hinged upon him: when he
was gone, the game was over. But he could only move one square
at a time, and was always on the defensive. The king had to rely
on others to keep the game going at all . . .

. . . at this moment, the lay-out man at the newspaper put
Benedikt's advertisement under the rubric 'Miscellaneous,' a sort
of curiosity shop in the personal columns. He boxed it in between an offer of maps of Poland and Czechoslovakia and the
description of an ideal girlfriend placed by a lonely unemployed
East German border guard, who felt misunderstood. Benedikt,
ignorant of the cost of advertising, had enclosed a large bill
when he wrote to the newspaper. It occurred to the lay-out man
that he could pocket the money, but then he read the message,
and pity made him behave. He selected extra-large print, called
'Emperor Size,' so the ad read:

UNMARRIED MAN WITH TERMINAL DISEASE
SEEKS CHILD, PREFERABLY TODDLER,
FOR PURPOSES OF ADOPTION.
WRITE WALLER, THIELSTR. 9, BERLIN 12.

In the evening, Herr Weltecke could not help taking pleasure in
the smooth gait of his Mercedes as he returned to East Berlin,

although the high-rises along the road were so densely packed
that they disrupted his radio reception of a football game. As he
reached his destination, he had a shock: at night, when all the
inhabitants were home, the parking lot was full of Mercedeses.
Herr Weltecke remembered he had been cheated. He gained
admission to the building, found the Golubs on the second floor,
eighth door to the left. Their room offered only a few square
metres for conversation, and those lay behind three beds and a
wardrobe. In the middle of this space stood four empty suitcases,
used by the family as chairs and a table. As Herr Weltecke entered, after giving one short rap at the door, they were lying on
their beds, reading German newspapers. Their child slept, tucked
in under several covers, despite the heat.

'I paid you far too much,' said Herr Weltecke. He described
his plan for royalty payments. He stood there in the middle of
their room, and they didn't even answer. He felt his mouth opening and closing for nothing, and indignity boiled up into his
eyes. Why was he putting himself through this? 'Too much!' he
cried. 'You must give me back two marks. Or I will report this
whole blasted place to the police.'

CHAPTER 5

Hurrying on: Benedikt has his future predicted by various acquaintances.
Opinions are divided

Now the countdown began to fatherhood, when society rages through the innocent lives of the parent, and he must try to keep his bearings in howling winds of advice from relatives and other strangers. Benedikt was naive about this. He did not expect the hubbub in the courtyard, a space controlled by housewives who actually shared his love of routine. He set about his day as usual, performed his rituals, devoted himself to a new task: reading his article about solitrons from the perspective of a father. But as soon as he supposed that the postman might be close by, his concentration flagged. Cheerfulness had crept into Benedikt's routine, destabilizing it more severely than illness had done.

He did not identify the sensation. He noted something benign in his mood that somehow transferred to his body. He felt his own blood moving, but not as a lethal coursing so much as a sweet, quick flowing. By the time the postman staggered up the street, bad-tempered as always, he got drenched by Benedikt's good mood. He stood there panting and amazed, hounded by unconscious memories of centuries of serfdom, early death, bad teeth, lost limbs, scourges, pestilence, and always being at the bottom, which he shared with the concierge, and muttered, 'Well, what have we got to be so happy about? Is the sun out or something?'

It was. The sun shone expressly, a hot grey stain on the

partly cloudy. Nevertheless Benedikt was in for a disappointment: 'Nothing for you today.' The postman staggered on.

Frau Bilka, the concierge, filled his place with her own complaints. The Poles were everywhere, they smelled, etc. She was tidy. She sniffed at her hands with satisfaction and said, 'Roast beef. I've been feeding my dog.' And what was he, Benedikt, doing hanging around on the street? 'Go and earn some money,' she advised. Benedikt knew about the money-mad proletariat.

'I saw your ad, Herr Waller. I wouldn't have put my name and address if I were you. You're going to be swamped with applicants. All sorts of scum, coming in and out of here,' said Frau Bilka.

'What does he want a child for?' she had asked the postman and several neighbours. They couldn't get it out of their heads: someone their sons' age coming down with a terminal disease, maybe that one popular with young people nowadays. And why had he signed with his name and address?

Gabi, the cashier at the grocery store who Benedikt had once taken to the movies, read his ad during a quiet moment at the cash register and felt chills she associated with deep-frozen peas down her spine. 'What a close shave . . .' She sought assurance from the photos of her husband and two sons that she always placed on the till before starting her shift.

Across the city, those who chanced upon Benedikt's announcement flinched, frowned, or pursed their lips, savouring their curiosity.

Benedikt Schmidt was scouring the pages for a new maid. Over the past week, his thoughts, irresistible as a simple tune, had returned again and again to his poor friend's fate, until he was so used to his own grief that he began to forget it. Then he saw the ad. He felt cheated. His friend was fishing elsewhere for sympathy.

Schmidt called him and, hearing the good cheer in Benedikt Waller's voice, said, 'I saw your ad. You must be crazy!' But then he calmed down, figuring that no one had ever found real happiness through the newspaper. 'What's happened to your theory about the difference between animate and inanimate objects being exaggerated?' he complained. 'Get yourself a doll.'

Schmidt hung up just as Herr Weltecke sat down next to the phone and willed it to ring. He, too, had committed his hopes to print: 'Seek villa or apartment building in the East. In good condition only. Trade for 220 midnight-blue Mercedes.' He leafed through the paper and his eyes stumbled across Benedikt's message. He called his wife. He called his daughter. 'Look at this,' he said. They stood around him, their heads bowed over the newspaper. Through the long glass pane of their living room, one could have seen them reading together, in the reflection of the trees, and in this pose they looked, for an instant, beautiful.

'This newspaper is full of such smut,' said Herr Weltecke, putting the page down.

Downtown, Benedikt was trying to make an appointment at the hospital to get the result of his blood tests. When the sky turned brown, the wealthy population mobbed the taxis, and not a few held the sudden influx of poor strangers from the East responsible for the overcrowding of public transport. As a taxi approached, Benedikt, trying to keep a toehold on the pavement, was spun about, pushed into the street. He cried as he went down, 'My wife is having a baby—I must get to the hospital!' At this, the others gaped, mumbled congratulations, helped him up.

The driver had the classifieds lying carelessly on the front seat. 'Do you have everything?' he asked. 'Nursing pads for leaking breasts, hamper deodorant, cream for cradle cap, zinc ointment for diaper rash, thirty days' worth of bathing salts to soothe a ripped perineum? It's a demeaning, disgusting business, you'll see.' He looked at Benedikt in the rearview mirror. 'Shall I drop you off at the delivery room—or back home and lock the door? It's not too late.'

In the clinic waiting room, the sick leafed through the newspaper. Some patients were cheerful, some very sad, others angry because they suffered the cruellest form of envy: they were envious of themselves, as they used to be, when they were healthy. Not Benedikt, who entered with the air of a bon vivant.

'Have you heard yet?' the nurse at the front desk asked him.

And he assumed his fatherhood was the news and said, 'Yes, I know.'

'How can you know?' She looked at his medical records again, scarcely believing it: the patient's blood count had improved. The specific numbers involved were just making the rounds of the various offices as a sensation.

'The news,' said the psychiatrist, stopping by, having missed this handsome, classically German-looking patient with his peculiar rejection of Germany, his motherland, 'is upbeat. We're all making progress. By the way, I was thinking about you, that you might like the East better if you had a look at it. Have you ever been over there—to the little villages? They're beautiful, untouched, just the way they were before the war.'

'Winning cells everywhere,' murmured the internist joining them. 'The medicine works.'

'I don't know how you do it,' whispered the nurse. 'Did you make a pact with the devil? Don't tell the other patients.'

Waller, Benedikt, just stood there, shaking his head at all of them, embarrassed by the attention.

'Your blood count is still a catastrophe, so your prognosis is still what we call grim,' said the nurse loudly now.

'So it is,' answered Benedikt, relieved, 'in the best of cases.'

'Don't start telling me about shorter life expectancy in the Third World,' the internist interjected. 'Or how you may actually live longer now because your chances of being hit by a car have decreased since you no longer cross at red lights. That's the optimist's line that really makes me sick. There are better forms of optimism—for example, simple hope.

'Perhaps,' he warned, 'you will be the very first patient to survive this disease! Bear that in mind. Next patient, please.'

Benedikt continued. 'My grandmother, for example, is already twenty years over the average life expectancy.' He sat there, his ribs visible beneath his shirt, ominous as prison bars, and he mumbled without any pride, 'My whole family is beyond any life expectancy. Eight hundred years old.' The nurse handed him his records to take to the eye doctor down the corridor. Nobody asked for an explanation. They tinkered with him, perplexed by this sudden recovery.

As he was leaving, his ad was being passed around the examination room. 'Look at this!' The nurses waved the paper at the physicians. 'That's our patient.'

'Being sick doesn't necessarily make them better people. In fact, it generally makes them worse,' said the internist, taking a look. 'Children and invalids are morally overrated. If you ask me, they deserve each other.'

Frau Golubka was also studying the 'Help Wanted' column of the newspaper. She underlined all job offers for piano teachers and maids. Her husband paced the room, skirting the furniture. Frau Golubka had spread the newspaper out on a suitcase. A box of instant soup mix and three bowls stood on another case. Their child played outside with a horde of others, occasionally knocking on the ground-floor window, pressing his nose against the pane till his parents noticed him; then he darted away. By the time he returned, Herr Golub was sorting clothes with small choppy gestures. His wife was staring at the soup-mix box, reading the line again and again, while listening to her husband complain. 'An incredible experience coming your way.'

He saw her lips move. 'Incredible experience,' she mumbled and this drove him to action. He swept the soup-mix box and the plates onto the linoleum floor and restored the makeshift table's original identity; he began to pack his clothes into it. His wife picked up the soup-mix box languidly and continued to read where she had left off. Their son looked through the window, from one to the other; he did not try to make sense of the scene. He existed. His body grew one billionth of a millimetre taller while his father packed and his mother studied a soup-mix box. After a while she looked up and saw what Herr Golub in his agitation did not notice—that he was packing not only his own clothes but also hers and the child's. She did not stop him. She smiled. Soon the case was full but there was still a lot of men's clothing left and he realized his error.

He saw that she was laughing. 'Be my guest,' he said. 'Laugh.'

He sank down on his knees in front of the bed, with his back turned to her. He had his eyes closed and his hands clasped together.

Frau Golubka stopped smiling. She was terrified. She reached across the room to run her hand over the brown stubble on his head. She asked, 'Are you praying?! Are you that desperate?'

He jumped up. 'I'm keeping my hands occupied, or they'd slug you,' he said, 'which wouldn't be right in front of the child.' He reached for the suitcase, lifted it high up into the air, turned it over, so that the clothes spilled everywhere.

He packed again, this time with forethought; he picked out all of the family's warm clothes, the sweaters, coats, and socks. He left the summer things on the floor. 'In two months,' he said, 'it'll be autumn. You'll freeze. Too bad.'

Dr Anhalt's secretary had clipped Dr Waller's ad and laid it on her boss's desk, but he had not bothered to read it. A few minutes later, a colleague called and said, 'I just heard Waller's put an ad in the paper soliciting for children. I think you have a scandal on your hands.'

Dr Anhalt rang Dr Waller at home and asked him for lunch. Then he worried that it might be awkward and invited Waller's colleague, Dr Graf, along. Dr Graf specialized in the number zero, a tall man who wore blue jeans and leather jackets to work but had such an elegant way of moving, that is, he moved inconspicuously, that one classed him instinctively as a gentleman. His elongated bald head, seat of his prodigious talent and cold reserve, held the mystery of a closed cathedral. His face had all the features traditionally called handsome, an aquiline nose, and strong chin, but his expression was generally so forbidding, despite a sense of humour, that few looked for long. Those that dared look remarked that his eyes were strange, although they could not say why. In fact, one eye was blind after an accident he'd had as a boy in Bergen-Belsen, but there was more to this strangeness than that, more than the early death of a wife he was said to have loved, more than the forty years he had spent in Germany without ever applying for citizenship, preferring instead the discomforts of statelessness—something he talked about endlessly.

All newcomers at the Institute eventually read the letter he had received from Bonn about the death of his parents, offering him compensation of ten marks a day for the length of their incarceration in Auschwitz ('not including the date of entry and date of decease') and ending with an invitation to apply for German citizenship.

Everyone at the Institute was similarly acquainted with his reply, in which he thanked the administration for its kind offer but turned it down, saying he could not imagine why anyone in the world would freely call himself a German. Indeed, he had written, he guessed that toilets all over the country must be flushing constantly as people disposed of their passports in the only appropriate way.

The prospect of a united Germany had so antagonized Dr Graf that it had moved him to action. He wanted a say in the matter: he applied for German citizenship. When he arrived at work he withdrew a photocopy of his application and flipped it open at his co-workers, as if it were a badge. Ever since the Wall had come down, he had been distracted. Instead of attending to his own work, he did some odds-and-ends chores with Dr Waller's solitrons that any research assistant could have done. And when he wasn't doing that, he was studying the classified ads in the newspapers, where the effects of the day were much more quickly noted than in the news. He was, for instance, the first to know about the declining price of East German cars on the second-hand market. By the spring of 1990, these mobile containers called Trabants were going for a token sum, and he predicted that by July they would be listed under the 'Items for Free.' He had a plan for them.

Dr Graf had not yet studied the classifieds when Dr Anhalt invited him to lunch. He had the newspaper open at the 'Cars for Sale' page as he entered the restaurant and addressed his companions. 'People are fascinated by cars because they satisfy people's desire to be four-legged.'

The others took no notice. Dr Anhalt was a trim elderly man whose eyes gleamed as brightly as his expensive teeth and who seemed dazzled by his own reflection, which he sought everywhere, in his glass, in the mirror across the restaurant, in his soup spoon, especially while someone else was doing the talking. But he could pay attention: Benedikt's placing immoral ads in the paper had made him have second thoughts about keeping someone on the staff who was no longer what he called a 'useful contributor.' He ordered the most expensive item on the menu for his guests.

'You're a wonderful mathematician, Dr Waller. But as long as you're between projects, why don't you referee other projects instead of just waiting for a paper to be published? Attend some conferences, write some reviews. Perhaps you'd like to give a few lectures. Tell me a bit about your life outside the Institute. Are you married—children?' Dr Anhalt was silenced by the sight of a meat press being set up over his soup plate. The waiter laid slices of veal inside, pressed them, and the broth trickled into the bowl. 'Twenty-five marks a serving, but worth every penny,' said Dr Anhalt. He forgot his companions. When the last drop was gone, he remembered them. 'When is your paper being published? What, you haven't heard from the magazine? Never mind, they'll publish it. With the usual fanfare. I think you should review regularly. The way others do. You're between projects. Say yes, and I'll order you another soup.'

To Dr Anhalt's amazement, Benedikt shook his head, finishing his broth with visible effort.

'When I ate here with Einstein, Albert said to me, "Gundolf, not even Mrs Einstein could cook like this. I'd trade my original manuscript about the theory of relativity for another serving."

And I ordered him one and said, "Albert, everyone knows you've misplaced it." Did you ever meet Einstein, Dr Waller? Probably you're too young.'

'I guess, probably so,' replied Dr Waller, daydreaming. Dr Graf got up from the table, with the classifieds, and said, 'I just have to make a telephone call. The first Trabants have made their appearance under "Items for Free"!'

Waller's too autistic to be a pervert, thought Dr Anhalt. But as he prided himself on his ability to communicate with even the most silent of scientists, he was soon casting about for a way to elicit Benedikt's confidence, find out about this pederast business. He knew that a well-kept secret could revive communication. 'I have a terrible dilemma at the office,' he said. 'Please don't tell anyone. One of our best technicians has tested positive for AIDS. I was going to fire him, but I'm a liberal man. And he's one of our best workers. I made him promise not to tell a soul. If word got out that my institute has AIDS-infected staff, no one would give us research money. Do you think I made a mistake?'

'I hope not,' replied Dr Waller.

'Now you have my most valuable asset, my reputation, in your hands. You could blackmail me. Tell me about yourself. Did you say you had children?'

'No. Here's Dr Graf.'

Dr Graf reappeared at the far end of the dining room, his expressionless face concealing surprise. He had negotiated the Trabant, leafed through the pages for more treasures, and read the obscure column 'Miscellaneous.' He had learned something about Dr Waller there. He had abandoned the newspaper.

An old woman who had tried to make conversation with him as he waited tottered after him, chattering to his back. 'Slow down, love. I want to tell your fortune. All you have to do is write down your name for me.' She waved a beer coaster. 'No, thank you,' begged Dr Graf. She had the seamless face of a fat child. She was still with him as he reached the table.

'Tell Dr Anhalt's future,' said Dr Graf, waving at Dr Anhalt.

'He has grand plans.' The old woman misunderstood his directions, went over to Dr Waller. Dr Graf tried to stop her, 'No, no, not that man . . .'

It was too late. The old woman was soliciting the sick man. 'Sign this coaster for me, and I'll tell you what your future holds.'

'It's no secret,' he replied easily.

'Go on, Dr Waller,' urged Dr Anhalt. 'But I get to keep the coaster afterwards, for my autograph collection.' He held out his gold fountain pen.

Dr Waller scribbled, without thinking, handed the coaster back to the fortune-teller, and said, 'Well?' He was used to hearing his future. Not only from the physicians. His sister told it to him constantly.

The old woman studied the signature. After a while, she pulled out a chair and sank down, losing optimism and altitude together. She stared at the coaster for a long time, while the lunch guests searched for something offhand and funny to say. Finally she spoke up.

'Someone is going to hurt you very much. And the pain will be far greater than anything you ever felt before or even imagined possible. Do you know what I mean? Terrible pain—oh, I am sorry.' She stared at the signature again and then she offered consolation. 'You can find relief, dear, you can.' She looked directly at Dr Waller for the first time: 'In the shade of a tree.' Then she turned to Dr Anhalt, 'Now some money for a beer, please.'

Dr Anhalt took the coaster, searching in his jacket pocket with his other hand. He picked out several smaller coins and placed them on the table in front of her. She looked at the pile, like a child at sweets: with satisfaction and a bit of anxiety. Then her expression changed. The years added on to her face at great speed: a frown placed wrinkles everywhere. She snarled, 'Small change!' lifted the end of the table, heaved it into the air, and the money and dirty plates showered down.

The group took advantage of the mess to disband. On his desk Dr Anhalt found the copy of Dr Waller's ad that his secretary had clipped for him; he assumed it was a scrap and threw it away without reading it. He sat down and remembered that he had a new addition to his autograph collection. He studied the coaster that Dr Waller had signed. It presented a puzzle.

He had written over a grey grease stain, the ink had run, each letter had blossomed, elaborating Dr Waller's simple signature. The coaster read:

Benedikt August Anton Cecil August Count Waller von Wallerstein

'A nervous breakdown,' said Dr Anhalt. 'We have to show him that we appreciate him.'

Dr Anhalt had a carton of caviar and three bottles of his favourite vodka delivered to Dr Waller. Schmidt sent him a huge bouquet of anemones, which his wife had recently designated Good Taste, and a note saying, 'To the new father!' Dr Graf parked two Trabants, newly acquired from East Germans embarrassed to own them, in front of Benedikt's house. He thought this would alarm the residents and cheer up his sick colleague.

CHAPTER 6

Seriously now: Benedikt thinks his plan for survival has backfired,
and perhaps it has, but perhaps it hasn't

That afternoon, Dr Anhalt followed Dr Waller home. The
city lay submerged in hot watery air; the upright walk was
no longer a natural form of locomotion, and each breath was
eventful. Despite the strain, Dr Anhalt wanted to talk. He stayed
so close to his companion that Dr Waller became anxious about
possible physical contact. In order to distract himself, he read
licence plates on parked cars, looking for interesting number
combinations. Dr Anhalt saw his gaze; he did the same. But like a
child with reading difficulties, he read aloud. When they reached
his front door, Dr Waller took the keys from his pocket, relieved
at the prospect that he would now be saying goodbye.

Instead Dr Anhalt said, 'Let's talk, Dr Waller, for a moment. I
know something about you. About the children. I can give you
some advice. Then you can give me some.'

Dr Waller's face betrayed no emotion; after all, he had none.
Any surprise or confusion was subordinated to the assumption
that Dr Anhalt was making the usual small talk.

'Let's go upstairs to your place,' said Dr Anhalt.

'My place,' said Dr Waller, 'is even hotter than the street, and
you're already very uncomfortable, Dr Anhalt, I can see that.
You'd be better off at the Institute, where it's air-conditioned. I'll
be in again tomorrow.'

But Dr Anhalt had made his decision. He was going to con-
fess. There was no turning back. Nor did Dr Waller have any

choice. His feet had already begun the climb upstairs. Dr Anhalt kept up, although he would have preferred to take the elevator, and the strain of hoisting his weight uphill made him forget his dilemma.

The two men reached the landing bristling with irritation and suspense, whereupon Dr Waller said, 'I have to go shopping—shopping must be very boring to you, a man of such sophistication.' He turned around and headed back downstairs, Dr Anhalt chugging behind. 'I suggest,' Dr Anhalt insisted, 'that I accompany you. I'd like to talk to you about some special transactions. I'm in trouble too, you know.'

The day continued to heat up. The carnival exuberance of the last winter, which had carried over into spring, had in the summer something strained and mean about it. The visitors from the poor neighbourhoods of eastern Berlin had little money to spend—they pushed and shoved through the shopping centres as though the aisles led through beautiful, thorny rose bushes. The small change of various currencies jangled in most pockets, marks from East and West, zlotys, kopeks. The bearer could tell them apart by their weight in his palm. A big department store was several doors down the street but Dr Waller rarely entered it. It was very crowded. Customers were looking but not buying and the staff were infuriated. Dr Anhalt led the way.

When they reached the middle of the crowded front hall he stopped, assumed the stance he used when speaking in his capacity as director, a complicated posture of repose, in which he threw his head back, turned his eyes upwards, crossed his hands in front of his groin until, although only thin air was supporting him from the back, it seemed he had reached maximum stability. 'My God,' he pronounced, 'my God,' pulling on his cigarette. Benedikt, caught on the hook and sinker of politeness, did not move away.

A map of Germany hung from the ceiling, the cities marked by twinkling lights. Several of the light bulbs had gone out and the workers were having some trouble repairing them. They climbed around on ladders and pulled and pushed the map until they realized it had a short circuit and was buzzing with a charge. 'Turn the juice off!' they yelled over the heads of the shoppers.

Down below, Dr Anhalt finally spoke. 'Tell me about the children,' he said. 'You're looking for children.'

'It was my sister's idea,' Dr Waller said. 'Nothing serious. But nothing came of it. One shouldn't listen to one's sister.'

Dr Anhalt drew on his cigarette. 'Shall we go somewhere quiet?' he asked. But Benedikt did not respond. He was monitoring the map, certain that it was about to fall. He did not want to be crushed by a map of this huge new Germany. Dr Anhalt kept up a conversation by asking him questions about his lifestyle, even about his sister, which Dr Waller answered with ingenuous honesty. Above them the workers fooled with the circuits, unable to figure out what was wrong.

Finally Dr Anhalt said, 'I'm actually quite desperate myself. As one desperate man to another, give me advice. I was a foolish young man once. I believed in certain things I don't believe in anymore. I got involved with people I shouldn't have. I helped them. I became their translator. I thought they had a right to know what everyone here knew. They were the underdogs.'

The workers abandoned the map. They came down off the ladder shaking their heads. Their Germany looked drab without sparkling lights. Dr Anhalt said, 'Let's go and see what's in men's wear.'

Dr Waller squeezed through the shoppers behind Dr Anhalt. Sweaters were on sale. Jackets.

Dr Anhalt fingered the cloth and said, 'I can tell the ratio of linen to synthetic just by the feel. Do I need a jacket? Actually, I do. But I shall live without this one. Let's look at the ties.'

'Once upon a time,' said Dr Anhalt, in the quiet, persuasive voice of the storyteller, 'there was a young prince who lived in great splendour, with every conceivable material comfort, but he had lost his health.'

He stopped at the tie rack and leafed through it, continuing, 'And the prince was willing to try every doctor and every remedy. But nothing restored the health necessary to enjoy his life, and he was very despondent. One day he was walking in his gardens, and he passed a pond full of very high reeds. He looked down and in the water he saw his own face crosshatched by reeds, as if it were very old and wrinkled. And this reflection spoke to the prince: "Your health can easily be restored: you must wear the coat of a happy man." '

Dr Anhalt went over to a large basket of sun hats. He tried on a cap. Leering at his reflection in the next mirror, he said, 'Do I need this? No!' He tossed the hat back into the basket and said, 'And the prince thanked his own reflection, and hurried back to his palace, where he ordered his soldiers and servants to find a happy man.

'But though they searched all the cities and villages for thirty days, they could not find one single man who would admit to being happy.'

Dr Anhalt moved on through the crowd, making sure that Benedikt could keep up with him.

'The prince was very sad and went for a walk in the garden, although he was rather weak now. And as he passed the pond, he saw that the reeds had grown thicker, and his reflection, which looked even older now, addressed him: "You must wear the coat of a happy man." Can you follow what I'm saying, Dr Waller?'

'Certainly.'

'Good. So the prince urged his men to resume their search and this time they scoured the countryside, the forests and fields. After many days and nights they finally found a man living deep in a wood who admitted to being happy.'

Dr Anhalt stopped and confronted his companion with nervous eyes.

'Triumphant, they asked for his coat. But the question puzzled the man who admitted to happiness. And finally he answered, "But I don't own a coat." '

Dr Waller's face was smooth and grey as an old stone.

Dr Anhalt concluded his fairy tale, making his point. 'I don't own a thing as far as science goes. I never did any research of my own. I have nothing to show. I gave everything away. On microfilm. To an officer. On a regular basis. When I was a visiting professor at American universities it was haphazard. The last time was on the sixth of November. They said I was indispensable.'

'I understand,' said Dr Waller. 'Don't worry. These things happen. I have to go.' He turned around.

'About your ad in the paper—' called Dr Anhalt. Dr Waller dashed off.

Back at home, Herr Waller found a note taped to the door:

> Per your ad: do you still 'seek a child' for adoption? I
> seek a dad for my wonderful son, who deserves a new
> chance, a new life. Perhaps you're the answer to all
> my smashed hopes.

The note was signed 'Jahn,' with a telephone number. Benedikt called.

A smooth, educated voice said, 'Excellent to hear from you so soon, and so punctually—let me get right to the point: would you consider an older child?'

'Older?' repeated Benedikt. 'How old?'

'I'm thirty-two,' he said.

'The matter has taken care of itself,' said Benedikt. 'Pardon me. Goodbye.'

The backfire, Benedikt grumbled, hanging up his jacket at home, makes a lot of noise and dirt and can cause severe embarrassment, even to bystanders. As he pottered over to his sofa, he debated what was worse: to make a decision, act on it, and have a lot of unhappy results, or to have fate, unasked, simply heap unhappiness on one. He had tried to influence fate, not a dishonorable practice, but fate had made a fool of him. Benedikt consoled himself: the ad was a mistake. But merely a waste of time, a touch of humiliation.

Scarcely had he recovered from the afternoon's shock, relieving his nerves by following his routine straight through into the
evening, scarcely had night fallen, putting up a wall between
himself and that awful day, than his doorbell rang.

His doorbell practically exploded. He was sitting on the sofa
when he felt the sudden ringing as a jostling inside his ear. He
became confused. Shush! Shush! he thought. Instead it came
shriller, grimmer, grabbier until he was deafened, whereupon it
turned into a current slapping against the door. He remained on
the sofa and enjoyed the inertia that could stymie fate: the door,
the disease. Perhaps he would never get up again. He would
remain there in the humble sitting position. He would not swallow or take the trouble to shift his arms. He could end the
struggle right now. Minutes would melt into months. He would
look out the manholes of his eyes. Without the slightest effort on
his part, he would disintegrate.

But his hearing returned, the bell volleyed inside his ear.
Instinctively, he turned his head to escape it, and in one motion,
he was at the door, pulling it open.

The caller did not take his hand off the buzzer, and when
the door stood open, the bell continued in a piercing dirge. A
child stood there, its palm pressed against the buzzer. Just because Benedikt had opened the door, the child saw no reason to
discontinue the noise. The woman patted the child's shoulder,
trying to get it to stop. Benedikt noticed her size—short,
stubby—her clothes—shiny black trousers, a peculiar black
shawl around her shoulders—and an acrid smell.

Then he took in the child, its thick brown hair that tangled
along its small shoulders, its black-rimmed glasses, eyes like blue
dabs behind the thick spectacles, its soft-looking nose. Something brown smeared at the mouth made him feel queasy. The
child looked very foreign.

The mother caught his attention again.

'We have come,' she said in an accent Benedikt felt could
rinse the West of any civilization, 'as you asked.'

Benedikt stepped aside and waved them in. It was the same

movement his father had used to welcome the impoverished, envious refugees from the lost provinces in 1945. Despite the generosity of his gesture, the wide sweep of that stick arm, the child did not move but hung on its mother's coat, its face warped with an expression of fierce disapproval. She turned, scooped her creature into her arms, and swung it over the doorstep. Once inside it stayed where it was, quaking on the wall-to-wall carpeting of Benedikt's foyer. The woman planted her feet wide apart on the threshold and turned her body back to haul two big, square, tan fake-leather cases inside. With an air of finality, she pushed the door shut behind her, straightening up. Then she sank down again, crouching at one of the cases, opening it, sticking her hand in, angling for something. Briefly, Benedikt expected a present for himself, the host, but she produced two pairs of grey, threadbare bedroom slippers. She closed the case again, stood up, sighed. Mother and child pried off their brown street shoes, placing them alongside Benedikt's collection of fine Italian loafers, and donned the slippers. The child looked at its feet, wiggled its toes, slipped a smile like a gold piece to its mother.

'Domici,' she said. Home.

Benedikt led them into the living room but he did not enjoy seeing it through their eyes, his simple brown sofa intimate as a bed, his few knickknacks on the end table (a Hummel figurine of a monk, a lamp made of illuminated plastic lemons), all presents from his sister, then his fake Christmas tree with the plastic bowl hanging from a branch, the turtle reeling around inside, his plain, practical carpeting, his books lining the walls, precious bibles of science, which they couldn't decipher, and his private notebooks (the male models hidden at the back), his desk at the window (even more intimate than the sofa), his computer (they might assume it was a television). Their interest pained him, until he noticed that the visitors did not seem at all curious. The mother's glance seemed obligatory, her smile formal. He walked them through the kitchen, from the end near his desk to the other end near the sofa. But even the microwave and the dishwasher did not arouse her interest.

He continued to the guest room, where he had never allowed anyone but his sister. The bed had been a housewarming present from his sister when he moved in, years before, and he had hung a Day-Glo map of the surrounding galaxies on the wall, expecting to tell her anecdotes about the heavens. That was before his interest in the universe had exhausted itself, when he realized that it was simply a location. Without asking, the Russian woman understood this to be her room. She collected the cases from the hall and began trudging back and forth, settling them down in the guest room without unpacking. The child followed her, an erratically moving obstacle that tangled in her feet until she spoke sharply, and evidently with an imperative, because it slunk to the living room and cowered in the middle of the sofa.

Benedikt stood in the entrance hall trying to make sense of the situation, with the Russian woman drifting around the room, hither and thither, light-footed despite the boulders on her chest. A wind whipped out between the snapping blades of her legs and the fluttering black jacket that bore an odour which Benedikt interpreted as dirty clothes and the vast toilet of the East.

Benedikt hurried to open the window. He did not see his colleague Dr Graf waiting for a parking space in another Trabant. The night was hot and the street smell washed in like clean water.

'What can I do for you? Money?' He put his hand in his pocket and searched for change. At the same time he was calculating how many bills he should give them; they were evidently poor, and he wanted them to leave again quickly.

'The child should eat something. It's hungry.'

The child should eat and then leave.

He imagined himself saying goodbye again, closing the door after them, after all, it was late, too late for visiting. They should be getting off to bed. They lived somewhere else, and they should return there. First he had to give them something to eat. When he saw the woman sit down next to the child on his sofa, he went into the kitchen. He found that he had nothing to spare from his carefully calculated weekend menu. With some diffi-culty, because he had never done anything like this for someone else, Benedikt spread a piece of bread with marmalade. He did not know what to do next. Put it on a plate and shove it in front of the child? He hesitated.

She came up behind him, looked at the bread, and said, 'Give me a plate, please.'

He always used the same plate, couldn't remember where he kept extra ones. He opened a cupboard at random. At once her arm travelled in front of his face, reaching for something; she withdrew a plate. 'The child,' she said, 'is thirsty.' She carried the bread away.

He had just enough milk for his morning coffee. He emptied this into a glass and set it down in front of the child on the sofa table.

'The child likes tea,' said the mother.

He returned to the kitchen, set water to boil, and imitated the way his sister made tea, one tea bag per cup. He heard her move around the room while talking to the child, who answered, a sound unfamiliar to him: voices in the apartment, and therefore unsettling. When he brought the tea, he suffered new noises, the jangle of cups and spoons, the shifting of feet, ghastly as a hor-ror-movie soundtrack. He suppressed his panic, stood up, came to them. Mother and child were occupying his sofa again, so he had no choice but to sit in the guest chair himself. He saw her put three heaping teaspoons of sugar in the child's cup. The child drank with concentration, producing a glugging sound, its eyes squinting at the bottom of the cup as it drank, its lower lip wet, its pose more desperate than graceful. Benedikt felt a strange mental prodding immediately familiar to most parents, but he could not identify it: pedagogic disapproval. Children shouldn't drink tea, especially with so much sugar. He had a load of opin-

ions on the matter that he'd been toting about without knowing
it. He said nothing and watched the child, who, without turning
its eyes from its cup, used its ears and nose and who knows what
extrasensory organs to keep its mother under tense surveillance,
ready at any instant to spring up and follow her. With equal
dedication, the child seemed to screen out its host, as if the
stranger weren't sitting there, within touching distance. Benedikt
had never paid attention to a child before, and he realized now
that he had no idea what one really looked like. He glimpsed its
hands on the cup, looked away again, and as if his impressions
were a kind of stolen goods, he studied them in his memory: the
hands were well-formed, with even fingers and very white skin.

Having drunk the whole cup of tea, the child devoured the
bread down to the bread crumbs that fell on the sofa, and used
shirt and trousers for a napkin. When the woman stood up, the
child reached her side instantly and they adjourned to the guest
room, closing the door behind them. Almost at once, they both
came out again, hunted for a toilet by opening doors until they
had found it. He tried not to listen. After they had returned to
the guest room, he lay down, curled up on the sofa, and pretended he was alone. His visitors would not permit him his illu-
sions—he heard a woman's voice singing in the bedroom. The
melody seemed to consist of random notes because he did not
know the song. After a while he heard the door handle turn
again. Some formal manner governed him more than any despair.
He uncoiled himself, and by the time she returned he was sitting
upright again.

She sat down in the chair opposite and said, 'He's sleeping.'

This information overwhelmed him. 'He! It's a boy!' he said.

'You want family,' she stated, looking at him. 'You're all
alone.'

'I'm ill,' replied Benedikt.

But the woman insisted, as if she knew better, 'You're alone.'

'I am ill.'

She looked sceptical.

Benedikt added, 'I wanted someone I could look at without

feeling ill. Excuse me. I didn't mean it that way. I had something else in mind. A child. Not an older woman.'

She looked him in the eyes, as if to assess his competence on the subject. Then she stretched her hands in front of her and studied them with mysterious satisfaction. The matter interested him, against his better judgement. She laid her hands carefully on her knees as if to display them. They had very wide palms and tapered fingers, each one different from the next, each tip facing a different direction, each fingernail dirty to a different degree, and the thumbs unusually long—his own fingers were so similar that his hand was a unified object. The strangeness of her hand confused him and he avoided her face. He could not have said what she looked like; he would not have recognized her in a photograph.

Benedikt argued, 'You are not what I had in mind. Please. I'm sorry. I want to adopt a child. I hadn't considered a mother to go along with it. I don't see how—you see, I have a sister who will be perfectly suitable.'

Her eyes became very peculiar, rather frightful. Her lips opened a bit; he could see one gold tooth off to the side of her mouth—the rest appeared to be various sizes and colours.

'If there's a mother to go along with it—well, why not? So, why not? I suppose it's more usual. All the better, but then someone who needs mainly security, a place to live, and a bit of daily routine. Yes—why not?—someone who wants a family life. I will look after the child's interests. But I have to admit, it worries me. This apartment is not that big.'

She said, 'I'm used to much smaller.' She suddenly laughed for no reason and repeated, 'Well, well, well.'

'How come you speak such good German?' asked the German. 'Russians generally do not.'

'I am not a Russian,' she replied, sounding offended. 'I am a citizen of the Soviet Union,' and then she added, 'unfortunately.'

'Well, what's the difference? You speak Russian. That's what counts.' His confusion at such presence of mind in a foreigner made him dislike her. He regretted this at once and asked in a tone as pleasant as he could make it, 'What's your name, anyway? I don't place any value on a name. But it's good to know.'

'Golubka. Marja. My son is Valerie.'

He found it a girlish name.

'What are you doing here in Germany?'

She smiled, keeping her lips shut, and shook her head a little, as if she found the question silly, or impossible to answer. He felt that the smile on her face was loosely attached.

'I suppose you like the shopping,' he said.

At this she laughed loudly, keeping her face absolutely still, opening her mouth wide, and making a hee-haw sound. 'But I don't have any money!' She seemed puzzled and not at all ashamed.

He did not ask more. It was none of his business.

'Don't be misled into thinking it's freer here,' he said, slipping into the tone of voice he had used when explaining the universe to his sister. 'The West has a terror of its own kind. Censorship, unemployment. The advertising industry provides thirty thousand jobs a year to those who'd otherwise be on the streets. And by the way,' he warned, 'I don't have a television.'

She looked at the turtle in its bowl, as if the reptile would give her information about this curious German.

'Perhaps you could work. Have you worked before? Had a job?'

She looked perplexed and repeated the syllables, 'Job, job.'

He tried again: 'Arbeit.'

She nodded. 'Arbeit macht frei.' Work is freedom. Her eyes seemed to beam with wickedness.

'Oh, come on,' he said. 'That's ridiculous.' He was infuriated. 'What will you do, anyway?'

'I don't understand, what do I do,' she replied.

'What do you do'—he permitted his tone to become aggressive—'you work at something, don't you? What do you do all day?'

And without hesitating, without any apparent planning or coquetry, she replied quietly, 'I exist.'

CHAPTER 7

*Picking up speed: the fact that the Russian mother exists quickly
begins to affect Benedikt. Can he get rid of her again?*

'I exist, too. I know because I'm ill,' replied Benedikt. 'When
every minute is unpleasant, you become aware of existence. I
exist more. And a lot of things about existence bother me.
Smells, for example'—he meant her smell, but politeness stayed
his tongue—'ugliness'—he was always polite to foreigners—'un-
evenness of all sorts, eruptions and excavations and concealments
here and there—I've no patience for any of that anymore.' His
patience with her now exhausted, he repeated, 'I exist!' But having repeated the word so often, he found it had lost its meaning,
turned into pure sound, ornamentation.

The Russian woman appeared to have a sudden attack of
shyness, or confusion. She gazed in his direction, her large lips
curved upwards at the corners in a set smile, and waited for him
to finish whatever it was that he was trying to say. After a while,
she seemed less animate to him, less of an intrusion. Her eyes
turned to Bakelite, her hair to a gleaming black-and-grey hood,
and the skin of her hands to plastic. Her lap of black acetate
trousers shone. He looked at her closely. He analysed the way
her hairline ran along her wide forehead and along the temples,
in a thick black mass. She had high cheekbones, very pale skin
with freckles, light-brown, almost orange, eyes, a sharp little
nose, and wide mouth. This face became very unstable during
conversation: the expressions that were apt to befall it dramati-

cally changed the relationships between the different parts, creating countless different faces. But now that she was feeling
somehow repudiated by him or perhaps just stunned, but in any
case was quiet and wasn't indulging her obvious appetite for
communication, he could see that her features were asymmetri-
cal, the nose bent slightly to the right side, the left eye narrower,
smaller than the right. The alertness of these two individual orbs
made matters worse, far worse—she was watching him, watching
him examine her face. At the same time, her smell reached his
nostrils, like two fingers poking into his nose, an odour he interpreted as decay.

He wondered whether she would use his bathtub. The idea
disgusted him. But it was not charitable of him. 'You can use the
bathtub,' he said, standing up. She remained seated, her eyes
turned towards him. He could not decipher her attitude. 'I have
soap, water, everything.' But she did not reply.

'Shall I tell you about my illness?' he asked. 'I'll explain it to
you.

'What I have is common. Dog eats dog, more or less. I always avoided taking any part in it. Found it uninteresting. Still
do. The medical side of science is tedious. What goes on inside
doesn't matter more to me than visna virus to a sheep, equine
infectious anaemia to a horse, caprine arthritic encephalitis to a
goat. And they don't matter at all. My monocytes and macro-
phages are infected. So what! I suffer defective chemotaxis, altered monkine production, enhanced release of interleukin-1,
cachetin, pyrogens, cell-killing. I'm passive as a battlefield. That's
existence. Two million people die every year from malaria and no
one ever worries about them.'

He went to his desk and stood with his back to her, scribbling something, while she waited patiently on the sofa. Finally,
he returned to his chair, sat down, and held up a page.

'This is the scene right now.'

He showed her the defender molecules of medication, their
atoms arranged in pentagonal heads, bonded against the invader.

'The figures do battle. The outcome is statistically proven. There's no question, the life expectancy of the host—that's me— is a question of two, three years. Burnt ground. Gutted interiors. If the host is lucky.'

She stared.

'Can you see what I mean?' he asked.

'I lost my glasses,' she said, 'twenty years ago.'

'You didn't replace them?'

'At the same time as I lost my watch . . .'

'You have no watch!' he cried. 'How do you orient yourself!'

'And my back teeth.' She said this matter-of-factly, as if she were reading off details from her passport.

'No teeth at the back! Why don't you go to the dentist?'

She waved her hand. 'What does it matter?' she said. 'I can eat perfectly well at the front of the mouth. And I can see well enough without glasses. And what do I need to know the time for?'

He had lost his place in his own tale of woe, so, although he was not curious, he asked, 'How did it happen? To your teeth. Did you have an accident?'

'No, no. It just happened. One day. They weren't good any- more, so it was no loss.'

'Didn't they cause you pain?' He felt something like curiosity.

'Earlier. A lot earlier. Then nothing.'

'It's like having death in your mouth, isn't it?' he said. 'You are a very old woman in your mouth. You must get new ones. It's possible. Old people have perfectly good teeth. And the child, he has good teeth . . .' He warned himself to avoid looking at her mouth.

'The child? Yes, he's fine.' She seemed surprised at the men- tion of the child.

'He should see a dentist.'

'I lost everything at once—I was eating a sandwich in a res- taurant, and the teeth were in it. I was surprised. I stood up right away and left. And didn't watch where I was going. There was a car. A Mercedes. A German. But it was my fault.'

'What happened? You dropped your watch and your glasses, and he ran over them?'

'My fiancé,' she said. 'Over my fiancé too.' She said it gaily. 'He was with me. He was upset about my teeth. I jumped out of the way. My glasses fell off. My fiancé was always slow. That's why he had borrowed my watch. It was useless afterwards.' She seemed to enjoy her own tone of voice. 'My mother lost a husband. Lots of Russians lost fiancés and husbands. I'm quite ordinary in that respect. It was a long time ago. One recovers, doesn't one?'

She stopped speaking, smiled at him, with the sole purpose, it seemed, of provoking a return smile from him. When he did not respond, she forced yet another layer of cheer into her voice to ask, 'What about you? What do you do, other than exist?'

He tried to alleviate the awkwardness he felt by explaining himself. 'I'm a mathematical physicist. I've been working on solitron research,' he said. 'My work is hard to explain. My sister always asks me questions like whether my work is useful, and I say no. She asks me whether she'll be able to understand it if she really tries, and I say no. Solitrons won't interest you, either. Although they're fascinating. They're theoretical particles. Nothing you'll find lying about in your home. But you can see them with a computer. I see them all the time.' She yawned. 'It's not interesting to you,' he apologized. 'You were probably never interested in that sort of thing. Perhaps Valerie is.'

'I am just very tired,' she replied.

'Then you must sleep.' He stood up, anxious that he had exhausted her and irritated that she was going to spend the night in his apartment.

'First, I would like to smoke,' she said. She withdrew a pack of cigarettes from her jacket pocket. 'It's my last cigarette. I have to stop smoking. It's bad for the health, isn't it?' She stood up, walked to the hall, to the front door, and out.

He heard her footsteps in the stairwell and smelled smoke. For a few minutes he was alone with a child in his home. It felt very odd to him.

She returned, nodded, and remarked, 'Thank you,' in a rather offhand way, as if she wasn't sure she meant it or found it an unpleasant sentiment.

'You're welcome,' he replied. He returned to the sofa, full of grim premonition. Having another person in his apartment disturbed him, like a strange penetrating noise.

From the sofa, he heard the bedsprings rippling, 'Exist exist.'

'She exists to make a fool of me!' Benedikt stammered into the telephone, concluding the whole story; he hadn't paused once, describing the ad and how his health had improved dramatically, but for what earthly purpose?! he cried into the receiver. Only to be stricken with a Russian family!

And the voice he presumed belonged to his sister replied, 'Wrong number!'

'Dolly, I'm in a mess.' He tried again, standing at his desk, hunched over the phone.

'Dial properly!'

'Don't disturb!'

'The nerve!'

He kept trying. His fingers jumbled the digits. He travelled through Germany via wrong number. Everyone was home, snarling at him as he broke in and entered. At the tenth stop, he reached his sister. Police sirens on the television, screams in the background; she was having a quiet evening at home with her husband.

'You have to help me!' he spluttered. 'I've got myself into such a mess. With a Russian woman.' He repeated the story: the advertisement (all her fault), the sudden change in Dr Anhalt on this account, the peculiar character who had contacted him, and now this female with her son. Maybe she had no idea how awful it was having a stranger around, anybody around, for that matter, using up the living room and needing help which he would give, of course.

'What do you expect me to do,' Dolly stated, unruffled.

'Persuade her to leave!'

'Why aren't you watching television?' she asked. 'Ah, maybe you don't need to. We're watching Berlin.' And he realized she was watching the news and the news was Berlin.

'I guess you forget I have no television,' he replied, hanging up in such a fury that the receiver fell into the wastebasket. He did not bother to pull it out again. He heard it beeping in the basket. He switched on his computer, listened for the start-up noise, as if under the circumstances even as stalwart a companion as his computer might balk. But it rattled and clicked and purred, and he could communicate, punching in to the electronic mailbox.

He typed rapidly, addressing the editor of *Annals of Physics*. The journal had always published his work; it had accepted his first essay when he was just twenty-five. The magazine was a home at the best address. Few, very few, kept a permanent residence there as he did. Some published occasionally, their very best articles. Most never got past the secretary's standard rejection letter. She was like an armed doorman. But Dr Waller did not even know the secretary. He addressed his correspondence directly 'to the Editor in Chief': he didn't bother to remember the man's name. He wrote in English, a language he had conquered without much interest at school, treating it as a minor puzzle, never bothering to learn proper syntax: 'Have you many Thanks for your Interest in my Work. I sent You *Observations on the Collision Behaviour of Solitrons*, in early November 1989, and would like to inform myself about the Date of publication of this work. With many Thanks.' Seconds later, a faraway secretary added the letter to a backlog of queries waiting for an assistant's attention. He picked the telephone out of the trash.

From his desk he heard the bedsprings in the guest room. The Russian visitor was trying to get comfortable. Was she having trouble sleeping? That was her problem! he told himself. She exuded restlessness, nervousness, even from behind a closed door. He was aghast at how much space she seemed to take up, acoustically and physically. The bedsprings creaked, 'Exist exist.'

Half an hour passed. He sat in front of the computer without thinking. Sickness had made an old man of him in that sense too: he could sit for hours gazing at his computer as if it were a fire in a hearth. The bedroom door opened and he heard her footsteps. She went directly into the kitchen. In the reflection of the windowpane he could watch her there, follow how she was looking around, putting her face close to the kitchen surfaces, the shelves. She opened the refrigerator, the bright light inside illuminating her face. Finally she got a chair from the living room and lugged it back into the kitchen, placed it under a set of cupboards, stood up on it to peer into the top cupboard. In this pose, her chest and rump appeared magnified. She stood there for an inordinate length of time, her face deep inside, inspecting the contents without actually removing anything. Finally she took something. He heard her fingers, the scraping of a box, and saw her mouth move. He wondered why her mouth was moving. It occurred to him that she was eating, and he remembered that he kept sugar cubes up there. He watched her leave the kitchen again, her mouth still moving as she headed for the guest room. The door opened and closed. The bedsprings again.

Dr Waller assumed the posture of concentration at his desk, facing the computer. He forced himself to recall his solitron article, the first sentence, as a kind of exercise, but nothing came to him. Instead, he remembered the argument he had won, in his mind, with Dr Graf about the solitary particle's utter immunity to change. Dr Graf had suggested that if more variables were introduced, then the solitrons colliding on screen might respond individually to their annihilation. The argument had broken out as Schmidt came round with his high-school students for a tour of the Institute—the dispute was actually responsible for the acquaintance.

'Dr Waller and Dr Graf,' the young teacher had interrupted politely, 'the particles are just theoretical, a computer model, if we understand correctly, two waves rolling towards each other, they don't really exist. But the way you are talking about them . . .'

Dr Graf had been sitting at his desk waving the computer printouts at Dr Waller and trying to ignore the young people. He always behaved as if students were a plague sent by God to test his endurance. Up to that point he had pretended they weren't even in the room. Suddenly he turned on them, on their teacher. 'Just theoretical, you say? So what's the difference? you'll ask next. Does a character in a novel exist? As soon as a character exists in the reader's mind, then he exists—in fact he exists far more than, say, my grandmother, who you Germans decided had no right to exist and who I no longer remember. By the way'—he addressed Schmidt directly—'one of your shirt buttons is undone. You'll catch cold.' Then he turned back to his calculations.

Dr Waller had followed the crestfallen teacher hurrying his students into the hall and apologized for Dr Graf. The next thing he knew, the teacher had invited him for an after-hours drink.

Benedikt shuddered remembering the incident. Dr Graf had not actually been working on solitrons at the time, he had only taken a collegial interest in the project after guessing that Dr Waller was not entirely well. Dr Graf was matter-of-fact about illness because he had experience—his wife had died of cancer. This misfortune lay more than a decade back, but Dr Graf had never remarried or talked about his private life. He had treated Dr Waller with the gruff directness that can be the subtlest form of tact, helping him with paperwork, calling it spadework. Benedikt, remembering this, felt a need for some sort of corroboration from the magazine. He always had a reply within half an hour to any letter he wrote. With a half-hour of dozing the half-hour was up and the magazine had not replied. Still he waited. It did not occur to him that the editors might be treating him like an ordinary scientist grovelling for publication. And he was not used to waiting: this was a departure from the norm. Being ill was much worse than he had ever imagined—the slothfulness, the patience, of it. That's why one was called a patient.

The guest-room door had opened again, and he heard footsteps heading towards the front hall and leaving the apartment again, footsteps in the stairwell. After a while, the front door creaked open and shut again, feet padded back towards the guest room, and as the door snapped shut the mailbox file on his computer began to blink. His fingers fumbled with the keys. A letter had come from the journal: 'Dear Dr Waller—' His eyes could not grasp the formal tone. He skimmed it, appalled by the lack of enthusiasm, the singular phrases—'A decision has not yet been made. Please have patience'—and finally, a secretary's name.

He pushed away from his desk as if it were suddenly contaminated. As he passed the bookcases his shoulder caught one of the shelves so that the volumes slid down one after the other, like dominoes, the pages of his scientific notations and his childhood drawings swirling around the room, a few settling on his desk, the rest all over the floor. This is an embarrassment, he thought, a setback. The illness!

An itching had seized his torso. He wedged his hand into his pants, hauled up his shirt, tried to scratch himself, saw that the snowy back of his hand was covered with red welts. He did not check closely. He did not care what his hand looked like. 'A fungus, *Candida albicans* again, aspergillus perhaps, or heat rash, or insect bites,' he was muttering to himself. 'But more likely the Russian woman is my punishment for twenty million Soviet dead, and then the nation rejoicing over reunification, and a football championship just when the rest of Europe is falling into bits and pieces!' He could accept the necessity of punishment intellectually, but he didn't like having it administered piecemeal. There was no doubting the correlation between the nasty letter from the journal and the appearance of this woman. What might she be up to? He could ask. As he headed in her direction, courageous as always, he imagined his end: the Russian woman getting up in the middle of the night and planting a knife in his temple. He decided to confront her.

He limped the length of his impeccable apartment, his handsome head drooping, to the guest room, pushed open the door, and saw the situation: she was asleep.

CHAPTER 8

Long-lasting sweetness: Benedikt dreams about his homeland

On a hot summer night, history rubbed up against Germany with the insistent, fake tenderness of a hungry cat. After dark, the crowd swelled at the central bank in East Berlin, waiting for midnight, when the national currency of the West would be valid in the East. All year the syllables 'Deutsch-land' had scraped and whined like millions of screech-hinged old doors wobbling in a draught. And on this evening, Benedikt changed into his white cotton pyjamas, having seen no reason to alter his routine for either uninvited guests or unwanted occasions. His gradual descent into sleep was heralded by a chorus of young males chanting to the rhythmic beat of their feet, *'Sieg! Sieg! Sieg!'* Their voices gradually grew softer as they turned a corner, changing to *'Eins zu eins!'*—one to one—the slogan of the Easterners who wanted a decent exchange rate of their savings into West marks. A current of applause and boohs travelled once down the street. In the sudden stillness the voice of the bouncer outside the Club Madamn boomed, complaining to someone that the clientele were no drunker, no hornier than usual, no more generous. His companion agreed and predicted that, in its final hours of use, the East mark would make a last surprise appearance in the West, even though the illegal moneytraders at the train station were no longer handling it. Meanwhile, the crowd at the central bank continued to grow, and towards midnight, their rejoicing became audible in the Western neighbourhood because of all the televisions tuned to the event. The volume increased as the jubilation spread, rushing in suddenly from the East like a wind: with the massive outcry from the central bank as the clock touched zero, the glass windows of the bank gave way to the weight of the waiting, the crash of glass merged with the shrieks of the onlookers, and the transfusion of Western currency into the Eastern system began.

He heard the television moderator rounding up the news, the quacking of the crowd, 'D-mark D-mark D-mark!' *'Eins zu eins!'* the jinglebells of good currency being tossed into wallets and pockets or dandled in fists, while lightweight metal pieces went splashing into gutters, a pounding and scraping as official buildings were vandalized by crowds, the barking of fireworks, the mooing of car horns, the baying of the boys scavenging for merriment, the neighing of the opposition. Bands of people trotted through the streets, the fireworks following them overhead. And then drums and electric guitars tuned up for a free concert at a nearby square, and an amplified human voice howled.

Benedikt lay in the deathbed position, his limbs and head heavy, when the public merriment reached his ears and travelled on to his brain, where it was greeted with stiff disapproval. He turned over on his stomach and jammed his head down into his pillow but his ears continued to relay irritating information from the streets. A curious thrashing noise joined in. He did not realize that this sound was nearby, very close, in his own living room. When it became very loud, he thought of burglars and turned over, hastily getting out of bed to look. He crisscrossed through the fireworks that tracked across his wall. He reached the living room. The Christmas tree was dancing.

The turtle was in full flight inside her container, hobbling around her plastic lagoon, and this caused her housing to swing back and forth.

'Frightened,' grumbled Benedikt. He returned to bed.

He did not share his sleep with dreams. I won't have them! Benedikt told himself, before losing consciousness. As if dreams were houseboys. And yet. They came from the street to fetch him. A trial was in progress. The man responsible for natural death had been tracked down by watchful citizens in the DDR. By the time Benedikt had reached the makeshift courtroom, the accused had escaped. The mob fanned out, narrowed down after him. Benedikt, hanging back, watched them pass. The wind created by their rushing bodies spun him around like a leaf. He found himself pressed to the wall that fenced off the Autobahn. He crept along till he reached a military watchtower positioned next to the improvised courtroom. He tiptoed up the steps and observed the scene from high above, through the window of the warm watchtower room, his mood pleasant, sleepy.

The hunted man was facing millions of charges of first-degree murder. The public was understandably anxious to bring him to justice, and they weren't waiting for the judicial system. He had little chance of getting away. The population of the immediate neighbourhood, having been alerted, had left their beers wasting foam in front of their televisions and joined the chase.

Benedikt spotted the accused as he took off at a run, heading west on one of the three roads that connected West Berlin to West Germany (the outside lane was much smoother because it was hardly ever used, since passing was discouraged by the authorities), with a crowd shouting and waving their fists behind him. He must have backtracked on the other side of an incline and skipped over the grass median strip, and in the foggy darkness no one but Benedikt saw him running past on the outside lane, heading east. He managed to reach the highway rest stop where they had held him before. Benedikt came down from the tower. He saw the man responsible for natural death standing in a line with a busload of Czech tourists, taking weak coffee and diluted goulash soup on his tray. But his hands shook like birds' heads weaving in panic, so that the spoons began to bounce on the tray and the noise made everyone look sharply at him. The servers recognized him. He abandoned his tray, ran for it, locked himself in a public toilet until all the footsteps had passed. But the crowd was waiting for him at the back entrance. In the dark they recognized him by the smell of lavatory on his clothes as he tried to slink past.

They brought him back to the cafeteria, Benedikt walking among them. They had set up the dining room for a trial; the Germans had arranged the chairs in an orderly fashion, but now foreign elements who felt there were not enough seats and wanted standing room only, and for everyone, began simply hurling all the tables and chairs out the door, so that they lay upside down in a miserable heap of metal in the parking lot. The accused was made to stand at one end of the room, Benedikt was allowed to stand next to him, in order to get a better look, and the accusers made rows like a congregation before him. It was a hot night, and the fog rolled into the rest stop and condensed on foreheads. The public moaned in enthusiasm, as individuals in the courtroom took turns calling out the charges in random order. (It was only fitting, shouted one, that the first charges were of German dead; later, one would proceed by continent.)

At first, Benedikt listened closely:

'In Henningsdorf on that dim, dismal afternoon of the twenty-fourth of April 1986, Ulrich Eduard Schmidt hung up his grey jacket in his entrance hall, on the coatrack he had installed himself. He smelled the dinner his wife was preparing but felt no satisfaction. She interpreted his expression as a lack of love, and to punish him she said, "Keep your jacket on, we're all out of beer, you have to go straight back out and buy some." He took his jacket off the peg, but then hung it back up again. He felt warm enough, despite the cold wind, because of all the stairs he had just climbed. His wife handed him a pail of garbage as he went through the door, and, under the surveillance of the neighbours, he heaved it high up into the air and emptied it into one of three courtyard trash cans. It was his last act as a living man. Within seconds of his turning away from the can, the accused, who several hours earlier had manipulated a fatty deposit into Ulrich Eduard Schmidt's major coronary artery, now hiked the victim's blood pressure. Schmidt suffered what the medical profession interprets as a heart attack. In a perfectly good man.'

The accused hung his head so that Benedikt could not see his face. The second accuser had already come forward and called out:

'On a lovely clear winter day, the fourth of January 1969, three-year-old Sunita Magalele, sent out to play in front of her wooden shanty . . .' but Benedikt's interest flagged. He listened again as the accuser described the sick pigeon that the small child had petted and kissed and dragged indoors. Scarcely had the bird died than the child developed a rash and a cough.

The third accuser was already speaking: Gemma Roberts-Winkler, a seventy-six-year-old resident of a Brixton old people's home, died after quarrelling with the barman in a pub about the quality of the potato chips.

Her son-in-law, Roger, had to be mentioned in this context—he had missed his flight to Majorca. He took a later flight, crashed. This was not just an accident; the accused had had his hand in this, too. The pilot had suffered a stroke!

Benedikt strained to pay attention, could not.

By the fifth natural death, no one could pay attention; even the crowd had lost its drive to bring the accused to justice: his deeds were no more a matter of interest than particles of dust settling into dust.

There were many variations on the theme, all with the same outcome. And the man hung his head in acknowledgement. Finally, Benedikt dared to look at him: he saw a simple peasant, with large hands, blue eyes, Aryan tower skull. And Benedikt thought: Perhaps it is not right to hate the German so. Perhaps the charges against the German are unfair. Why shouldn't Germans have their happiness at reunion?

And his dreams brought him back to his bed, released him, in the accustomed position. The morning had driven people from the streets, which were littered with the waste of festivity. And he sensed that he was not alone, even before his memory returned with the data. He did not follow his routine. He crept out of bed in his white pyjamas, strode to the guest room, carefully pushed open the door.

The room was unrecognizable—the suitcases had apparently exploded, spewing grey polyester and acrylic. Several tins of fruit had rolled into the corners.

These people are generally unfit, he thought. Always sleeping. The woman slept, her back turned to the door, beneath the map of the galaxies. Her hair lay in a black mass on the white sheet. The child lay facing her, his body tucked into her body, his head next to hers on the pillow. They were holding hands. He could not identify the gesture although it seemed familiar. Then he recalled having his hand held once, twice, by his sister.

CHAPTER 9

Resolutely: fate has its way with Benedikt. He objects,
but cannot find words or actions to oppose it

His stare roused her like a hand. Her legs stirred, she rolled over, turning her face to him, her yellow eyes glared at him, her beak opening, cawing.

He hit her with words, he pummelled that bird face with the ugliest words he could think of: 'You roost here like street pigeons! What a mess this is! Filthy! Debris! You rot!' He stood in the middle of the apartment and it no longer felt like his own. His sister's room had passed quickly out of her possession, into someone else's, that of a woman he did not know, whose name he could not pronounce, who was unfamiliar to him. Who was regarding him with fear, as if he were threatening her, and he retorted, 'I am not threatening you!'

He was not angry, just frustrated, as if a scientific problem were taking its time getting solved and he had to try different methods. His guests were not rot. They just needed help. They needed to be educated. They needed to share his possessions. Well, why not? He stroked his lower lip, which was bleeding where his teeth had cut into it.

'In the West,' he said, keeping his voice gentle, 'we have cupboards and wardrobes. We take care of our belongings. We don't hurl them carelessly around. This is not outer space, where it doesn't particularly matter. This is confinement, and we must treat it with some sort of respect, caution . . .' His voice was very soft now; his words came rapidly, relentlessly. 'And in the

West we get up in the morning and attend to our business—' It occurred to him that these Russians had no business to attend to. 'One gets up even if one has no organized life. One gets up. There is always something that has to be done. The day has its demands. For example, one has to wash. In the West, one washes every day and changes one's clothes.' He gasped. 'Please, clean up here now! What a mess it is! And then—I don't know.' He moved towards them.

The two strange guests had a bizarre reaction—their faces scrunched up, water spilled from their eyes. He was unnerved. 'Stop that!' he commanded.

In response, they sent the sheets flying like the swooping sails on a turning schooner; they abandoned ship, dived over-board, sheets, blankets, pillows dragging on the floor. They scrambled for the door. He swung around to close it. The child was faster. He zigzagged around one side of him, while Marja tried the other side. Benedikt managed to block her path. He was surprised and relieved when she backed off, allowing him to slip backwards through the door. He locked it from outside.

She bombarded the door with her fists and feet. The child took refuge on the living-room sofa, where he cowered, mewing and sniffing. Simultaneously, the doorbell began to ring, a thrust-ing in his ear, and Benedikt cried out, 'Not another one!'

He hurried to stanch this most unbearable of noises. An old woman stood on the threshold in a starched black-and-white maid's uniform. 'Pardon me, are you "Doctor of Physical Mathe-matics, Benedikt Waller"?' And stepped in. She carried an enor-mous handbag of fake crocodile skin, which she deposited next to his regiment of loafers.

Neither the pounding on a far door nor the snivelling of a small, foreign-looking child squeezed into the corner of the sofa, not even the distraught man in pyjamas, discouraged the old woman from coming right in, deep inside his territory, wafting down onto the sofa next to the child without being asked, and squawking her biography. She was the real McCoy, a storyteller: plot had priority over the universe. She had a list in her hand with the names and addresses of scientists in the western part of the city.

'They've been very generous,' she said. 'But my pension is no longer enough to support me. My, what a noise! The state was generous. Four hundred and fifty marks a month! Before, that was worth something. Now, it won't get you ersatz coffee. But I can tell you a few stories for a small price. It will enrich you. I was Dr Albert Einstein's maid. Fräulein Schulz. He called me Bertha.'

She cocked her head for an instant towards the guest-room door. 'Noisy, these new apartments, even in the West. You hear everything your neighbours are doing. Now, I know how much you scientists admired him. And I can tell you the most fascinating private details about him. What he liked to eat. How he walked around in his blue-and-green-striped morning coat, without a stitch on underneath. And so on. I admit I knew Mrs Einstein even better. I spent all the Berlin years with them.'

One last thud on the door. 'Oh, Mrs Einstein, she was a good soul. I always thought the prizes and medals should go to her, because without her he'd have got nowhere.'

Benedikt watched the child quailing next to her on the sofa, either afraid to move or perhaps figuring politeness in the form of playing dead would control the situation. After a while he swung his legs a little, stopped abruptly, resuming his rigid pose, and soon swung them again. Benedikt thought the child looked different in the morning: in daylight, the lines of his small face were easier to follow, although the brown hair fell over his forehead and encroached on his cheeks. The child's features were too vague for Benedikt to define, but the dark-blue colour and angular shape of his eyes were emphasized by dark lashes; he realized the child was not wearing his glasses.

'If you want to hear details about Professor Einstein, I can tell you them. Every single one. But I can't just give them away,' the old woman continued. As Benedikt did not reply, she offered, 'I can also cook and clean. As I said, I've had years of experience with Professor Einstein. This place could be shipshape. And I don't mind looking after children. I adore children, really. I have a way with them. Perhaps you need to think about it. I can wait here for your answer.' Benedikt had gone to the guest room and was unlocking it, while she simply talked on.

When Benedikt opened the door, Marja stumbled out, wearing a greying pink bathrobe, her face red and sweaty. He apologized. 'I'm sorry. I didn't realize it was locked.' Her son hurtled past him to cling to her thighs. She stroked his head. He watched, suddenly greedy for details: the way her fingers wove through the thick brown strands of hair, reached down to his earlobe, caressed that too, and then patted his cheek. The certainty with which her fingertips negotiated this surface, as if they were seeing and tasting it, struck him as unseemly. It was not her own surface, after all. Finally her hand reached for his hand, and then her arm lifted up and away from her, stretching his arm with it, so that he had to let go of her legs.

Meanwhile the new visitor had arisen from the sofa and toddled over to her big bag on the floor in the hall. She bent over slowly, spreading her legs to keep her balance, and began rummaging inside the bag, which appeared to be full of more black-and-white uniforms.

'By the way,' she disclosed, 'I also have a relic with me that I'm willing to part with.' She retrieved a plastic shopping bag, slowly righted herself, and opened the bag. She waved a navy-blue tie with red polka dots. 'Mr Einstein's favourite tie,' she said. 'Complete with a gravy stain. I couldn't get that out anymore, try as I might. And he said, "Throw it away, Bertha." But of course I did no such thing. I kept it as a keepsake. He wore it to so many distinguished occasions. But now I'm too old to appreciate it, and I think I'll sell it to someone who really would like to have it. What about you, sir?'

Bertha Schulz made coffee and toast, bustling about the apartment with authority, setting places around the coffee table in the living room. While waiting for the water to boil she sauntered around the living room, marvelling at all its treasures. She seemed particularly impressed by the Christmas tree, with the turtle's plastic bowl hanging there.

'Oh my,' she said. 'We have those at home, too, but not in private hands. Is it dead?'

Benedikt had a look. The turtle was still huddled under its shell. Probably it needed to recover from the previous night's excitement. When Bertha carried in the coffee, the Russian mother and her son sat down on the sofa. Bertha wedged herself in next to them. They feasted, while their host paced in a ragged ellipsis around the room, going from the sofa to the desk, through the tunnel of the kitchen, back to the sofa again. In the corner of the sofa, the old woman was scribbling notes, listing the dishes Einstein had liked which she was prepared to cook for Dr Waller. She also had a list of her financial requirements.

'I can live in,' she said, 'starting today,' as he plunged past.

'Einstein was a very gentle gentleman,' she called as he approached again. 'He liked to pace too, but in a grand way. Well, he wore slippers. And he was rather fat. Not like you, sir. But my cooking will do the trick.'

On his third round she said, 'He had a sense of humour . . .' Her voice dropped to a penetrating whisper. 'He liked to tickle me!' Benedikt pictured Einstein panicking at the sound of this stupid talk, and he felt he must do something to protect Einstein's honour. Almost anything was legitimate. A sense of mission, of rightness, cleared the debris of impressions that had collected in his brain. As he passed the sofa again and heard Bertha still going on about the tickling business—or was she talking about money now? The Russian woman was listening attentively!—he plucked Bertha from the sofa and shook her. Her head whipped back and forth for a while and then he dropped her back down onto the cushions, whereupon she whined, 'My pension is suddenly worthless.'

At once the Russian asked, 'How much do you get a month?'

So Benedikt turned on her, picking her up with one hand. With the other hand he slapped her face as hard as he could. Righteousness was a physical power. Still his guests did not stop their chitchat. He let go of Marja, ran to the hall, and hoisted the mirror off the wall. Returning to the sofa, he smashed it down over the Russian woman's head. What was her name? Marja. A hideous name, left over from the religion. The sound of breaking glass caressed his ears, and he saw her expression of surprise as her head emerged through the jagged glass, wearing the mirror as if it were a collar, oh, what a backfire of her plans. Then he grabbed Einstein's gravy-stained tie, knotted it around Bertha's neck, keeping his eyes on his own hands as he pulled the tie tight.

She lived on. Marja, too, was immaculate. He ripped his computer mouse out of its sockets to flog them, but it flew out of his hand. So he hauled Marja up out of the sofa, carried her over to his desk, and pushed her head through the monitor, like a loaf of bread shoved into the oven. As the monitor imploded, her head disappeared and her body began to burn. He turned around to get a pail of water to douse it, but suddenly the women were fighting back with their fingernails, with fists. The child was nowhere to be seen. That was good. He did not want the child around. It was none of his business.

He strangled both women at the same time, using one hand for each neck; he could certainly be strong when he needed to be. Afterwards, he carved their limp bodies up the way he had seen his uncles treating a stag they had shot—slashing open the belly and scooping the guts out into a pot. When he was finished, he dragged their empty carcasses to the balcony where he had breakfasted with Schmidt and threw them overboard, one after the other. They turned onto their stomachs, and swam in the air, breaststroke, their faces free of all malice. They managed to reach the balcony railing. They hung onto it with their ugly hands. He placed his palms on their shoulders and pushed them off backwards, far out into open air again, but they just swam back; he had to keep swatting at them, and then the telephone rang.

The women did not move to answer the phone. They stayed where they were on the sofa and watched his expressionless face and his pose of complete rest as he stood outside on the balcony. Finally he responded, coming inside, moving towards the desk, picking up the phone.

It was Dr Anhalt. 'Are you coming to my place this afternoon? I have something to discuss. We're forming a committee of distinguished people in favour of Berlin's becoming the new capital of Germany. I've nominated you for membership.'

CHAPTER 10

Presto!: Benedikt makes a fast decision. He retreats

After he'd hung up the phone, his system registered that he had not actually murdered the two women. His heart began swinging in his chest and was joined by the pulse in his wrists and his neck, silent bells across the entire landscape of his body. At the same time he became aware that he had made a decision; his brain presented it to him, without any deliberation, as if a court hearing had taken place in his subconscious and his fate been sealed. And he passed it on to the others, his tone urgent. 'Please pack your things, we're leaving.' He drove them, Pack pack pack! like a rooster bullying his hens, and they ran squawking in all directions. Quick quick quick! We should leave before it's too late.

He packed his clothes, too. He faced no decisions: he packed everything, and everything he had fit easily into his one big case: the black suits, the white shirts, the plain underwear, the white pyjamas. 'Hurry!' he called, stuffing several notebooks and his solitron calculations into the case and pulling the plug out of his computer. He did not tidy up. He did not check on the turtle. He left everything as it was.

He had them all together in the stairwell: an old woman, a younger one, the child, and himself, four people: the little family. And then he moved them down the steps, locked the front door, scolding, Go go go! And they did as he commanded, they yielded to his tone.

As they entered the street, he saw that the financial union of

Germany had already left its mark on his street; overnight, it had been transformed. Actually, what he saw was the culmination of days of work for Dr Graf. The zero specialist had pursued the classified ads for Trabants in the 'Items for Free' column, made phone calls, collected the cars, usually from distant, unfamiliar addresses in East Berlin. He had returned with each car to Benedikt's street, where he waited for a parking space with the patience of one who is glad not to be at home. Dr Graf had no family left besides a stepdaughter who no longer spoke to him. Against his will, Dr Graf often pondered this. Collecting cars and anticipating his upcoming German citizenship kept most of his unpleasant thoughts at bay.

Dr Graf's persistence in relocating the Trabants, symbols of Communist inferiority, was rewarded on the eve of the currency reform. That night, many drivers vacated choice parking spaces in order to drive around town. The mathematician had succeeded in filling the last space except Benedikt's own with scrapmetal, lollipop-coloured East German cars. Benedikt's elegant downtown street looked as though it belonged in East Berlin. This was a good send-off for Benedikt, making him doubly glad to leave the city, as he thought, for good.

And so it happened that Benedikt did what everyone else was doing: he took to the pan-German road in a German car loaded to the hubcaps with suitcases and passengers, stepped hard on the accelerator, which wasn't so easy for a man whose leg muscles were wasted, who could not take for granted that he would be able to budge a pedal at all, including the brake. Far more peculiar and dangerous to Benedikt, though, was the sensation of having passengers in his car. It had been years since he had shared a space so small for more than a few minutes at a time. After his trip to Switzerland with his sister, he had always driven alone—he had declined to take taxis with others to meetings, preferring to walk. And now it had come to this: a full car, with its warm thick air, a sauce produced by so much breathing.

He opened the windows and gulped the exhaust fumes from the highway.

It was the first summer in his memory that travel across Germany was a private affair and not subject to any government restrictions—one did not need to discuss it with anyone. Moving from place to place had become politically insignificant, and because it was allowed, many Germans behaved as they had after the war, trekking restlessly about the country in caravans, often undecided as to which location they wanted to call home. Benedikt, at least, had a goal. He could have discussed it with his passengers, the route they were taking, why, or where. But he did not. He was not being secretive, either. It just did not occur to him that they might want to know.

He had encouraged the child to sit in the front seat next to him, but then the skin on his right arm and his shoulder registered the child's nearness, tickling him. The awareness that he was in charge of a small boy created an uneasiness others would have called joy. Nevertheless, he was relieved when the child stood up, turned around, and scrambled over the top of the seat into the back, where he settled into his mother's lap. In the process he scuffed Bertha with his little sandal, leaving a grey mark on her smock. She yanked her handkerchief from her purse and began scrubbing the mark so violently, bouncing up and down in the seat, that he accelerated in order to push his passengers back into their places.

He felt guilty of anger, craned his head around to look at the backseat—he didn't know how to find someone in the rearview mirror—and glimpsed Marja. Her features were organized into a dazed expression.

Facing the road again, he asked her, 'Are you admiring the landscape?' He wagered another look around at her.

She was smiling a brilliant smile that he recognized as artificial and said, 'I'm thinking.'

'All the thinking on the planet adds up to only two point three grams of energy,' he said.

'I'm thinking how nice if you had a car accident,' she said.

He found her reply nonsensical, attributed it to her poor grasp of German, and concentrated on the potholed road surface. But his mind was not lulled, nor his impatience stilled. He felt the presence of the others as a storm of sensations. The child produced a lot of sound: writhing on the seat, chaotic muttering, whining.

Bertha did not stay silent, either. She accompanied the boy's noise with a steady murmur, reading the road signs in a gentle, warning voice.

'No right turn permitted,' said Bertha.

'A hundred kilometres an hour speed limit?' asked Bertha.

'It's not in effect anymore,' answered Bertha.

'No one knows the traffic laws anymore,' scolded Bertha.

'A state without laws starves,' sighed Bertha.

'The child needs to eat,' said Marja, and Benedikt was struck by the repetition of this phrase.

After this, all were silent until they reached the East German border, with its recently abandoned guardhouses. Thereafter, the road became streamlined, black, smooth as glass, and they made quick progress; his car had a strong motor. He tried to see the child in the rearview mirror but all he could find was Bertha, her square face under an abutment of grey curls, a forehead with two deep vertical lines in the middle, as if her nose had slid down through it before getting wedged between her full jowls. A thick set of eyebrows gave her shy but eager eyes some shelter. She was regarding the landscape carefully, like a nun watching a man in a bathing suit.

She repeated, 'Where are we going?' but again, he ignored her question, not realizing that it was addressed to him.

And Marja said, 'The child is hungry.'

They stopped at a restaurant. The sensation of appearing in public with a child exhilarated Benedikt, and he wondered whether he would ever get used to it. The child was not impressed. He hovered at his mother's side, while Bertha proclaimed her delight at the cleanliness of it all, the dazzling formica tables.

' *"Erlebnis Gastronomie,"* An Eating Experience,' Bertha read in a sad voice from a poster on the wall. 'I have no money on me.'

Benedikt did not respond to the last pointed remark, which was really a question. He sat down at a table and the others followed suit, Bertha next to him, leaning over his lap to adjust his placemat for him. While he studied the menu, conversation lapped at his ear until Marja repeated, 'The child is hungry.'

He shook his head in surprise and said, 'Then it should eat.'

She looked at Bertha for assistance. For an instant, the two women were united in their uncertainty about who was going to pay the bill. They raised their eyebrows and their palms at each other, and with this exchange they agreed just to carry on, eat, and see what happened. When the waiter came, Benedikt ordered soup for them all.

'Don't like real china,' said Bertha, when their food came in plastic bowls. 'Afraid of dropping it.'

'Why, you'll want to know,' she continued. 'During the war, I worked for another scientist. A man who was not at all fond of Einstein, oh no, he wasn't. I lived in. Kept everything so clean they used to say, Let's eat off the floor tonight! But of course they always used the best china in that family. Even when the city was being bombed, they lived normally. We always had excellent food. It was 1943 when I started work there. I had been there over a year. One day I was taking away a whole trayful of their best china to wash. They'd had a lot of visitors to lunch. Bigwigs.' Bertha loaded an imaginary tray in front of her. 'Soup tureen, ladle here, soup bowls and glasses there. They had settled down in the drawing room with coffee, and I carried the dirty dishes out into the kitchen. And I was just a bit short of the kitchen table when something caught at my shoe. The missus was always very careless about leaving things lying around. She must have left something on the floor. I tripped. All that china smashed! But they didn't hear anything. They were having their coffee. And I had such a fright, I just ran out the door and didn't come back that night. Their best family porcelain. An heirloom.'

She shuddered, remembered her soup, took a spoonful, and

continued. 'But I'm honest. I felt bad just running out on them, leaving all that broken china. And my clothes, of course. I was live-in. I spent the night wandering the streets, wondering what to do. I knew I had to go back and explain. And the next morning, first thing, I headed to their house. "It's all my fault, I'm so terribly sorry," I practised saying on the way over. But when I got there, the house was gone. It had been hit by a bomb that night. Everybody was dead.'

The others had finished their soup. 'Ach, I'll hurry now,' Bertha said. A family of Poles had come in, their conversation a thick slick on the surrounding hubbub of German.

'We're very generous to the East,' commented Bertha. 'The Poles are greedy. They always exploited us. Bought us up. Everything we had. All they think about is money,' she said, swallowing. Marja stared at her. Bertha hesitated. 'You're not Polish, are you—?' She bobbed her head at Marja.

Benedikt worried that Marja might be offended, then he worried that Bertha might be offended by Marja's response, by the way the younger woman laughed under her breath and regarded the elderly German matron with mocking orange eyes. He did not know much about women but he felt that a specimen as ugly as Marja should not think badly of others.

'Where are we going?!' asked Bertha again.

The next hours passed uneventfully, except for a slight altercation between his passengers when Bertha asked Benedikt to turn on the radio. He obliged, and pop music crashed into the car, whereupon the child clapped his hands over his ears, crying out as if he were in pain. Marja snapped, 'Turn it off!' with such authority that he obeyed immediately. He might have asked her why, why so adamant, it's just ordinary music, one can endure it, but then he had to pay attention; it was time to leave the highway. After following a country road through open fields for several kilometres, through a little town with a pretty square and old houses, he turned into a narrow lane that led through a forest where the trees became dense as the local Sunday church congregation. Just when the passengers had grown used to the monotony of driving through the dark woods, the car burst through into sunlight again, travelling along a country lane now, through cultivated fields and, later, overgrown meadow.

The road ended at a gate and a high red-brick wall. Two stone knights guarded the top of ornate wrought metal, capped by a crown. A garden lay on the other side of the gate. A gardener stood nearby tending vegetables.

When he saw the car, he straightened up, looked troubled, approached, and shouted through the bars, 'What do you want?'

Benedikt got out of the car. 'I am Count Waller von Wallerstein,' he said slowly, the words cumbersome in his mouth. 'I've come home.'

part two

CHAPTER 11

Without regret: Benedikt returns home

He had all the keys. He'd taken them when he moved to Berlin, and kept them at hand, a rattling mess in the top drawer of his desk. He opened the three locks of the gate, ignoring the astonished gardener, pressed down the resisting handle (his palm retained the impressions of that hot heavy steel in all its variations, from the first time he had swung on the handle as a small child trying to budge it). He looked forward to the graceful swing of the gate, but why not? The clack of the latches roused the dogs in the distance. The air was sticky with plant life—it stuffed his nostrils with blossoms, wet grass, and wood; he inhaled through his mouth. He trod back to the car, his limp making him teeter, yanked at the car door handle, noting the paltriness of its modern design, catching his reflection in the window, his face silver and shiny as a five-mark piece in the sun. He drove through the gate in second gear, hesitation making his foot wobble on the accelerator so that the vehicle bucked. He had to get out again, skirting the glaring gardener, to close and lock the gate.

Now the car was fumigated with flowers. A tar road led for almost a kilometre past the gardens that bloomed in full force, with purple stock, towering pink phlox, vats of oleander, with larkspur and bindweed, on to the deer park, through another, simpler gate, behind which the dogs waited. They chased the car along the fence that kept them off the road, all the way to a fast-moving stream, swollen in July, which had once served as a moat.

The water steamed. He kept his eyes from the dark slab walls of the building ahead, suddenly afraid of their familiarity. At the same time he became aware of how much smaller and less imposing it was than the reflex of his memory asserted, no more than a large country house, really. He accelerated. But the car reversed, its wheels caught in a muddy pothole and spinning. He had to stop, swing the wheels back and forth, navigate to the side of the road. He drove across the stone bridge, to the pebbled clearing next to the entrance, where he parked in the shadow of the building, turned the motor off, and, realizing that he had reached his destination, shrugged his shoulders.

They left the sunlight and entered the stairwell, a cheerful place after a seventeenth-century uncle had widened and brightened it, dressing it in marble, alabaster, and gold. An eighteenth-century offspring had chided his lack of imagination, had gone back to work on the stairs, twisted the banisters, added stone angels here and there, pulled out the length of each step to slow the pedestrian down, and filled the empty space between the ceiling and the tallest man with bouquets of crystal. The stairwell intimidated some visitors, impressed others, but to Benedikt, it only possessed a cloying familiarity. 'Sorry. All this fussiness,' he mumbled to his guests.

He hurried up the stairs, remembering the different faces of the steps, their veins and dents. The stairwell led to a door, a last outburst of baroque in the design. Behind lay a large high-ceilinged salon, which the late nineteenth century, with its presumption of permanency, had filled with furniture so heavy that, after it was removed again in the twentieth, the stone floor retained deep impressions of it. The chandeliers were switched off, and the warped glass in the high narrow windows allowed little light to pass through, so the room was dark and, like Benedikt's feelings, an apparently empty space filled with obstacles.

He could make out no details, but memory helped him, and he sensed them all: the closed concert piano in the middle of the room, a long curved wooden bench with a high hard back next to a fireplace, a number of high-backed wooden armchairs in inferior positions around this. At the other end of the salon he could make out a white vertical line, where light broke through the double doors leading to his grandmother's room. The old dining table was visible as a dark interruption of this bright line. Each corner of the salon had a small door, one opening to a passageway that led to the kitchen, another opening directly into the chapel, a third into the living quarters, and a fourth into the narrow winding staircase of the tower, where Benedikt had lived. When a light went on in the kitchen corridor, the walls of the salon began to glow. The portraits of Waller von Wallerstein ancestors hanging there became visible, so that Benedikt was suddenly surrounded by his relatives.

He felt ridiculed; embarrassment made him talkative. Benedikt addressed his companions and introduced them to his family in an earnest, polite manner, pointing to the pictures: 'That's a great-great-grandfather on my father's side.

'The third sister of the man who laid out the gardens.

'A distant relation who once visited—he was Count of Auschwitz (couldn't have known, really, what lay in store).'

Benedikt steered his visitors' gaze around the room, giving equal time to every portrait, making no distinction between those faces that braved the centuries in simple ebony frames and those that had massive golden fortifications.

Despite the overcrowding on the walls, Benedikt's relatives showed no signs of dissatisfaction; the expressions they directed at the world were haughty or complacent or slightly bored, and not at all dangerous, like those of customers having their hair coiffed at a beauty salon. But in the middle, historically out of order, hung a portrait Benedikt had never seen before. It had rough edges, with a row of nails hammered into unpainted canvas at the sides. This puzzled Benedikt until he realized that the picture was simply not framed; he had never seen naked canvas before. The painting depicted a man of such commonplace features that Benedikt could not identify him: his eyes were simply dark circles, his hair a dark mass, and the outline of his well-proportioned head and shoulders merged with his sackcloth-coloured background, as if he had pushed forward briefly through a jellylike substance that clung to him. On closer inspection Benedikt saw that his ear was formed like an inverted G clef or a violin scroll. No, the man in the picture was not common at all. And despite the lack of expression in his features, he was apparently undergoing paroxysms of emotion because his skin was bright red, as if he were suffering a monstrous attack of embarrassment.

'And him!' said Benedikt, astonished. 'I don't know him at all. A modern picture.' He found the face attractive. Then he felt annoyed and suspected the red man was his sister Dolly's idea.

'Well, we'll stay here,' he said. 'Why not?'

'My apartment in Moscow was warmer,' complained the Russian, shivering.

Benedikt and his visitors became aware of a creature in a maid's costume watching them from one corner. An electronic beeper sounded from her, and she hurried down a corridor and picked up a wall telephone. She spoke, listened, hung up the phone, and marched up to the intruders.

'Who are you?' she demanded.

Benedikt considered for an instant and then he pointed to the portrait of the red man who could not tear himself away from his background.

Since an argument with her granddaughter about a Gobelin tapestry that Dolly wanted for her television room, the Countess had declared that there were to be no more visitors at Schloss Biederstein, neither family nor acquaintances.

'I'll live alone,' she said. 'The old live alone.'

Once, Dolly had just shown up, but the old woman had refused to buzz her in or speak to her on the intercom linking the front door and her room. Dolly had rung the bell until Liesel had let her in, and then made a nuisance of herself tottering on a ladder in the great salon trying to hang up a modern portrait she had brought along. None of the staff would help her, even the chauffeur refused to give her a hammer and nails, so before she even got started, she had to drive back into town to buy them.

Liesel didn't tell the Countess what her granddaughter was up to. When the bedridden woman asked about the pounding and scraping in the salon, Liesel said Dolly was there, but she could not identify her activity and she had no time to enquire, she had mending to do. The Countess rang and rang her bell. Liesel didn't dare answer; later, she pretended she hadn't heard the ringing over the pounding in the salon. After that, the Countess threw away the bell and the front-door intercoms and had a system of telephones set up all over the house, with electronic beepers for the help. But Dolly didn't visit again.

The Countess never saw the new addition. Shortly after the picture went up in the salon, Liesel died. Liesel had raised the Countess as a child, had moved to Schloss Biederstein when she married, had raised Benedikt's father and then Benedikt. Between children, she looked after the Countess; she sacrificed her life for the family. She enjoyed self-sacrifice *per se*, but also the power that she wielded and the knowledge that, when she was gone, the Countess would be unable to replace her, because she was the only true friend her employer had ever had. When Liesel was gone, the Countess moved farther on into her isolation. The double doors to her room were kept shut, and the staff went in and out through a small back door leading in from a dressing room, a passageway so small that those of normal stature had to bend down to squeeze through, so that visitors entered the room with a show of humility.

But for over a year, the only visitors had been employees. Once a month the board of managers who ran the estate came to report to her. Once a season she had the piano tuner come. Her son had played badly but gladly. He had exercised his flair for composition during the war writing up-to-date victory songs for the military bands and choirs at the front. Because of this talent, he was considered too valuable to be sent to the front. His mother had tolerated his songwriting, and secretly—she was not given to admiration—she had loved his playing. After his death, the piano was kept tuned but closed, so that no passersby could tinkle wantonly around on it, as they are apt to do. The children and the help unconsciously steered a path around it because the shiny black silent box had the aura of a casket. Even after there were no more passersby, the piano tuner came, listless as a social worker who knows his efforts make no impression. Twice a year his chords would wrack the salon, followed by a Brahms waltz he could play blindfolded and earplugged. He closed up the piano quickly and sent a bill for his services; he did not want to wait there one extra minute to be paid.

There were no other intrusions at Schloss Biederstein. The owner remained formidable in appearance, her face well preserved, her hair thick—even the roots were stubborn, sending out grey-yellow tones into the mass she wore pulled tightly into a bun. But if she was vain about it, she wasn't interested in impressing anyone other than herself—except for fate, perhaps.

Once when a maid commented, while combing her hair, on its phenomenal colour, she remarked, 'Everyone is afraid of time, but time is afraid of me.'

When Liesel was still alive, the Countess sometimes asked the old woman to keep her company during dinner. Now the Countess, her head slightly elevated on a podium of pillows, ate her meals, heavy with cream and starch, alone. She sipped the gravy and in the kitchen they kept the meat for themselves. 'My appetite's gone,' she complained, her mouth dusted with cookie crumbs. Her stool, reported her personal maid, a trained nurse, resembled mouse turd.

After Benedikt had left, most of the others had retired and decided they wanted to live with their own relations. Nor did their children want to take over their jobs, as was expected of them; instead, they studied or moved away. They found the old house eerie and country life boring. The help that replaced them had no feeling of belonging and, therefore, none of obligation.

They did not want to live in. There were rumours about ghosts; stories about how a tray laden with the oldest porcelain suddenly took off from the big table, into the air, touching down along the floor, smashing everything; anecdotes about visitors who felt burning sensations in their hands and feet. No one wanted to risk that. Furthermore, the remainder of the old guard was hostile to newcomers. The death of Liesel, who had been critical of everyone, old and new, high and low, had been the final blow.

Finally, the Countess fired everyone and acquired a new set of staff through the classified ads of the *Deutschen Adelsblatt,* where only nobility dared advertise. The new retinue of help all belonged to the nobility themselves. They had no names and no faces, as far as the Countess was concerned, not even the Biesterfelds, who had actually left years earlier. The Countess rehired them, pretending not to know that the Biesterfelds had been part of the family for generations, all very small, all tending to hunchbacks and talented hands. The Countess never referred to the past, and the Biesterfelds never referred to it, either. They allowed the Countess to address them as 'Cook' and 'Chauffeur' respectively; the others were also called by their jobs, 'Nurse' or 'Maid.'

One morning 'Maid' brought her a new supply of pastries and chocolates and the news that there was, after more than a year, a car full of visitors.

'Send them away,' she had replied, her calm a toppling monument. 'At once! Or I shall become upset!'

When she registered footsteps in the salon, approaching her room, she repeated her order on the internal intercom without asking who the visitors were. With satisfaction, she noted Maid speaking sharply. But this was followed by the soft, shy male voice she hadn't heard in a long time. She picked up her bedside intercom again. Maid scurried to the phone ringing in the corridor and heard the rasp of the Countess in her ear. The old woman wanted to see her grandson at once.

Maid was infuriated. 'The Countess will see you, but . . .'

she said. 'We go in through the back. And they wait.' She meant the others. 'Please don't let the child break anything. The piano stays shut. The chapel stays shut.'

Benedikt turned to them, wanting to make up for the maid's tone. 'Sit down,' he begged, 'I won't be a minute.'

Benedikt proceeded on his own, stooping through the low doorway to the Countess's bedside, sensing her authority over him as if it were a drug. He advanced blindly through the room until he reached the foot of the bed, when he turned his body and face towards her.

Had she changed? He did not look for changes; perhaps he feared them. Her arms sheathed in the black wool of her robe lay on top of the purple bedspread. What lay beneath was hard to define. When he finally looked for her eyes, he found her staring at him.

She had to strain to propel her whisper. 'What are you doing here?'

He was ill at ease, realizing that she did not consider this house his home. 'I wanted to stay just for a while. And then I'll. . . . And then I'll . . .' He didn't finish.

'You're bringing the city with you, aren't you?' she sighed. 'Sharp footsteps mean city shoes.' He saw that hesitation and self-doubt had found no place to settle on her soft wrinkled cheeks, because they were still guarded by those cunning blue eyes. 'Two pairs of sharp shoes and a child's pitter-patter.'

She turned to Maid. 'Have the guest rooms on the second floor made up for them. Plain ones or what do you want, Benedikt? Who are they?' And Benedikt told her that they were acquaintances staying with him, his guests, wherever he was.

The Countess wanted to see them.

He returned to the salon, where his guests were posed on the bench, tense, ready to continue the journey, like passengers waiting for a bus that will arrive any minute. At his request, they followed him.

The head of the Countess's bed was positioned directly to the left of the door, so that, stepping into her room, a visitor first saw the foot of the bed, but by that time he had already placed himself within striking distance of her countenance. Benedikt's grandmother did not shift her position when they entered. She was holding a pack of tarot cards, shuffling them slowly, making a sound he associated with her being awake, but similar to her snoring when she slept—a rustling noise, followed by a short panting as the cards were laid on the blanket in front of her, seven or ten or twenty-one times, depending on which method of divination she was up to. As the visitors arranged themselves in a line at her feet, the child pressing himself into his mother's side, she looked at each face in turn, while her hands pulled out a card from the deck. She glanced at the cards, nodding her head as if she were receiving answers. Marja observed this with a smile Benedikt found condescending, a declaration of undeserved independence, even superiority. Bertha looked abject.

The Countess beckoned Benedikt. He had to bow down, so she could reach his head. 'Are they from Silesia?' Her words were a boiling breeze in his ear. 'You know I despise Silesians.'

Then she addressed Bertha. 'I hope you had a pleasant journey.'

'Fräulein Schulz. Very pleased to meet you,' said Bertha.

'The old woman speaks a revolting kind of German.' The Countess spoke directly into Benedikt's ear in her penetrating whisper. 'I wouldn't even have her as a refugee. And her dress is worse than what your aunts' maids had when they came from back east. And the other one is a Communist.'

'She's Russian,' he whispered back, a bit bored now, afraid she would ask him for details about his visitors. He couldn't remember anything else.

'This is bitter company,' she said. 'You might have spared me. I'm too old for this sort of turbulence. See to it that I don't see or hear them. And having a child around will put the last nail into my coffin.'

Bertha could not decipher the Countess's words. She stood at the end of the bed, and desire to please straightened her spine, travelled to her heels, making them click together sharply. Bertha adored an authoritative tone. She sidled closer to the bed, explaining, 'Pardon me. I didn't work just for Einstein. I worked for a prince of sorts. First I had another scientist, too, who always used to say Einstein is overrated, he stole his ideas, and so on. He even had proof. He used to tease me for having worked for Einstein at all. And then, for the last twenty years, I worked for a prince—'

'No prince ever had the stupidity to become a scientist,' whispered the Countess. 'We used to say, "Getting a D in science is a matter of honour." We were proud to have servants who were smarter than us.'

'Prince De Broglie,' said Benedikt, apologetically; his grand-mother's ignorance was forgivable but he had to set the record straight. 'Nobel Prize in Physics, 1929.'

'No, no, my first employers were scientists, not the prince, oh no, he wouldn't have bothered, he was a normal prince: he ruled. He was a politician. Herr H., I called him, I worked for him at his hunting lodge. The state's real mistake was being against capitalism and private property. But he had a beautiful house for his own use, where I worked. He was very kind to me. He always gave oranges to the help, eight of us, to take home to our families. I had no one and had to eat them myself. I'd get sores on my mouth.'

The Countess's ensuing stare had an unusual effect. It did not force the victim to lower her head. Instead, Bertha gazed with a kind of formal rapture directly at the little black nuggets in the Countess's eyes. Over in the northeast, where she came from, one was used to authority: it did not intimidate, one rode it out like a big wave as far as it could carry. When it lost power or was about to crash against an obstacle, one hopped off and looked for another wave to ride. One assumed that some celestial force was responsible for tides.

'The hunting lodge was wonderful,' Bertha declared, 'but it wasn't as good as this. I am so glad to be of service to you. This system is worthy of my utmost efforts.'

The Countess said to her grandson, 'I would like to speak to you alone.'

Bertha murmured, 'Of course', pivoting, her head turning like radar as she took in all the details of the surroundings. Marja grabbed her son and followed Bertha into the salon, where they waited again until Maid appeared and summoned them to the second floor. They found their bags set out in adjoining guest rooms along a wide, chilly hall. Bertha was extremely pleased with the new arrangement and declared it even better than expected. Her room was next door to Benedikt's—she would have no trouble looking after him. The simplicity of the wooden furnishings perplexed Bertha, as they were no better than what she was used to. But the bathroom caused her joy: it was large enough to dance in, and dance she did; when she discovered it, white and gleaming with fixtures, she performed a waltz, as she had learned at the Emy Goering Dance Academy. Two dance steps brought her from the bath to the sink, where she fingered the thick towels hanging there and twirled to the toilet, where she skidded, catching hold of a vertical pipe with both red hands, screeching with pain and pleasure that it was hot, hot water! When she regained her balance she fought for breath and saw that she was not alone. In the sink mirror two faces peered from the door.

'Isn't it what you've always wanted?' said Bertha, turning to Marja.

But Marja only grunted in disapproval. She spoke a few words in Russian to the child, who giggled, staring at Bertha. They disappeared.

'The Russians,' chafed Bertha aloud, hoping Marja would overhear, wherever she'd gone to. 'Russians, Russians, Russians. I'm going to keep this place spotless.'

Downstairs, the Countess and her grandson had not spoken. She had laid out an ordinary deck of cards and was studying it, ignoring Benedikt, who did not move away.

Finally she looked up and declared, her voice stronger, 'Benedikt, you're so thin. What's the matter with you? Are there food shortages in the city again?'

He did not answer for a while and she mumbled something about the prince of clubs aligning himself with the ace of spades, to everyone's detriment, and he enquired, 'Is there no one left?'

She understood his question. 'They're all gone,' she whispered. 'Except Cook and Chauffeur. Alfred and Gerda. The Biesterfelds.' She repeated their name several times, 'The Biesterfelds,' as if she enjoyed hearing it, and then she continued.

'They were gone for a few years. Alfred had a young girl, eighteen years old when he met her, a seamstress over in town. She liked him because he was nobility, and because he had a good car but mostly because he was so helplessly in love with her and referred to every hour without her as a "dark time." Of course she minded about him being so small, and about the hunchback. But she was a good Catholic girl—she felt guilty about having a physical aversion to him. He kept trying to kiss her, and she avoided his kisses until he reported to her that his wife had predicted that the young woman would never kiss a man who was so much shorter than she. Then the seamstress bent down and kissed him. Later she sewed him a whole new set of clothes that played down the hunch with special padding to lift the shoulders around it, and went with him to a shop where they made built-up shoes so that he was as tall as she. But she didn't want to marry him, either; she was afraid of what the children would look like, and he kept insisting. He told her only the nobility understand what love really is. She believed him, and then she didn't and then she did. She was so confused she came to see me and told me the whole story. She had heard about the cards. I refused to advise her, but when she was gone I laid hers; they were fine.

'But after she'd changed her mind about five more times he had an attack of pride—you know how proud he is, about being a von Biesterfeld and driving a Mercedes—and to show her up he went back to Gerda, who'd never stopped waiting for him, living in town, three doors down from the seamstress. Gerda had a sense of timing; when two years had gone by and Alfred still hadn't married the girl, Gerda knew he never would. She looked around for a new position for herself where he could join her. She put an ad in the paper, and I hired her again. When Alfred complained that the seamstress had been chasing him all along and called the two years with her "the dark times," Cook came and asked me to hire a chauffeur, and so I hired him back too. And it was a good choice. Cook told Chauffeur that Seamstress hadn't accepted him as he was—she hadn't realized that inside his hunchback were his angel's wings—and threw out the padded suits and the built-up shoes. Together, they considered that poor girl the devil incarnate, and ever since Seamstress picked up and moved to Berlin, they've been perfectly happy. I'm glad they're here again. Mind you, Cook is more difficult than ever. Migraines and despairing about the morals of other people and going on and on about the beauty of Chauffeur's driving. The rest of the staff are easier. But I don't know them.' The Countess was barely audible. 'I don't want to.'

'I will go and say hello to Gerda and Alfred,' he said. 'Goodbye, Grandmother.'

'The Communists will have their meals separately,' the Countess hissed as he was ducking out the door. He hesitated, waiting for her to finish.

'This is worse than after the war. But don't let her cook in her room, either. Remember the fire that those disgusting little von Leopolds started, boiling potatoes on the second floor? Your guests should eat in the kitchen with Staff. That leaves you alone in the salon.'

'All right, Grandmother,' he said, and shuffled out.

A few hours later, Benedikt had his meal in the salon, under the gaze of Maid, Cook, Secretary, Chauffeur, Dogkeeper, Nurse, and Gardener, who took turns peeping at him through the round window of the swinging door to the kitchen corridor. They were waiting for him to finish so they could proceed with their own routine. Under normal conditions, they worked until exactly five minutes before five, when they gathered around a worn oak table in a kitchen alcove, waiting for the bells and the clocks to strike, whereupon they sat down together, a family of subordinates. But on this afternoon, they entered the kitchen alcove and had a shock.

The foreign guest was sitting down already, waiting with her son. She had her back to the door as they came in, presenting a helmet of black hair and a vulnerable neck. The Russian woman did not suspect the impression she made. She did not turn her head as she heard their footsteps. Staff stood on the threshold to the kitchen and felt the newcomer was unbearably presumptuous, waiting for them to join her at the table, forcing them to say 'Guten Tag' first. Staff resisted. They waited in the doorway until Maid pushed them aside, coming in from the salon with Benedikt's dirty plates. Staff gave up. They advanced to the table, mumbled grudging, incomprehensible 'Hello's, which the guest did not return, no, instead she smiled stiffly up at them, perhaps wondering why they did not sit down. When they had all pulled out their chairs and lowered themselves to her level, she sniffed the air and announced, as if it were of interest, that she and the child were hungry.

Cook was heard to gasp loudly from the stove. She was sentimental about children to hide her fear of them, but she believed that physical senses like hunger were mystical and should not be discussed. She was so refined that she often did not eat for days. In particular she scorned meat, preparing the venison the hunter brought her without even tasting the sauce. She was always trying to be kind. It was her form of sadistic tyranny. She held money in greater contempt than anyone else did (her father had been a society dentist, she knew what it was like to have money) and she often regretted aloud that she was not doing more for humanity. This was the only self-criticism she willingly paid, because it bought her the right to think badly about others. She did not verbalize what she thought, though. She was silently severe, her most forthright expression of criticism a gasp, followed by a visible effort to control her disgust.

Her hands shaking with controlled outrage, she placed a cut

of beef on the table, and everyone watched the Russian mother place a modest amount on her own plate, but then pile her son's plate to the brim in order to eat what he could not finish. The help spoke about this afterwards, long afterwards, after Marja had retired with Valerie and Bertha had been frozen out of their company by dint of no one's responding to a word she said. They sat at the table and mocked the new arrangement with the bitterness that lies at the bottom of unwelcome responsibility. It was one thing coming to work for an old bedridden countess, quite another to serve her peculiar grandson and his most peculiar entourage. It was early evening by the time they had finished their conversation, but as they prepared to get up from the table, they began it again with new energy and remained seated. They just had to make sure to be out of there by dusk; the others pitied the Biesterfelds, Cook and Chauffeur, for living in. They couldn't have slept a wink in that place.

Of course the house was Chauffeur's home, from cradle to coffin, and the couple did not mind being alone there. At night they drove out any spirits by odd sexual practices (normal sexual relations gave Cook a backache) and by commiserating about peculiarities she picked out in others. She was so astute that she could recognize sexual 'overripeness' or 'coldness' in strangers, even those she only knew from television talk shows, and once she had pronounced an opinion, she never doubted it. She was seventeen years Chauffeur's senior, and by covering her forehead with a curtain of evenly coloured blond bangs and her eyes with large-rimmed glasses and her cheeks with rouge and by shaving her armpits and her pubic hair and never allowing him to see any more than that part of her naked, he and she could both keep up a pretence that she was a little girl.

Chauffeur was much the way her father had been: by turns overly attentive and then aloof. He was tiny, but his head was virile, with thinning blond hair, a thick moustache, sharp-edged features, and pale-blue eyes that he turned away from others, as if he were bored, or beamed directly at them in a tense stare. He was not very communicative. His pride, so often sullied because of his stature, had become, like a dirty vest, the first characteristic others noticed about him. Forced to participate in conversation at mealtimes, he bragged in a monologue about little things, about the garage he had fixed up for his Mercedes, his lack of curiosity in people, his clever hands, the way his body never sweated. He was even quite handy at *bon mots* but ruined their charm by asking, 'Wasn't that clever?' One never rebuked him or tried to trip him up. The Biesterfelds had a hereditary claim to authority; they were the last in the dynasty of servants; they embodied permanency.

Benedikt passed by the kitchen and overheard their discussion without interest. He was looking for the boy. He found Valerie with his mother up in their room, standing at the window looking out. Marja was smoking. Their door stood ajar, and when he appeared on the threshold, she extinguished her cigarette in a porcelain eggcup, an heirloom.

'My very last cigarette!' she said. 'Chauffeur gave it to me.'

'You don't have to stay here all day,' he replied. 'You can go wherever you want.' He was anxious to show the boy the tower clock and his telescope at the top of the winding stairs.

But she said, 'I'd rather see the garden.'

He assumed he would just take the boy alone, but his mother came along anyway on the pretext that the child didn't understand any German. Of course the boy stayed within easy clutching distance of his mother; he even tried to match his footsteps to hers. He showed no interest at all in the house, but he forced them all to a standstill when they passed the salon piano. His feet just stopped moving there. He stood with his back to the keyboard and looked at the ground, refusing to move on. His mother put her hand under his chin to raise his head. His eyes, shielded by his glasses, seemed to Benedikt uncanny attributes. He whispered '*Royal*,' as if she might have overlooked it. Her mouth laughed, while her face frowned. Then she gave a sigh, a sound Benedikt had heard in movies when the wind blew over a deserted battlefield. The child seemed upset and pulled on his mother's hand to move on. They strolled around in silence; the guests did not pose any questions and the host did not offer any explanations. When they reached the stairwell that led to the tower and she saw how steep the steps were, she refused to climb them.

'I prefer the ground,' she said. 'I get dizzy, and I hate it.'

He did not wonder why. He said, 'One time shouldn't bother you.'

But she stood her ground, saying, 'No. Not one time. Never. I get *very* dizzy. I have a phobia.'

Out of politeness, he asked her why, why a phobia; he did not anticipate understanding fear, nor did he want to.

He didn't pay much attention when she explained. 'It's a secret I keep even from myself. I'm afraid of a lot of things,' he heard her admit. Or was she bragging? 'Small places. Being closed in. All things unnatural: airplanes.'

He gave in.

'We'd like to go outside,' she said.

'There's much more to be afraid of outside,' he warned her. 'Don't go near the pond. It's a killer pond. People have drowned in it. The reeds pull swimmers down. The pier is roped off. And don't get lost in the woods or the deer park. The deer are rutting now. It's dangerous. There are hunters about. They imitate rutting noises. Don't get in their way when they shoot.'

But Marja, it transpired, had an affinity for the outdoors. She ventured out there with her son, and the gardener, coming inside for a drink, reported to the staff that the Russians had gone to the deer park, skirted the very edge of the pond, before disappearing into the woods.

Benedikt sat on the bench in the salon waiting for them to return, listening to the deep breathing that heralded his grandmother's evening nap; the Countess would be up again soon, ringing for her dinner. When Benedikt heard the front door slam and two sets of footsteps on the stairs, he left his post. Hurrying to the guest-room corridor ahead of them, he grabbed his suitcase. He could not imagine sleeping in the room next to Marja's. He dragged his suitcase downstairs, meeting them on the stairs. He wanted to look at the child, but his gaze was literally knocked away by the pungent smell of heated unwashed clothes coming from the mother. They merely passed each other, nodding acknowledgement, the boy looking straight ahead. Benedikt continued across the salon, up the narrow staircase, past the garret with the huge clockworks that ran the tower clock, to his old room.

The door was closed, the room hot and dry and dark because the sun was behind a chimney. A cloud of dust rose as he sat down on the bed. It seemed more spacious to him now that he had grown so thin, but also harder on his bones. Someone had covered the rickety wooden table he had used as a desk with a red-and-white-checked plastic tablecloth. Sitting there, he could see the driveway below; his car looked out of place, a machine from the future. The setting sun moved out from behind the chimney, was lanced by a turret, and spilled its thick hot yolk all over the roof and into his room.

He unpacked, laying his last research results on the table. He saw with satisfaction that his work no longer fitted his desk. The mass of paper seemed proof that he had been right to leave home, returning with a title that really mattered: Doctor. At once, he felt ashamed of such superficial pride. 'Doctor,' he reprimanded himself, is an ugly word. He was going to cut down on his sleep here: five hours would do, with a break after two and a half hours. The time had come to resume thinking about solitrons again. His work was like a foreign language he hadn't spoken or heard in a long time.

Dr Waller remembered his dilemma, that the American magazine had not made a decision. But his computer was no longer linked up, the mailbox was dead. There was no point in working. He was sure that the solitrons were a great contribution to mathematics. Surely his greatest. That gave him a feeling of accomplishment, even as he remained idle.

His first day at home ended on that note: he fell into a

satisfied sleep. He woke up after two and a half hours with his mind sharply focused on his astonishment that he had a child now. It did not matter that the boy could not speak to him. Dozing, Benedikt pictured the child facing him, addressing him. He could not understand what he said. He stared at the little lips intensely. They were forming the word 'Papa.'

CHAPTER 12

Dragging: some changes in Benedikt's life are inevitable, some unpredictable

A week passed, or perhaps it was even two or three, or a month. He was like someone swimming underwater, who feels others as a stirring, a current created by a boat passing overhead. Far away the days washed up, like waves against a beach, dumping all sorts of worthless paraphernalia; the others rummaged through the hours, looking for something worth saving. The staff had soon learned not to talk to the grandson. Even the Countess, after berating Benedikt from her bed about his abandonment of the family, by which she meant Family, no longer called for him. Still, she gathered reports from Nurse and Maid and established his routine, studied his horoscope and the cards, and one afternoon she summoned him again. He stood at the foot of the bed, where she tried to pierce his indifference with the sharpness of her gaze, complaining about what she termed his strangeness, his detachment, his reclusiveness, his spending all day up in his room.

Finally she posed a question. 'You're not turning into a version of me, are you?'

He accepted this comparison politely, did not place any value on it, dropped it down deep into his subconscious, where even his memory would not find it. The sun went up and the sun went down. He did not work, but his internal state was tense, tautly strung, as if he were in the middle of some fascinating project. He did not recognize it himself, but he was waiting for something to happen. He lay on his bed and waited. Often, surprise that he had a family flickered in his consciousness, quickly became a bonfire of astonishment and fear, before he quenched it with the indifference he always kept at hand. One morning he sat down at his desk and wrote a letter to the editor of the journal, giving him his new address and asking him to send the galleys of his article on solitrons. As he shuffled downstairs for breakfast, he heard a strange sound, a melody sung in a high, simple voice, a voice without strength but nonetheless penetrating: a child's voice. He stood and listened until it stopped. As he began to move it started up again. He had never heard a sound like that. At first, he found it simply shocking that a child could produce such a noise.

Somehow, after that, changes began. His lack of interest in his work suddenly needed no explanation: he was absorbed by this creature, this child. He tried to appease his interest. One day, he drove to a bookshop in town and requested literature on children. The salesgirl directed him to children's fiction.

He returned, baffled, and protested, 'Please pardon me, but I'm not interested in stories,' and he could not help adding, 'not in any form; mankind would be better off without them. Stories are even more damaging than small talk.'

She thought the customer thin and obnoxious. She sent him to Child Development. He bought every book written by a doctor, laboured home with them, shoved aside his solitron calculations to make room on his desk, and began to study. At once, he was confused. Some of the texts seemed to consist entirely of anecdotes, gossip about children. Others were as full of theories as a mathematical text, but without any of the beauty. He kept reading.

Marja saw him hunched over a book at the dinner table. She inspected the title, drew back, and laughed. 'What are you reading books about toddlers for!'

The age difference had not seemed important to him. He peered at Valerie, but she placed herself in front of the child, hiding him from view with one of her black polyester outfits.

If she had a jealous interest in not letting him near the child, the child was her best ally. He kept a space of several feet cleared around him, where no one else but his mother was allowed. He would not even bestow a glance on Benedikt. He shivered when anyone looked at him. When Benedikt passed him on the stairs or in the salon, he shrank to the side. Benedikt did not consider behaviour something that could be influenced. He accepted the boy's aversion, as he accepted everything about the boy, because he did not comprehend it: his behaviour, his thick brown hair that grew so abundantly on his head, the volatile facial expressions much like his mother's that registered his strong feelings about everything, his short, fuzzy arms and legs, the smooth knees sticking out beneath his grey or green shorts, his white shirts always hanging out on one side, the socks baggy at his bony ankles, the way life fuelled those limbs. Benedikt's impressions were based on rare sightings; most of the time, the child was an image passing through the salon, a voice in another room.

One afternoon Benedikt hazarded into the kitchen to tell Cook that, from now on, he would eat his meals with the help. She was taken aback. She wanted no part of any more new arrangements. She carefully put down her chopping knife while she considered whether to proclaim a High Festival of illness for herself. But Benedikt had already left the kitchen. Thereafter, he saw the boy three times a day, sitting at the far side of Marja at the kitchen table. Valerie seemed to require all of his mother's attention at meals; he ate very slowly and never, or so it seemed, without urging that often sounded like scolding. The others termed him a bad eater, but they did not meddle; mealtimes went quickly.

Benedikt established that the 'family' had also settled into a routine, although time here was dictated by lack of obligations, and in between the minor constraints posed by the rising and setting of the sun, they could do what they wanted. Bertha went up to Benedikt's room every morning, made the bed for him, handed his laundry over to Maid, and got down on her hands and knees to wash the floor with a wet rag. Bertha was not used to idleness. She was like a hunting dog kept indoors. She spent the rest of the day waiting in key places of the house for something of interest to happen. The staff knew her kind and snubbed her. They could not place Marja, therefore they could not snub her, and she caused them considerable unease. But Marja did not seek their company. She had taken to exploring the surrounding landscape like a cat who needs to know. On one of her trips she discovered a pig farm. She and the child had spent hours watching the farmer, and soon enough they were helping out. This did not improve their smell. When they came home for the midday meal, the others edged away from them.

One afternoon Marja returned with a bag slung over her shoulder that squirmed and oinked. The farmer had wanted to butcher a runt. Marja had intervened and taken the little pig home. Gardener made a pen for the pig, after admitting he was a nice fellow who smelled like a wild pig, that is, of bouillon cubes. So Marja had already instigated changes in castle life, forcing it to include a runt whom she named Hans. She plundered the kitchen for leftovers to feed him, was seen walking him around the courtyard and, once, dandling him on her lap on the salon sofa. Gardener soon lost his patience. He said if Hans ever ventured into his flower patch he would shoot him on the spot.

Bertha was the next to voice dissatisfaction with the situation.

'About my salary,' she said at lunch. 'It shouldn't be less than what I was earning at my last job, should it?'

Benedikt went into town and opened a bank account, transferring money from his account in Berlin.

'Home,' proclaimed Bertha. 'Home is where you keep your money.'

He transferred just enough to pay Bertha the sum she had requested and to have cash in his own pocket. He asked Marja how much money she needed, but she looked offended and replied that she didn't want any at all. 'But,' she added, 'Valerie needs new shoes.' His sandals had ripped, and they barely stayed on his feet.

Benedikt took them to town, enjoyed the spectacle of a little boy having his feet measured and trying on various shoes. Marja was not in the slightest bit interested or choosy—she was prepared to take any. Soon the salesgirl cast an astonished look at Marja's worn pumps and declared that she needed new shoes just as badly, forcing Benedikt to buy her a new pair as well. He was not used to paying for other people; he found it rather pleasant. He did not expect her to thank him, and she did not. She asked him to stop at a grocery store, where, with his money, she purchased cigarettes, several bottles of cola, and bags of sweets.

'There's a shortage of this at your home,' she explained.

More changes followed. One day there was a newcomer at the dinner table. Dolly Sieseby, having heard that her brother had turned up in Biederstein, had sent her eldest daughter, home on holiday, to look after him. Isabella was twenty, a modest, quiet, bookish, and extremely pretty girl. She was tall and blond, and even Benedikt noticed that her torso, in her ladylike dresses, had that perfection which in men and women is characterized by their having some perfect features of the other sex: her shoulders were delicate but strong, her chest unobtrusive, her waist small, but so were her hips, and her arms and legs would have been beautiful on either sex. She took her beauty for granted, made nothing of it. She was studying ancient Greek and Latin and was glad to be around that uncle named Lämmchen she had adored from hearsay only—he had never visited them. But when one scolded her for her intellectual interests, his name came up as a warning, and she had always longed to meet him. News of his illness had filled her with strong emotions. She wanted to cure him, at least make him feel better, by being the only one, so she thought, who understood him. His illness, also the impending loss, impassioned her. She arrived, accepted his lack of interest in her, felt that she had known him forever. She made no efforts to socialize with the others, nor did the others make an effort either; no one really liked her, and even the Countess, who was fussy about looks, remarked to Benedikt, 'She is still too young to have an interesting face.'

The house was large; Isabella was given a room at the far end of the guest wing and tolerated. Benedikt had been annoyed to see another face at the kitchen table, but she made no attempt to get friendly with the child (as the eldest in the family, she was quite bored by small children) and he found her mute interest in him easy enough to ignore.

Finally, the biggest change of all occurred.

One morning the Countess rang for him and said, 'I hear the Communist and her child chattering. And—' She stopped. He expected complaints. She stared at him, her eyes still as window-panes while some storm raged inside her. When she finally spoke, a kind of defiance thickened her tone. 'I hear the child singing.'

'I'm sorry, Grandmother,' he said automatically. It hadn't oc-curred to him that it might disturb the others.

The Countess shook her head. 'He has a lovely voice,' she said. 'I would like to speak to him. Have him and his mother come here now.'

'I don't know where they are!' he protested.

'I can wait,' she replied. 'When you're old, waiting goes faster, because you've seen it all, seen it all . . . but sometimes you get a surprise.'

He did not wish to keep her waiting. He did as she asked, although he had to surface briefly from his isolation. He had to fight his dislike to go into Marja's room, where he felt forced to view the neatly made beds, a pack of cigarettes on one night-stand, the grey bedroom slippers at the door. No one was there. He turned away at once.

Bertha, her hand full of sewing, caught him in the corridor. 'Marja is always in the deer park,' she said, reproach festering in her voice. She suspected the deer would be disturbed by a child.

'Thank you very much,' he said, retreating. And although he hated going outside, it did not cross his mind to displease his grandmother. So he went, hugging the shade of the building, squinting in the direction of the deer park.

He saw her emerge from the trees, coming towards him, a

colourful handkerchief tied around her hair and knotted under her chin. She walked slowly, as if she was enjoying it, the boy trotting behind her.

Benedikt intercepted them, passed his grandmother's wish on. He did not take part in the meeting or wonder what came of it. He forgot it. He enjoyed a period of quiet, several days, or possibly weeks, without changes. He stayed in his room, appeared for meals, controlled his sleep, controlled his thoughts, limited his impressions.

He did not notice Bertha approaching the Countess, with a forward motion so slow that it was taking days to negotiate the threshold. She knew she was not welcome. She peeked into the dressing room, analysing its contents from afar. Her rubber-soled feet made little squeaking noises at the entrance. Within a few days she had made it brazenly all the way into the dressing room and was pottering around there, investigating the corners. She grumbled aloud. It was not as clean as it could be. She and the Countess belonged to the same generation—they knew the value of cleanliness. She savoured the word '*Schmutz*,' dirt, noting the way it made one's mouth form a kiss. She wanted the Countess to hear her, so she could pass on her observations about Maid's laxness. She neared the entrance to the bedroom at the side of the Countess's bed: she could see the Countess's hand, the rings, on the cover. Bertha had a shock. Next to her bed, facing the door and looking straight into Bertha's peeking eyes, was the Russian child.

Bertha staggered backwards. She hurried to her room and had a nap.

That night Bertha made discreet enquiries among the staff: did the Countess often allow children into her room? The staff paid no attention, nor did they observe the way the Russian mother chuckled into her soup. No one would have believed that the Countess could take an interest in a child or that this very shy, strange child might repay her interest in kind. Unobserved, the child slipped downstairs in the mornings, scooted into the Countess's room, sat down on the chair or jumped up and stood next to the Countess until she ordered, 'Closer.' He watched the bony old hand reach into the folds of her sheets and pull out half-melted chocolates. Then he allowed her to pull him right up to her, allowed her to pry open his mouth by pressing on the jaw bones, the way she had done with her favourite dogs as a child, and shove the chocolate in.

He trusted her. He let her caress his thick brown hair and touch his cheek. He waited for her to pay attention to him, waiting with his talent for patience, sitting in the chair while she read or studied her tarot cards or lay dozing on the pillows or stared out the window without seeing a thing, because she was thinking hard. He waited patiently while something momentous moved inside that old brain, until finally, after several days or weeks of this, she sighed and spoke up, loud enough for the child to hear, loud enough for Bertha, rummaging through her dressing room, to decipher, loud enough for Marja, waiting in the salon, to register, loud enough for Benedikt, coming downstairs for lunch, to understand.

'I have made a mistake. I have sinned against the Father but also against my grandson.'

Sun up, sun down. Benedikt did not note the speed with which his grandmother, despite a certain geriatric drag, was rushing through changes, careening (still in the supine position) to her destiny.

One morning she had Secretary call in to the local employment office to announce a job vacancy for a children's tutor. Then she summoned Benedikt and gave him orders. After lunch, Cook and Secretary, Maids, Nurse, and Gardener assembled in the front salon. Benedikt served them sherry in their uniforms and passed on his grandmother's message in a voice weak with annoyance, for he did not like giving orders and found the matter ludicrous.

'The Countess wishes us,' he stammered, 'to dine together this evening in the salon as a family.'

At once, Cook had a migraine. She set her sherry glass down carefully on the stone floor (she liked sherry) before sinking dramatically onto the wooden bench, clutching her forehead. The others watched as Chauffeur's hands closed with practised caution on her thin body. They had seen this drama so often by now that they knew the dialogue by heart.

'I'll be all right,' groaned Cook, 'tomorrow.'

Bertha finally saw her chance. 'I'll cook.' And she added ominously, 'My gentlemen adored my schnitzels.'

For the rest of the world, it was an ordinary day. One day like the rest. But Benedikt was nervous. He heard Bertha muttering to herself in the kitchen, 'Wait till she tastes this, just wait!' as she dropped the first breaded schnitzel into the pan, where it created a pandemonium of sounds and smells. She began opening tins of red cabbage.

Benedikt stalked into his grandmother's room, wanting to ask what exactly she had in mind, what had got into her. But his question was magnified into speechless astonishment at finding Marja there. She was sitting splat on the end of his grandmother's bed, while the boy was perched near her pillow, leaning against the Countess's arm, his stockinged feet up on the covers. Marja regarded Benedikt with obvious impatience, hoping that he would leave again. He realized that he was interrupting a conversation.

'Don't the visitors bother you?' he asked.

The Countess said, 'Valerie is welcome anytime. And Marja too.' As she spoke, she grasped the boy's shoulder from behind, which he did not seem to mind: he seemed used to it.

Benedikt asked Marja to come with him into the salon. She came, reluctantly, hanging back at the door. 'Ah, my grandmother is very old,' he said.

When she did not react he said, 'She's a bizarre old woman. Don't let her annoy you.'

Marja snorted, 'I don't know what you mean.'

He started to walk away, hoping to coerce Marja into following him by asking, 'What do you talk about?' but Marja just stayed in the doorway, remarking, 'I have to go back—I'm having tea with her.'

He stopped. 'Let me talk to her first, please. Wait outside.'

He returned to his grandmother's bedroom. She must have identified him from the tap and swoosh of his limp, because her voice, in a powerful stage whisper, reached him passing through her dressing room. 'Did you know: she's not a Communist at all!'

The word 'she' irritated him.

'Well, I am glad you like her,' he lied. The word 'her' felt like a burr in his mouth.

'Have you never asked yourself why she speaks such good German—have you never asked her? Because her mother was German! But she didn't like the Nazis, or they didn't like her, and she went to Russia . . . I believe she may have been one of the Chosen People.'

He turned and left again, brushed past Marja, without saying a word, hurried to his room, where he tried to find peace, could not, came downstairs, and drifted around the salon, trying not to hear but nevertheless listening intently to Marja's halting voice as it issued from his grandmother's bedroom. Suddenly he noted a singsong whimpering that he did not recognize, either. His ears recoiled, although the sound was soft, rather pleasant. He strode towards his grandmother's room, flung himself inside.

The Countess was laughing.

He retreated again.

'What an extraordinary life you've had!' the Countess called with a full voice.

How can she be so self-deprecating! chafed Benedikt, with a tremble of class consciousness on her behalf. He pooh-poohed his grandmother's interest in Marja's private life. As he dragged himself up the narrow stairs to his room, the Countess's laugh pursued him. He sat at his desk, leaned on his solitron calculations, and felt safe from the goings-on below.

He could not interfere as his grandmother reached one outlandish decision after another. 'I have decided,' she said to Marja, 'to teach you a few things. The most important ones first. In this country, women are expected to smell like flowers. You must wash and change your clothes every day. You've worn the same outfits since your arrival.'

Marja did not protest. Her arrogance had melted in the warmth of the Countess's interest, although a slick of cynicism still remained in her eyes. She listened intently.

'A little vanity is a good, natural thing. Makeup, that's disgusting, that's unnatural. Now, do as I say—'

And she directed her into the dressing room, to a wardrobe in one corner. Inside lay a collection of clothes neatly wrapped in tissue paper. There were hand-embroidered blouses, skirts, underwear, scarves, the clothes of a young woman. 'Take them out,' she called.

Marja unpacked everything on to the purple bedspread, where the old woman looked through them, sitting up, leaning forward, independent of the pillow. She picked out a plain white silk blouse and a long skirt and instructed Marja to put them on.

Marja complied. She stepped out of her trousers and pulled up her shirt. While her arms were knotted over her head, her audience examined the heavy white body, with its precise contours, the blue veins of her breasts, the rounded belly, the baggy white underwear, and slender legs. For an instant, she was imprisoned, squirming, in her shirt. The Countess and the Russian boy looked at each other slyly and smiled. As the cloth finally slipped over Marja's head, freeing her, her audience quickly looked away again. Satisfied that no one had watched her, Marja quickly dressed in the Countess's clothes. When the Countess handed her a hand mirror from her night table, Marja turned away, tilting the small mirror about, studying herself from every possible perspective. Beneath the thin cloth of her shirt, the straps of her brassière were visible cutting into the flesh of her back. She kept gazing into the mirror; she could not satisfy her interest until Valerie grew alarmed by her self-absorption, by her posed smile, and the Countess suddenly snapped, 'Don't be so vain!'

Meanwhile, Bertha's red cabbage was rumbling in its pot, gathering force. All at once, the smell of a festive meal in East

Berlin, cooked cabbage, burst through the house. Staff remained stoic. The smell swept away Benedikt's thoughts about abstract particles as if they were flimsy bric-a-brac. Only the Countess was too preoccupied to notice.

Marja had, at the Countess's request, hauled one of the heavy armchairs from the salon to one end of the long table and positioned it in front of the Countess's closed double doors. The chair had massive ebony arms, an austere seat, and a high back. When Marja returned to report that the chair was in place, the Countess's face turned white with fear and determination. 'You will help me sit down there,' she whispered. 'I will eat with the family.'

Marja could not gauge how astonishing this wish was. In a still, small voice the Countess spoke to Chauffeur on her intercom, ordering him to open the double doors. The help were dressing for dinner, taking off uniforms, and stepping into a uniform look (plain skirts and flowered blouses on the women, cheap conservative suits on the men), while Bertha was drizzling parsley on her schnitzels and boiled potatoes. Benedikt was putting away his solitron collisions as Chauffeur began to pry open the bedroom doors. He resorted to a hammer, pounding and cursing, while Bertha, grumbling about having to handle china, set the table, which was Maid's duty, but Maid was primping. When the doors finally budged, the dogs began to whine and the Countess thanked Chauffeur and asked him to leave the salon. Marja and Valerie needed a quarter of an hour to move the groaning, giggling Countess from her bed to the table.

She cursed, using words she had secreted in the back of her memory as a child, and then remarked, 'I am fighting with my own position.'

When she was finally in place, she dispatched Marja to a cupboard at the other side of the salon, where the best dinner service was kept. The old brass dinner bell hadn't been rung since a Sunday afternoon lunch decades earlier, a meal that had lain so heavily on the stomachs of Benedikt's parents that they had decided to take a drive to Lake Konstanz afterwards, an excursion that ended in a fatal argument. For decades the dinner bell had waited mutely at the back of the cupboard. The Countess rang it herself, a signal that reached the dinner guests putting the last touches to their clothes and prompted Bertha to heap the serving platters and carry them in to the salon table. Afterwards, she did not return to the kitchen but propped herself behind the window of the swinging doors to see the effect her meal would have.

Bertha watched Cook, followed by Chauffeur, three maids, Nurse, Secretary, Dogkeeper, and Gardener, advance, festive and unsure of the situation. They gaped as they saw the Countess already seated at the head of the table. From her vantage point, Bertha observed that Dr Waller came in last, his face thinner and more drawn than usual. She noted the sudden widening of his eyes, the tremor of his mouth as he registered his grandmother's presence. Bertha thought it was the sight of the potatoes that was affecting them adversely. A thin medley of meek voices reached her ears as the guests exchanged civilities.

'They're saying the meal's not good,' despaired Bertha, 'that it's not enough and that the meat is cold. I should have made more potatoes . . . and kept the schnitzel in the oven.' She began to whimper behind the door. 'Oh how silly of me . . .'

Then she cheered up, seeing the Countess reach for a schnitzel, drop it on her plate with a pleasant, rollicking thud. The old woman sawed merrily with her knife until she had a piece of meat on her fork that she led cautiously to her mouth. The others watched, fascinated. Her mouth opened, revealing a bit of tongue. The piece moved inwards, the lips closed. The fork was withdrawn. The Countess was chewing, her gaze introspective. The others began reaching for food, loading their plates. But now the Countess was turning pale, and an odd noise came from her, as if air were rushing into her head, and it seemed as if her head was growing bigger. Her hands went to her mouth in a gesture of politeness.

She expanded.

CHAPTER 13

*Interruption of a silence: Valerie giggles twice while
stillness regales the Countess with memories*

A fter a while, the Countess gasped several times—was it
astonishment, wondered Bertha, at the taste of the schnitzel?
Was it regret, thought Benedikt, at taking part in this dinner?
Her gasps were loud, way over the threshold of politeness.
Thereafter, she was silent.

She stared straight ahead, her mouth slightly open, like an
elongated rip in a piece of tissue paper. The company settled
into inactivity and silence.

Silence, Benedikt mused, is the most fragile substance. By
describing a silence, the author is already violating it. But there is
no musical or literary notation for utter silence, because the silence between two notes is a rest, and in a rest you can feel the
rhythm. A real silence has no pulse. And, as any physician can
tell you, anything without a pulse creates a problem. After Euro-
pean monks had figured out how to notate the relationship between different notes, it took them another six hundred years to
develop a notation for the length of each note. No sooner had
they done that, than they began to count the length of a silence
between notes. They intended to control silence. After all, silence is the domain of the most volatile mental activity.

Silently but rapidly, the Countess was going through
changes. The only external indication of this was her complex-
ion, which became, as her blood was said to be, blue. Her companions waited, their senses saturated with the smell of bacon

and cabbage. She was staring with plain hatred at the silver platter that held the schnitzels. The platter was the most recent
addition to the household. It had joined up in 1918, at her wedding, the gift of the Countess Waller von Wallerstein, the
groom's grandmother, who had done her best to talk him out of
the wedding because the bride's families, the von Umpfenbachs
und zu Rheins, were wealthy but on the lower rung of the social
register.

'Weddings and funerals are the most important occasions in
the lives of our family,' the elderly snob had sniffed. 'Births are
less important because they don't guarantee the other occasions.'

The bride was the daughter of recent-money aristocracy; her
grandfather had built hotels in south German resorts. The platter
had the Waller von Wallerstein crest engraved in the centre; it
was still unused a fortnight later when the groom fell while patrolling a Belgian street for snipers; he was the victim of a freak
accident involving a black cat and a plate of hard-boiled eggs set
out to cool on a windowsill. The widow had thought briefly
about sending the silver platter back, giving up her married
name—she didn't mind marrying into a title but she didn't want
to inherit one—then she suddenly had other worries. These worries made a proper widow of her, set her fighting for his standards, abiding by Count Waller von Wallerstein's silence, in
which she heard hourly his high-pitched voice advising, steering.
The social register listed a son eight and a half months after his
father's demise, the gap between ø and * representing months of
panic because in the eight times the marriage was consummated
(fitted into the three days and nights of his military leave) she
had done everything she knew to prevent a pregnancy. But what
had she known? Forty years later, as the pressure increased on
the Countess's chest, she remembered his weight on her.

In the silence the Countess was not able to blush or flush or
control her thoughts. She recalled The Eight Times chronologi-
cally, beginning with the strange unpleasant smell of her body
when it was unclad. And then the smell of his body (not quite as
bad) and, through eyes screwed shut but opening of their own

accord, the glimpse of him (oh, how gruesome!) that explained the feel of him. At the time, she had been so amazed by the unnaturalness of this behaviour that she had experienced love-making as one protracted assault on all her senses. Yet in retrospect, she could remember those eight episodes precisely enough to order them in time and thus tell them apart: two before breakfast, three in the evening, three in the middle of the night.

The last time had been particularly rough. Although he was shorter than she, it seemed as if he was sawing her in two. She had felt sorry for him. Perhaps that was her first feeling of love: poor, insensitive boy. She did not want to make him feel bad by hopping up afterwards and washing him out as fast as she could. She lay there fighting her disgust. He did not seem even to notice her dishevelment and odour. Perhaps, she thought, education had stuck better to him. She had been taught not to notice herself at all. Now and again, she had sinned, stolen a peek. She had a general idea, from looking downwards. She knew, too, that there was more to it than met the eye from this perspective. She also knew what Down There felt like through underwear and a skirt. Uninteresting, of course.

As the Countess was lost in thought, the silence at the dinner table in Schloss Biederstein was broken by the child tittering twice. No one shared his humour. No one explained. As soon as the silence was restored, it droned on. The guests glanced at the Countess and then turned their heads away. In the silence, Benedikt saw for the first time the exact bend of the silver fork handle, the millimetre-sized crown beneath the prongs, the tendrils of the initials, WW. He heard like a full modern orchestra the syncopated clack of the clocks, sensed the cold corrugations of the stone and the warping of the windowpane. He actually craned his head to study the portraits, musing about the colour of the backgrounds, the frames, and then he saw the brown rafters in the white ceiling, like a huge wooden cobweb, and turned his attention back to the platter, the schnitzels covering up the family crest.

When the old woman gave several more gasps he remembered her and realized that she was, for some reason, not breathing correctly. He decided he must tell her something amusing, something to jolt her out of this peculiar mood. He cast about for a topic. The Countess gasped again and was submerged again in her silence.

As the pressure continued to build in her head and chest, the Countess became younger: tall, boyish, pointy-featured, with an impish smile on her thin lips and a chesty laugh. Her parents were terrified by her enthusiasm for life and protested that her stubbornness, dangerous in a man, was inappropriate in a woman. At least they were not surprised when she disappeared in 1917, just sixteen years old, to be a volunteer nurse in a lazarette run by Benedictine nuns on the front. They did not know that she was running away from a short, pale, delicate army officer named Waller von Wallerstein who kept visiting her. He wanted to introduce bigger bones and blond hair into the family stock and proposed marriage, but she preferred a man's adventure. When she left home she believed that she believed in God, but, faced with danger, she lost her belief and decided that only pure will could protect one from harm.

One evening a report circulated in the field lazarette that a Russian soldier dying of bubonic plague had been driven away by the doctors. She went looking for him in the dusk and found him several hundred metres from the lazarette, sprawled in bushes wild with insect life. His face and hands were covered with sores, his eyes swollen shut. She sat on the ground with his head in her lap for a while, and then, when it was dark, she helped him back to the lazarette and laid him fully dressed on her own bed. She combed his hair and patted his hands. When he moaned, she kissed his forehead. She sat with him until he finally died, and then she called a doctor. The Russian was the only man she had ever willingly taken into her bed, but that didn't interest the others. They hauled his body out of there in a hurry, berating her as they went. The doctor came to talk to her with a priest. The doctor told her to pack her bags and leave, she was fired, but the priest kept interrupting him to insist that first, first he should hear her confession, give her extreme unction. She refused them both, leaving the lazarette without her bags or last rites. Back at home and healthy in Hamburg, she heard that five nuns had contracted the plague and died.

By that time she had already agreed to marry Fürst Waller von Wallerstein. He had kissed her. She remembered the sensation of his wet lips, the stubbly coffee-brown moustache covering her mouth. One could not simply wash that away. And then it turned to cherries. She was small, wiry, master of a hard, boyish body. She climbed into the top branches of the cherry tree and feasted on the fruit. It was her grandmother's tree. Her grandmother had forbidden her to steal, but it was a hot summer day and she could not resist the climb into the branches. Suddenly her grandmother was standing below shouting. As the girl wound her way down the tree, her grandmother was picking cherries from the ground and putting them onto a plate. The cherries were full of worms.

'As punishment, you will eat these,' the old woman said.

She had to sit skewed on her grandmother's gaze and eat them all, swallowing the wriggling worms whole. She told her grandmother that they tasted delicious. No sooner had this sentence left her mouth, than she vomited. She could not be made to eat anymore and was put to bed with a fever which her grandmother said was God's punishment for disobeying.

Nausea wracked the Countess. This gave way suddenly to a delightful sweet taste in her mouth. She felt warm all over, and the warmth came from milk in her mouth.

She heard the sound of a voice that was soothing and without precise meaning, like a lullaby. She did not identify the speaker, Benedikt, as he pleaded, 'Grandmother, you know that I'm ill, I have a touch of cancer, something like cancer. Grandmother, listen to me! It's fatal. I hadn't told you. We didn't want to shock you. I'm not going to live as long as you. Well, we can't know, I might . . .

'Grandmother . . .'

She savoured the stroking of the familiar voice and the atmosphere of the milk, until her mouth was suddenly dry again, as if it were being sucked out. Her body was wet.

She felt herself squeezed from all sides. She heard the hammering of a heartbeat. Then she knew nothing but the sensation of pressure.

The Countess's flesh and the chair collaborated: they held her upright. She had spent the last twenty years of her life lying down. Now she died, regally, sitting up.

CHAPTER 14

Gravely, majestically: Benedikt takes part in a family ceremony

When family feeling is stifled, its release can be explosive. During her last years, Alice Waller von Wallerstein had neglected the family; she had not invited them to the castle or taken up their invitations. Her granddaughter had tended to her husband's relations, while Benedikt had disappeared altogether. Family felt its union eminent when it saw the newspaper obituary of a deeply loved Countess Waller von Wallerstein, née von Umpfenbach und zu Rhein, which had the biggest headline in the regional newspaper on that particular day, bigger even than an advertisement supporting German reunification.

At once, all over Germany, in parts of Austria and England, family energy began to accumulate. When it had reached a highly charged state, the bells in the castle tower began to vibrate and clang, unfamiliar cars created wind turbulence in the streets of Biederstein, cumulus clouds trembled on the small town's narrow horizon, and the roses swelled up on local trellises.

Ceremony is the link between the past and the future, ceremony is the present intensive. When pomp was detonated within the containment of the family, everyone's thoughts rattled back and forth between past and future.

That the death was a bit bizarre would not normally have put anyone off. The story of a death belongs, in any case, to family lore, and telling and retelling it, leaving out all the really telling details, asserts family feeling. She had, it was chorused, choked.

In the company and full view of her servants and grandson. A relatively quick death, at a grand old age, and she hadn't been up to much lately, anyway. Must have been an unpleasant scene for the staff, interrupted dinner. Afterwards? Well, afterwards, her grandson drew up those shocking invitations.

'Afterwards' actually lasted several weeks, beginning with the Countess's last breath. Immediately afterwards, it had been the company's turn to gasp, wait, and then snivel. In the face of this implausible event—death—time had jerked and stopped like a train inching along a bad track. The witnesses were alarmed, shrieked, and then sank into an interim of indifference, in which their fingers tugged apart their paper napkins. Their alarm asserted itself again slowly, growing until it was powerful enough to elicit a new shriek. Napkins stained with gravy and cabbage lay shredded all over the table, red-and-brown confetti.

Only Marja had shown no signs of this natural shock. She remained aloof, like a professional. It was Marja who made the diagnosis. She jumped up from her chair while the others were still watching from their places, rushed over to the Countess, and slapped her full in the face. When the Countess failed to respond to this insult, Marja pronounced, 'She's dead,' which the others interpreted as 'ШИЗ ДЭД,' failing to understand the Russian accent or her sudden authority. There was nothing ceremonious about the way they listened to Marja's pronouncements and then followed her orders. Chauffeur and Gardener behaved like schoolboys, heeded her words, and went to work (oh, ghastly lack of ceremony) extricating the body from its chair. This so exhausted their strength that they did not dare carry her far. They cleared a space on the table, bedded her down there, and waited for further instructions. She looked entirely natural lying there, as if the table were made for her. The true lady looks good under any circumstances.

It was Marja who organized the subsequent transport from table back to bed, with the help of the tea trolley—horrible, unceremonious scene, not intended to be kept by memory, but memory snatched it in as many perspectives as there were witnesses. Gardener and Chauffeur hoisted the Countess up, one holding her shoulders, the other her rump. Maid caught her legs just as they swept off the table, taking several glasses with them. Together, they heaved her over onto the tea trolley, their palms repelled by the feel of her, given her condition. During the last seconds of this journey, Benedikt added his fingertips, holding up her gown so that it did not brush the floor. With the trolley wheels groaning, they transferred her back to her bed.

The others remained seated, kept still, not wishing to rouse their fear with activity. The entire staff stayed overtime. Bertha and Cook were the first to leave, after saying goodbye to the Countess, each after her fashion: Cook stood before her and shivered violently, while Bertha picked up a bottle of perfume from the bedstand, let her fingers hover shyly around the dead woman's ears, until she found she was too afraid to touch her, so she pocketed the flask.

'I have pains,' Cook told the Countess through clenched, chattering teeth, 'in my arms, in my legs.' The two women retreated to the guest wing: one heard them complaining about death the whole way, their syllables tangling.

'I always retired,' pronounced Bertha at the top of the stairs, 'before my employers got that far. My last one got axed while I was with him, but that's different.'

After his grandmother was restored to her regular surroundings, death gave her an inexplicable authority, even greater than life had, and Benedikt heeded her unspoken wish to notify the family at large. He realized that her social register was missing. There were more of these on a special shelf in the hall, but Benedikt knew she had used her own copy as an operating manual. She had written comments in the margins. It had to be found.

A search ensued. Neither Secretary nor Maid could remember seeing it. Cupboards that had been closed for twenty years were broken open, brooms swept under beds and sofas, even the kitchen was scoured. In the process, her will was located in a desk drawer in the library, along with guest lists she had kept to document all of her invitations. An hour passed with the survivors picking through the house mumbling, 'It has to be somewhere,' until Marja finally thought of pulling the Countess forward and looking under the pillow, where she had kept her tarot cards. Marja pulled out the volume, dated 1917, the year of her marriage. The green cover with its golden crown in the middle looked new, but as Marja lifted it up over her head in triumph, she felt the thickness shrink in her grip. The Countess had not seen any reason to consult her register in recent years; she had lain on it, and as Marja held it, the pages poured down over the deceased in a grey powder.

The staff could take no more. They excused themselves. Another ghost had been added to the regiment patrolling the house.

Valerie had curled up like a little dog on the hall bench and fallen asleep.

A physician arrived to fill out the death certificate. He threw back the bedcovers, scrutinized the body, and pronounced: 'Rings.' And then: 'No necklace, no watch.' He wrestled with her fingers. 'Oil!' he commanded. 'Bring me some oil.' Only Marja obeyed him, procuring salad oil from the kitchen. The physician handed Marja his booty, the Countess's engagement ring and the double-stranded widow's ring she had acquired soon afterwards.

Marja passed them on to Benedikt, remarking, 'She would have insisted I wear them.'

The physician made a few phone calls, arranged for a funeral home to pick up the deceased in the morning, and ordered the family to bed.

Benedikt remained with his grandmother all night, watching as death had its way with her, stealing her temperature by two degrees an hour, spattering her hands, propped on the bedcovers, with blue spots, and distending that poor purple face until it had no definable contours at all. He sat on a stool at the foot of her bed and leafed through her old invitation lists. The size of this collection of names impressed him; she had lived in an invisible city.

As the hours passed, Benedikt made a decision: he would make up for his own neglect of the family. But the invitation he sent out a few days later was taken as an affront. The invitation and the goings-on after the death were highly irregular. They would tarnish any ceremony, clog it up, making it unable to lock the past to the future. The list of relatives unwilling to attend the family celebration included barons, dukes, counts, and countesses, and one prince from Austria. The reason given by all was shortness of notice. Family heritage required protection. Tradition was the benevolent dictatorship of the dead over the living.

In all fairness, the family could not and did not blame Benedikt for wanting to respect the old Countess's will, in which she ordered cremation and 'unaccompanied burial' in the same grave as her maid Liesel. The villagers, however, and the staff denounced him for this, for deferring to his grandmother's senile sentimentality. After all, he was a fully grown man. They had their turn at horror. Liesel's relatives, her nephews and nieces, conferred telephonically and roundly refused: a countess had no place next to their aunt. Liesel belonged with her own family. When the local priest heard of their efforts to block the burial, he sighed with relief. And this sigh, transmitted on wings of gossip, elicited more sighs of relief: the priest was on the villagers' side. The case rested.

The heir did not know what to do. He took the plain brown-paper box that held the tin of his grandmother's ashes and placed it on the dinner table, there where the schnitzels had stood, and forgot it altogether. He ate his meals opposite without paying the slightest attention. Then his sister, the Countess of Sieseby, Freifrau von Hagelberg, took command. She arrived at Schloss Biederstein with a flashlight and a shovel. At midnight she met Chauffeur and Cook in the hall. She collected the box and drove out to the cemetery where Liesel rested. Cook had a weeklong migraine afterwards, which is how the story got out, because Chauffeur described the events preceding the headache to the village doctor, akin to opening a faucet of disapproval that soon flooded the village with details. The Countess of Sieseby had made the cook hold the flashlight while the chauffeur dug a hole into Liesel's grave. Then she had torn the cardboard box open so carelessly that bits of its brown-paper wrapping roosted and fluttered around the cemetery for days. She had prised the lid off the tin inside with a can opener and tipped the ashes into the hole. As the ashes poured downwards, Cook began to snivel.

'Oh, stop it!' snapped the Countess. 'Who knows whose remains these really are. Surely not my grandmother's!'

The villagers took the Countess of Sieseby to be, in ascending degree of evil: callous, indifferent to tradition, and strange; but her brother, they said, was worse. Within days of the death he was putting his crazy ideas into practice. Remarkable, his agility at this—who would have thought.

He had systematically kicked over all legal and moral barricades.

First, he had cornered the administrator in charge of marriage licences during the man's lunch break. What brilliant timing: the poor man had just bought himself a meat-salad sandwich. It was lying on his desk.

'I want to marry as soon as possible,' Benedikt had said. 'What are the requirements?'

The administrator tried to rid himself of Benedikt by passing forms to him. Benedikt filled them out with alacrity and pressed on. 'She's not married. Really. I don't understand these forms at all.'

And who does? thought the administrator.

'There's no point in requiring Frau Golubka to have all the documents sent from the Soviet Union. They don't exist in the shambles. They will never get here.'

It was hot. The administrator had a fear of food poisoning, and he judged that in another ten minutes his meat-salad sandwich would be dangerous. He decided to take Benedikt's word for it that his fiancée was not married. The adoption of the child could take place right after the wedding. He picked out his first free date in August.

'I trust you don't want a church wedding,' he said, stamping the forms.

With this Benedikt proceeded to the church and found the priest with a half-eaten meat-salad sandwich. The priest was still recovering from rumours about the Countess's burial. He did not want to mess with the Waller von Wallersteins any more than necessary. He agreed without hesitation to marry Benedikt in the castle chapel. But he'd like to baptize the child before the legal adoption, even if that was officially none of his business: he had his principles. The child was already seven, it was high time.

'Maybe he knows more about God than we think,' he said. 'Say the word "Bog"—that's Russian—and watch his reaction.'

Benedikt agreed to start Valerie off on religious instruction at once. He used this as a vehicle to tell Marja about their upcoming marriage. They had finished dinner, and in silence he had accompanied her and Valerie through the hall, and onwards, and as they reached the guest wing, she stopped walking and looked at him quizzically: why was he walking with them?

And he said, 'Valerie should see the priest tomorrow. He needs to be baptized before I can adopt him, even if we are married.'

She did not seem to understand him, which he attributed to her poor German. She just nodded, grasped her son's hand, and hurried away with him to their room.

'But I am married!' she said a day later, same time, same place, her small, expression-torn face now full of innocent amazement. 'On paper, and otherwise. How can I divorce my husband when I don't know where he is?'

He thought he saw something strange happening in her eyes: a blurring of all the alertness, confusion. He was ashamed of himself. He was being too forceful. Perhaps the matter was hopeless.

'Conventions don't count,' he ventured, giving it one last try.

'If you want to, we can get it annulled, cancelled—I mean, does it really matter? That was in Russia. Your husband's not here. I need an heir. Your son will be looked after his whole life. I don't just mean financially. I mean aesthetically. You don't want to throw away an opportunity like this.

'Your name will be Count Waller von Wallerstein,' he said to the child. 'You must practise saying that.' He turned to Marja, 'Can you translate that, please?

'The child is a perfect specimen of a Waller von Wallerstein. He's got that thick hair, and he'll be tall,' he added.

'He'll be very dark-haired, you'll see, as he gets older,' replied Marja.

'And his eyes are such a deep-blue colour—my mother apparently had dark-blue eyes.'

After the priest met Marja and Valerie a few days later he did not mention the need for religious instruction again, and Benedikt sent out the wedding invitations he had written two weeks earlier. Although she had never actually agreed, Marja did not protest, either, when he told her, 'The date is set.'

Their life together proceeded with few changes. He had wanted to buy her a wedding dress but she refused. She preferred to wear one of his grandmother's dresses. 'It'll be just as good, I'll fix it,' she said, her gaiety settling the question. She picked out another outfit from his grandmother's fifty-year-old collection, and he agreed that it would do. She did not want a ring, either. 'They bother me when I'm using my hands.' He didn't know what she could be using her hands for, and they reached a compromise: at the ceremony they would exchange his grandparents' wedding rings. She would wear hers for the duration of the day and then give it back to him. Apart from these negotiations, they rarely saw each other; their routines did not intersect.

His interest in the event itself soon waned, and he told his sister the news in the hope that she would volunteer to look after the organizational chores. So it was Dolly who opened the letters of reply from the relatives in which they regretted, in a unison of polite coldness, that they could not attend. At least two aunts had contacted aide-de-camp gossip columnists in order to insist that they, too, boycott the wedding. That was how the press got wind of it. Journalists are human. It was a good story. A great story. The only explanation for a count's marrying a Russian was that she was a countess. But she wasn't. The only other explanation was True Love. The Count must be head over heels to be kicking over family tradition like that.

The chapel was going to be crowded. Most of the Berlin acquaintances Benedikt had invited agreed to come, their curiosity complicated by what Dr Graf called 'class self-consciousness.' No one had suspected that Waller actually belonged to a different species. Benedikt Schmidt was hit hardest, the invitation leaving no doubt about Dr Waller's contempt: the name on the back of the envelope reading 'Count Waller von Wallerstein.' He invited his wife along. As for Dr Anhalt, he cancelled his Sunday tea party and took his car to the car wash. Dr Graf, glad to have something to do on a weekend, also decided to go, while the internist who had treated Waller, Benedikt, showed the nurses his invitation, enjoyed their urging him to take a needed break, but never seriously considered attending. With the exception of Dr Graf, who had no sensitivity to rank, the others, including several additional colleagues from the Institute, were incredulous about suddenly coming into the acquaintance of a real count, proud that they had never taken his status into consideration, as if this proved their lack of snobbery. With these thoughts glittering in their studied equanimity they set out on the long journey southwards which they felt would contribute to the settling of class differences.

And although the list of relatives unwilling to attend was long, pages long, there were a number of family black sheep willing to leave their golf games and their jobs (some had to work, some simply preferred to), as well as several illegitimate children who never missed a family event, especially when they were not invited; this contingent including an occupational therapist and a *maître d'hôtel*. Two spinsters with religious ticks that undermined their senses of propriety came, and two elderly homosexuals, one of them a cleric, the other a dentist, the latter married, and a whole minibus of English cousins who were over in St Moritz anyway, as well as a Mike Wallerstein, grandson of a New World buff who'd taken up farming there in the twenties. America had leeched class consciousness out of his genes; his descendant was over on a package tour and simply stopped by to see what he called his 'roots.'

Just because the rest of the family stayed away didn't mean they weren't curious. For days after the invitation had gone out they wondered (in ascending order of importance) about Benedikt, the rest of the family, the estate, the castle. There were a lot of Waller von Wallersteins but only one ancestral home. When a distant cousin joked that Benedikt, obviously still a wild man, might turn the little castle into a home for Cossacks, no one laughed. They suspected others of attending. And when they had confirmation, they enquired as to what kind of presents they planned to bring, huffy that Benedikt was depriving them, by behaving too absurdly, of the chance to satisfy their curiosity.

'Maybe,' said cousins, aunts, great-uncles, once, twice, three times removed, hearing about Benedikt's new Russian, 'she's an Obolensky.'

'I guess they're curious,' said Marja, standing in front of the altar with Benedikt, rehearsing the ceremony the night before. 'And their curiosity will not be satisfied by looking at me.' Benedikt paid no attention to her conversation, nor did Valerie, sitting in a pew behind them. The child was uninterested in the proceedings, apathetic. Marja hadn't noticed him lately. She was preoccupied. Events had pushed her son out of the heat of her maternal attention. She was out of reach for him, too, being carried in the middle of a great, stately commotion.

'Perhaps,' she said, 'tomorrow will never get here.'

The next morning was as perfect as anyone could recollect. The sun had come up, so it seemed, a full hour early, but without being a bully about it. The sun had a pastel strength; the air shimmered with cool humidity, as if it were the year's first warm day, or the last. Good weather can whip the emotions, and many of the guests who had set off on their journey the day before had woken up in nearby hotels, pulled back the curtains, and felt protected from any more irregularities by the pretty sky.

I am glad I brought my yellow dress after all! thought the Countess Dolly, although I am expanding like a good dough around the middle. With a good stout girdle I will look fine. Like a girl. And my pink stockings—lovely! And she turned over to watch her husband snore, slowly, regularly, pompously, as the healthy do.

The Berliners in the Pension Biederstein found the climate charming. Dr Anhalt lay in his single bed, the fresh sheets caressing his large body until he had an unusual surge of feeling for his wife, grateful that she wasn't along to discourage him. Right next door, Dr Graf woke up with his usual sadness as a companion, while two young colleagues, sharing a neighbouring room and a research project, began a pleasantly heated discussion about the use of probability theory in predicting the success of a marriage. Benedikt Schmidt was just arriving in Biederstein. He and his wife had taken the overnight train and they were miffed that no one had met them at the station, although he had told the groom, his old friend, exactly when they were arriving.

'You see how he is!' said his wife. 'Calls himself your friend!' They took a taxi.

By late morning the cars from every side and end of Germany were converging on Biederstein, where shortsighted pensioners, could spot an out-of-town car by dint of not recognizing it, since every car was associated with someone, like a favourite hat or cane. The bells rallied like artillery. The cavalcade of traffic moving through town and out again, past the castle gates and the gardens, was not greeted by the dogs because they were assembled with Dogkeeper at the side of the entrance stairs. The guests went inside once, marvelled, deposited their gifts, had a good look at the table set up discreetly in the hall, assessing what the others had brought. The relative from America, who was by far the wealthiest there, had brought a coffee-table book about the Midwest. The Count of Sieseby and his wife had brought a television of modest price. Dolly arrived with her children and a video camera with which she intended to capture everything.

As her first chore, Dolly took command of the little Russian child, who would not budge from his mother's side on the hall bench. She saw that the child was not well. She felt the weakness and coolness of his hands. At first she attributed this to his being Russian. Then her common sense intervened. She walked the child over to her own brood, an impeccably dressed quintet, three boys, two girls, all of them tall for their ages, slender, fair, with the vague features of a small-boned breed. The robust little boy wore what looked like a miniature clerk's outfit: straight-cut trousers of cheap cloth, a white shirt, and sandals. But he was handsome, his posture very straight, even as he twisted his head around to check his mother was still on the bench. He trained his deep-blue eyes in her direction even though he could see very little because a photographer had asked him to remove his glasses for the occasion.

Dolly organized the company, sent them back out to the courtyard, where they milled about. Most of the children were clad in the clothes they had worn to a recent wedding. For the adults, there had been confusion about whether to wear black, and some did. The Berliners kept to themselves, their faces complicated by their intellects, their clothes urban and rather out of place though expensive, while the relatives socialized, Benedikt's sister in the thick of things. The bride stood far off at the boundary of the courtyard, out of the shadow of the house, in the sun, studying the ground, the very small shadow she cast. It was midday.

The priest was waiting in the sacristy, playing through the ceremony in his mind. He'd had a blackout at his last service. He had forgotten protocol and text and couldn't say whether he was running a wedding, a baptism, or a funeral. He had studied the congregation, and halfway into his wedding ritual he'd switched to a mass for the dead. No one had picked up on it except his mother. She attended all his services; she always had butterflies beforehand, although she took beta-blockers.

CHAPTER 15

Volubly: Benedikt expresses some ideas about child-rearing.
This makes Marja nervous

A nd the boy won't suffer the way I did . . . he won't live with the dead . . . untiring creatures . . . taking his air . . . sharing his meals . . . looming in his brain . . . with their sketchy personalities . . . Uncle Edmund . . . such a gourmet . . . he could tell you not only which spices were in the sauce . . . but also the age and sex of the deer he was eating . . . Great-Aunt Alois . . . who was so pious at twenty-five that ten white doves circled over this roof . . . tipping off the family . . . when she drowned . . . during a swim . . . after a heavy picnic lunch . . . oysters and champagne . . . five hundred kilometres away in Monaco . . . Great-Grandfather Hermann August . . . "a man of courage" . . . who rescued Great-Grandmother Augustine . . . "a woman of grace" . . . as well as Great-Aunt Helena . . . the "pretty, unmarried daughter" . . . and the "imposing" Great-Great-Aunt Helena . . . rescued all three from a wild boar that attacked them . . . they were strolling in these woods . . . the boar was maddened by the campfire songs they sang . . . Great-Grandfather kicked the boar between the eyes with his hiking boot . . . may these stories never reach his ears . . . nor shall Valerie Count Waller von Wallerstein ever have to start calling the staff by their last names . . . the day he reaches a certain age . . . the way I did . . . the cake has been eaten, the presents admired . . . come here, my boy . . . you're ten years old today . . . and from now on . . . you will refer to Liesel as "Frau

The organist was already at his post. He had his girlfriend with him and played some rhythm and blues with the electricity turned off to amuse her. He got carried away and the keys made a racket, which set the priest's foot tapping without his being able to identify the source of the beat. When the organist heard the bells in the tower ring, he snapped the switch and began to play for his money. The Countess of Sieseby gave a signal and the procession travelled back inside, through the hall, and into the chapel, taking their places: the immediate family occupied the first aisle, then the servants and their relatives (in order of length of service), finally the rest of the family, and way to the back, the friends from Berlin.

The Count of Sieseby, Freiherr von Hagelberg, known as Hackse, remained outside in the courtyard with Marja. When all footsteps had ceased, the organist played a new tune and Benedikt entered, alighted like a ghost at the altar, his black suit fluttering, his face immobile as he steadied himself at the altar railing. The assembled attributed his thinness to his work, to his health, to his rank, to his sudden marriage, and these surmises were distributed evenly among the groups.

The bride stood in the courtyard, smiling shyly at the circling news photographers until Hackse Sieseby came for her. He was a gentle man, big and beefy although well over sixty already, with natural good manners. But an evil spirit caught hold of him suddenly, and instead of going up to the bride, he simply called her from the stairs, 'Come on, then.'

She obeyed. With each step forward she was leaving something behind. As she proceeded towards her new brother-in-law, she passed the dogs held by their trainer and they jerked their noses in the air: they smelled fear.

Herbert" . . . to Alfred as "Herr Biesterfeld" . . . and they will
call you "Count Wallerstein" . . . or, for short, "sir" . . . and my
son won't have to tolerate the chauffeur speaking to him in public . . . as if they're strangers to each other . . . followed by
secret confidences when the car door is closed and he slips mentally into the familiar low gear, the *"Du"* form . . . don't take
your grandmother too seriously, little one, she'll forget about the
broken vase, here's the church now, mind you behave yourself,
goodbye, sir, I'll pick you up punctually, sir.

   'None of those vain class distinctions . . . and no conventional religion . . . as a kind of paramilitary training . . . Hail
Marys from flailing lips . . . knee-bends at the altar . . . and no
adoration of useless manners . . . and no, if he doesn't want to
finish his mashed potatoes . . . well, then, he won't . . . no
sitting him in the corner with the silver bowl of cold, stiff potatoes . . . watered down by hot tears . . . and the hours pass like
an enemy . . . smelling of cold gravy and plaster . . . and no
taunting him about his interests, if he has them . . . they're
allowed . . . a noble thing . . . interests . . . strong ones . . .
and no hunting if he's not inclined . . . holding his ears when
the guns fire . . . posing with the hunter over the dead animal
. . . keeping his eyes averted, afraid of feeling sick . . . afraid of
doing the wrong thing: crying . . . nor will his bad behaviour be
punished either, after a tribunal of servants and relatives decides
. . . the servants actually having no say in the matter . . . how
many with what object . . . the cane, the open hand . . . I was
never naughty, never once . . . I was worse . . . I didn't believe
but I behaved . . . no temptation . . . does that sound unnatural? I was not energetic enough to oppose them but my sister,
always . . . Grandmother was the highest judge . . . visitors had
honorary jury duty . . . the butler, Heinz Umpfenbach (no relation to the von Umpfenbachs) . . . was the hangman. At least
once a week, Dolly had a punishment coming to her . . . what
had she done? . . . stolen jam from the kitchen . . . talked back
to Oma . . . made faces at the swans . . . mumbled her prayers
. . . my grandmother always said . . . "I was the same way or

worse! One has to learn, as I did!" . . . then she called out her sentence . . . Dolly was urged to walk of her own accord to the little parlour, which everyone referred to as the punishment room . . . a waiting room with plush sofa . . . her screams were shrill . . . I suffered for her the most excruciating pains . . . "Shush! Shush!" I begged . . . she returned with a purple, tear-stained face . . . until one day, I intervened . . . ever so slightly . . . Dolly was already ten . . . in fact, these occasions were seldom now, seldom enough to make me notice them even more . . . when I said something disparaging . . . something about cruelty and the Germans . . . my grandmother realized that my sister had my sympathy . . . so she proclaimed that I was to watch . . . I was forced into the punishment room . . . made to sit on the floor . . . while my sister bent over the back of the sofa, but just before she put her head down, she winked at me . . . he lifted the cane high up over his head . . . it whooshed down into the pillows . . . a walloping sound . . . she screamed . . . her face was purple from . . . making herself scream . . . and the tears . . . of repressed laughter . . . made her skin sting . . . I had to go and see my grandmother and report . . . my sister had repented . . . oh what a farce! I will not lie! I told my sister, I will tell her the truth . . . Here Heinz fell into a panic . . . he whipped me across the neck with the stick . . . then he fell on his knees in front of me . . . he apologized, grovelled . . . I did up my shirt at the collar . . . so that no one could see the red slash across my neck . . . I lied to my grandmother . . . that was MY childhood. I'll have none of that for my son, oh no. His will be much better.'

The others were eating, picking through a banquet menu, a reproduction of what his grandmother had served for her son in the spring of 1948: chicken soup, roast goose, mashed potatoes, jam tart, champagne. That wedding had been big, very big; all the city dwellers had come because they knew the country relatives had something to cook.

Several of Benedikt's guests were delighted by the menu because it brought back the most succulent memories.

'The most extraordinary meal I'd had in three years!' cried one fat elderly uncle always called Bopo. 'I remember every mouthful! Although there were only three bottles of wine to go round, and no coffee, the cigars were so stale, after years of being hoarded, that they cracked in your hands!' He uncorked another bottle of champagne, called, 'Today! We waste it!' and splashed some on the floor. The others followed suit.

Benedikt stood in the doorway of the chapel, speaking to no one in particular, the priest and the bride on either side of him, the boy standing in front of his mother, his hands at his sides, his eyes almost closed. A group of photographers from the glossy magazines danced about, snapping their cameras. His sister, Dolly, had been filming the family but she put the video camera down when the groom began talking about her, and after he had finished, she shook her head angrily, remarked, 'I don't know what you're jabbering about!' and moved away quickly, her feet rapping the floor.

When the photographers' cameras weren't snapping, the bride dabbed furtively at her son's mouth. The boy's lips glistened with spittle, his chin was inflamed from being wet for so long. The priest followed Marja's hand and observed this with interest; he couldn't remember drooling at that age himself. He concluded the child was backward in his development. It made no difference in the eyes of the Lord. He studied the bride. She was flushed. High blood pressure, he thought, or a vodka habit. The photographers left, looking for fresh game.

'I would like to speak to the child alone now,' the groom said. He did not know how to proceed. He might have taken Valerie by the hand, but that gesture was foreign to him. He might have said, 'Follow me, Valerie,' but he knew Valerie wouldn't follow him, even if he understood him. So he repeated, 'I would like to speak to the child, alone,' addressing the priest, who responded promptly, grasping the child and saying, 'Come on, then.' He moved him firmly along, away from his mother, into the chapel, Benedikt following.

When Benedikt had taken a place in a pew, the priest released Valerie. The child moved closer to Benedikt's knees. His face was dulled by some sort of exhaustion. Benedikt wanted the boy to say something to him, he wanted him to say 'Papa,' he wanted to hear that voice say 'Papa,' but the boy said nothing. Benedikt would not use force, and he considered suggestion force.

After a while, the priest, watching them just sit there, intervened. 'I'd like a try. Permit me,' he said. 'I am the Father as well. Come, child.' Benedikt stood up, moved out of earshot, allowed the priest equal time. The priest pictured himself in an old masterpiece: holy man with a savage child. He whispered to the boy, 'Behold, ye heathen, listen and learn.' He couldn't afford to talk like that to a child who understood. Benedikt was out of earshot.

The boy had his dark-blue eyes nearly closed. By cocking his head, he managed to keep his mother within his line of vision just outside the chapel door. His mouth was dry again. When the mother approached the doorway to see what her son was doing, the priest put his fingers to his lips and waved her away.

Marja, seeing Valerie in the power of the uniformed man, might have snatched her child away, but a fear of authority sat in her muscles and hindered this reflex. She looked around for a form of salvation.

She saw the piano.

Benedikt returned to the boy standing with the priest and said, 'Allow me, Father.'

The priest sighed; he was hungry, anyway. He left the chapel, striding to the banquet table, where he attended to a generous helping of goose. When he saw that he was being watched by several cameras, he twiddled his fingers at the lens and winked, his mouth full. Just a few days ago he had suffered second thoughts about this hasty, disorderly form of matrimony. But after Benedikt contributed a sizeable sum for a new church roof and insisted that the priest was doing the family a service they could never forget, the cleric felt much surer that it was the right thing to go ahead with the ceremony. If the marriage was unorthodox, at least the spread was conservative, excellent.

Benedikt had sat back down in a pew, the boy standing close to him, his body shaking slightly. 'Say "Papa",' ventured Benedikt. He waited. Nothing. Then he continued his monologue:

'And I'm going to do everything for you . . . you will have private tutors . . . your education won't be left to chance, to the roulette of teachers and comrades . . . why should you spend your waking hours in the society that chance brings you? . . . on weekends, children can come and play . . . related children . . . or the children of the help . . . and the old staff who used to work here . . . they should all return . . . it is their duty . . . they have their own traditions . . . working for us . . . my family gave their families a roof over their heads . . . nourished them . . . the whole area lived from the organization, the family Waller von Wallerstein . . . with its seat at Schloss Biederstein . . . providers . . . ours was a benevolent government . . . personal . . . no one was overlooked . . . even the wild animals were counted . . . fed through hard winters . . . the old ones were shot in the summer so that they didn't suffer starvation . . . they didn't take advantage of it, and Valerie . . . you won't take advantage of it . . . the family will thrive . . . we'll have mealtimes in the hall, the way my father did as a child . . . I didn't have parents . . . but Valerie has . . . you will become a part of my family . . . it will become your family, my great-aunt is . . . your great-great-aunt . . . my great-grandmother, your great-great-grandmother . . . there's no harm in . . . knowing a few things about them . . . what they were like . . . it was a long time ago, but . . . they lived here just as you do . . . and it's useful to know how they lived . . . what they thought . . . some were courageous . . . some pious . . . others culinary geniuses . . . they all slept here, and hunted here . . . they went to church here, lived and died here . . . and church . . . why not . . . it's a rhythm . . . one doesn't have to believe . . . that's not the point . . . no, you shouldn't believe . . . but you should practise . . . if you want to go hunting, why not . . . it's an old tradition, you're part of that.

'And . . . you will learn that there is a difference between the chauffeur and you . . . that difference is simply that you belong to this family . . . and he belongs to another family . . . and that these families are intertwined . . . to be sure, but the chauffeur's family has his traditions . . . his great-great-grandfather worked . . . for my great-great-grandfather . . . my family gave his family . . . a roof over their heads, nourished them . . . his family supported ours . . . they didn't take advantage of us . . . and we didn't take advantage of them . . . we are not imaginable without them . . . and they are not imaginable without us . . . but we're two different families . . . and it's preferable that way . . . so if you say "Sir" to the chauffeur . . . because it reminds you . . . of both of your histories . . . why then, there's nothing really wrong with saying "Sir" to him, especially since you both know that it doesn't mean anything . . . more than a respect for both of your families . . . Biesterfeld . . . or the gardener . . . can be responsible for punishing you if you misbehave . . . because I don't intend to punish you . . . or anyone else for that matter . . . ever . . . and they'll have no compunction about it . . . you'll be starting with a private tutor soon . . . mealtimes in the hall . . . and mass on Sundays . . . we'll keep all that up . . .

'And what was beforehand, you'll forget that after a while, you're young. I don't remember my parents at all. I think we should say from now on, yes, your life begins today, we can forget everything else.

'And now I would like it very much if you could say "Papa" to me, or "Father," whichever you like.'

The bride, Marja Waller von Wallerstein, was approaching the piano. She did not turn around again. She did not see her new husband talking with such energy into the ear of her son. She did not see the people in the room, she did not see the room. She saw only the piano.

CHAPTER 16

Wild steps: the wedding guests and the newlyweds take certain liberties

As Marja moved towards the piano, a strange wilful look on her freshly married face, the society asserted its right to party. An apparently aimless emotional collision of two persons there, a random matching of fantasies, occurred, a movement that would later cause a violent jerking of Benedikt's life—but he didn't notice it, being in the chapel with the child, nor did anyone else beyond those two colliding notice it, and even they did not imagine the consequences of their actions.

The company was expanding like a huge, heated molecule, liable to break down into its various components. The teenage family members flew towards each other, were propelled as a group to the outskirts. Having no qualms about helping themselves, they adjourned to the alcove where the wedding presents were stacked. They manoeuvred the television out of the pile, examined the white ribbons with which Dolly had trussed it for decoration, snapped them off. They carried this fabulous booty down the corridor. They set it down on the hall table, in the middle of the feast. The television did not work; an extension cord had to be found, the antenna had to be adjusted. Several young men busied themselves with this.

The other guests streamed around the house, filtering outside. The sky had clouded over, slammed shut, and the heat increased. Dolly's husband, Hackse Sieseby, and Uncle Bopo marched a platoon of men who had changed their Sunday best for green camouflage jackets, trousers, and galoshes. They had screwed green-feathered hats on their heads and slung binoculars over their shoulders. Hunter waited for them on the lawn, feeling grumpy, because there was a dreadful city slicker along, a dentist from Saarbrücken, who'd never been out on a shoot before. And as if that wasn't enough, Benedikt's city friends surrounded him, demanding to be taken along too. Hunter was annoyed by their strange clothes, by their odd, long-winded way of speaking. He snapped his hearing aid off and shook his head to indicate he couldn't understand.

Isabella was just joining them after fleeing her own age group, and she said, 'You have to ask my uncle for permission.'

'Someone ask Dr Waller!' commanded Dr Anhalt, anxious to show the hunter, whom he considered an uppity employee, his rightful place. He leaned backwards and waited for volunteers, one hand winding his tie around his finger, a warning sign to the others that he was about to brag about his tie again—it had belonged to Einstein, everyone knew by now, he had bought it, gravy-stain and all, from Einstein's maid, after the Wall came down. But Dr Anhalt was intent on solving this minor administrative problem before discussing his tie. 'We'd like to go. Who will ask Dr Waller?' he called again. This time, Schmidt volunteered, and Isabella volunteered to accompany him—she'd show him the quick way inside. She had seen Benedikt go into the chapel with his son.

They had a bit of an adventure together, marching through the kitchen, skirting Bertha, who was organizing the maids, having grabbed authority as if it were a dish towel to wave in their faces. By the time they reached the chapel, Schmidt had recognized a certain physical similarity between Isabella and her uncle and, therefore, between Isabella and himself. She was as tall as he, as blond, all the more feminine for it in the ladylike clothes he associated with aristocracy, a pink, tight-waisted jacket with large buttons and a wide stiff skirt. Her face had the same design as his, the features distributed evenly, as if they'd been planned with a ruler. The round eyes were more alert than her uncle's: they followed what was going on with eagerness to be pleased by what she saw, an expression Schmidt interpreted as humility. As the two reached the chapel they heard Benedikt's voice inside.

'I'll wait here,' said Isabella.

Her company made Schmidt feel much surer of himself, and he went in. He was glad of an excuse to speak to his friend, anyway. He found him in an odd pose at the end of a pew, the Russian child standing next to him, his face grey and drawn. The child did not respond when Schmidt approached.

'Benedikt, the others have never been on a real hunt, and we'd like to go along,' Schmidt said, keeping his voice hurried, self-assured.

Benedikt didn't even look at him. He answered, 'You have to grow up hunting to understand it. You'll hate it.'

Schmidt persisted, 'I think we'll love it. We may never want to do anything else.'

But Benedikt met his jocularity with an indifferent stare.

Schmidt retreated to Isabella, who suffered a massive attack of sympathy for him, and consoled him by suggesting, 'Well, let's have a hunt around the house instead.'

Out on the lawn, waiting for her husband to return, Renate Schmidt, an angular blond good at sports, good at rules, was being treated with condescension by Drs Anhalt and Graf and the three other scientists from the Institute, who found her uninteresting and therefore abhorrent. She recognized this, knew that there was nothing she could do to reverse the direction their opinions had taken, fought gallantly, with small talk about holidays (after the horrors of teaching).

Schmidt had still not returned, and the huntsmen began mounting their vehicles. The hunter, Herr Flick, turned up his hearing aid again so as not to miss the Count of Sieseby's call to start the car, which was the first step in a hunt. He had gone deaf working for Hackse, who used to steady his gun on Herr Flick's shoulder. The hunter had concealed his deafness for several years. When it became obvious, Hackse fired him. Dolly had intervened, insisting that her husband pay for a good hearing aid. As soon as Herr Flick responded again, turning and coming when called, Hackse reinstated him. 'Hearing aid off,' he always called, before resting his rifle on the hunter's shoulder. Now he cried, 'Herr Flick! Let's move.'

A caravan of gaudy vehicles bumped and sloshed through the fields that led around the woods. The huntsmen kept their binoculars aimed through the car windows at the forest, searching for signs of elk, while they chatted about nature, about money.

The Berliners gave up, moved on. The huntsmen's wives settled into the white garden chairs placed under umbrellas on the lawn, watching after their husbands with the conspiratorial mirth that male vanity always aroused in them. They soon realized that a male had wandered into their midst. Dr Graf had dropped behind Dr Anhalt and Renate Schmidt, backtracked towards the wives, and sat right down on the last vacant seat, endangering it with his size. Asked, he reluctantly gave his name as 'Graf, Albert.' Forced, he proved delightful company; he could handle a whole circle of women without losing his poise. Having no respect for them, he became intimate with them.

'All these beautiful women, dressed so badly,' he began, turning his good eye in their direction. 'Countess Sieseby, you should be in strapless, hugging dresses. High-heeled shoes,' he said to Dolly, whose good-natured face glowed.

After a few more such comments, he sprang up again, bobbed his head, and fled, having suddenly exhausted his repertoire and fearing boredom. They watched him leave, felt disappointed, at the same time relieved; one couldn't relax with men around.

Dr Graf began searching for the Berliners, who had taken a stroll around the house. For the moment, they felt at the bottom of the pecking order, a condition they, as intellectuals, hadn't experienced since they were children. Indeed, their professional lives were in many ways devoted to making up for those social slights received in childhood. Suddenly they were suffering this awful feeling of ostracization again. And without being able to fight back! Because one's brain was a useless organ here that aroused pity, if not repulsion. They skulked from portrait to furniture piece, unsure whether to view them as art or family lore, murmuring, 'Interesting,' or 'Fantastic!' They reached the stairwell, where they surprised Schmidt and Isabella leaning on stone angels, talking, more than talking really, having discovered that Benedikt's health affected them equally, a delightful discovery. Schmidt remembered the hunt and hastily explained that it had been impossible to talk to Benedikt at all—Benedikt just wouldn't listen, having (understandably) more important things on his mind than doing his closest friend a favour. The eminent scientists were disarmed by Schmidt's modest manner and found his boyish good looks rather touching. They settled around him at the top of the stairs, included him in their conversation, elbowing Isabella out, and creating a wall over which Renate Schmidt glared her disapproval.

And by and by, Schmidt, following the conversation of the learned men, dared to speak up again. He was driven to it, in fact, by the pressure of his strong feelings on the subject: they were talking about their ambivalence towards foreigners.

And Schmidt said, 'It's taken me a long time to admit this even to myself. But one shouldn't fight one's feelings by suppressing them. And I've learned to say that, frankly, it bothers me that there are so many foreigners around, speaking a language I don't understand, practising customs antithetical to mine. If I wanted to live with Turks, for example, why, I could move to Istanbul.'

In the ensuing surge of agreement, Isabella found a small cranny between the men through which she could watch Schmidt. But it was the friendly attentiveness of the distinguished scientists that prompted Schmidt to go on.

'I had an ugly but illuminating experience recently. I have American stereo speakers—I brought them back with me from New York one summer. There's only one repair store for them in Berlin, and that's in Kreuzberg, a Turkish neighbourhood.

'The speakers are cumbersome to carry, and I was lucky to find a parking space right in front of the shop. As I started pulling in, an extended Turkish family suddenly hopped into this empty space, waving their hands at me and shouting, *"Nein! Nein!"* They were waiting for some uncle to come from Istanbul, God knows when he was going to get there, but they were holding this parking space free for him. I nudged them aside with my car, very gently. And then this young man comes up to the window, he wants to say something to me. All right, I rolled down the window and said, "I'm just parking here for one minute, I have to drop something heavy off at the store. And then I'm leaving again. Just one minute." Reasonable of me, I thought. But this young man— he swung his fist at me and he said, I'll never forget his words, "Nix minute. I smash your puss." ' Schmidt shrugged his shoulders. 'Communication is just not possible between these people and us.'

Dr Graf was preparing to launch a vitriolic attack against Germans, against reunification, against schoolteachers in general when he saw that Schmidt's wife had found her way to her husband's side again, and this struck the Hungarian as a powerful and just punishment.

Schmidt did not accept his due. He said plaintively, 'Do you think you could find a phone and call home, see how the children are doing with your mother?'

The others would not get off easily for having listened to Schmidt: providence sent a group of Siesebys past them, their conversation strafing the intellectuals:

'He becomes a duke,' laughed one elderly man loudly, 'then a lord, just because he conquered Europe. His relations have never set foot here. Weren't invited.'

'The Hohenzollern are particularly ridiculous,' agreed another.

'Age still has value in our circle,' concluded a third.

The Berliners drew closer as a group, felt a rather pleasant sense of indignation that made them smile at each other, which Isabella did not understand. She was a good daughter, she had never questioned her family's way of speaking, nor did she admire it, she simply accepted it, the way she accepted the behaviour of others in general. By incremental degrees, Isabella had moved closer to Schmidt, and when she sat down on the stairs, he sat down next to her. His wife was nowhere in sight.

Soon another group of relatives passed by, this time of mixed nationality. They were quarrelling with an invisible enemy. The subject was hereditary peerage.

'Most of us are decent, responsible, even very nice people,' said one English lady. 'The fact that there is a loser, it's only temporary in the long run, and it doesn't mean that everything that's been accomplished should be ignored. Every human being, every family, can have an off day or an off generation.'

'This talk about accidents of birth is disgusting. I don't believe that God has accidents,' agreed her German cousin. 'And lots of people who start out in a questionable way—I'm thinking of someone involved in today's ceremony—end up very good people.'

Outside on the lawn, beneath the umbrellas, the wives of the hunters, including Dolly, flipped through magazines the Countess had brought and snacked on bits of conversation.

'I had a dream last night that my analyst said . . .'

'I called Obolensky in New York. He's never heard of her. A Golubka. He says there's not even a middle class left in Russia.'

'My analyst . . .'

'I think it's unfair that state insurance pays for analysts. It would be much better for the psyche if they paid for facelifts.'

As they chatted, the ladies did not read idly. They turned to the advice columns and then the horoscopes. They looked up their own, then their children's, then those of various men of interest, and finally their husbands'. They checked to see what Venus was up to. They hoped that Dolly would offer them advice on their constellations but she did not. They had all, at one time or another, asked her in a jocular tone, not believing a word of it, for advice. They had dug out their birth certificates to look up the hours of their births and then casually mentioned them to Dolly. She had declined: 'It would be unprofessional.'

Only the true disbelievers, like her husband and brother, did she regale with information. 'Benedikt's poor little Venus is stuck in his fourth house, where she doesn't feel at all well,' she murmured to herself now. She looked at the sky and decided it was time to warn the others. She cleared her throat to speak. All the women looked up.

Benedikt Schmidt's elbow brushed Isabella's upper arm quite by accident. This was bound to happen sooner or later, they were sitting so close to each other.

In the chapel the groom had stopped talking to the little boy. He was very tired. For the past week he had prepared himself for the ceremony by limiting his sleep to four hours a night that he divided, waking himself after two hours, always at 2:00 a.m. and 5:00 a.m. In between he read his old scientific publications, as an exercise, his satisfaction that he could still understand them masking a latent fear. This habit kept his brain in a strange twilight between sleep and wakefulness, so that the extraordinary reality scarcely affected him.

His bride had reached the piano. She loosened the constraints, her fingers threw open the cover.

The hunters had abandoned their horsepower to hike through the woods. Beneath the cover of the trees they could no longer follow the dour colouring of the sky. They passed through a fenced area with feed troughs where the animals were penned up for the winter.

'They can't survive by themselves anymore,' explained the hunter.

'They rely on us for help.'

Hackse Sieseby turned around suddenly. 'You've reminded me. The portfolio. I have to discuss something with the groom. Silly of me.' He excused himself.

The hunter was satisfied. He could turn off his hearing aid again. He led the others along a small trail to the hunting platform; he reminded them that they had to share one gun. He worried about quarrels.

On the staircase, Isabella shifted her position slightly, her thighs were now separated from Schmidt's by five millimetres. Heat bridged the distance.

The hunters' wives regarded the Countess Sieseby, hopeful for a wise word about the heavens, and she finally spoke up: 'It's going to rain,' she said. 'I can feel it in the paper. Glossy magazines are real barometers, they get statically charged. We should go indoors.'

The others were alarmed.

They thought about their hair, and then their husbands. Perhaps the men would be struck by lightning. Their married lives passed in a second before their eyes, and then the long minutes of fantasy about their widowhood. They felt their grief. They wondered which dress to wear to the funeral. There was a rumble of thunder. They thought about their hair again. The rumble became louder.

A noise shattered the hall.

The bride had sat down, and now she began to play—but perhaps 'play' is the wrong word. The ladies on the lawn were startled by the sudden explosion, or so it seemed, in the normally quiet castle. The magazines dropped into their laps, their mouths closed, they tipped their heads sideways, listening. They assumed Benedikt had switched on a stereo. Classical piano music? Not very pleasant or cheerful. Perhaps modern. Sounded rather like jazz. No doubt about it: jazz. Peculiar. Perhaps the boys had fixed the television—that was it. Perhaps there was something good on. The bride attacked. She sat far away from the instrument, as if she didn't want to get too involved with it, leaning back, watching her hands dance on the keyboard in front of her, excited by her own hands, enthralled by what she heard. She moved forwards, she looked upwards, unseeing, her torso apparently charged, swaying slightly, back and forth, sinuously, with the grace of an animal restored to its natural environment. What her hands were doing struck the observers as unrelated. Somehow, she produced riotous music. The audience could not place it. Classical, to be sure. Schmidt was torn between sensations: the music and the girl sitting so near to him. He knew what was going on. He could have her. He had a low threshold for sexual vibrations, he could pick them out almost before they began.

He stood up, looked down at Isabella, and said, 'I have to go and listen.'

The English relatives simply raised their voices: 'The Winstons go to a self-catering flat in Nice. We go to a hotel ever so near the beach. The French have a talent for hoteling. It's charming, the Norfolk.'

'What time d'you go?'

'Early. February.'

'It's a lovely time of year.'

'Last year I had a superior view from my bedroom.'

'I don't think I did.'

'No, you didn't.'

'You had to go to a corner window, and then you could see it all. Lovely. I'm just thinking of the breakfast in the hotel. There was nothing you couldn't have.'

The Berliners had split up into those who wanted to listen and those who treated the conversation as a dog a bone, unwilling to let go.

Dr Graf, standing at the foot of the stairs, was growling at the others. 'The night the Wall came down, imagine how people really felt: statistically, every sixth rejoicer must have had his doubts; or worse, his panic. Every sixth person had actively supported the East German government. East Germany was a nasty little family, the system was typical of family life, where tattling is a kind of custom that holds the kin together. And in their zeal,' railed Dr Graf, 'the goody-goodies tattled the dullest details of their brothers' private lives.'

'How do you know?' asked Dr Anhalt, infuriated, held back by the fact that the man was a foreigner.

'Because they always do,' replied Dr Graf, turning his back, sated, heading upstairs to the noise.

Schmidt was standing over Isabella, who remained seated on the steps. He had forgotten the illustrious scientists. His fondness for music was a stronger force.

'Sounds live,' he said. It was something he knew about. He turned to Dr Anhalt. 'I was going to be a pianist but then I had no connections in the music world, so I couldn't get my foot in. In retrospect, I'm glad I went into teaching.'

The others smiled, charmed by his frankness. Isabella sighed that life could be so cruel, and he looked down at her, and repeated, 'I'm going to go and listen.' She understood his invitation, took the lead, picked her way through the others heading up the stairs. He caught up with her at the last bend of the banister and said, 'Let's listen unobtrusively.' She savoured the word 'unobtrusively' as if it were a strange glistening jewel.

In the hall, four cleaning ladies hired for the occasion appeared under Bertha's lead, lugging huge vacuum cleaners that could suck up puddles. They took positions at each corner of the hall, where they plugged in their instruments. At a signal from Bertha, they simultaneously flicked their switches.

The priest had returned to the chapel, closing the door against the sudden roar of the vacuum cleaners and the driving piano. He approached the Count and his son and spoke officially. 'It will be my duty to prepare him for the sacrament of baptism.' He looked at the boy and addressed him. 'You will perceive water on your head. But much, much more is happening to you.' The priest realized he wasn't in the mood for this. He wished he could go home. His mother was waiting for him. He pictured her sitting at the kitchen table, peeling potatoes, waiting. He sighed and left the chapel, returning to the banquet. Benedikt remained with the child standing as far away from him as he could.

'Valerie, say "Father," ' whispered Benedikt. He did not dare speak up, afraid to shock himself. The child stared at the closed door. 'Say "Father" to me,' pleaded Benedikt, speaking up now. 'I want to hear what it sounds like. What if I can't get used to it? What if it makes me ill just to hear the word? "Father, father," ' he repeated, listening. 'It should come from your mouth. You don't understand, do you? Maybe your first German word will be "Father"!' He opened his mouth wide on the syllables. ' "Faaaather." '

The boy staggered, bringing him closer, so that he stood sideways between Benedikt's knees. Suddenly, he was near enough for Benedikt to see his ear, a pale piece, very perfect in its elaborate shape. Benedikt addressed this directly. The child's saliva dribbled on Benedikt's hands. It was sticky.

Benedikt stood up, trembling with disgust. 'My God, my God, it's got on me.' He opened the chapel door and saw the female forms hovering over the floor with their vacuum cleaners.

'Frau—Frau—' he called in their direction.

Bertha responded at once.

'The child must be cleaned!' he said. He spat on his own handkerchief and rubbed the spot vigorously, smelled it, and blanched. He looked for water to clean himself, headed through a small back door into the sacristy, where the priest changed his clothes. The room had a bed, a cross on the wall, the white walls of a hospital room. The window was open. He intended to close it but was distracted by the way the trees were shaking in the wind. He sat down on the stone window seat. Sleepiness spilled over into his impressions. He heard music. Music, like taste, had never interested him, because its form was not apparent to him. He remembered Liesel, his grandmother's favourite maid, taking him on a visit to her niece who lived in the village, and the two women listening to a scratchy old record of heroic-sounding songs, and Liesel saying, 'That's your father playing the piano.'

Bertha was nudging the little boy along in front of her, loath to touch him. Valerie's face was a sheet of sour spittle, an odour Bertha recognized: hunger. His eyes were worn and dry. The cleaning ladies vacuumed.

Meanwhile: a stag was making its way through the woods, a handsome brute in his prime. He smelled something that alarmed him, impending rain. The hunters heard rustling. Visions of deer danced in their heads. 'Make sure it's not a dog,' whispered the hunter, refusing to hand over the loaded gun to Bopo, who kept reaching for it. Bopo flushed, cursing the hunter's memory for other people's mistakes.

Up on the landing in front of the hall, Schmidt turned to let someone pass and accidentally leaned against Isabella, his side against her front. His arm slipped around her waist, as if to steady himself. For an instant, his face was close to hers. This was the dominant seventh chord, the boulder let loose at the top of an incline, the point of no return.

Marja did not notice Valerie passing behind her back. The pianist had forgotten her offspring. By the time she turned her face from the keyboard to the chapel door, it had opened and shut again. She did not see him being steered along the wall towards the corridor. Bertha took him to their bathroom, that spacious, white-tiled pleasure dome. The child's salivating infuriated her. The sink was too gentle. He needed to be convinced somehow. She could convince him. His mother would be grateful. The Soviet Union would be one man cleaner. It was a start.

Bertha prodded Valerie over to the toilet, forcing his head down till it was deep into the bowl. He did not resist; he bent his knees and hung in her grasp. And this absence of normal repugnance angered her, while simultaneously horror at what she was doing—oh, he was forcing her—enraged her. She held his torso between her knees, put her left palm on the tender valley at the centre of his neck, pushed down where the hair grew in wisps, and with the right hand, she flushed. When the water had stopped splashing down on his head, she flushed again. 'That's what I'm here for,' she said, flushing again and again, 'to clean up, I'm the maid, the old-maid maid.'

CHAPTER 17

*Wilder still: the liberties that certain humans
take affect the animal kingdom*

Made unafraid, the bride no longer played to disturb her
public. She played what she knew of Germany; she played
Beethoven. The portraits of ten generations of the family made
up the front row of her audience, their faces dry and cracked but
glistening as if time were a great heat that had baked them. The
cleaning ladies drew nearer to the piano with their roaring vacuum cleaners. Marja had thrown her head way down again towards the keyboard. Tears dripped down her cheeks, hung at the
tip of her nose, and a grey stain widened under each arm of her
wedding dress. She opened her eyes, looked down at her left
hand again as it executed a leap to another octave, regarded this
hand with astonishment and approval, closed her eyes again. The
cleaning ladies converged on the piano. One cleaning lady
vacuumed beneath, another dusted the top, a third polished the
legs, and the last stood behind the piano stool and mopped
underneath it.

Benedikt was still sitting in the sacristy window. He heard
the rhythmic pounding bass notes and imagined that the past
had caught up with the present acoustically: his father was playing martial music. A draught pulled the window further open,
smacked Benedikt's face with the smell of rain. He did not turn
away. The brown sky rumbled.

'Now I've had it,' muttered Benedikt. 'Oh, it's going to finish
me off yet.'

A few raindrops pelted in through the window, messengers of more to come. Benedikt did not move. He felt offended: nature forcing an unwanted intimacy on him. He was going to get wet.

The hunters huddling in their wooden fortifications heard the wind hiss in the leaves and rattle the branches. They tensed up. Herr Flick held the gun loosely on his knees. He was daydreaming and did not turn on his hearing aid.

The wives reached the hall, their magazines crunched in their hands. The pianist sensed an accumulating audience: the thunder outside sounded like applause. Her play became more exuberant. Her left hand drummed the bass notes.

Benedikt followed a sudden shuffling noise that was breaking through the piano music, growing louder, closer—footsteps. He realized he was not alone.

'I wanted a little word with you,' said his big fleshy brother-in-law, Hackse Sieseby. 'We must talk about your portfolio. I have to go to Frankfurt tomorrow to settle our affairs and then I'll look after yours too. I'll do what's best for you. I have one major idea.' He cradled a briefcase. 'You need someone to look out for you. You've a responsibility to the family now. I'm going to recommend you invest in American stocks. The dollar's at an all-time low. And everything's much too risky here. You see, I'm not a real speculator! No risks!'

Hackse pulled an advertisement from his briefcase: 'You're just going to love US Surgical. The stock is the nearest thing to greased lightning on the New York Stock Exchange. It can make you rich or send you to the intensive care unit of your local hospital on any given day.' He looked at Benedikt. 'The range has been a hundred and thirty-four to forty-four this year alone!'

He kept talking: dividends key ratios shareholders data market value shares outstanding insider net buy. At some point he must have stopped; he was gone.

Benedikt, propped in the window seat, watching the woods, a scraggly army whose victory was its existence, finally localized the source of the music—it was issuing from the trees. In the torrent of rain, it seemed the forest was playing Beethoven.

Benedikt was not alone in thinking this. Any creature with a hearing apparatus could hear a version of what he heard, and the rest could feel it. Velvet worms, millipedes, crustaceans, diplurans writhed in terror or hopped and froze. A fairy fly, a mother-to-be who had faced all sorts of horrors in her lifetime and had had the classical miserable childhood of all fairy flies, living off the stolen eggs of other insects, spread its fan-shaped hands when the wracking rhythm began and had a miscarriage. The leech felt the pounding of the earth rhythmically and curled up. Natural phenomena, inherited memory told it, never last more than a few seconds. Seconds were the limits to its memory. It forgot the pounding that preceded it; the leech could only feel ten bars of allegro at a time. At some point it tried to get away. It wound around in the earth, heading downwards.

On its way through shallow dirt it passed several arthropods, who considered themselves the most successful of all living things, because they could subsist on anything, even stale cookies. But this: no. They had not been exposed to such strange rending of the atmosphere before. One roach that had broached a clearing had a shock. It picked up speed on its tripod gait, zipped this way and that, trying to shake off the pounding decibels. There are three thousand five hundred races of cockroaches, and this one individual was about to have all the bad luck.

The butterfly's feet were vibrating so hard on the flowers that he could not taste properly and lost his appetite. The antennae of a family of mosquitoes began to buzz. The entire group headed for a bush. They crouched on the leaves, buffeted by their jiggling antennae. The grasshopper swayed on a long comfortable blade of grass, the tiny membranes of cuticle on his sides ringing with this strange rhythmic noise. He couldn't help himself: his back legs hiked up and began rubbing the wings; they began to sing. The praying mantis had more self-control. It raised its wings, rubbed its abdomen against them, the warning colours flashing on its wings.

The pygmy white-toothed shrew, a furry beetle patrolling an acoustic landscape of grunts, whistles, bellows, rustling, and vibration, stopped short. What the devil? Man, most likely, was liable. Finding his droppings and discharges everywhere was bad enough; now this. The fish searching for food near the banks of the pond felt the low tones as a tickle; he fled to deep water, where he found it was not as bad. The dogs back in their field along the entrance road stopped and sniffed the air, finding no olfactory explanation for the jangle in their ears. They did not bay, they adjusted to it.

The bats who shared the house were the closest to the source of these bewildering sounds. They were accustomed to all sorts of horrid decibels—alarm clocks, dinner bells, boiling fat, rattling pots—but most of these sounds were pitched high enough to be bearable. Whereas this—this was a feeling in the bat gut. Like bat diarrhoea.

Even the house itself responded, the wood and straw and old mortar shifted, groaning and creaking.

The Berliners, trying to amuse themselves, headed towards the din in the hall and observed the scene with detachment, emitting a range of soft noises, from snorts to grunts: 'Extraordinary!' 'Fantastic!' and 'She's not half bad!'

Only Schmidt was not impressed. He sulked, muttered, 'Just dreadful,' and later, 'Is this a joke?' and began tapping time with his black shoe. His shoes proved that her play fluctuated in rhythm.

'She has no regard for the most elementary rules of tempo!' hissed Schmidt to Isabella, who did not know better and agreed. 'Where's the pulse?' cried Schmidt. 'And so unclean! Half the notes are wrong.'

But the pianist was no longer really among them. She seemed to hover above the piano stool, her mouth twisted in a witch's grin, her hands whirling about, abracadabra, an enormous wailing and crying coming out of that instrument. Some fled, while others remained to listen against their better judgement. Because what she played was recognizable but not recognizable either: it was different, and this difference antagonized the audience. They cast about for reasons. Unwilling to name the playing simply different they said, 'Third-rate.'

'There are probably more third-rate pianists than people in the world,' said Dr Anhalt.

'Of course.' Dr Graf was embarrassed about his initial show of enthusiasm. 'You're right. Although . . . her playing does have a certain vitality . . .'

'Undisciplined Russian emotionalism, you could call it,' said a young colleague,

'There's a market for it.'

'Perhaps Russians shouldn't play German music,' said Schmidt seriously. 'They just can't understand it. The culture is too different. How can someone who's never been to Vienna understand Mozart or Beethoven?'

'Or if they do play German music, they should do it back in Russia,' said another.

'Can't someone tell her to stop!?' cried one of the ruder of the young cousins. 'We want to watch television!' He had finally managed to fix the antenna.

'She could teach, of course,' said Dr Anhalt.

'Why should she? She's married to a rich man. She's well off now,' said Schmidt bitterly.

It began to rain heavily. The rain took potshots at Benedikt, still sitting in the window. Out in the forest, it drummed on the hunters' heads and drew a curtain around them. The hunters almost drowned in the smell of wet leaves. When the dentist thought he detected movement, he grabbed the rifle from the hunter's lap. Bullets crashed into the path below and struck a passing cockroach, spewing roach parts for metres beneath the leaves. The noise was interpreted by wildlife within a square kilometre as danger; they froze and then bolted away from the

source. The whole forest reeked of barbecue. The hunters'
mouths watered. The smell carried all the way to the house and
brushed Benedikt's lips. He licked them. He thought he was
hearing things now: a strange, high-pitched croaking nearby:

'I will tell my wife you are my little sister now and nothing
more. Nothing more. Why shouldn't I call you my little sister? I
was curious about you, and you satisfied that curiosity. Now we
are brother and sister. And I would like to kiss you, as a brother.
A little more than a brother.'

Benedikt shook his head to clear out the sleep.

'I think about you all the time. You are there when I wake up
and when I fall asleep. I am very unhappy. You are a poison in
me. But I don't let on. Because poor Gerda, she suffers if I suffer.
That's real love.'

So it was Chauffeur. He was using the sacristy phone, in a
little alcove by the entrance; he had not seen Benedikt leaning
against the wall, seated at the window. And Benedikt listened,
without understanding the terms that Chauffeur used.

'I had feelings for her once, too, very strong ones, especially
before I knew her. Then Gerda sated them, and we belonged to
each other. I always fetched her aspirin when she had headaches.
And she ironed my shirts. After a while, I barely noticed her.'

In the silence, Benedikt was wrenched by confusion. He was
accustomed to incomprehension when people (Schmidt, Dolly)
spoke about their feelings. But now he had an inkling of understanding, as if he were listening to a foreign language that he
would one day speak fluently himself. Chauffeur's voice continued, in an arrogant, know-it-all tone.

'It is far better to live with someone you do not notice. Yes,
of course I noticed you. You distracted me, because you talked so
much. I could scarcely drive anymore. I was glad when you were
talking to someone else, then I had a moment of peace and quiet.
And I liked the feel of you. The skin on your face was so tight,
my hands remember it. And your body's sharp edges. My palms
are longing for that feeling. You like to hear that, don't you? Ah,
you are not like me. You don't question yourself the way I do.

You are full of self-satisfaction, satisfaction that you exist at all, it oozes out of you. You call it happiness. For a while, I was persuaded. Gerda taught me that suffering is a higher state of being, an art, proof of good character. If it weren't for you, we would get on. She likes sex with my gear-shift hand. She says it's mysterious, like in church.' He laughed his high-pitched bitter way. 'You don't like church, I know. You're not deep. You're charming, and you can sew, and people like what you sew because you're charming. You have the vitality common to women. It protects you against strong feeling . . . I remember how you said once, "In heaven there's no music, just laughter."

'Gerda couldn't believe anybody could say such a thing! She said, "What a monstrous woman!" Well, why shouldn't she have her opinions about you? She has deep feelings, like a little girl. Like a good little girl: she always behaves correctly, even now: she hates you and not me. She loves me so much that she is willing to do everything for me. She is learning to sew, she will sew as well as you. She has taken to wearing her hair in braids like you do. We do not talk, we get on. And she accepts me as a sick man. Corroding inside. A sizzling sound. From the wound you made. You made. She gives me little presents. She knows how to satisfy me as a man. She irons my shirts again.' Benedikt cleared his throat. Chauffeur held the receiver away from his ear. He heard the music and the rain and relaxed.

'I have to go,' he said, his voice very tender. 'Do you miss me, little sister? Would you like to see me? I can't talk to you now, because I have important things to do. Maybe we can see each other soon. I would like that.'

The child was lying on his bed, where Bertha had left him, his soggy head and body too heavy to move. He was aware of the hostility of the force called gravity. He heard his mother's playing through the walls, and above him the pounding of the rain. He experienced his own sadness self-consciously: 'I am sad,' he whispered to himself. The fact that he was sad did not affect his mother; she continued to play. She continued even as the television began to work.

'Someone tell her to stop now, we want to watch TV.'

'Stop! Stop!' they shouted.

Finally Dr Anhalt took the initiative. He went over to her, bent down, and tapped her smartly on the shoulder. He backed off as she suddenly lifted her hands from the keyboard, looking dazed, as if she'd been slapped out of a trance. When she realized where she was, she remembered her child. Her subsequent smile contained a kind of arrogant apology. She had forgotten her son entirely. She made no sound: her wail of remorse was internal. Her heart was a strange organ.

CHAPTER 18

The maternal heart, fluctuating

The bundle lies square in the middle of things. It is edible but not highly prized in sated societies because its flesh is tough from overwork. A muscle wholly devoted to routine, subject to the orders of a motley, quarrelling ministry of emotions, it responds instantly when told, Speed up! Slower, now! Nevertheless, no matter how much it works, the heart remains an attractive organ.

The maternal heart has particular allures. It stays hidden behind the adornments of the chest, which are clamped, in Marja's case, into a stiff cotton-and-steel construction from the Countess's collection, dated 1935. This ingenious contraption lifts and presents the contents on the pretext of concealing them—it draws the viewer's eye to that very spot concealing the heart.

As with all truly precious things, it is better to picture the heart than to see it. Beneath grey skin and bent rib, stringy tendon and wobbly fat, this ladylike organ lies wrapped in a special stocking of its own called the pericardium. The pericardium is a sensitive, sheer garment, streaked in mature years with a pretty yellow buttery cream; it should never be tampered with. The maternal heart snuggles inside this, a velvet-skinned, irregular-shaped violet body whose different parts have various duties, affecting their physiognomy. The right side, which controls unoxygenated blood, is slimmer than the left side. It has the lighter workload, the cushier existence, it deals with the 'have-not' blood, the 'spent-everything' blood, sending it over to the lungs for oxygen. The left side controls the oxygenated 'rich' blood, forcing it to the remotest corner of the body, and its tissue is thick and red as a housewife's hand.

The heart's most important partner is the lung. The two are connected by proximity—they are practically touching—and necessity. They execute a series of complicated steps with such dexterity that it is impossible to say whether the lung is leading and the heart following, or the other way around. As with all relationships, pressure makes the system work. The heart vessels containing the spent blood are under low pressure. They are soft, pliable, their activity passive; all they do is come into contact with the high-pressure lung. The lung cannot resist, drawing the carbon dioxide from the 'spent' blood, while oxygen spurts from its high-pressure system into the heart vein's low one. The lung behaves ostentatiously, making the outside walls of the chest heave. The heart works modestly, meticulously—when it has given up its rubbish, two heart veins leave, one from each lung, carrying blood truly oxygenated and red as the most expensive lipstick. They unite at the left side of the heart, where the fluid gushes like so many compliments into the left atrium. Two little flaps there, silken, white, and tissue-thin, wait until the ventricle is full as can be, it can take no more, then they flip over neatly, closing the opening, the no-more-for-now signal, and this decisive setting of limits makes the muscle contract, in the healthy adult, about sixty times a minute. Is the number a coincidence? The tempo changes constantly, just as the tempo of time passing changes. Marja's heart, when she is playing the piano, flutters like a hummingbird's wing.

The heart has a chaperone, the vagus nerve, stationed in the organ itself, who sees to the rhythm: even minute fluctuations of rhythm can cause havoc to the heart. The chaperone relies on electrical impulses to enforce her authority; the entire surface of the heart is a positively charged field. But almost everything can go wrong. The heart has many enemies, internal and external. The outer garment can suffer epicarditis, but so can the myocardium, '-itis' being the furious syllables that spell inflammation and destruction caused by hordes of bacteria. Or a bit of fat can land on the delicate flaps and stick there, corroding them, or it might build up on the walls of a large vein or an artery, plugging up the byways.

Anything sudden is offensive to the heart. A bolt of lightning, for example, is a real enemy. It travels through the body, singeing just several grams of fibre on its way, tolerable unless it reaches the heart. When this happens to a very large creature, say an elk, the heart itself remains in its organized state but the muscle's routine gets disrupted. Fluid is carried in the wrong direction, and the rhythm goes all unsteady, inebriated, euphoric. A bolt of lightning affects in a quick way what long-term emotions can do: it is the fast-forward version of a 'broken heart.' Emotions can be very bad for the heart.

And yet, according to the anthropologist, emotions, like our sense of pain, help the species survive. Where's the proof? The proof is: otherwise, we wouldn't have them. Not every animal seems to profit from certain emotions. The heart of the squid does not speed up at orgasm. We know very little about the emotions of animals that can't communicate with us. The day of Marja and Benedikt's wedding was a day of maternal tragedies for many. As an example: for a roach that lived practically under the same roof as the Waller von Wallersteins.

The roach is indestructible as a species. This does not make the individual roach safe from the Bitter Word. The roach had lost her entire last brood to a grape. She had laid her egg in an enclosure she took to be uncommonly suitable, being smooth-walled and cool and dark even during the deadly hours of daylight. The walls smelled perfumed. This enclosure came to the attention of a local child who liked to play with the old tree stumps. The roach's nest was inside what he recognized as a Coca-Cola can. He brushed away the dirt blocking the opening and tipped it upside down. At once the tiny white baby roaches appeared at the hole. They swarmed around the top of the can, the sunlight darkening them, turning them black, until he swept them back inside and plugged the hole with his thumb. The child was armed with grapes. He decided to feed the roaches. He forced a grape into the container. The baby roaches nibbled at the surface, bursting several minute capillaries. They drowned in the juice. The mother roach was not aware of her loss. She spent a large part of her life, several minutes, looking for the can. Then she forgot her progeny. She went foraging for her own dinner.

Now comes the bad luck. The cockroach, having lost her offspring, lost her life. She was strolling along minding her own business, when providence paid her back for her indifference. The dentist sprayed her with buckshot. She lay on her back kicking. Perhaps her life passed before her eyes in a series of sensations. Then her personality dissipated. Her legs curled up towards her belly; she became a shell of her former self. This was of course merely a case of hard luck, two bouts of misfortune affecting the same family within an hour of each other. Victims of casual violence, or over enthusiastic care. Heartbreaking. But maybe not. Perhaps the cockroach mother is the most sentimental of living things; perhaps she scales high pinnacles of passion, and falls into deep trenches of remorse; perhaps her emotions are all the more intense because her memory is so short. On the day of Benedikt's wedding, there was a rash of violence in the forest.

Conventional opinion has it that the animals were not disappointed, that they did not expect either better or worse.

Animals, qualifies the hunter, do not anticipate death. Therefore the hunt is not cruel in the same way that it is cruel to chase a human being. The fox or the deer does not know what the pack of dogs will do. His fear is merely a reflex. Fear, admits the hunter, is a highly unpleasant sensation, on a par with pain. The animal does not recognize the muzzle of a gun. He is not knowledgeable. But when he hears foreign or loud noises, he responds with fear. He must feel fear because otherwise he would be careless. Fear is what the newborn feels when he is hungry, and the hand of hunger begins wrenching at his stomach. He does not know that he must eat. He feels this ghastly sensation and he responds with terror. Fear is the first emotion that the human being feels, and the first emotion that a man of courage must suppress. Those who do not feel fear will soon make a mistake. Those who do not have feelings are at a disadvantage from the evolutionary point of view. This is something that the Countess knew, but not from a book. She knew it instinctively. But in order to induce feeling in her brother, she would have to start with the basics: fear and loathing. Love can only develop where hatred has trampled open the soil.

Mother love lies square in the middle of things. Like all complicated mechanisms, it tends to slip easily into imbalance; there is always either too little or too much of it. At the same time it has a great external stability; like all dungeons, it tends to trap what has wandered or been pushed into it. The wounded child listens to his mother playing the piano while he lies exhausted on his bed. He does not comprehend what just happened to him, but he knows that it was humiliating and wounding and that his mother did not prevent it. If someone were to hold her head instead of his in the toilet, the wound would be more obvious to him; he would fight the aggressor with every weapon at his disposal, the whine, the shriek, the little fists. He would not fight for himself with such vigour, because he doubts his right to. He expected his mother to intervene for him, to function.

She did not. As he remembers this disappointment, he is so aghast that his limbs begin to thrash, and this thrashing eventually brings him to a standing position. He wobbles back to the bathroom. His head is wet and cold. He feels queasy. He has not eaten anything for days but his stomach is bursting with water he swallowed in the toilet, and his nose still stings from the water that ran back out through his nostrils. He retches. Afterwards, he feels better but terribly sleepy, so he lies down on the bathroom floor and immediately falls asleep.

Bertha is down in the kitchen, hating the child for forcing

her hand. Bertha has never had her head washed in a toilet, but she has had her mouth washed with soap: Bertha was small once and her bulk now is a clever disguise of the fact.

Bertha loved her mother, and then her father came into the range of this stirred-up love, where it hit him, too, and soon afterwards, her older brother. This brother mothered her when necessary; she called his motherliness brotherly. Bertha's beloved brother became a Catholic priest. Bertha wanted to spend her life with him, but she had no natural inclination towards the Church. Once, basking in the sun on an early summer day, she asked God whether he 'wanted' her too. She was eighteen years old. God gave no answer. She thought she would make it easier for God. She said to Him, Very well, you don't have to say anything, just give me a sign if you want me. At once, Bertha felt a terrible stabbing pain in a back tooth. She took this to be confirmation of God's wish; she signed up with the same religious order as her brother's. The day she was packing her bags to leave home, her brother was assigned to East Africa. She would never see him again. Bertha unpacked again and went to the dentist, who extracted an impacted wisdom tooth. Her feelings for her brother had reached saturation point; she became indifferent. Nor would she ever love a man. Why bother with all that disappointment? Bertha's mother had told her once, The longer you love a man, the more watery this love becomes, the more grey and loose.

Bertha's mother was a small-town housewife who cultivated homilies in a little sunless patch that lay in the shadow of the monstrous construction of her accepted ideas. Her husband hated this show of independence. Is it possible to love sincerely someone you have known for long and to whom you are bound by law, she asked the priest? And he gave her one hundred Hail Marys and told her never to allow such thoughts into her brain again. But she could not prevent them. As she was preparing soup, unpacking and thundering a slab of beef heart onto her cutting block, she turned to her children and asked, Is not the loving spouse's heart, in the best of cases, an insensate, worn-out muscle? And then she sawed the heart into pieces. Bertha was not extraordinary the way her mother was. She became afraid of her mother, even as she acted on her mother's advice and never married, never expected anything from love either for a man or for a child.

After 'cleaning up' Valerie, she laid him in his bed and told him to stay there. She returned to her post, organizing Maid, satisfied that she had done the right thing.

Valerie eventually woke up on the bathroom floor and could still hear his mother's playing through the cold tiles. He understood without being able to explain it, the way children understand the adult heart, that for his mother, music was an appetite that diverted other appetites into lesser channels, and even her maternal feelings were subordinated—in short, her hearing devoured her other senses, including her sense of propriety and responsibility, including her mother love. He heard the notes and longed for his mother, holding on to the notes with his hearing, allowing them, dulled and distorted through the floor, to caress him; he had already forgiven his mother.

He would forgive her any- and everything. When Dr Anhalt's eighty-year-old mother finally dies a pleasant death, the middle-aged son weeps and cannot sleep because she is gone. When his wife left him he was unbearably offended. But sad? He conjured up the good times they had shared, and thought: So she is turning her back on that, the stupid cow! And he is indignant, but not sad. He soon finds another wife.

The chauffeur, Albert, decided many years ago never to marry. Then he met Gerda, the cook, who was just five years younger than his mother and much like her, only much more so, more elegant, mysterious, opinionated, more disapproving, more prone to headaches and fits of helplessness: more like a little girl. The fact that Cook was older made him feel safe with her— chances were, she would age before him, which restored to him the power that her moral superiority and worldliness (he knew a great deal about cars; she knew a little about everything) gave her, so that their relationship balanced, still balances, is harmonious, from his point of view. The fact that Chauffeur had a hunchback made Cook feel safe with him—chances were, he would stay faithful to her, even when she was an old woman. Cook for her part enjoys caring for Chauffeur the way girls like to look after their fathers, enjoys his dependence on her. She loved him once as a man—with her headaches she even forced the paternal attention she craved out of him—but he gave her so many reasons for irritation that after a while the very sound of his high, thin voice aroused her disapproval. But as the familiar object of her annoyance, he is dear to her, and besides, he can drive a car. She has never lost her admiration for his quickwittedness at the steering wheel, the ease and elegance of his driving. The passengers don't even realize when he steps on the brakes. He does it so smoothly that Cook starts to cry, because Beauty is beautiful, and this equation makes up for everything else in life, including all his other follies, not to mention his angel's wings. The habit of being married to Chauffeur connects her to her youth after her body, turned hard and brittle from inside, as if filled with twigs and wet foliage, no longer can; he is a prop to help her imagination, so that her face, when she checks in the mirror, still has the pretty smoothness that recollection, the best cosmetic, restores to it. She'd prefer her father any day. But he is dead, and he is staying that way. Like the best marriages, the couple's relationship has the stability of a stranded boat. Given the choice between sitting there for ever in an unmoving vessel and trudging through the uncomfortable but safe ankle-deep water to land, they'll stay put. Chances are.

Dr Graf's wife, Hannah, was a ballet dancer who controlled her daughter, Klara, by confiding complicated adult secrets to her about marital unhappiness. After Hannah fell in love, she no longer needed a confidante. Klara had loathed her stepfather because her mother was so crazy about him. The first years of this marriage, the couple had behaved, in Klara's adolescent eyes, like teenagers—it had turned her stomach. She used to go into their bedroom when they were away to open the bulky bag of contraceptives her mother kept in the bathroom, glaring at the ingredients—with a fury about her lack of control others would call jealousy. Dr Graf had not taken a particular interest in his stepdaughter. They had avoided each other. But when Frau Graf was dying, they looked after her together. The patient dozed all day, and when she wasn't dozing she was often aggressive, because she was in pain, and when she wasn't in pain, she was sentimental. 'You were my greatest joy in life,' she said to her daughter; 'You were my greatest joy in life,' she said to her husband. Klara was twenty-five years old, and not as talented as her mother. She was making a career anyway on sheer will power and diligence. Her movements were deliberate, conscious, timed; they imitated, in her own mind, the movements of her mother. After an initial phase of shyness, Dr Graf liked to watch her do the most ordinary things.

The day that Klara's mother died, he had decided to cook for Klara. He made cold cucumber soup. He was chopping and dicing and sautéeing shallots when the sick woman started complaining about the heat, the strong afternoon sun coming in through a small opening in the drawn white curtains, the smell of onions. Klara drew the curtains all the way shut, turned on the fan in a corner, and went into the kitchen to her stepfather. Her mother's voice was weak; one could not hear her over the frying onions. Dr Graf felt his stepdaughter come in without hearing her, her footsteps were so light. He was glad, staying at the stove stirring the onions. She came up to him, leaned her head against his shoulder, and then years of repulsion and the nearness of other emotions sent them on a cluttered path to tenderness.

After her mother died, Klara never visited her stepfather again. She stopped dancing. She became fat. She had no boyfriends. She studied pharmaceutical science and worked in a pharmacy. Her colleagues considered her cold-hearted.

The groom, Benedikt Waller von Wallerstein, was sitting in the window of the sacristy, so worn out by lack of sleep and excessive socializing (by his standards) that he began to dream. He dreamt that he was standing in front of his father, but he did not reach any higher than half way up his father's flannel trousers. His father's voice addressed him, congratulating him on finally having a child to carry on his name. At once his mother came up from behind, a giant figure in a loose white skirt. And she lambasted his father. Was not Lämmchen's work as good as having a child, since it bore his family name in the same way?

His father retorted that he was beginning to think his family was of no significance to her. She bent down to Benedikt, squatted so that he could look into her face, but it was so near to him that he could not identify any details other than the absolute familiarity of this particular arrangement of eyes, nose, and mouth. She was handing him his own manuscript about solitrons which he had submitted for publication. When he took his eyes off her to look at his manuscript, she used the opportunity to disappear.

He began reading the familiar text. In his dream, he realized that someone had written annotations in the margins. He looked more closely and saw that the old-fashioned handwriting belonged to Albert Einstein. Einstein himself had read his manuscript and provided comments. It was a great privilege. Benedikt was suddenly wide awake with curiosity.

And he read: 'One must be careful about colliding with women. There has been much experimentation. The usual method of colliding and then continuing as before is unreliable. My observation is that, inevitably, bits of the man get tangled in the woman. If he keeps moving away from her, he will suddenly find himself popping apart, and the noise this makes startles the local people for miles in every direction. It sounds like gunshot into a flock of sparrows.'

Einstein was making no sense. The paper began to slip out of Benedikt's hand. He tried to catch hold of it. But it twirled away from him, went flapping out the window like a bird. He leaned way outside after it, and this act provoked a lightning flash. Simultaneously, he felt rather than heard the crash of thunder and then a strange pounding as the rain turned to hail. Benedikt disliked the out-of-doors but he felt no fear. He remained there, hanging half way out the window.

The wind had slipped underneath the roof and was prying off one tile after another, exposing the attic. The hail pounded on the attic floor and rain accumulated until several old cracks on either side of the massive chandelier gave way to the pressure. Brimstones of wood splinters, mortar fragments, and ancient straw from the stuffing poured into the middle of the hall. The weather had free access to the house, the wind gave a shriek, the hail bombed through, and the rain that had collected in the eaves cascaded down through invisible seams along the walls of the hall. Random hailstones bounced off the piano onto the key-board. The hail was louder than the Beethoven had been, more percussive, equally abnormal: out in the forest it caused countless casualties, and the survivors had no one on hand to interpret the meaning of it at all. The bride had disappeared, the guests settled into the dry corners. At the dining table a consensus had been reached on which programme to watch. The chandelier lights stayed on, and the atmosphere won a new kind of elegance.

But a chilling fear of becoming an item in the headlines had set in. The journalists took notes and the photographers pictures, calming their nerves with the knowledge that if they survived they would make good money. These imagined headlines served the same purpose as the notion of hell and salvation had once done, sending fear into otherwise courageous hearts. A person in an uncertain situation adjusts his sense of danger according to what might be written about his plight:

CASTLE COLLAPSES: WEDDING PARTY TRAPPED!
MAIMED! KILLED!

or shown on the evening news:

> The commentator (as the fireman points to the bod-
> ies): Huddled in a corner, the victims had apparently
> sought comfort . . .

'If this storm is bad enough it will give the right wing new impe-
tus,' declared Dr Graf. 'They profit the most from chaos.'

Dr Anhalt replied that a house that had survived eight hundred years had surely been through a storm or two, but Dr Graf
ignored him, remarking that freak accidents caused livelier obitu-
aries than any other form of death. Schmidt and Dr Anhalt both
thought to themselves that at least their mothers would be
pleased to find out what company they were keeping.

The relations stayed cool—they were inured to country life.
'I hope,' said one Sieseby teenager, 'that the roof holds over the
television.'

'Hail,' said Dolly, 'is terrible for televisions. It should stop
now.'

The hail obliged, but another clap of thunder seemed to
blow open the sky as if it was a water pipe. Only the side of the
hall with the television remained dry; all the guests huddled together. They were forced into proximity by the weather rather
than by the wedding.

'You don't wear the same dress as your friend. Why do you
wear the same eau de cologne?' Dr Graf asked Dolly.

The rain washed down the portraits, collecting in the trough
of the ornate frames, so that each picture had a seascape at the
bottom. The red man's face seemed to swell up on his unframed
canvas; the colour was water-soluble.

One of the wives wondered loudly what the flood could
mean about the wedding, bad or good luck?

'It's an omen: late fertility. Rain just before autumn,' hazarded one of the hunters' wives.

'Benedikt,' said Dolly, 'is going to learn how to swim. Because I do wonder where he is. That comes from having his moon in a quadrant with his Mars today. And the bride, for that matter, is also missing.'

One heard her footsteps down a corridor, and she appeared, her white dress wet on the shoulders and down the back where she'd been rained on. She strode right up to the priest, who was making his peace with the Lord at the table and had his mouth full of meat again.

She addressed him with a most menacing expression. 'What have you done with my son?'

'I saw one of the women taking him to be cleaned up,' he replied, swallowing. 'He was filthy dirty.'

'What is it: filthy dirty?'

'Don't you know!' he marvelled. 'Dirt?! His face was covered with a kind of slime. It wasn't appropriate for a conversation with his father. I want to begin his religious training soon, simple Hail Marys, and such.'

She sneered, and the priest flinched. She was a scoffer. They were the worst. 'Play us another tune,' the priest begged. 'He'll be right back.'

As if to reward him, the chapel doors swung open and Benedikt appeared, a shadow in the dark chapel. The relatives, swinging their heads in his direction, gave him a standing ovation that ended abruptly as the hero on their programme was cornered. They returned their attention to the television; their hands fell silently to their sides.

The priest was more interested in the host. He considered that it might not be Benedikt over there in the gloom: it could be a theophany. The priest, who dealt in the fantastic, was not frightened. He reasoned that God would never appear to him, especially not in front of others.

Benedikt took a few steps into the brightly lit hall, and saw the havoc there, the ripped-open ceiling, the rain running over the portraits, the red man's cheeks drained of colour, the red fluid dripping from the unframed canvas, trickling down along the wall. To his sleepless eyes, the puddles of water on the floor formed a frozen sea, the chandelier a constellation of stars. He began to shiver. He realized that he was shivering in front of a lot of people. Then he yawned, trying to inflate his mind, to raise it up out of the mire of sleep. The yawn came as a long drawn groan out of his mouth, so that the crowd turned its many heads towards him, and one after the other they all yawned too. He mumbled, 'I'm so terribly tired,' but the heads were already winding back to the television and meanwhile the door bell had started ringing, like the fire alarm on a distant ship sinking at high sea.

No one paid attention. Finally Bertha came in from the kitchen, glared reproachfully at the mess in the hall, and went downstairs to answer the door. She returned with a brown envelope. 'Express letter for you, sir,' said Bertha. 'The postman wanted to wait out the rain here but I said no, there's a wedding party going on.'

There was a lull in the action on television while Benedikt stood mutely holding the letter.

Someone remarked, 'Hey, the rain has stopped!' Relief came as an anticlimax.

'Must be the letter. Saved our necks. What's it say?' called someone.

'Read! Read!' cried another.

The groom was staring at the envelope.

It was from the magazine. Finally, he ripped it open and withdrew the standard letter inside. An apology. They were not going to publish his article. There was evidence contradicting his theory. It would be posted separately. That meant it was heavy. Photographs. When it became clear that the letter was not important enough for Benedikt to read aloud, someone turned up the volume of the television. The audience began shrieking and clapping their hands, several cried with horror: the hero had just died in an ambush. Their cries merged with a faint wailing that began upstairs.

The bride had found her son on the bathroom floor. She picked him up in her arms and carried him downstairs, and as she reached the hall her sobbing and moaning startled the crowd. Benedikt looked up from his letter as she marched up to him, the child like a drowned bird in her arms, his long hair slicked over his face. 'This place,' she snapped, 'is going to kill my son.'

The company compressed, became a crowd, afraid of this new danger, the child, with his blue lips and dazed eyes.

'He wouldn't eat. He hasn't eaten for weeks. And now he doesn't answer me. He won't talk! He hasn't talked in days and days,' his mother whimpered, realizing that she had overlooked the child entirely.

Benedikt remarked, 'Communication isn't everything,' the letter dangling in his hand.

'My son. My son won't speak anymore. He hasn't spoken to me in days. My son. No sounds come out of his mouth,' she moaned.

He heard only the possessive and it sounded ugly to him, the ugliest word he had ever heard. 'My son.' The possessive was a bleating curse. But he knew no remedy for it. 'Bring him upstairs,' he said, 'up the stairwell, to the tower. I'll show him something extraordinary—he'll forget himself. My telescope. I haven't seen it yet myself. And we'll look at the big clock.'

She didn't want to go upstairs. She seemed terrified at the suggestion. 'No, no, it will make no difference to him,' she said. 'He doesn't care. Just look at him.' She shook him in her arms and wailed, 'Valerie!' He didn't answer, his eyelids opened wide and shut again.

At once, Dolly took action. She marched over to the bride, swept the child from the woman's arms, slung him over her shoulder, and headed briskly towards the stairwell. 'Benedikt,' she ordered, 'come along.' Brother and sister climbed up and around the narrow winding steps until they reached the look-out window at the turn of the stairs. Dolly said, 'Look, Valerie. You can see your mother, down there.' Dolly felt the boy lean over her shoulder, to look down. She fought for balance, the child stretching, pulling her backwards. 'Benedikt, take him,' she cried.

Her brother was coming up from behind her. The boy was craning his head through the little window as Benedikt approached slowly, moving closer and closer to the child. Valerie saw him coming, looked down at his mother and then back at Benedikt. His energy had taken refuge in his eyes now. He allowed Benedikt to decrease the distance between them while his eyes shoved him away. He was pure rejection, anti-magnetism.

Benedikt's arms were travelling through the air towards the boy when there was a huge bang downstairs. He had just about reached the child when the front door flew open and the hunters entered. They were dragging the stag they had found. It smelled roasted. Benedikt's hand was closing on Valerie's shoulder; he could feel the warmth of the small body. The huge animal had been hit by lightning. God was a hunter too. The stag had had his head down; his antlers were intact. The hunters held the creature upright, and fear entered the child like a foreign spirit. Benedikt's hand had not yet closed on his when Valerie threw back his head and his terror came out of his mouth in a mighty cawing.

Having given this sign of life, the child freed himself from Dolly's grasp and Benedikt's proximity by fierce kicking and writhing. He bolted down the steps again, scuttling to his mother and leaping into her arms as if he were saving himself from drowning. He held on to her, blubbering and babbling, while the company turned away in embarrassment. Only Dolly kept her eyes on him, shivering with the urgent sympathy she felt for all helpless creatures.

But to everyone's surprise, the mother addressed them with quiet triumph and relief. 'He says he's hungry.'

Now merriment, after so much danger withstood, united the company, made them equals. Even the journalists felt warmly towards their hosts, like kidnappers consorting with their hostages.

Dr Graf, finding himself in a crowd of women, remarked to Dolly, 'Did you know that we're related?'

'You don't say,' she returned, surprised.

'Yes, indeed,' the tall man with the magnificent skull assured her. 'When I was at primary school my parents took me to a little town on the Ostsee called Sieseby. When I got home, I wrote a school essay about Sieseby. So in a sense we're related.' He glanced down at her and smiled sweetly.

Cook was just putting in a special guest appearance. She had spent the afternoon having a headache after discovering a set of built-up shoes secreted in the back of Chauffeur's wardrobe. There was a bunch of folded-up letters stuffed into the toe. She had read them. They were the kind of sentimental letters unabashedly sentimental people write, full of easy affection. 'She's chasing you again!' cried Cook. And Chauffeur did not argue. With detachment, he watched her take to her bed. After a while he went through the motions of feeling sorry for her, and although she knew he did not mean it, she pretended to be touched by his concern and said she felt better. 'Let's join the others,' she said.

They strode into the hall, Chauffeur trotting to keep up with her, just as Gardener came in, reluctantly, and the hired cleaning ladies, giggling with uneasiness, and Dogkeeper, full of self-importance, and Hunter, his hearing aid turned on high, in his soggy fatigues. The merriment soon reached into the very crevices of the human soul, that is, even Bertha was touched by it, tossed her apron on the piano, and gulped champagne with her superiors.

And into this happy group came Dolly, Countess of Sieseby, Freifrau von Hagelberg, bandying her video camera and filling the room with her bright yellow, sweeping gown, her pink nylons glistening with sweat. She surprised Benedikt by no longer paying the slightest attention to the child, as if he had miffed her with his behaviour. Instead, she filmed the guests, and Benedikt sitting on the bench, resting, and Marja pacing around in the background. When she wasn't filming, she was watching the Russian woman, never letting Marja out of her sight, walking behind her, far enough behind not to be noticed, consciously or unconsciously imitating her step, imitating the way she leaned against the piano as if it were a dear friend, more than a dear friend. Dolly's thin lips twitched in an imitation of the bride's closed-lipped smile of ironic humour or uneasiness.

The tower clock struck eight times and the groom began hoping everyone would go home. His sister was watching her own film when she called her brother urgently to the camera. 'Come quick and look,' she commanded. 'But she is sexually attractive, Benedikt. Very,' said his sister. 'I bet her Venus is in Scorpio. Just look at her.'

CHAPTER 20

For the advanced only: slowly, but with overtones and undertones.
After the party is over the aftermath begins

M uch later that evening, the guests[1] promenaded down the stairs to the front door, while a friendship between two guests[2] tightened like a noose.

[1] The Berliners, including Dr Anhalt, who was tired out from taking mental notes on who he had seen and what they had said and from realizing that no one wanted his notes (he was no better than the average chronicler now), Dr Graf, in a bad mood because he had enjoyed himself and hadn't planned to, and the married couple Schmidt, Schmidt anxious to get his wife back into the hotel bed and fast asleep, so he could manage a rendezvous; the staff, including Maid, anxious to go (the husband waiting for her at the gate, because he considered the environs dangerous), Gardener, who never felt well inside the house, Dogkeeper, who would have preferred to stay a while longer, Hunter, inclined to believe that lightning had struck the elk as a personal favour to him; his sister's husband, Hackse, their children, except Isabella, who had arranged to stay for one more night and then return home—where was Dolly, was she outside already?

Assorted other relations, the older ones weary but gay, the younger ones annoyed about a wasted day, the English cousins disappointed that they had not been asked to stay the night—there seemed to be a lot of space; on the other hand, the thought of the hotel breakfast made going to bed a pleasure—the journalists, hauling their impressions like heavy equipment: this simple true love story was rather complicated; Dolly, hanging back because she had forgotten to tell her brother something; the USA cousin, an early-to-bed man himself, knowing he would be tired the next day, but it was worth it, he would describe this event to all his friends, after the Colosseum, Trafalgar Square, the food in France: a country-style wedding; Uncle Bopo, with stolen silverware clanging in his pocket; the priest, who had prayed with such concentration when the hail storm began that he was rather exhausted, overworked.

[2] Schmidt brushed Isabella's cheeks with his lips; he was reckless, but his wife, never expecting, was unsuspecting.

Chauffeur was holding the door open, and the groom, positioned on the threshold, prepared to shake hands. As they reached the host, words[3] like the rain still in the trees shook off their lips, and he smiled without answering.

His sister[4] went out last, Chauffeur let the door swing shut again, and they returned upstairs, where Cook was waiting. The two couples[5] murmured 'Goodnight's, the von Biesterfelds slipped away quickly, Benedikt headed for the wooden bench,

---

[3] *Auf Wiedersehen.*
Fabelhaft.
Es war fabelhaft.
   Congratulations!
   You have a great place here: *Wunderbar!* I don't envy your maintenance costs. You got enough help now with the cleaning up? Thanks a million. It's been really memorable.
   Look at the sky. *Wie schön! Auf Wiedersehen.*
   I wish you all the best, really and truly. Psst—Caroline, don't forget to shake the bride's hand, psst, Caroline! Over there, the bride! Goodbye. And we look forward to seeing you in Scotland. You must come. And you can stay with us, you don't have to go to a hotel or anything.
   Let's see each other again soon!
   Congratulations Dr Waller! Shouldn't I call you Dr Waller von Wallerstein? *Doch* No? We must discuss your pension.
   Fabelhaft. We survived. *Auf Wiedersehen. Auf Wiedersehen.*
   Look. The stars! Full moon, nearly. Enjoy. And all the best.
   We stayed a little too long. Because of the weather. Time for bed.
   Remember. Our grandfather Wallerstein always said: 'Marriage is like life. Only it never ends.'
   I just want to wish you a smashing wedding night, Lämmchen.
[4] Like a neon light, so that everything seemed duller, darker, after she was gone.
[5] Chauffeur was thinking that Seamstress might easily marry one day, and jealousy descended like a devouring hawk. He knew there was only one remedy for the emptiness in his affections: take Cook on his lap upstairs, play 'little girl' games with her, in which emotions were not required; Cook was wondering whether she wasn't running out of laxatives; Benedikt was marvelling at the child's face, turned to alabaster because he was so tired; Marja realized she could soon be released from the prison of her wedding dress and savouring a smoke in one of the closed guest rooms where she kept an ashtray and her matches.

sat down, and watched Marja's slow, triumphal march through the hall towards the stairs with what he now thought of as his son, holding the child's hand as though that were the only natural position for it. Bertha was already in bed upstairs, philosophic about the day's events.[6]

Left alone, the groom listened to the clock,[7] waiting for each new tick as if it were a stupendous occurrence; in the silence

[6] The bride had, from her point of view, everything. Try to find the worm, the hook in it! She had a wealthy husband with a life expectancy as short as her affections for him were small. He was too skinny to betray her or make excessive demands, or in fact any demands at all. She had a house without a mortgage and in no danger of being confiscated by the state. She had servants to look after all her menial chores. She had had had. She did not have to give. She had no obligations. She could cultivate her hobbies. She could exist in style. Disgusting.

[7] He did not hear footsteps. He was staring in the direction but did not see the couple meeting in the doorway at the top of the stairs. His eyes told him: there is something over there, but the couple kissing made no sense to him, had no context, it was like a hieroglyph on a vast empty page. He did not notice them disengage and hurry on tiny vibrating footsteps up the stairs to the guest rooms, nor did he see the man return down the stairs alone and head for the door. The visitor was more observant. When he spotted Benedikt on the bench, he took a few steps towards him, then a few steps back. It was Schmidt. He had crept out of the hotel room, left his wife sleeping. His mouth, his skin still felt the impressions of his triumph. That Benedikt didn't know annoyed him. He should know. It was a paramount part of the triumph. He should see for himself: Schmidt's lips were slightly swollen and sticky from so much kissing. He had made a woman out of the girl, without even penetrating her. There was time for that later.

Benedikt's mouth was moving: those thin lips, that had never kissed anyone, fluttered like a pale moth on his face. Benedikt Schmidt moved closer, trying to overhear him, but all he could make out was 'universe.' Schmidt found it implausible that a newly made groom should be thinking about science on his wedding night. It ruined his triumph, made him doubt Isabella, made him instantly regret spending so much time on a seduction; Benedikt Waller's passions were more consuming than his own. Benedikt Schmidt faced a new onslaught of envy. So instead of confronting Waller with his pleasure, he skirted him, slipped out the door, trembling a little, hoping that strong feeling could guard against the presence of ghosts.

between, the universe expanded one billion miles, so that contrary to popular conception, each second was really a very long unit of time.

By and by, Benedikt looked up at the portrait of the red man, whose face had been washed away, denied the right to exist independently of the clock. There was nothing left but a red smudge, not even signs of long-forgotten embarrassment. Benedikt had not told the psychotherapist everything. The destruction of the portrait made him aware that, at a great distance from the present, a hideous embarrassment festered in his memory.[8] He changed the subject. He looked at the portraits of his ancestors. They had survived the rain, they would survive the Flood.[9]

Benedikt remembered Chauffeur, his heated conversation; he thought about Marja's gyrating facial expressions. Then he looked around at the portraits of his family members, at their

---

[8] The closed chamber of his earliest experiences was not soundproof. He heard his own voice crying out there. Although Benedikt was not a memory acrobat, the occasion was within reach of his ear, and if he wanted to, he could grasp it with his sight: from the vantage point of the backseat of a car, with his sister just a baby next to him, he could see two huge figures in front, leaning towards each other and then away again. Their hands flailed, their voices lifted in a chaotic, unmelodious exchange.

Suddenly the car swooped like a bird up into the air, turning around, spinning. He would have heard his own child's voice calling, 'Goodbye, Mami!' and he could recall that his fear was subordinated to such embarrassment about his sentimentality that he was determined to forget the episode.

[9] No, they wouldn't. Only a good theory, Benedikt knew, can achieve immortality—it lives on like an amoeba, changing forms. But nothing dies so completely as a theory that doesn't hold up. It doesn't get sent into oblivion, it just disappears: no one remembers it, it leaves no survivors, it leaves no footnotes. It does not make the Flood. So much for Benedikt's pet theory. As for Benedikt himself:

If he doesn't die of his disease, then he will catch another, at the latest he will die of old age, and if that doesn't catch him either, well, barring some sort of catastrophe that takes care of this earlier, at the latest five million years from now, the sun will swell up and swallow the earth, hook, line, and sinker, Benedikt and the portraits of his ancestors right along with it.

unchanging expressions, and he recognized that he did not feel any more than they did. Despite his protestations, he was indeed a perfect specimen of a Waller von Wallerstein. He had always taken his dead relations to be alive around him. Now he realized he had been wrong, it was the other way around—it was he who had been dead around them. He had never lived. But now he intended to.

Benedikt, soothed by the apparent simplicity of his own ambition, fell into a deep, dreamless sleep in which his pulse rate kept up neatly, evenly, with the tower clock.

part three

CHAPTER 21

Powerfully: Valerie develops. But Marja grabs all the attention

Valerie Count Waller von Wallerstein, not yet a German citizen but now the rightful heir to the estate of his adoptive father, eyed the stones on the bank of the moat, picking one so sharp-edged that it cut into his fingers, clutched it nevertheless, and sent it with all the strength of his small arm into the window. He was aiming for his new father's head.

As the stone smashed through the glass, Benedikt's face appeared in the middle of the flower-shaped hole, staring out, his hand on his forehead. The assassin called, 'Sorry!' and scampered away, stopping every so often to turn back and shout, 'Sorry! Sorry! Sorry!' ducking his head, as if someone were liable to hit him.

The thought that in time his apology might lose its power made him break into a run. At the same time he scorned the word; it represented to him the weakness of the German language, because the Russian equivalent seemed much more serious, weighty, and he could never have used it as lightly.

Some words had a power he considered magical. Just thinking of the name 'Moscva,' for instance, elicited such a warmth in him that his impressions of the place melted, and he could not make out any details. Then he tore at the air in front of him, scratching it like a cat, screeching, or he marched around like a soldier preparing for an invasion. Whenever he saw his new father he uttered a string of syllables culminating in *'nyet, nyet, nyet!'*

His handsome face was soon marred by a black eye he acquired from a run-in with the handle of a door he was preparing to slam. He played ever more roughly, sought out the local boys at a nearby farm, and when introduced to the grandsons of the gardener, who had brought them around expressly for the purpose, bullied them in Russian. He learned German, so it seemed to the Germans, on the spot, and used it to call, 'You're all assholes,' or 'foreign scum,' having learned the latter from the gardener's grandsons, who had applied it to him. He stole any small change that was left lying around and fiddled with the telephone in the salon or the sacristy, apparently making random calls to listen to the voices at the other end, hanging up with a shrieking laugh.

Most of the adults working at Schloss Biederstein avoided him; the cook could catch migraines from seeing him without prior psychic preparation. At meals, Maid, who now served them formally at the hall table, refused to fill his plate after he had formally tipped his portion into a plastic bag, saying he needed it for the pig. The gardener, who still kept the runt, warned him that he would shoot the animal if he ever found him outside his little pen. And if he grew, then he would shoot him, for that too. The pig was not going to get anything more than the leftovers.

'The pig is growing now,' Valerie taunted him. 'He is still hungry—you have to feed him more.'

Gardener began to fear the child. He kept away when the boy was around. When he heard piano playing in the house his nerves started to sing along, because it generally meant the boy was on his own. Soon, he was always on his own; the bride played the piano more and more, from dawn to dusk, so the child's assaults became unpredictable.

When Gardener complained about this in the kitchen the other staff corrected him. She was often with the child. She had a way of paying fleeting but intense attention to him, listening to him when he spoke, as if his words were prophetic or of inestimable wit; but she ignored him the rest of the time. In the evenings she put him to bed unlike other mothers. Bertha reported that she had seen her hold Valerie by the shoulders and shake him into the pillow.

When Marja noticed that Bertha was spying on her at bedtime she explained, 'I told him that's how Germans always put their children to bed. And that they fall asleep at once. In Moscow he made me tell him stories for hours. Now I don't have to. Just a shake, and off he goes.'

Of all the adults there, only Benedikt behaved fearlessly. Again and again in his awkward, ignorant way, Benedikt proffered friendship. If this was in the form of a helping hand at dinner, Marja intercepted it. If he spoke to Valerie when the child was unattended, she appeared suddenly, interrupting. But if Benedikt approached the boy, and his mother did not show up at once, then Valerie ran for her. He refused the most normal eye contact. He rarely spoke to the adults but they often heard him: he had a charming singing voice of piercing sweetness. Benedikt began listening for it and once asked him to sing. 'Nyet nyet,' he screeched. He sang a fragment when no one was expecting it, watched Benedikt's head crane in his direction, and stopped again. He took to humming under his breath when he saw Benedikt coming, singing a few bars outright as Benedikt came nearer, and then clamping his lips shut. He looked directly at Benedikt only after an attack, in order to assess the damage he had done.

After pitching the stone and watching the splinters of the window explode in Benedikt's face, he took a few steps in his direction, turned, and ran. He ran long after his 'Sorry's were exhausted. He kept going; he ran towards Moscva. This time his memory did not buck and shake him off course. He was bounding up the subway steps into the wind of the big street—he slowed to a walk. He was a little afraid of what he might find so he dawdled for a while at the subway exit, watching the cars catapulting past, jolting the pavement. Finally he followed the pull of familiarity up a side street to a square park. The scraggly grass there yielded generously many treasures his parents called rubbish—no present handed over by an adult would ever give him the same satisfaction. Seeing this playing field was not enough: he trod on it, felt the texture of the surface beneath his sandal and then the dust between his toes. He knew exactly how it lay, uncomplaining, flat, friendly, when he played football with the neighbours. Finally he headed towards the orange entrance door of a modern tenement.

The darkness of the stairwell pressing against his eyes, he continued blindly towards the steps, his feet recognizing the way. He stomped two flights upwards making as much noise as possible because the echo was so lovely, found the middle of five buzzers lined up vertically at a door. He never had to count up and down, because each buzzer was broken in a different way; the Golubs' consisted of a bare wire that one had to manipulate inwards, whereupon it sent a shriek through the whole building. At once the front door of their communal apartment swung open on its own. He was greeted by the familiar sound of five televisions on simultaneously, one in each room, all tuned to the same programme, and then he had to laugh with pleasure seeing how the entire length of the corridor was lined with shoes and slippers.

It was lit with one weak bare lightbulb that swung from the high ceiling. The bulb was closest to Ivanov's room, so he had more light than the others, and since this was unfair, Ivanov had agreed (after a lot of bickering) to be responsible for replacing it. Lightbulbs were rarely available in the shops but Ivanov worked in a well-lit factory where bulbs were replaced the minute they went out. Every few months the hall remained dark while Ivanov was at the factory with the hall bulb, 'replacing' it, by swapping it. Once he was ill for several weeks, the bulb went out, and he forced Valerie to take the bulb to school and replace it there. Valerie hadn't dared—he had brought back the dead bulb and stolen one from his father's secret supply under the bed. The sight of the bulb brought back a sudden anxiety about this theft, but he calmed himself, inhaled the pungent smell of shoes, of mouldy rugs and books, of a chemical agent against bedbugs. He walked self-consciously on the rectangular gold-coloured rug covering up the smooth speckled linoleum, checked to make sure that its peculiar design had not worn away entirely, no, it was still there: the orange-and-brown rectangles with grey petals growing out of them. The walls of the hallway were hung with coats and bathrobes, but it also had something special, that other corridors did not have: a sword, a real sword, with a long curved blade and a mean-looking bare handle, affixed to the wall parallel to the floor, ready to slice people open; Micha Salmanovic, a retired engineer, had acquired it—he refused to say how—as a young soldier fighting against the Muslims in Middle Asia.

Valerie reached the second door to the left and turned the big brass door handle, slipping inside. No one was home, but the television was entertaining the furniture, as it always did when no one was home. The wardrobe stood in the middle, with the same scratch marks, the cracked pane on one door. The left side contained all their clothes, the right side stored trinkets, six crystal glasses of various sizes, a chess set, a metal clown on wheels with a drum in front that he could pound, a toy that had made daily excursions down the hall, pulled along on a string, until old Salmanovic lamed him by stuffing a piece of cotton into the clown's arm joints and wheels, an action he thought kinder than scolding the small child about the noise. Books in all sizes and on all topics were kept on Valerie's bed and taken down in the evenings when he went to sleep. The TV stood on the table, in the middle of the room, and they ate their meals around it.

Valerie was glad to see the brown piano, which was still missing the two lowest keys and had one broken-off key in the middle. In fact, the child did not like the piano, seeing it as his rival, and he refused to play. But he was proud of the way his mother could negotiate the potholed, sharp-edged keyboard without hurting her fingers and of how she laughed that she had developed a new technique for playing dangerous instruments. After a descant C key went missing altogether, she had started the hunt for a piano repairman, given up, and she simply sang the missing tone whenever it was required, even at high speeds. Not everyone was impressed. Only one neighbour did not mind her playing, but he was a singer, and when he had visitors in to rehearse duets, the neighbours up and down the whole house turned up the volume on their televisions to protest; it could become very noisy. The singer eventually moved out, trading his room for one less modern but more central, leaving Valerie's mother to be the noisiest person in the house.

She kept playing, even after a delegation of representatives from the compound of buildings stood outside the door, grinding out complaints like a one-legged accordion player:

'What are you doing to us!'

'Doing to us!'

'Mozart is all right.'

'Bach is all right.'

'But Stravinsky—no.'

And a more conciliatory voice had suggested, 'We know you are allowed to practise at night at the music school.'

His father had yelled at them promptly—they had no business talking to a great artist that way, while his mother cooed assuaging noises behind him.

Valerie's father would do anything for his family, including make a fool of himself. His temper often saw to that. Valerie was proud of his father's bad temper, even when it was directed against him; it dissolved quickly, like a tablet in hot fluid, but it made him sweet afterwards. One just had to wait his tantrums out, then one was rewarded with a nectar of repentance and generosity. After shouting at the neighbours, Salmon Golub insisted his wife practise at the music school, and he picked her up in the evenings there, so that she didn't have to walk home alone. He was a philologist; he worked at the central library.

Valerie did not like to think of his father, for fear of having forgotten him altogether. When he dared, his memory produced a smell. If he persisted, memory, under pressure, recalled a presence, an occupied spot at family conversations, at best a vague form; no more. So Valerie thought instead about his bed in the corner of the bedroom, the frayed green blanket, and then, all of a sudden, he saw his father clearly: asleep on his side, his face

battered by the pillow, his hand dangling over the green
rug . . .

Valerie was walking aimlessly now, and the house in Biederstein exercised its gravitational pull; without planning to, he had
made a circle through the woods, coming out at the entrance to
the vegetable garden. The runt, Hans, grunted. The child increased his pace again—he swooped past the pig pen, opening
the gate with a practised flick of his fingers. The pig had really
grown; his eyes jiggled seeing the opening in the door. His step
towards it was drunken with hope. Soon, he was feasting on
some roses. The gardener was alerted by his grunts of satisfaction.

Valerie carried on. At the front door of the castle he heard
the piano. She was playing. She would not have noticed that he
had misbehaved. His 'father' was sitting in the window, holding a
big bath towel against his forehead, reading again. This so enraged the child that the relaxed muscles of anger began to tense
up again and he looked for a way to relieve them. He searched
for another stone. By the time he had found a big round one, his
target was no longer sitting in the window. Valerie guessed he
was down in the hall somewhere. He threw the stone at the
metal front door. The clang made the crows fly away, cawing.

She was playing the piano and hadn't heard the glass break or
the clang of the front door and didn't suspect a thing until
Benedikt appeared, his face even whiter than usual, pressing a
bloodied towel against his forehead. Her hands flew to her mouth
in horror, which saved them some damage, because he marched
right up to her and slammed the piano lid shut. 'I suggest you
return to Moscow,' he said. 'The child will be fine here with me.'

As she did not reply he cajoled, 'I will pay for your journey.
Airfare.'

She shook her head dully, shocked, but stubborn. 'No. I
won't go back.'

'Are you afraid of going hungry?' he demanded. At once he regretted his question. 'I'm sorry,' he said.

'What happened to your head?' she asked, in a noncommittal tone. He was too proud to tell her of this defeat. 'Something in the window, don't understand myself,' he mumbled.

'I can bandage it for you,' she said, sounding more polite than concerned.

But he waved his hand. 'I can fend for myself.'

Benedikt returned to his desk and his reading, his forehead bandaged with a huge poultice he had found in his grandmother's First World War medical kit. He heard their voices outside, in front of the window, both very agitated. Benedikt concentrated; he tried to block them out; he could not. He heard the sound of her voice, sharp with threats, whetted by frustration as she saw her threats were useless, and culminating in a slap. At once her voice turned whiney and panicked, as she repeated, 'I'm sorry,' in Russian. He heard how misery replaced frustration. He knew enough about diplomacy to recognize that Marja was torn by respect for Valerie's incorruptibility and a desire for peace. It was a bad mixture for negotiations. He blamed the boy's past for somehow interfering with the present. He had no evidence for this other than the fact that both mother and child remained strange to him. He had assumed that after a while they would become familiar. When this proved not to be the case, he sought the blame in Moscow. He thought so often about this Moscow of his imagination that he too effectively called it into existence at Schloss Biederstein.

The Golubs' life, in his mind, was squalid and impoverished. He pictured their home in Moscow—a high-rise, the kind that stood in East Berlin, one in a row of buildings lined up like soldiers along a huge boulevard. On the second floor: three rooms, a tiny kitchen, not much different from his own in Berlin; Benedikt was not well acquainted with East Bloc poverty.

As he sat down with his family at the long table in the hall he pictured a Russian dinner: coarse, famished, dull-witted diners wrestling for small portions of potatoes and fat, gulping them down with the abnormal hurry he felt was typical of the hungry. In the West, we eat slowly, thought Benedikt, watching Marja snap at Cook's dainty vegetables and venison. 'The fork belongs in the right hand,' he explained to the child. But the mother's table manners were worse than her son's. She wasn't awkward so much as indifferent, and she seemed irritated by his intervention. 'What does it matter how you hold a fork, as long as you can eat with it?' she asked, when he offered to teach her the proper position. Nevertheless, she held it the right way after that, although it seemed to cause her some difficulty, and the attention had made her self-conscious: she took bites, glancing around her to see if Benedikt was watching her, which of course he was. Promptly, food toppled off her fork and into her lap, and she laughed unhappily. He was pleased that she even noticed; she was generally too absentminded to pay attention to what she called 'little things'. He had extra napkins brought to the table, big linen ones. Occasionally, she used one. He imagined her sitting in a Moscow cafeteria, eating off a metal plate, her treacherous teeth sinking into a sandwich and staying there for good.

He pictured Valerie at school with hundreds of dirty children learning Communist passwords to happiness, Valerie coming home again with a gang of others chanting the passwords. Benedikt remembered his grandmother's wish and hired a tutor for Valerie: an unemployed teacher, an unimposing, nervous young man, who did not want to begin until the school term officially began, because he needed a holiday. 'Teaching is incredibly strenuous, and you need the vacation in order to be able to concentrate on your pupils,' he explained. He came around to meet the boy and spent most of the time with Marja, who asked him for help pronouncing certain words; he worked with her all morning, while the boy played outside. The word she absolutely could not say was 'Glück' (happiness) and it seemed to present a pleasant intellectual problem for him. All morning Benedikt heard her efforts, 'Glück Glück Glück,' and the noise of the boy kicking a tin around the courtyard.

He thought the boy must have picked up his behaviour from

his father. He pictured Herr Golub as a rough-skinned, tall, strong man with a bottle of vodka under his coat, shouting at his son, smashing windows when he was annoyed. 'In the West,' Benedikt would say, 'we do not shout or smash things when we aren't happy. Oh, and in the West we go to dentists.'

He wanted Valerie to go to the dentist. Marja could go as well. They didn't want to. Marja resisted passively, avoiding the conversation, refusing to call the local dentist for an appointment. When he made appointments for them both, Valerie began to shriek and cry, and when his mother had calmed him down, Benedikt promised, 'If you go without being afraid, then I'll do anything you think frightens me.' He could not name something that frightened him.

The boy replied at once. 'I go to the dentist—and you take me home.'

'This is your home,' responded Benedikt, more puzzled than hurt, picturing the seedy high-rise, the florid-faced Communists from which he felt he had rescued the boy.

'Then you swim in the lake, through the dangerous part,' demanded Valerie.

Benedikt agreed, neither frightened nor really expecting to fulfil his end of the deal. If Valerie went to the dentist, he promised, on the next hot day he would jump into the lake, the most dangerous part.

The dentist was more interested in Marja's mouth. He had never seen anything quite like it in such a young woman—such a waste of beauty, he complained. He wanted to make everything new. It would cost quite a lot, but it was going to be worth it. 'It's just not done in the West,' he complained, 'running around with such bad teeth. Quite apart from the effect it has on one's eating habits.'

The dentist soon had the town gossip wound up and tisking away about the Countess's teeth. Russia! The dentist saw no hope of salvaging what she had. He pulled ten teeth, including the remains of her back teeth, and filed down all the rest, all in one sitting, fitting her at once with provisional jacket crowns in front

and temporary sets of false teeth for the back which made her
gag whenever she spoke and must have caused her severe pain
(she did not complain). She looked nauseated and did not dare
speak at all. At dinner time, she had to excuse herself every few
minutes, she was so uncomfortable. Benedikt was forced out of
simple politeness to worry about her teeth, to bear her feelings in
his mind, to encourage her constantly to keep wearing them.

After a week had gone by, Marja stopped wearing the back
teeth altogether and missed a dentist appointment; he was going
to start work on the permanent set of dentures. Her spanking
white front teeth flashed when she spoke, so that her mouth
looked extravagant to him, the lips fuller. This change either
annoyed or embarrassed her, because she now kept her lips
shut when she smiled, which heightened the ironic potential of
that face.

He begged her to return to the dentist. He lectured her.
'This is not Russia! You will be considered repulsive here!'

She went every other day, sullen, recalcitrant, blaming Benedikt for the misery the false teeth caused. At least the weather
was unseasonably cold so he didn't have to go swimming. Every
day Valerie dashed out the door before breakfast to check on the
sun and returned crestfallen because it was chilly. There was
even a frost, putting the gardener into a terrible mood, and all
they ever seemed to talk about was Marja's teeth.

Marja seemed to deflect in her own direction any interest he
took in the boy. When he asked after the boy's musical education, she described playing Brahms for him when he was a baby.
Asked whether he was interested in math, she answered, 'Yes,
he's excellent. I was very interested as a child, too, and had the
best marks in the class.'

He wanted to show Valerie some mathematical tricks. After
the child had finished dinner he pushed a pencil and some paper
over to him. 'Think of a number,' he suggested, 'and divide the
number by three.' The boy shook his head and looked away.
Benedikt did not persist. He was puzzled by something. His
memory for numbers had let up so much that he could no longer

do the calculations in his head, because he could not remember the figures. Numbers had a pattern to him with aesthetic value, each one very different, very individual. Some number combinations he found audacious, others gorgeous, or awkward, or chillingly ugly. But now his brain refused to hold on to them, even if, like ordinary people, he hooked them up to primitive milestones—twenty was five less than his birthdate, the twenty-fifth; eighty-seven was two more than the number of centimetres over a metre that he stood; and so on—they disappeared, like drops of water into a lake, indistinguishable from each other, and he could no longer do the simple calculations in his head.

Marja took over. She knew the system—she could do complicated sums without writing them down, without being a mathematician. Meanwhile the boy had taken the paper and was writing something in Russian. He sat bent over the table, his tongue sticking out the side of his mouth, frowning, the pencil in his fist, straining to push the tip over the page, as if he were moving a boulder.

When he had finished, Marja picked up the page and read aloud, translating, 'Dear Papa, come here, I am sad—'

She chuckled, and patted the boy on the head. The boy made an infuriated grimace and ran away, babbling something. She followed him. She soon returned, picked up the page, folded it.

'Do you intend to send it?!' Benedikt cried.

Later she showed him the envelope Valerie had addressed himself. It read in German, 'To my Father in Moscow.' She reassured Benedikt. 'Don't worry, it won't get there.'

He was ignoring her to the best of his prodigious ability to ignore people. But she continued to force herself on his attention. Her presence was everywhere, the rounded but delicate figure in his grandmother's old-fashioned dresses, moving about the house, or sitting on the living-room bench, cuddling the boy ('My son!') or the runt Hans, who oinked with bliss at the privilege, or in position at the piano, playing with a kind of wanton self-confidence, despite her complete lack of professionalism, the big square hands jutting out of the delicate sleeves, asserting themselves.

Once he came downstairs and interrupted her playing to ask, 'What did you do all day for Valerie in Russia?'

'For Valerie?' she returned, looking up from the keyboard. 'He went to school. And I worked.'

'What was your profession?'

'I am a pianist,' she replied, with inexplicable self-satisfaction. 'I played in restaurants, in hotel bars. I played in department stores. Morning concerts. Culture for the people; the salesgirls did their nails or knitted, or they just slept. I played in nuclear-power plants, including Chernobyl, in the entrance hall of Building 2—the accident had nothing to do with my playing. Later I accompanied singers and children. Revolutionary songs. The only place I never played was in a big concert hall. I don't know why. Ask the agency in Moscow that made decisions. They will tell you that I wasn't a virtuoso, the way others are. Even though I am good. Really very good. Please believe me. You can't recognize that. The agency turned down all requests for concerts. My mouth got in the way of my hands.' She had a way of speaking about herself in a cheerful tone of voice, as if to say, It's the way I am, and therefore it's fine.

He despised her talent. Talent was a presumption on other people's admiration. Talent should be kept to oneself. She seemed to prefer to play when people were listening. She became bolder and bolder. She asked him whether there was a store somewhere nearby where she could buy music. He hedged. They would have to drive to a big city, he said. And then the weather turned warm again.

One morning during breakfast, he heard a car in the drive. Soon the doorbell rang. Valerie hopped up, bolted downstairs to open the door, while Benedikt, fearing a visitor, was already hurrying to his room, lying down on his bed. After a while he heard footsteps on the stairs, quick steps, light steps: the child. The steps came nearer. Benedikt didn't move, watched the door open.

Valerie stood on the threshold. 'It's hot outside,' he stated. 'You can swim today. Here's a letter for you.'

Benedikt was overjoyed at the friendliness of the child's gesture, bringing him his mail. 'Thank you, my son,' he burbled, unsuspecting, pleased at his triumph. He stood up and collected the letter. It came from the magazine in America, the heavy envelope he had been expecting. There were photos of his solitrons. His theory had been disproved by pictures, fact making a farce of theory. The solitrons collided, and then they either disappeared, well, he knew about that, or—they changed. They merged, and did not part again, they became different, more elaborate. The scientist was a young man in upstate New York called Einstein. He had changed his name, claiming to be an illegitimate son of the genius; the only thing he could prove was that his mother had been a waitress in Princeton. He had repeated the solitron experiments on his own computer, using a wider range of speeds, faster and slower. Then he had reconstructed the scenario with an electronic synchrotron. He had made photos of the results. They showed the most extraordinary results. When solitrons collided, they grew tails, wavy lines: they became complicated, and some became beautiful.

'And this afternoon,' leered the boy, 'you'll swim.'

The piano roared in his ears. Valerie had disappeared again.

Benedikt reached into his wardrobe, fished out the gravy-stained tie that Bertha had sold him for 100 marks, a week's pension. He lay flat on his back in the monk's position, with his eyes closed; he concentrated on Einstein.

I need your help, sir!

CHAPTER 22

Keine Ruh in Tag und Nacht: *Einstein's ghost is fed up
with being asked for advice. Nevertheless, he gives some*

He was walking through the gardens of his country house. As
a spirit, he was always conjured up as a wise old man, that
is, five decades past his most inventive age. But nobody liked to
appeal to a peach-fuzzed young man anyway. Collective memory had a vague image of him: short—up to Benedikt's collar-
bone—wild-haired, jug-eared, as if to make more of his cranium,
pin-headed. He had an impish smile that went on and off like a
newborn's, according to inner impulses, strains of melody, or the
pleasant straining of his gut. Just now some music was going
through his head, winding around with a simple harmony that
had once been forbidden by the church, millenniums ago, because it was so pleasurable, and then, after the ban was lifted,
used so much that serious people considered it sinfully trivial, but
Einstein adored it. Thirds.

Suddenly he felt observed. The skin on his head had goose-
bumps. He had not had this feeling lately. Someone watching
him from a great distance. God, probably. He said a little prayer
asserting his love, his modesty, and his intentions. The sweetness
had gone out of his walk. Malevolence set into his mood. Then
he realized he was being pressed for advice again. But not quite
in the usual manner. This petitioner had an uncommon psychic
strength, which is why Einstein had mistaken his identity. But his
request was prosaic. The usual. Woman trouble.

Marital problems, raged Einstein. Didn't I have enough of my own!? One of the many drawbacks of fame was the desire it roused in women to have children with the holder . . . The correlation between successful men and successful offspring was practically nil; it was, in the likeliest of cases, a coincidence. Talent landed like lightning in a dense forest of trees. There were too many variables, including the child's talent getting crushed by the nearness of someone else's talent. The best chance of having a successful child was to make sure the father was unknown and driven by lowly ambitions, like making money. At first Einstein had felt grateful for the offers of some attractive women; later he felt merely flattered; ultimately he felt disgusted. On the list of problems posed to him constantly, the ones that interested him least were: Children, bottom of the list, and women, next to the bottom. Strangely, the number of petitioners seemed to grow by the years, his popularity rivalled only by that of Bach and Shakespeare (the religious founders didn't count since it was their business and it served them right). Once Einstein got on a complaining jag, he couldn't stop. He felt like a monster mutating in all those memories. Conditions had got worse since the last generation that might actually have seen him alive died out, and the following generations worked him over from reproduced photos and nostalgic hearsay.

Einstein knew that all those who presumed to understand something about life after death were making an elementary mistake. The fact was that human beings had a certain amount of good and a certain amount of evil in them. And what was lopsided in life could still be balanced out after death. So the worst human beings became, in the afterlife, the best spirits, while the kindest grandmother became the most hateful influence, spewing wickedness to her relatives. If you want to ask someone for advice and help, then ask Hitler! he suggested to this extraordinarily wilful beggar, lying flat in his castle bed concentrating, evoking the spirit of Einstein's genius. He was certainly getting in the way of Einstein's peace and quiet.

There were six petitioners on him right this minute: an ambitious physics student in Tucson enquiring about help for an eleventh-grade project; a Japanese housewife trying to understand the universe while vacuum cleaning; a Jewish opera singer in Sheepshead Bay, New York, who had an audition at the Met the next day; three other scientists with dull theoretical problems . . . actually, it was a slow day. Benedikt had more mental energy than the others put together, Einstein admitted grudgingly. He decided to give him a tip about affections, though it had nothing to do with hard science:

> Any strong emotion is like a tone of music: it makes memories along the entire range of one's history resonate. No tone exists by itself; there are no pure emotions. And these memories carry other emotions, including hope, disappointment, and rage, so that the feeling of love in an adult is always a violent chord.

But now he was bored again. Tired of being a rubbish dump for physicists and their petty problems. And about this Benedikt (Oh, of what earthly interest is a German anyway!)—if he so badly wants to love a child, then I suggest he clear the path of people who also love the child. Get rid of the mother. There are ways! Then you'll have the child. Daughters are better. I never had any luck with sons. Daughters are almost as good as sisters. Get rid of her. I always left my wives in Switzerland. And now leave me in peace! Me in peace! In peace. Pieces.

CHAPTER 23

Allegro assai: fear

'**H**elp me!'
Several hours after Benedikt made his decision to get rid of Marja, his palms and the soles of his feet began to burn. He did not know whether his body or his mind was to blame, and in the ensuing confusion he ended up shouting for help, his cries carrying from his room, down the staircase, into the hall, echoing into every last nook and cranny of the castle, like a wind that has torn loose inside.

The night before they had eaten roast pork for dinner. Marja had been hungry. When Valerie had left the table after pudding, she mentioned that the pig, Hans, had grown really insatiable. Perhaps it was time to slaughter him. Benedikt felt ill; he changed the subject.

He went up to his room and sat down at his desk to work out how to turn Einstein's advice into action. At this point, the feeling of sitting at a desk was still the most comfortable sensation he knew, being barely any at all, the slight pressure on the bottom, the occasional stirring of his legs, the feet way off down below, on reserve duty, lazing about, the elbows mirroring the angles of the knees, the hands agreeable on a smooth surface or overseeing the distribution of paper, the direction of the pen, with languid movements, the body adrift in contemplation.

He had maintained this position all morning. Finally he had invented a plausible scenario for losing Marja without harming her much, or at least without seeing the harm done. He had poked around in his memory for an ideal location to execute this, and coincidence rewarded him, calling attention to a certain Swiss town, Marienfels. The name had a bitterly familiar sound now which he could not have suspected twenty years earlier, when he had spent a night there with Dolly. The memory of that previous visit did not cause more than a slight twitching of incipient embarrassment, which he easily suppressed. He delighted in his choice because—the wonders of coincidence!—the town had a gondola lift that dangled the passenger over an abyss. Anyone troubled by heights would certainly refuse to go on it, would be weakened into agreeing to all sorts of other unpleasantries, anything in order to avoid that confrontation with emptiness. As he deliberated, Benedikt's plans seemed to scald his hands and feet. At the same time, he could barely feel them anymore: his hands lay on the desk in front of him and felt as if they were, like some gondola swinging over a forest fire, floating on burning hot air.

The weather on this particular morning had turned ideal for swimming. In fact, it was warming up as each minute passed. The sun appeared to be increasing in strength. Anyone afraid of that ultimate catastrophe when the sun swells up and swallows the earth would be getting nervous now. But it was more prosaic than that. The sun commandeering the sky sent the heat like so many marauding parachutists down over southern Germany, onto the green cover cascading beneath. The flowers enjoyed it, the phlox released its perfume in a seizure, the stock swooned. The heat moved on, caressing the larkspur and the bindweed until they bulged and the roses nearly ripped themselves open, the heat rolling on through the vegetable garden where Valerie was playing with Hans. The boy wore a beige cotton outfit, with wide-legged shorts and a tight jacket, that his father had worn in the fifties and his grandfather in the twenties. The seat was black with mud from his squatting in the pen. He sat next to the pig and drizzled dirt through his fists onto the animal's back, the pig neither objecting nor answering when the boy addressed him. 'Hot today. Father has to swim.'

The heat, having failed to bother the boy or his pig, travelled on, circled around the big house from all directions, slipping inside through its windows and cracks, beneath the doors, whirled into the kitchen, overwhelmed Cook peeling potatoes, who sagged into the chair and tinkled complaints, 'headache,' 'stomachache.' The heat sped up now, had the maids from behind, all three at the same time while they were bent over dusting the chapel, took Marja playing the piano, who sighed and cursed and gave up, dragging herself up the stairs, travelling with the heat to her room. The heat spread out there, wallowing in the sheets of her bed, and then climbed lustily along the outside walls of the castle into Benedikt's room. Anyone watching would expect this to be the climax of the story, Benedikt grabbed from all sides by the heat that was lacking in his heart and forced outside to the lake.

Not a bit of it. He sat so still that the heat could not get a hold anywhere on him—it just slipped off, leaving an aura of coolness around him. He had other worries. He was trying to make sense of his body. He was aware that, while he had been planning a journey, the illness inside was heading out for unknown regions of its own, perhaps to the end station. After a while, he became annoyed. He was going to be a package again, something to be transported to the hospital and opened and closed, slit and punctured, shaken and straightened, talked about, observed, taken too seriously and not seriously enough. He had a vague desire to protest. He managed to stand up, to wobble forwards to the staircase on his burning insensate feet.

As he clutched the banister and looked down at the stairs, he recognized that they had become a barrier to him. Now he had the impression of mentally trying to push something away, shake something off, something that had no form and could not be shaken off, something that was in his mind and therefore unavoidable, something invisible that raked him and pumped air through his larynx, so that a weird groan issued out, which his mouth formed into syllables, 'Help me!'

In short, he was afraid.

'**A** m I . . .'

Benedikt was trying to speak to Chauffeur from the back seat of the Mercedes. But the words wouldn't leave his lips, and Chauffeur did not notice. He was so frightened by Benedikt's condition that he lost all self-consciousness about his driving. He rocketed down the tiny country lanes, ran over curbs, changed into the wrong gears, accelerated roughly. He knew all the clinics in the area because Cook had tried them all at least once, finding them all wrong, that is, not one doctor had ever found anything wrong with her. He headed for the nearest one, a rural public hospital. When they arrived, Chauffeur opened the car door for him, and Benedikt, cowering inside, unable to move, posed the question again that would not leave his lips. Chauffeur rushed for an orderly.

He watched as Benedikt, eyes now turned to the orderly, mouth open, trying to speak, was rolled away. Chauffeur did not wait to fill out the admissions forms for him, he was feeling queasy and not at all in control of his emotions. He drove home the same artless way. Real illness deeply upset him; he preferred his wife's kind.

The patient kept trying to speak. He was moved from the emergency room, jabbed and prodded as he went and attached to tubes by rubber-gloved hands swinging from green-clad figures with masked faces, spinning him down the hall, upwards and downwards. He strained to force sound out of his mouth, but the words 'Am I . . .' would not come. The admissions doctor accompanied him, running next to his moving bed, and saw his lips twitch but paid no particular attention. The patient was being raced not into intensive care but into isolation; during the summer, the clinic did not take chances on unidentified men of sexually active age who might come from a city.

He tried to speak over and over again, but his voice would not leave the aperture of his mind. The ward doctor didn't even notice. A red-haired, overweight young man from South Africa named Ribbontrop, with a face long and sad as a gnu's, was tired of being asked about his family history, and even more tired of the heat. The hospital ward had a dozen ventilators pushing the hot air from one stagnant pool to another. He lifted the patient's green hospital top gingerly, placed his stethoscope on the grey hairless skin of the chest, and listened to the heart and lungs.

'Careful,' he said to himself. 'Careful. There's an off chance that this fellow is highly contagious'—there was just no telling anymore—'a statistical chance.' The patient was breathing irregularly, pulling in air and not letting it out again, his mouth opening and shutting like a fish's. Finally the doctor remarked, 'Please, breathe as normally as you can, d'you hear me?' barely glancing at the patient's face.

As the doctor puttered around, the patient wrestled with his voice, but the words caught in his throat and tore on the first syllable. Dr Ribbontrop was glad to leave, whistling a little under his breath, his legs swinging, his arms jaunty, his feet clicking like hooves on the corridor, taking his precious agility for granted. As he travelled along, the patients watched with respect. They classed any being that could move independently as extremely lucky, worthy of admiration.

When a nurse came to check the patient's intravenous drip he resumed his efforts. The nurse saw the patient's mouth opening and straining, but she thought nothing of it. Patient had come unaccompanied: no one had asked after him, no visitors, no phone calls. She changed his bedding, using her arms and hands in the most complicated manner, fluffed his pillow, looking him in the eye and murmuring, 'You're a silent one, aren't you!'

Benedikt had a fever. Dr Ribbontrop and his colleagues established that the fever was not related to the polyradiculitis. It began when the sensation was returning to his hands and feet as a prickling, as if they had been frozen. It seemed to the patient that the fever originated in his forehead, an aggressive visitor who made himself at home everywhere, who poked down to one's torso, sprawled along one's legs, occupied every corner of one's body with his hot fetid presence. The intravenous drip was removed, and someone told him he would be eating and drinking normally soon, as if ingestion were a patient's ultimate goal. It was not. Speech was primary—he wanted to be able to cry out for help. He wanted an answer to his question.

He did not fight his dependency on the hospital staff. Instead, he welcomed it. He allowed his food to be brought, his bottom to be washed. One of his hands had swelled up when the IV slipped out of the vein, and he allowed a young woman nurse to massage his hands.

His question stayed locked in, pent up. The next morning, when the Yugoslavian cleaning lady came to mop his room, she noted his efforts at once. She moved close to his bed, leaning on her mop, watched his lips, asked, 'What are you trying to say?'

This solicitude sufficed. He released the words: 'Am I going to die?'

She considered. 'Not yet,' she grunted, bending down to mop under the bed. From beneath the bedsprings she called, 'What do you do to make a living?'

And he replied, 'Mathematician,' hoarse, but edged with pride.

When she emerged she looked at him closely and bragged, 'I thought maybe something like that.'

She looked at the machinery with tenderness and admiration and also responsibility, knowing that she was a part of the apparatus. And this shamed him—he did not like to think of himself as costing so much, the price of her wage, the machines. He was a great expense. 'Am I worth all this money?' he begged.

She straightened up, leaned on her mop, considered carefully. 'As a mathematician, no.' She hesitated. 'As a human being, maybe.' She picked up her bucket, turned around, added, 'What is it, a mathematician?'

Soon after, the fever drew away and feeling was restored to his hands and feet, but he found he was weak. And weakness was not just the absence of strength but a kind of debris left by his unwelcome visitor, the fever. The nurses and doctors congratulated him on his luck—they seemed genuinely astonished. He could walk on his own within two days. He used the opportunity to visit the medical library, where he looked up the drug that had helped him: Erythromycin. He chanted it under his breath, again and again, 'E-ryth-ro-my-cin.' But he was aware of the clean freckled hand that had administered it, personally. He did not like this awareness of his dependency. He went back to the library.

$C_{37} H_{68} NO_{13}$, he learned, can be shaped in the desired atomic hook-up into 262, 144 different structures, derived from the many possible ways to couple right- and left-handedness at its eighteen chiral centres. The medicine was hopelessly complex, a monster of electronic configurations and bonding. He went back to bed and waited eagerly for lunch.

After lunch Dr Ribbontrop said in that lazy, bored way of his that if Benedikt wanted to, he could go home now. The patient rejoiced with caution. He was better, but he had experienced fear, and the feeling stayed at the rim of his consciousness, ready to tip back at any time.

CHAPTER 24

Binding: Benedikt and Marja re-enact the pietà.
Einstein is watching. He is not impressed

The taxi driver had taken the plastic shopping bag of Benedikt's possessions, medicines, magazines out of the trunk and set it down on the first step of the stairs, where the morning sunlight sloshed in a hot sauce. As he left, circling the drive, spewing gravel, he had regarded the tall thin man trying to lift the bag. What use was such a house if you had no muscles in your arms? Benedikt, unable to budge the bag, finally abandoned it and undertook the long trek up the stairs, taking off his jacket to lighten his load and draping it around the shoulders of one of the stone angels at the bottom of the stairwell. An observer who had known him for a long time, unlike the taxi driver, nearly wept at the sight of those thin legs struggling home, the hip bones swivelling visibly beneath the dark wool cloth of his conventional trousers, the delicate Italian moccasins heavy weights on his feet, his face turned upwards towards his goal, as if he were pulling himself along by looking at it, his hand clutching at the balustrade like a child his mother's slippery, unreliable fingers.

Chauffeur, peeking from the bottom of the stairwell, closed his eyes to calm himself. He had known Benedikt since the boy was born, and he had never taken the slightest interest in him. But now that Benedikt had departed from the norms of his own age, leapfrogging even Cook's age group, becoming a weak old man in front of Chauffeur's eyes, he had forced his humanity on him. As Chauffeur watched him going up the stairs, he tried to banish this feeling of sad superiority, reflecting that, at the moment, everyone he knew well could rouse his sympathy merely by walking away: the characteristics of their gaits, splayed or straight feet, empty-handed or struggling under a load, betrayed their vulnerability. As if my gaze were a weapon, the chauffeur scolded himself, and the object, merely by being unaware, were my victim.

The observer's pity was in a sense squandered, because Benedikt's weakness did not worry him, any anxiety on this account being subordinated to his pleasure, after two days of incarceration in a hospital bed, at being a free man again. And it is in any case one of the primary pleasures to come home. Any dog feels an agreeable sense of accomplishment and relief just by reaching his favourite rug.

By the time Benedikt had mounted the top step and moved forward to the next obstacle, the heavy door, he no longer even noticed the strain. He was too absorbed by something that he heard: the child's voice, singing. The beauty of this sound lay in its transience: no sooner had it reached his ear than it was gone; he could not hold it, inspect it, tire of it. His physical collapse made even more of the two-day separation from that voice—he would have followed the melody blindly, over cliffs and into deep water. In order to be one step nearer, he flung open the heavy door.

At once, darkness enveloped him. The singing was close by. He stepped as lightly as possible into the room, but the child was suddenly silent, and he heard its feet clip-clopping away across the stone floor. He stood there, unable to make sense of the room, distracted by his disappointment.

He sensed someone near him, moving through the darkness, setting the darkness into motion. He felt a hand groping for his own. At first he assumed this was a handshake, but the hand stayed closed in his, and he did not question its authority, although he knew that it belonged to Marja. He allowed her to lead him, until her hand came undone in his palm again, travelling lightly along his arm, fluttering along the cotton sleeve, settling briefly, pressing slightly.

The windows hung in the blackened room like five similar portraits depicting various intensities of sunlight warped by old glass. When the bench bumped his shins, she said, 'Sit down a minute and wait.' The bench was hard against the bones of his buttocks, as he waited the way old people wait, floating on time, satisfied at how easy it was to stay afloat. She returned, giving another order, 'Stand up.' He obeyed the hand on his arm, standing exactly where she positioned him while she patted and fussed with the bench, until she commanded, 'Sit down again, and then I'll help you lie down.' She had covered the bench with a blanket. Her hands gripped his shoulder, leading him downwards, until he was stretched out. His weight held him there long after his better judgement had prompted him to make at least a weak effort to raise himself again. He felt far off a jostling at his feet, and his shoes dropping off, and then his head being grasped and lifted and released again on a pillow. He could not stay above the watermark of consciousness: he slipped beneath, he fell sleep.

When he woke up, she was sitting next to him on a chair, very close by, a soft dark occupant of his line of vision. She bent towards him, sponged his lips with a wet cloth. 'I'm not ill!' He struggled upright, and she muttered, 'You didn't get this by not dressing warmly enough.' That bit of common sense defused any rebellion. He let her have her way with him. 'Lie down!' she said again. And he lay back. His illness seemed to spread out, relax inside him.

When her hands began tugging at his limbs and torso, he did not resist. He permitted her to roll him this way and that. He did not know what exactly she was doing to his body, but he didn't question it. Gradually he felt suspended and utterly still. He smelled an odour he knew he considered repulsive but somehow he no longer objected to it. He inhaled it gladly. His tactile sense took stock of the situation and gave evidence of a springy softness against his chest. He thought it was a pillow at his side. The cloth itself seemed to stroke his cheek. He basked in a warmth that enfolded him without touching him, like an invisible blanket. He felt precisely that he existed.

A while later, a light went on in a corner, then another. Maid tiptoed about. The child clattered down the stairs shouting, 'Mama!' singing mightily, banging a fist on the piano. Benedikt heard Marja's voice very close to him, almost as though it were underwater, a rumble, which made the pillow next to his head shake. It did not rouse him enough for him to make sense of the situation. He enjoyed the sound, and then again the child's high voice chattering in Russian. As answer she suddenly grasped Benedikt's hand, held it up. The boy was nearby. Benedikt could smell him, an odour of sun on skin, and earth; he must have been playing outside. Why were his own hands being held up in the air? He realized Marja was showing Valerie the marks where the intravenous drip had been.

The child disappeared. A blue curtain neared Benedikt's face, a glass of water was pressed to his lips. He drank, aware of the square hand with its strong fingers and very soft skin close to his mouth. He was tempted to kiss it, to show his respect. Far away a television or radio chattered, and he welcomed it, because he could identify it—the fact that he had heard it hundreds of times and was hearing it again pleased him.

By now the pillow, the active hand had also become utterly familiar sensations. The hand smelled salty, of strong broth, he thought. He recognized it: old sweat. He sniffed for it. When he looked up he saw Marja's bosom and face from an odd perspective, from below, the line of her shoulder running into a long sinewy neck, the underside of her chin, an earlobe, the black tendrils of hair at the temples. He realized he was lying in her lap. He admitted a strange sense of dependence others call gratitude.

Gratitude, chuckled Einstein, who was following developments, is like a gleaming unknown berry in the forest—it can be nourishing or poisonous. Benedikt did not recognize the danger.

Nor did he object to his situation. He lay in his wife's arms and fell asleep. Much later that evening, he became alert enough to want to free himself from her comfortable lap. She did not restrain him but helped him sit up on his own, and then she stood up and left the room. He did not miss her, but he wondered where she had gone to.

Cook appeared and was genuinely concerned, shaking her head so that her bangs danced around on her forehead. She wrung her hands and groaned, 'I wish I was a nurse instead of a cook.' She had made soup for him, a dish she said she had invented, and soon Chauffeur came slowly across the hall, bearing a tray with a gilded tureen, a ladle, a matching bowl, and a monogrammed napkin and spoon.

The soup had at least satisfied Cook's artistic ambitions—all its ingredients were chopped up in exactly the same size. He ate with intensity, each spoonful seeming an affirmation of his returning strength, and did not mind that the Biesterfelds stood there watching him. Meanwhile Marja reappeared with Bertha's radio, switched it on, twirled the knob until she found a station with classical music, an orchestral work she apparently recognized because she clapped her hands in delight, and then she began to dance, an appalling clownlike dance. She pursed her lips in a pointy smile, tipped her head slightly, her eyes narrowed in a familiar expression he had always interpreted as self-satisfaction, as her full body went weaving about on delicate limbs, sending the blue cotton of his grandmother's old dress flapping. The child giggled and tugged at his hair in a fit of suspense, delighting in his mother's show. And Benedikt watched every movement she made, greedy for details of this entertainment.

That day the relationship between Marja and Benedikt became apparent. It was ghostlike to be sure, but it moved and breathed, and he could not ignore it. And this figure would inhabit the same room as he did, move next to him in the hours that followed the sweet relief at having recovered from his illness. When he went to sleep or got up in the morning, it was there, a presence in his thoughts. When he sat down at meals and Marja had not come, he wondered where she was, as if she were attached to him by an emotional elastic that went taut and pulled at him whenever she was not close by. He read in the hall or in his room and she sat next to him, invisible but tangible, she followed him to the toilet, commented on his production, and made him self-conscious whenever he even thought about her son. And with each hour this relationship to her seemed to get more powerful.

'Relationships,' sniffed Einstein, an old sufferer, 'are like living beings, with their own drives. They feed themselves, develop, each at its own pace, and like all living things they have an infancy, a youth, and inevitably they grow older. Often they die before the people who brought them to life.'

The relationship of Marja and Benedikt went unnoticed in its infancy, calling attention to itself when it had reached an uncomfortable, half-grown state, full of vitality, with criminal tendencies, provocative, dancing around, a pubescent monster. How can one get rid of an offspring that lives on its own? Impossible to murder it! It would resist a premature death, it would put up a big fight! All this was clear to Einstein, who could not entirely forget Benedikt and noted how he was suffering with this peculiar new companion. Einstein had experience—he had learned the hard way that relationships are more permanent beings than ancestors, that they go on existing after the persons who brought them to life are long gone.

Einstein liked strewing theories and hoarding the real truth for himself. He did not tip Benedikt off to the fact that there is an afterlife reserved exclusively for these strange beings, relationships, sources of feeling converted into energy, experience into a spectral mass. The evil ones among them, reeking of disappointment and hatred, come into one side of this afterlife, a place where bad feeling rages at maximum temperature. The good ones, usually young things snuffed in their flower, forbidden love affairs or old friendships based on mutual admiration and goodwill, come into another: 'And if there is such a thing as paradise,' Einstein sighed, 'then you can only find it there.'

CHAPTER 25

Smoothly: love begets confessions and all kinds of nastiness

That same afternoon that Benedikt lay on the sofa at home watching his wife dance, another kind of dance was taking place a few kilometres south of Schloss Biederstein, at Dolly's big comfortable house, in Lindau, where Hackse Sieseby had his vine-import business. Isabella, moping around at home until the university term started—she had few friends—had a visitor.

Dolly Sieseby had quizzed this guest, learning that he had come all the way down from Berlin to visit his parents, who turned out to live 200 kilometres further east. She recognized the broad-shouldered blond man, quaking with virile energy in a tight silk polo shirt and white linen trousers, as her brother's friend Schmidt. She asked him whether he could babysit for Isabella for a few hours, while she took the smaller children swimming. Schmidt thought she was reminding him of the age difference and was irritated; he did not like to be reminded that anyone was younger than himself. Cause enough for envy that Isabella was so pretty. Dolly deposited an armful of videos into Schmidt's lap—he had made himself at home on the sofa— obliged him to give her a critique of the films she had made of Benedikt's wedding, and left with her horde of children.

Schmidt and Isabella were not opposed to this small assign- ment. They put the first film on, sitting together on the sofa. They watched for a while until Schmidt jumped up with a gasp of exasperation and pushed the fast-forward button, and they both had a giggle, what a joke! But then, the wedding was a joke, was it not? Was there any evidence of happiness and love there or just the correctness of ceremony?

. . . The couple at the altar snap their mouths open and shut—lipreaders should guess what they're saying: maybe 'Ja, ja,' or 'Ha, ha.' Clap their naked hands together. Somehow, gold rings are involved. Peck once at the air near each other's cheeks, then they snake past the camera, never looking at each other once. The camera veers behind them, showing their backs, fleeing, into a rainstorm of confetti thrown by Dolly's children, the camera panning across their wild whooping faces, glimpses of the tired, glassy-eyed face of a boy different from the rest, standing on the sidelines, confetti turning to mud in his tightly clasped hand.

Flutter. Static . . .

The camera zigzags, apparently frantic. Finds the couple. Society newspaper photographers whisk in and out of their presence, like feeding fish. The groom's arm, at a command, yanks out, touches down around her shoulder. The camera appears to have an attack of laughter or heaves, suddenly bobbing up and down. Then it faces the floor . . .

The home audience had a laugh about that. But sitting on the old corduroy sofa close to Benedikt Schmidt was no laughing matter to Isabella. Isabella's whole being strained for union with him. She wanted to give her thoughts and her long perfect body to him, a spasm of generosity—if only he would accept! She touched him lightly on the forearm, awed by his short-sleeved blue shirt, astonished by the arm, incredulous about each freckle and each unique strand of blond hair growing there, the broad veins, the muscle, mostly from hauling the trash down to the garbage cans and tossing his brats in the air, but also from playing squash three times a week with another teacher. He did not respond to Isabella's fingertips brushing around there, his irritation at the film drowning out corporal sensations.

'Is that love?' he asked. 'It's grotesque. A travesty!'

'Terrible!' answered Isabella.

He felt contempt for her readiness to agree, for her naive

unselfishness. He remembered being that way with her uncle. He understood Professor Waller's behaviour for the first time: naked affection was not attractive. One had to keep it clothed. There was no affection so lovely that one could tolerate it nude for long. He recalled how Benedikt Waller had turned him out of his bed on their first night together, and then—he remembered one indignity after another. Memory ripped open this past hurt so that he felt Isabella's hand on his forearm as solace, and now he forgot his antipathy to her. At the same time he imagined that her parents had returned home and were watching them from the doorway, the children gaping, the mother interested, her father, the strong old man, his chest heaving with anger (and suspense) at the sight of his daughter making love . . .

Schmidt's sudden passion more than made up for its delay, in Isabella's eyes. She allowed him to pull her impossible dirndl-like frock up, right there on the shabby tan sofa, while the wedding ran on in fast-forward, his passion stoked by the certainty that the family was watching. The beautiful young woman was beyond caring about her parents; she experienced a fit of generosity so sweet, so overwhelming, that, in the process of giving, she gripped what she could of him. But all of a sudden, she felt his passion dwindle. She had nothing left to hold. He lay on top of her, made feeble motions, apologized. He blamed his lack of passion on a lack of concentration, on the situation.

'I'm a real tiger, otherwise,' he said. 'But here, on a sofa, with your parents walking in any moment and seeing us . . .'

She was confused and horribly embarrassed about her own willingness to forget this situation, her parents, about her lack of poise. She said nothing, waiting for him to get them both out of this jam. After all, he was older, a man—what use was strength if not to save one from disgrace?

He rolled off her, kissed her without conviction, and said, 'Quick, get into your clothes before they burst through the door. Christ, everything's all wet.' He dabbed at the sofa with his polo shirt.

Now, at last, she was no longer interested in her uncle. The moment Schmidt had slid into her, he had driven out of her consciousness all other affection she had felt for other men, her brothers, her father. Marvellous, the power of the shared shame one called intimacy.

'There's another matter that should interest you,' said Schmidt, buttoning his trousers, standing up, running a hand through his thick blond hair. 'The inheritance. Your uncle is flinging it away. The castle where your mother grew up. And your family.'

'It's not love at all,' said Isabella. 'I thought it was, I don't know why. I never questioned it. But he wants that child, you're quite right. Oh, my God!'

And then she repeated, 'Oh, I don't know,' a fragment that had accompanied steady sighs of confusion ever since she had met Schmidt. Everything had gone so fast that she had had no time to savour all the impressions she had registered, the details of his body: the chest, giving off a magic heat, the hair growing with precise boundaries, a map of his masculinity, his sexuality, so authoritative, not like her father's.

They sat in front of the television, leafing through women's-magazine articles about the recent true-love wedding of Count Waller von Wallerstein and a poor piano-playing Russian. The articles were short but comprehensive, the family lineage precisely conjugated, like a complicated irregular verb, through every turn and exception. There was speculation about the bride's family background—were the Golubs politically or professionally prominent? The bride had refused to comment. One thing was clear: she was proud to be part of this family, and she was going to do everything to keep up family tradition, including playing the piano just as Benedikt's father had done. There were small photographs of Benedikt as a child, his father playing an upright piano in the foreground, beaming into the camera, the soldiers crowded around him, a double-leaf spread of the wedding party, and several snapshots of the guests, including Isabella, as the most photogenic of the lot, and Schmidt either near or next to her. Schmidt and Isabella searched the photograph for signs of their future love. They found them in Isabella's modest expression in that otherwise endearing face—she had the smooth dense skin of a child, eyes so large that they seemed to hide her thoughts like screens, the regularity of her features producing a kind of plain prettiness or pretty plainness that stole the show from her intelligence.

Cleverness was evident in her mouth, which had many different poses, and the proof of her emotional state now was that her lips were always parted slightly, like those of any idiot. He wondered in a fit of irritation whether he would be the tiger if she didn't worship him so. He remembered the look of her legs with her frock pulled up, heart-shaped knees. She was tall, he reminded himself, as tall as he, as tall as his wife. But this did not impress him.

He chided himself for what he thought must be honesty: he simply did not desire someone he did not love. He remembered when the Wall went down and the street was suddenly full of brawny young workers from Eisenhüttenstadt—he had not paid the slightest bit of attention. Instead, he had devoted himself to an elderly man he had met in a café where he had gone just out of curiosity. He was an extraordinary man—a really famous professor of sociology, a friend of Adorno's. Unattractive, but it hadn't bothered him in the slightest. He had treated Schmidt with respect. Unlike Professor Waller.

'We must do something. We mustn't just wash our hands of it. I keep thinking of that poor child. Valerie. Immoral, really, to do nothing,' he added.

'But what?' she said.

Finally Schmidt concluded, 'I suppose one could inform the officials that Benedikt has an infectious disease. Not which one. That would bring the whole family into disrepute.' (He thought that she might consider him open-minded and generous to have anything to do with such an ill family at all. At the same time, his heart ached that she was impugned.) 'It would be a scandal. But you know, villagers know how to deal with scandals. And the Institute where he worked in Berlin, that's a little village, too.

Gossip is a powerful moral force. I think it's been developed just to save the species. But, Isabella, you'll have to pass the information on, not me. I mean, it's in your interest, not mine.'

'But how?' she asked. 'Should I just ring his institute and say by the way, about your Professor Waller . . .'

'No, no, you should write a letter to the editors of these magazines. Tell them the facts about this true love. They'll write a big article about the mistake they made. Actually, you're right about the Institute—hey, it's a good idea—you could come to Berlin and make an appointment to see them.'

'I could call Dr Anhalt right now,' suggested Isabella, anxiously. Her mother had the telephone number of the Institute in her address book. 'I'll make a date to see him in Berlin.'

Dr Anhalt was unpleasantly surprised to hear from Dr Waller's niece. She wanted to visit him. The gravity of what he feared her call meant pulled him downwards into an expenditure he otherwise made only for tax-deductible visitors: he decided to invite her to lunch. As he spoke, his hands turned cold, his heartbeat rapid, a dangerous condition for a man of his age and constitution. 'I have a funny story about Einstein and just this restaurant,' he blurted. His voice over the telephone was laden with dignity he no longer felt. Fate was tugging at him in a most bossy, unpleasant manner.

After he'd hung up, Dr Anhalt realized he had to do something to placate fate. He was a very vain man, that is, he was fond of himself and did not like to do the object of his affection any harm. But some forms of harm were worse than others. He did not want a big show when his relationship to East German science, as he thought of it, came out. He was still sitting in his institute, in the big leather chair of the chief, when something between desperation and hope waged a battle and reached a compromise.

Dr Anhalt grabbed his favorite prop, a fine calfskin briefcase from Florence, and took a taxi home. The spacious apartment was quiet. His wife was away visiting relatives. He had some pills to calm himself down if the day had been exhausting and he could not sleep. The look of those pills always reassured him: snowy-white compressed-powder relaxation. He took twenty of them.

Dr Anhalt wrote a note: 'My beloved Wife, My chronic depression leaves me no peace. I have put an end to myself. I swallowed twenty ten-mg Valium. Farewell.' He put the note in his jacket pocket, with his passport. Then he left the house, went for a walk, not entirely aimlessly; he kept within a five-street radius of a big hospital. He fell asleep at a red light.

Back at Lindau, Schmidt had been ill with envy at the ease with which Dr Anhalt, such a distinguished man, had invited Isabella, an unknown young girl, to lunch. Women had it easier. 'Maybe those kinds of men always like you!' he said. 'Famous men.'

'Once,' she admitted, 'I spent a whole evening with a really very famous man.'

Isabella had told the story:

. . . she had met a visiting writer at a university party after he'd given a reading. Everyone was in awe of him. He was French, small, balding, but very nice somehow, because he was so sure of himself. This gave him a kind of strut and a very straight back, as if he could easily bear the weight of the additional success surely coming to him. He was a Jew, Isabella added with respect, as if this were yet another intellectual qualification. The writer had stood about chatting after his reading. All the women were looking him straight in the eye and pretending to be in such good moods, until he had felt utterly trapped. He had suddenly turned to Isabella, whom he called 'Frau von Whatsit' as if he were trying to insult her, and said he was tired. 'I'm already asleep, but no one notices.' He asked her to drive him back to his hotel. Isabella was so flabbergasted and honoured she said yes, of course. They left, and on the stairs she remembered all she had was her bicycle.

She did not apologize or explain. She offered him the luggage rack. He had not expressed any surprise either, sitting down sidesaddle like a lady, laying his arms around her waist, and off they went. She could feel his hands waking up on her hips and belly. When they reached his hotel he invited her up for a drink. She could not say no to such a distinguished man . . .

Isabella paused to see whether Schmidt was interested. 'Go on go on go on!' he cried. He did hate suspense of any kind.

She continued:

. . . as soon as they were upstairs, he had undressed hurriedly and asked her to tuck him into bed. He climbed in, she tucked the covers around him as she always did with her little siblings, and he said, Now a bedtime story. As she cast about for something, he began talking himself, telling her how many centuries old fine Jewish families were, and what distinguished ancestors most had, he himself came from generations of Germans, he was as German as she, he swore, and then he interrupted himself, the curtains were not closed, it was bothersome. He hopped out of bed, jarring Isabella off too, and tugged at the curtains. But they wouldn't close, because one of the rings was tangled up at the top of the very tall window. He fumbled with it, stood up on a chair, stark naked in the window, but could not manage to shake the curtain loose. Finally he came down off the chair and asked if he could try sitting on her shoulders, she was so tall. She did as he told her. He mounted the chair again, made her stand in front of it with her back to him, and then he straddled her shoulders. She held onto him as he strained above her. It was useless . . .

Schmidt had stopped paying attention, nervous now.

'That's what happened. The curtain was really broken. I couldn't help him. So I went home,' said Isabella.

The film was running on and on, through several reels. 'I'm hungry,' complained Schmidt. 'Don't you ever eat here?'

They went to the kitchen and helped themselves to a big pot of stew.

They ate standing up and giggling about their hunger, forgot the unhappy incident a few minutes earlier. He tickled her to see if she would spill stew, she tickled him back; they ended up in an embrace, both holding their bowls behind each other. They kissed; heated, he ran his hand around her shirt, gasped what a shame he could not have her then and there, 'Look how hard I am.' He made her feel the evidence, and finally, reunited by this annoyance that they could not satisfy their desire for each other, they spoke with passion about Benedikt's marriage, his relationship to the Russian woman, his sickness, and the need to save those three from each other.

'Sometimes one shouldn't mind one's own business,' said Schmidt.

'Immoral,' agreed Isabella, who had never used the word before and felt it a rather alien notion, 'to do so.'

'There's the board of health too. And when you come to Berlin, we can see each other again. We just have to plan it. I can't keep coming down here to see you, anyway.

'And now let's finish the films so we can compliment your mother.'

CHAPTER 26

Slow rocking: Benedikt sets forth his plan to get rid of Marja

Benedikt gained back his strength in a matter of days; he enjoyed convalescence, as if the absence of pain proved the absolute value of living. Early one morning he woke up in the tower and spotted the road map of Switzerland spread on his desk. Although it was dark, he felt tired of sleep. The night had been soggy, the day would be worse. The boy would start asking his mother when 'Father' would finally go for his swim in the lake. He looked at the map and remembered his plan. He had little experience in making decisions for others, and so he assumed that if he'd decided on something, that proved it was right. He was well enough now to carry out his plan.

He went to their room, knocked on their door with his skeletal fist, and called, 'Please get up now. I'm taking a trip. To buy you the music you asked for.' He waited, and added for honesty's sake, 'I'm taking a roundabout way there. I'll drive where it's cooler. You're coming along.' He did not ever say 'we,' it was too strange a word.

She came to the door in her bathrobe and slippers. She screwed up her eyes, ran her hand through her hair, and tried to make sense of his fast way with words, ' "Roundabout"?' she repeated.

'Music,' he said. 'You wanted some music.' She did not protest or appreciate this. She showed neither pleasure nor worry, she didn't seem interested, she didn't enquire, ask, 'Where are we going?' He wouldn't have told her; someone as frightened of heights as she was might balk at the mention of mountains. 'We'll leave when you're dressed.' He managed a glimpse of the boy in a heap in his bed, his arms flung to the side, his face without glasses uncanny, so small.

Benedikt was scarcely excited—he stuck to his plan as if he were following a script. He went to the kitchen and ordered the cook to prepare a large picnic. She suffered a headache. Chauffeur had made a surprise proposition that soon they might take a long trip to Berlin, to see what was left of the Wall before it was gone altogether. She suspected he wanted to know what was left of his feelings for Seamstress.

'The seamstress,' he said, 'she thinks of me still. But no, I won't see her. I'm faithful to you. Although, if we're there, I suppose I could call her, have coffee with her. Ten minutes, no more.'

'But what will you do when she lunges at you—full of longing? I'm here for you always, I love you, but on one condition: there's no one else. One kiss and I'll leave you and never come back. But I'll probably die from a heart attack first. My chest is so tight. And also my head.'

Her voice had a natural vibrato that came from her quivering body. He couldn't afford just to lose her. There was no one else. The seamstress's letters were not so specific about whether she wanted him back. She might no longer want him, prefer someone else, for all that he knew, be madly in love, she was such a tart. Ah, but he wanted to see her.

'All that I want is to travel with you, drive with you next to me. Berlin in the night is a city unmatched,' Chauffeur replied. 'I'll pack for us both, you'll have nothing to do.' And of course she was caught in a vise.

Cook went to his wardrobe and took out the last pair of make-you-tall shoes he had hidden in there, the toe stuffed with letters. They were old ones, she'd read them before. She replaced them inside and toted the lot to the trash. On the way back she passed him and snarled, 'Not on your life will I drive with you there.' She knew he would sulk but he'd come round, he had no one else, just his car.

She still had to make Benedikt's lunch. She was not in the mood for great art. She got the old wedding cake out of the freezer where Bertha had stored it, for economy's sake. It had formed a strange sludge, and the wax couple adorning the middle were frozen in icing up to their knees. She packed a hamper with several containers of chopped specialties, picnic plates, cutlery, cups, and a bottle of juice. She felt it immoral for others to think about food when her head was unwell. But her pride in her talent was roused, so she added a tablecloth fit for a lawn, being green—colours should match—with the Wallerstein emblem embroidered on it. She carried the hamper herself to the salon table, set it down there, sat down as well, positioned herself with her head in her hands, and waited for someone to ask how she felt.

Bertha was first. She identified Cook's ache from the opposite end of the hall. The elderly Bertha was never inclined to waste sympathy. She saved it to spend on herself. She too could have headaches. Bertha slipped behind Cook into the Countess's room. How strange, how unchanged! The bed was turned down, the pillows still plumped. The house was entirely quiet. Bertha thought it an interesting room. Herr H. had arranged his personal videos down in the cloakroom. Her rump touched the edge of the bed and felt this a sign to sit down. Cook just outside could not bother her there.

Bertha was cross with the cook for teasing her about an old garbage bag. She had acquired the bag on a trip to the nearest big city. When she arrived, the local museum was lit up with posters and lights—they were having a bash. An artist whom everyone knew was attending his own exhibition—she admired the bakery bags he had painted.

Bertha addressed him. 'Pretty bags,' she exclaimed. He heard from her accent that she was a Saxon. Faraway Saxony . . .

'You're from the East!' he exclaimed. 'I'm glad you could come.' Generosity was widespread that year. He picked out his prettiest bag, signed it across one long side with a fillip, the signature famous, and gave it to her.

'For you. Welcome.'

Bertha had taken the bag and hurried away. She bought herself chocolate for the bus ride home and packed it inside. And when she was home she had an idea: it fitted exactly into the wastebasket in the bathroom. Herr H. had always liked bags in his wastebaskets.

Cook had found out and thought it a shame that the East German citizens had no idea. She said it just once, but once was enough. She'd never get solace from Bertha again.

Benedikt also ignored Cook's condition. He thanked her for taking the trouble to make them a lunch and struggled alone with the hamper downstairs, to the car, where Marja and Valerie waited, gnawing on chips and tippling soda. Marja was lighting a cigarette butt she had saved. 'I'm all out,' she said, blowing the smoke to the side, so that it wouldn't get in his face. She had dressed herself and her son in the clothes they had worn to the wedding—Marja in her white dress, the boy in grey flannel trousers and white buttoned shirt. They sat in the back.

· At midmorning they left, driving south. Nearing the border to Switzerland, Benedikt asked for her passport. Marja surrendered her Soviet document, gold hammer and sickle embossed on the cover. He tucked this into his shirt pocket, next to his own. The guard waved them through, not suspecting his plan. When he stopped to get gas, he asked them to stay in the car. He strolled to the other side of the station and disposed of her passport, inserting it into the slot of a metal trash can already filled up with wrappers and leftover sweets and ice cream. The wasps swarmed out of the slit as the document landed.

It was noon when they turned off the road and onto another that led along hills that seemed trapped at the roadside, a landscape where any natural incentive to grow had been thoroughly squelched by middle-class Swiss industriousness, mowed, ripped out, clipped, badgered into submission. Marja remarked, 'They keep nature inside concentration camps here.' Benedikt, used to

remarks of this sort, ignored her and savoured the knowledge
that soon he would no longer have to ignore her.

On the left side of the road, the hills became steeper, the
villages stationed like watch towers. They stopped at a restaurant, used the bathrooms, and the child wanted chocolate. Marja
complained that she had no Swiss money, in fact she'd no money
at all. This news put her husband into a quandary. He did not
want her hungry but knew she was helpless without any money,
and that would be best. He gave her some francs, just enough for
the chocolate, but she bought herself cigarettes first and addressed him, her mouth full of smoke, 'I need more.'

They continued, drove south, turned off the highway and
onto a road that went winding in serpentines alongside a mountain, where man's power was useless: he had no more than the
right to pass through. At first the road was packed in by forest
and chasms and waterfalls. Later the landscape grew bare, the
cliffs leaned in menacing postures over the road, signs, beaten up
by the weather, warned about rock slides and avalanches. Marja
was silent. He thought she was probably fighting the terrible
panic she felt—he knew about fear now. The altitude change
made the boy feel unwell. He complained that his ears hurt, and
Benedikt stopped by the side of the road and told him to yawn.
Valerie cowered, his hands over his ears—pain made him docile.
Benedikt, driving again, observed this with wonder and fought
satisfaction at finding a means to control the child's moods.
Marja scolded in Russian, but he didn't respond, his face un-
harmonious, his eyes all askew, his mouth pulling up at one side.
When the pressure inside his small ears equalized suddenly, popping, he cried out and smiled in relief. Still, he worried that it
would return, sat back in the seat, watching the road with anxiety. His fear had at least calmed down his mother.

Finally they came up through the clouds like a plane. The
sky had a blue so intense that the child winced again, so that
Benedikt, watching him, swerved and slowed down. Valerie was
staring outside: the blue of his eyes seemed to draw the blue

from the sky. His mouth fell open in wonder, the teeth lay inside like little white stones. They soon cleared the tree line, the road levelled off, and they reached the pass, the ground a flat surface smeared with old snow, wearing a thin beard of vegetation. Further along a glacier had poured in a slow torrent from a peak and was receding again, at the speed of a metre per century, leaving behind a track of rubble and rocks.

'Up at its top,' Marja remarked, as if to distract herself from her fear, 'land has the silence and brilliant colour of deep sea: the same blues, greens, and blacks.'

She was no longer afraid. After all, the ground there was flat, one couldn't fall off, one did not have to fly. She wanted to walk on the glacier. He felt patient with her, strange as her wishes were, parked at the side of the road, and let her get out with their son. He watched them amble around, Valerie moping a bit at her side, sneaking a look at the snow. Almost slyly, as if it were a matter of pride not to show too much interest, he was picking up stones from the glacier, dropping a few in his pocket. When Benedikt turned on the ignition they scuttled straight back to the car. It was not much further now to what he considered Marja's stop. He imagined that on his return he'd be in the car with his son and Marja would be on her own. He'd been alone for most of his life and preferred it that way. As they came down from the pass, a fork in the road made him slow down, but he not only slowed down but stopped, as if to draw the finality out of what was in store. One road was wide and well travelled, leading to Italy, the other was small, and led to a town at the foot of a mountain, where Benedikt parked. Through the window, his wife spotted the gondolas. The mere sight of them worried her. They rocked in the wind and they whined.

The town square was decked out for festivities. Long tables were set with check tablecloths, and platters of cheese that the farmers had brought, and bread that their wives had baked for the town's nine hundredth birthday. The villagers strutted about with suppressed joviality; their costumes restrained them. They had on their family clothes, the older the better, submitting to layers of cloth pulled tight to highlight the waistlines on women, the calves on the men, as if these were the characteristics one needed to know to tell the sexes apart. These costumes were taken out of storage once every few years, aired for a day, but neither the clean mountain air nor the heavy use of eau de cologne could rinse out or drown out the mothballs; the village square on its birthday smelled like an attic.

Up a slight incline, the ski lift ran like a factory belt, even though most of the gondolas carried no one at all. 'Since you don't like heights, you can wait for us here. I'm taking the child,' Benedikt said. 'You wait right down here.'

'He won't like it either,' she said. 'We'll wait for you here. Besides, he is hungry again!'

'He'll like it a lot,' Benedikt promised. And then a moderate postponement of his plans occurred to him, a treat for Marja before he left her. 'We'll have lunch, we'll eat first.'

Together they carried the basket that Cook had prepared. He led them out of the square, and over a field, through a forest, remembering the way without effort: his sister had forced him along the same path decades ago. He had conceded to all her demands. Over the years this journey repeated itself as a vague memory. He remembered the fright he had felt as the very last time he'd been frightened at all: he'd absorbed enough popular culture to fear that the landscape would stir up romantic ideas in her like a hornet's nest. He had kept a great distance between them, avoided all bodily contact with her, and said not a word till she finally conceded to his terrible mood and suggested they turn back again. He had no idea now as to why he wanted to return, twenty years later, following an impulse, like any subordinate carrying out orders, in this case the commander unknown, out of reach, inside himself.

The path crossed a wide field. They sauntered abreast of each other, the hamper swaying between them. The child stayed to her far side, and Benedikt tasted the joy he would feel when this woman was no longer blocking the way emotionally. He imagined her gone, and the air was much clearer, easier to breathe, and next to his son's feet, treading the path, he pictured his feet and they picked up and set down, they no longer limped. But the path now posed dangers. It became very narrow, running alongside a gorge. There wasn't a railing, the incline was steep perpendicular rock, with a furious river roaring below. One wrongly placed foot and your feet were no use, only wings would transport you. He remembered his sister skipping about on the edge; she had always loved danger as long as she stayed in control. It was odd that Marja, who must have been terrified, did not complain, did not show any signs of discomfort. Perhaps there was no point in showing it—going back down would be worse.

Eventually the path turned from the ravine, through a wood, and came out on a field of wildflowers, surrounded by sawtoothed mountain peaks gleaming in the sun. There were no houses in sight. Benedikt's legs were beginning to hurt him, his limp became audible. She looked over at him with a frown of concern and suggested, 'Let's have a rest.'

He realized that she had been worrying about him so much that she had forgotten her own fear of heights.

Affection, like nausea, travels through human psyches in waves. Benedikt tried not to notice.

They searched for a tree to serve as a parasol but found that the sun was polite, even at noon never forcing itself on those in its presence, and so they set down in a field. Marja unfolded the tablecloth, neatly unpacked the artwork of Cook's chopped-up fruit, chopped-up meat, and pudding, the sludge of the cake, fully melted. The newlywed couple in plastic was gone, sunk to the bottom of the bowl.

They sat down around this. Valerie proved not the slightest bit hungry, but Benedikt urged Marja to eat, knowing it could be a while before she had her next meal.

She fished the drowned couple out of the cake, held it aloft, and addressed it. 'There are stores here, of course, where music is sold. The cows and the bees line up, eager to buy.'

Benedikt nibbled, in order to give an example of what should be done now rather than talking. He did not enjoy knowing more than she did about what lay ahead, wielding power over her, but he had no choice. And forced by disquiet he too began talking, he asked her if she'd ever seen such high mountains before.

'Much higher,' she said. 'We've much higher mountains at home. I travelled a lot there. I had something to do. I have nothing to do here. But at least in your house, I can play. Here in the mountains I can't even practise.'

The boy was far off in the field picking flowers. He returned once in order to hurl a bouquet in his mother's direction, then ran off again, embarrassed perhaps by the niceness he'd shown.

Marja accepted the gesture as sweet. She spread the bouquet on the blanket, inspecting each flower, saying '*Schön, oh wie schön,*' seeming to mean it. She picked out a larkspur, crowded with tiny white petals, and she started to rip it apart, petal for petal, mumbling in Russian. The child drifted back, stood nearby, his eyes turned away, surreptitiously listening, as Benedikt was.

Marja soon noticed and said, 'Even numbers mean bad luck, and odd ones mean good luck.'

He felt this a put-down. 'Numbers,' he said, 'individual numbers. More special than people. You brutalize them if you sort them like that. Valerie must have a favourite number, let's ask him.'

'Favourite number,' she said lazily, plucking the larkspur bare. 'Valerie, tell us your favourite number. My favourite number is one. An old classic. Valerie's favourite number is "more." And yours, Benedikt?' She had never addressed him by name before. All those weeks she had somehow avoided it. He had never noticed, till now. The sound of his name in her mouth simply shocked him, a sudden calamitous intimacy. She'd finished her task, the flower was bare, she tossed it away in the grass. 'Good luck,' she said cheerfully. Valerie left, went hopping away on one foot.

After a while she packed up the basket, put everything back, and stretched out at the edge of the tablecloth. He sat with his legs crossed and watched her. She was murmuring something. He listened.

'You know that your grandmother told me things I was never supposed to tell you. Funny. Maybe I'll tell you. I don't think she will mind.'

He listened.

'Your father,' she said, 'didn't die in that car crash at all. He survived. He was lamed. In a wheelchair. The day he came home, it was cold, it was winter. And he disappeared. They found him much later. He had gone in his wheelchair out to the lake, and onto that pier. Maybe he wasn't so skilled with a wheelchair, or he was weak. And it rolled off the end of the pier. It landed upright so his head and his waist were way above water. But cold, individual number, it was five below zero.

'Your grandmother said every day afterwards she could hear very clearly the creak of his wheelchair rolling along on the planks of the pier—only Valerie's singing made her forget it.'

Benedikt was annoyed at his grandmother's confidences. He didn't remember his father. Why should he care how he died?

Marja went on, 'Funny thing, about luck. I've got good luck. For example, I've witnessed two people choking, but nothing bad ever happened to me, I always see bad things happening to others. My sister was married. Her husband was a cellist, and everyone liked him. But she fell in love with a fireman. My parents were angry. They wouldn't allow her to leave the musician. "You're trading a Stradivarius for a water hose!" they screamed. "Forget him, your fireman!"

'He was Latvian, a brute, by the way. He didn't fit into the family at all. But my sister insisted. She said he was nice, and so handy, could douse raging fires, cut accident victims from cars, knew all sorts of tricks about keeping people alive . . . We met to discuss the matter with her. I was forced to go home back to

Leningrad to assist on the project of bringing my sister back to her senses. My mother had cooked. We sat down, all the aunts and the uncles, the brothers and sisters. We talked. It was my fault, as usual. I told a bad joke. And we laughed. Everyone laughed. We all laughed so hard that we cried. We were bent over, holding our stomachs. My father was blue in the face. We thought: Well, from laughing. But then he was making such weird gasping noises. Maybe from laughing. We stopped and we watched him. He was blue in the face. And my sister ran over to him, her arms circled his chest from behind. And she squeezed with her fists deep inside him. Till a sausage came popping up out of his throat. Her fireman taught her that, how to stop someone choking. After that, we all begged her to marry him. Too bad I never asked her to show me that trick.'

Her voice was inaudible now, although she kept talking, the stories bubbling out of her. She lay stretched on her back, her legs crossed, her eyes closed. Then she was quiet. She turned on her side, her head in the crook of one arm, the other arm stretched over to him, palm upwards. She slept. Valerie crouched down at her side, at her back, and continued to pluck at the grass, talking in Russian, occasionally singing a snatch of a song under his breath, refusing to look at his father. Soon he was bored, he seized fistfuls of grass, and then he moved off a few metres, searching the ground for something of interest. Benedikt had nothing better to do: he studied her hand.

He remembered how skilful it was, and thought he saw proof of that in the strength of the palm, the length of the thumb, while the perfect half-moon on each nail was a sign of her grace when she played. The wrist was not strong, and the arm was slight, with very white skin. He followed the flesh to the sleeve, he inspected the neck, then the crescent of cheek, the jaw's geometry, the swirl of her ear. He saw them all as a series of lines, abstract, unrelated, until all of a sudden, they came into focus as something: a face. The skin had a dusky colour and texture; she was, he recalled, much younger than he. Her face was familiar, her hand was the servant and lord of her talent, her body had warmed him. He thought it was marvellous, really, what she could do with her hands and her body. He found he admired her.

After a while, he moved closer to her, in order to see her more clearly. He looked at the inside of her arm, while desire to touch what he saw brought his fingertips right to that surface. But it proved very smooth, and smoothness feels empty, as if nothing is there. He looked at her face. His fingertips travelled the length of her cheek, were about to touch down.

Her eyes opened suddenly, two dazzling suns sliding out from the clouds.

CHAPTER 27

Frantic: Isabella sets all sorts of cogs into motion, without realizing it

The tarot cards were giving Isabella advice. The dialogue of the cards and Isabella's fingers rent the entire house, with its peculiar thunder of shuffling and then of fate slamming the selection downwards onto the coffee table with a snap-snap-snap.

All day long Isabella sat on the beige living-room sofa, her feeling of space distorted by the awareness that he, Schmidt, had sat on the sofa, gulping the very air of old cotton curtains and Dolly's spice collection. She asked the cards again and again for their opinion, and then they became her way of keeping tabs on his exact state of mind:

What is he thinking this minute?

And the cards always gave an answer. She did not accept the answers that said he was happy. She shuffled and pulled again, so that it did not take long for her to establish that he longed for her, that he thought compulsively about her day and night, that his happiness was her happiness, and, what's more, they were going to have a child together. Whereupon she packed her suitcase and told her parents she was going to spend the last few days of the holidays in Berlin, stay in her uncle's flat, he wasn't there, clean it up for him.

Dolly said, 'Call him and ask him for the key.'

But Cook reported her uncle wasn't home—that same morning he had taken his family on a trip, information that made Dolly look old and worn. This condition was aggravated by her daughter's insistence on leaving right away.

'We don't want you to,' said Dolly, speaking for her husband, who hadn't a clue. 'Not on your own, with nowhere to go, other than to that man, Schmidt—I can never remember his first name.'

Dolly knew that her daughter had a good heart, that she was intelligent and beautiful, and that none of the above protected a young woman from harm at the hands of a man she happened to like. Dolly believed in the necessity of disappointment, or life would be dull—she had never given her children what they wanted for Christmas. If they still longed for the same thing when Easter came, then they had a fair chance of receiving it; more likely they had to wait until the following Christmas. She didn't dally with Isabella's problem. She was busy with her younger children who had started the new school year, and she considered her eldest daughter 'out of the house,' even if she was still living there during university holidays.

Nor did Dolly question her daughter's obedience. This had practical grounds: Isabella had always had money in her pocket. Dolly had seen to that. It had been her strategy. Then, if she ever needed leverage over her daughter, she could withhold funds and the girl would be helpless. Not only did she forbid Isabella the trip to Berlin—from the moment her daughter had broached the subject, Dolly gave her no more money.

A miscalculation: Isabella was so well protected that she had no fears about being poor. She had some money, not enough for the train fare perhaps, but nevertheless: enough. She slipped out of the house in the evening, left a note for her parents on her desk saying that she was going to Berlin to clean up her uncle's apartment. At the wedding, Dr Graf had mentioned that he had the key. She would be back in a few days.

By the time Dolly found the note, Isabella was on the outskirts of Berlin. She had not really had to hitchhike. She had simply walked for a while through town and stopped the first car at the first red light she came to, knocked on the window, and asked the astonished driver if he by any chance was on his way to Berlin. Two hours earlier, the young driver had been released from prison after serving five years of a ten-year sentence for armed robbery. He had discovered Jesus in the process. His mother had picked him up from prison with a new car, and driven him home, and said the car is for you, to make a new start. The young man was driving aimlessly around when the blond young girl with the innocent face knocked on his window. He thought she looked like an angel. He thought this might be a test from God. So he said, 'Sure, I'll take you to Berlin,' and he drove very carefully through the night with his precious cargo, determined to make a good impression on his Saviour. He was afraid to look at her for fear of having his eyes burned out, much less talk to her, so that the conversation that Isabella initiated never got beyond his hurried, 'Uh-huh,' and she soon gave up. He dropped Isabella near her uncle's apartment, did not pay the slightest attention to her protestations of gratitude; he was in a hurry to call his mother, explain, and get back. It was already late morning.

Isabella called Dr Graf at the Institute and asked if he by any chance had the keys to her uncle's apartment. He did not.

Isabella hinted that she needed a place to stay for a few nights in Berlin but Dr Graf, picturing her in her pink wedding costume, offered, 'I can recommend some cheap pensions. If you need help with the cost, I'll gladly pay for it.' She accepted; he cursed the necessity of seeing her to hand over the money.

'I'll find a place, and then come to see you. Unfortunately, I haven't any money whatsoever,' she said without any qualms, adding in all honesty, 'just enough for this phone call.'

She hung up, and despite her fatigue, she spent the next hour hiking to Schmidt's address, a neighbourhood with playgrounds for the children, which she treated with the respect of a pilgrim for his destination. She sniffed the air, took in the details of the cobblestones, his, his, his. Then she backtracked to the city centre, checking into a cheap pension as Isabella Sieseby. The manager gave her a map of Berlin and recommended a tour of the Wall, but she had not the faintest interest. Instead, she lay back on the bed or sat at the desk or stood in the window or just paced, while imagining Schmidt, Schmidt just coming home from school, tossing his children in the air, kissing his wife, watching television with her, sprawled next to her (she must be beautiful!) on the sofa. Nonetheless, her own claims to him were strong. 'We're going to have a baby.' Or were they?

Isabella took her grandmother's tarot cards and asked them how long it would be before she had his baby. The cards were not good at dates. When the cards told her he would be home and glad to hear from her, she dialled the number he had given her 'for emergencies.' He did not seem to be surprised at her voice. Nor very interested either. He said, 'I'll come by and see you in the morning.' And there was nothing else to say.

She hung up and thought: Twenty hours, impossible length of time, such suffering! Hours insurmountable as walls and jail bars. What do you say, cards? But the cards were annoyed at being asked twice. They gave lousy answers. She became so tense that she called him back. This time his voice was slightly unfriendly, harder.

'I've already called the Institute,' she said, 'to tell them about my uncle. I'm going to see his colleague Dr Graf later.'

He replied, 'I thought you were going to write to those magazines.'

'I'll do that too.'

'Good,' he said and then he added very softly, so that someone in another room could not hear, 'you can let me know tomorrow what they say at the Institute.'

'Fine, then,' she said.

She knew she had let him down, because she hadn't written those letters, as she had promised.

'Dr Graf, this is Dr Waller's niece, again, Isabella. I've found a hotel.'

'How is he?'

'Well, that's what I wanted to talk to you about anyway. You know that he's very ill.'

'Of course I know.'

'Do you know what he has?'

'Miss Waller. We are all going to die someday. If you want to talk about it, give Dr Anhalt a call.'

Dr Graf wanted nothing to do with a young woman. His stepdaughter was still a problem for his conscience. It had been so singular that nothing afterwards could compare. Worse, the episode remained fresh in his memory. He could not eat without thinking of it. Nevertheless, like a moth drawn to fire, he apologized to Isabella for his rudeness and invited her to have lunch with him at home. He hadn't had a visitor in years.

Isabella came, dressed, to his distaste, in one of her dirndl frocks, shyness bending her graceful back into a slouch. From her point of view, the lunch was not a success. Everything she said about Dr Waller bounced off the man, who made no secret of his incredible lack of interest in her, his hurry to get the meal over with (why had he bothered to invite her?).

> He's got a horrible illness.
>> 'Umhum. Umhum.'
>> Now he's married. But he's going to die soon, it
> was immoral of him.
>> 'Umhum. Umhum.'

Dr Graf, too, considered his invitation a failure, but because his guest had not succeeded in interesting him. He could not even follow her conversation. His own 'Umhum's covered up the same old thoughts:

> Dying Hannah, bad-tempered Hannah.
>> And Klara here next to me.
>> 'Blah Blah.'
>> Hannah could not see us. I kissed Klara.
>> She did not talk as much.
>> 'Blah Blah.'
>> Afterwards she became fat, and could not dance
> anymore.

'It is impossible!' cried Dr Graf, hovering at the stove, managing to look elegant even in an old apron. 'I cannot listen to you and cook at the same time.'

She was offended, sat in the living room waiting for him to finish cooking, but when he was finished he did not pay attention to her, because he was eating his soup. 'Shouldn't talk when eating,' he said. 'It ruins the enjoyment.'

Food was all he cared about! she raged, eating as quickly as she could.

When they were finished, he took her plate and said, 'I'll show you to the telephone. Call Dr Anhalt, talk to him. He's your man, he runs the Institute.' He was fighting a terrible urge to kiss her. He hadn't kissed a woman in years; he did not know how to.

'But I've already made an appointment with Dr Anhalt,' replied Isabella. 'He's taking me to lunch tomorrow.'

'Did he say something about veal soup?' asked Dr Graf.

'How did you know?'

'I'll show you to the door now,' said Dr Graf. 'Here, take this.' He shoved a great deal of money into her hand. 'That should do, shouldn't it?' She pocketed it without counting.

Back at the pension, the sound of tarot cards being shuffled at a hysterical speed alerted the owner to something fishy going on. It was important to eavesdrop. She heard the phone: 'Dr Anhalt. This is Isabella Sieseby. Ah yes, Isabella Countess of Sieseby, yes, that's right, Count Waller von Wallerstein's niece. I'm in town and will meet you tomorrow as planned.'

The landlady had a pleasant shock. She recognized the name. She hurried back to her room and fumbled for her magazine. The family had been mentioned recently. It had interested her. The bride was Russian. And there was a photo of her playing the piano. In the text she read, 'The bride playing the diabolic variations.' In the background she saw the pretty young Countess listening.

The landlady deliberated about placing a call to the magazine. Was it not newsworthy—a countess visiting the big city? She imagined having her pension mentioned in the magazine. It was certainly worth risking a call. The telephone number was listed right at the front. Obviously, the editors relied on the public for information.

'Hotel Central, Frau Wirth speaking. I wanted to pass on that the Countess of Sieseby is staying here.' She hung up, thrilled to have talked to the press personally. They seemed interested. They had taken her telephone number.

The magazine had a journalist in Berlin who had flubbed an interview with a film star. His editor told him he might as well have a word with the Countess, who knows, maybe there's a picture story there. The journalist and a photographer arrived while Isabella was having a lot of trouble formulating a letter to the same magazine. She was about to give up. She was about to call off her relationship with Schmidt—she really hated writing letters, and if that was the condition, well then, she realized her dream was hopeless. Realism was just nudging Isabella back to the dry shore of proper behaviour when the landlady, bristling with hope and excitement, showed the journalists to her pension-room door.

Isabella guessed that Schmidt had contacted them. She felt hope again—he was obviously understanding about her inability to formulate.

She had little instinct as to how to handle the predators. They stood about the room while she sat at the dressing table, her fingers working the tarot cards. They were excited: the story that she was too shy to tell, that nevertheless came from her in fits and starts, was much better than they had expected. They gathered that her uncle was terminally ill, that he had never had a girlfriend before, to her knowledge, he had been 'married to mathematics,' that he did not care two figs about his family or the family history, that he had no 'normal' relations with anyone—she could not say more beyond that an old German family was being decimated. Isabella did not enjoy this story *per se*. It was not her idea of fun to tell strangers who had no idea of her family, their way of life, their responsibility to others, over centuries. But when she spoke, she heard Schmidt speaking, and she loved Schmidt and loved hearing him speak, so the words she used were his words, her voice was his voice, and her inflamed passion added a vehemence even Schmidt did not feel about the subject.

After the journalist had heard everything he wanted proof, or at least specific details. She was refusing to answer. He kept asking, but she resorted to small talk about her wonderful family:

> Which illness? Come, tell us, which illness?
> 'Blah Blah.'
> Is he homosexual? Dear girl, you must say. Dammit, it matters!
> 'Blah Blah.'

Isabella felt trapped and embarrassed. The photographer found her facial expression especially lovely like that, as she sat at the dressing table, the mirror reflecting her graceful back as a trellis for her blond hair, while the front view showed her long white hand cupping a face that seemed to them to embody the mystery of the aristocracy: the simple features, eyes that betrayed no emotion. But in fact she was longing for Schmidt and wondering why her longing did not bring him to the door at once. There was a knock at the door. Relief streamed: that it worked, that wanting the man she loved made him listen, made him respond, made him come to her. She watched the journalist stand up to open the door, her eyes suddenly expressive: shining with joy.

It was another reporter.

The landlady was keeping busy. She had even roused a couple of foreign correspondents from prestigious daily newspapers. Germany was a popular beat that year. And the second one to visit managed to break Isabella's reticence. He was a pale-faced American who had climbed young to the near top of his career, where there was no shade and no cover from other eyes and the sun of his colleagues' envious attention. And then he had not managed the peak. This gave him a weatherbeaten, downtrodden air, that mixture of arrogance and fatigue that Isabella identified as fatherly. She poured out her heart: about her uncle, about his illness, about the refusal of the Russian child to go near his new father, and about her uncle's complete lack of interest in the mother—the marriage was a farce, there was no love involved. She mentioned her own love for her uncle's best friend. She did not care anymore whether someone knew or not. The colleagues who followed received fluent versions of her story. Talking to them proved a good way to fill up the afternoon hours. It occurred to her that her parents might be worried; then she hustled the thought from her mind.

Dolly was indeed worried. She had no idea where her daughter was. She had called Dr Graf in Berlin, interrupting him as he watched a sports show. She heard the game in the background, she knew what that meant. 'I'm terribly sorry,' she blurted.

'Think nothing of it,' he replied. 'I was always the one who had to answer the phone if it rang during a football match at Bergen-Belsen. By the way, your daughter visited me just an hour ago.' He reported that he had given her money. Dr Graf was terse. He did not want to be bothered. He did not know where Isabella was staying. He promised to call Dr Anhalt in the morning or meet them at lunch.

Dolly had called the chauffeur, Alfred von Biesterfeld, and begged him to drive to Berlin as quickly as possible and pick up Isabella. Chauffeur had agreed at once. Cook had no time for a tantrum. It was better to make herself indispensable—while he was changing the oil in the car, she packed Chauffeur's suitcase with his nicely ironed shirts, and then she packed her own and announced she was coming along.

At that very minute, on a mountainside in Switzerland, Benedikt was looking into the yellow eyes of his bride, his fingertips brushing the velvet of her cheek.

CHAPTER 28

Forced: a climax, but rather different from the planned one

N*ein, nein!'* she bellowed, and slapped at his cheek. 'Never touch me!' She beat at his hand. Her face had the texture of a lily, her features set in a pattern he did not recognize. 'Swine!' Her arm swung. She was standing up over him, and he could no longer analyse what was going on. The blows were falling on his head, shoulders. As he fell over they picked up speed. They melted into one long continuous pain up and down his back.

He tried to roll over and stand up to escape them, managing to haul his knees beneath him. He knelt before her. She kept swatting him, her nails cutting his cheeks, his neck. He heard her say, 'I am not a hostage of gratitude!' He was astonished that she knew such complicated words in German. She kept going, each emphatic word fell on a blow: 'I take it back, all I did for you. I was there for you any time you wanted me, I played for you, all day, you could hear me, I agreed to stay with you, to marry you, look after you when you were ill. And I'm not grateful, no, I'm not, why should I be?' He was standing up. The blows fell on his back, her nails scratched his arms, his face. She could not stop.

But after a while, he no longer felt the blows or his own surprise. He stood there, his head thrown back, facing upwards, studying the sky with a kind of abstract interest. He noticed something peculiar happening: very slowly, as if a giant paint-brush were sweeping over it, the expanse was turning green. He regarded this transformation with fascination; it was, after all, the first time he had deliberately looked at the daytime sky, only to witness a natural phenomenon. He wondered what might have triggered this sudden change at the atomic level. Finally he understood the green: he was lying face down in the grass.

His face began to burn. He felt an ant whisk away. Something crawled inside his pants, and a wasp seemed to explode into his ear. He flipped over and sat up, his eyes greedy, grasping for the sight of Marja and Valerie. His gaze was not rewarded. His gaze prowled among the peaks, looking for movement, the white flying flag of Marja's dress. He stayed on the ground with the insects munching on him while he grilled the scenery for details. There were none. A farmhouse lay like a boulder at the bottom of a mountain peak. Terror moved as if it were a living thing inside him, the fear of having done something with irreversible consequences. Marja and Valerie were gone. The mountains stood about him, witnesses to this laughable human drama and emitting silence, a complicated code.

He staggered after them, downhill, along the path, along the chasm, chanting to himself as he went, 'Careful! Careful!' gravity tearing at him, until he was no longer in control. He could no longer keep his feet under him. He flew.

The oompah-pah band greeted him, lean old men with strong white teeth and faces hard as rinds. The villagers in their costumes twirled around him, singing, their lips glistening with soup. He adjusted his eyes to respond only to a young woman with a dark-haired boy, and his ears to the sound of Russian. The music stopped and a voice cried out in Swiss-German, 'Nine hundred years ago!' Benedikt was pressed away by the crowd that released him at the edge of the square, only to be swept up by an eddying stream of hikers in gaudy sportsmen's dress. He was washed up at the entrance to a restaurant; he went in.

'There's no room for you!' called the waitress gaily. 'Do you want to wait?'

He stood and waited. Newcomers pressed in behind him. After a while he found himself sitting down at a table with two middle-aged men exuding the cautious self-satisfaction of older but still healthy animals. Benedikt belonged to a different species, and the waitress punished him for it by ignoring him. The two men at the table extracted photos of children from their wallets and exchanged them, studied them, as if they were yet another bit of important evidence that they were living well. They pointed at details, discussed them in Swiss-German, a language guttural, hostile to Benedikt's ears. The waitress served them and skirted the German.

'A tea for me, please,' he called after her. She did not acknowledge him.

The two diners fed, their conversation temporarily stopped. Then they pushed their plates away, lit cigarettes, and began discussing business in High German but with Zurich accents. They were lawyers. One of them unhappily explained certain changes in inheritance law. 'One has to warn the families to start moving the money out as soon as death gives a signal that it's waiting,' he said.

No one could make sense of the thin city guest suddenly standing up, this movement throwing the table forwards so that it crashed against his neighbours' full bellies. He held his mouth wide open, but nothing came out. After a few seconds, the restaurant was riveted by the sound of a grown man yowling, a terrifying sound, a perverted yodel.

The waitress felt it was her fault for refusing to take his order. Oh, those Germans.

'Home home home home,' he chanted, stepping on the accelerator. He had the hope, based on no evidence other than hope, that they would be in Biederstein. He hurried to them, he soared through the late afternoon by car. The evening came up from behind as he turned off the mountain road, back to civilized lowland again. It was dark as he reached the German border, where the prowling guards did not bother him. He arrived in Biederstein, had trouble unlocking the gates in the glare of the car headlights, and enraged the dogs by driving past so fast that the wind in his wake blew them about. The house was dark. He parked, got out of the car, but did not go inside. Instead he picked his way along the path towards the lake. In the night, there was life everywhere, it flew and wriggled around him, brushed and stung and clung to him, while the mud of the foot-path sucked at his feet. He reached the pier. The planks creaked as if someone were moving along them.

The lake jutted into the darkness like a sharp-edged obstacle. He passed the pier, found the edge of the water, crouched, and dangled his fingers into the brine. The warm water exercised no pull. He was scared. He drew formulae on the surface with his index finger, and they turned into identical waves, drifting into the reeds.

He undressed, folded his clothes, and laid them on a patch of grass behind him. He went into the fetid, warm lake. He pushed off. Great fear made him fight the water, and his strokes became choppy, panicked. Nevertheless he forced himself forwards, to-wards the dangerous reeds. Within seconds he was up to them, swimming through them; they reached for his face and shoul-ders. They caressed him. The temperature was even warmer there and the stagnation suffocating. The clouds broke open in one spot, and the moon beamed through. He had the desire, which he identified as absurd, to say goodbye to the sky. For the meantime he kept swimming, waiting for the lethal pull of the water, struggling against it as much as he welcomed it.

part four

CHAPTER 29

Hesitantly: Benedikt makes some decisions. He visits his sister
and finds his relationship to her changed

When Benedikt cleared the reeds, his surprise could not have been greater had he walked on the water. He became aware of his breath, dragging, pausing, his arms and legs following the same rhythm. He took no movement for granted; he deliberated each one. He had spent long enough in the suspension created by repetition. Now, each stroke was an answer to a question, and each answer provoked another question: Shall I stay above water for one more stroke? Yes. And again? Yes. And what about now? He was moving forwards. Soon he reached an area where the water seemed thinner, clearer, like mountain air—Marja had been right—and he kept going, sensing as he swam that he had a kind of grace in the water that he did not have on land. The moon placed a halo around his head; he crossed the depths, a modulation of the word 'death,' without any fear. The water grew colder, it washed over and under him, anaesthetizing his skin. As he reached the middle point, where the lake was at its deepest, he felt himself in relation to the lake and the reeds and the water, that he was their equal and all together they made a small part of a whole that he could not know. This equation struck him as inexplicably lovely.

He might have stayed far out in the middle of the water until the calm but insistent hands of fatigue pulled him down, but he did not. His body made the decision for him, paddling back the way he had come, leaving behind the clear water, ploughing back into reeds and the soupy water near the bank. As he pulled himself up on dry land, his body became heavy, graceless again. It had apparently wanted that. He collected his clothes from the grass. Their dryness put them into another category of being. They turned wet and weighed on him, cold and without mercy; his trousers would be violently creased.

He paused to rest between each step and wondered anew whether to continue. The outdoors had patience with him now—it did not hurry or frighten him, the stranger. The sky wore the mild night like a huge old scarf, thinning out here and there and at the edges where light came through.

He crossed the gravel drive and began the slow climb up the steps, first to the front door, fumbling with his key in the dark, then on up the marble entrance stairs. As he opened the door to the hall, he heard faint snoring. He was not surprised by the sound he had always considered the soundtrack of the hall when his grandmother was pursuing her favourite activity. He guessed that he was imagining it. He switched on the chandeliers, but the sudden illumination was uncomfortable as a fever. The snoring was definite. It occurred to him that he might be afraid of finding some version of his grandmother. Then he scoffed. 'I have no more reason to be afraid of her dead than alive,' he announced and went to her room. The bedroom lamp was burning. There was a large fat figure buried in the bed, her face hidden by a book, two hands holding the book in place. He stared at the hands and could not identify them. His grandmother's rings were missing, and the skin was not wrinkled so much as stretched and red. He lifted an edge of the book and saw Bertha.

Should I mind, should I care? he asked, without minding or caring at all. If his grandmother's ghost had not chased the intruder away by now, then she couldn't have minded either. He turned back, through the flagrantly lit hall, leaving a trail of water on the stone floor. Hope that Marja and Valerie were upstairs sleeping began like a question that, receiving no answer, evolved into a statement, and as he reached the corridor, turned into a demand. Inconceivable that this should be refused. He was relieved: somehow, they had managed to find their way back home! From far off, he saw that their door stood ajar, a bad sign. Disappointment drew into his brain; hope expelled it again. He shuffled closer.

At the doorway, he smelled her, a smell so familiar that he closed his eyes for an instant to savour it, turning his head in the direction of the beds. When he opened them again he was shocked to see that the beds were empty. Their grey bedroom slippers stood at the entrance, eloquent as abandoned houses.

He hung on to the brass doorknob to steady himself. Disappointment travelled through a secret system inside he did not know: he could feel it going from his eyes downwards, following the bloodstream, throbbing down into his fingertips and toes.

He let go of the door, he turned away. Hope can be, like silverware in a land of starvation, a petty luxury. He looked into the other rooms, all empty. He checked the way dogs do, sniffing and peering everywhere until he found the von Biesterfelds, each in a single bed placed at opposite ends of the room, guarded by the infantry of Cook's medicines, her battalion of cosmetics shining on the shelf above the sink. The room, like a box, contained the strewn details that made them a couple: books on meditation, on car design, on art; clothes. For ascetics, they had a fair number of possessions. Benedikt stood there for a long time, studying this matter. Then he had a shock. His eyes refocused on the beds. They were empty too.

His legs began to tremble from standing for so long, and he finally continued on to his room, where his own empty bed waited for him. Sleep, he thought, is a journey that I would gladly undertake. But remorse can lurk like a stowaway between the sheets, and once I have cast off, it will come out and frolic.

He had a fit of silent petulance: I won't set foot in this room ever again! Fatigue and despair waged a silent battle and despair came out a clear winner, sending him tottering back downstairs, through the hall, out into the night that gave him a dark hostile welcome, now that he had allied himself with the indoors again.

He got back into his car, drove fast through the countryside, to the outskirts of Lindau. He parked in a street full of glossy cars. He rang the bell of his sister's house. His own tactlessness was completely beside the point to him. Her hunting dog made a big hullabaloo at the door. Benedikt and this creature waited for Dolly, who finally arrived, fearless about opening the door in the middle of the night—she was always fearless but sleep made her reckless. She stood there blinking at him, her sleepiness bandaged by her bathrobe. He blurted that he had lost Marja and Valerie in Switzerland, but she did not seem to comprehend or care.

'Hurry up,' she said, holding the door. As he passed her on the threshold she felt the dampness of his clothes and asked, 'Did you try to walk on water?'

She led him to the guest room on the third floor, without asking him how it had happened; he couldn't have answered anyway. He kept one hand on the wall as he walked in case he fell over, but she didn't notice. She gave him a pair of her husband's oversized pyjamas and showed him to the bathroom, admonishing him to hang his clothes up on a clothesline there, running him a bath, pouring something in that produced choking floral fumes and a dangerous foam.

'Is this where the mouse died?' he asked, remembering.

'What mouse?' She looked puzzled.

'The mouse that prayed.'

'Mice can't pray,' she commented. 'This'll warm you up, and I don't expect you'll have trouble finding your way to your room— it's directly next door.' She did not kiss him; he thought perhaps she was annoyed.

He waited for a few minutes, sitting on the edge of the bath, fully dressed, and listening for the periodic drip of the leaky tap. After a few minutes he slipped out of the bathroom without letting the water run out again, realizing Dolly would scold him for that in the morning, and glad, because it guaranteed conversation; for some reason, he feared he might not see her otherwise. He saw the guest room with dismay, its small narrow bed with a gristly old mattress, the bare, dark plywood wardrobe, a narrow, low armchair, a big television like a huge eye in one corner.

He might have stood there all night wondering whether to lie down, but his knees decided for him, seeming to pitch him downwards on to the bed. He lay there, all the lights in the room on, fully dressed, and waited for sleep. Insomnia, he scolded, is a condition much like waiting on a cold windy corner for someone who doesn't come. He had never waited for anyone. Benedikt, who had practised not sleeping in order to think more clearly, now found himself thinking very clearly indeed about his loss, and therefore yearning for sleep, as a way of forgetting. His clothes had dried on him.

He entrusted himself to his legs again, crept through the house, so strange to him, and so familiar to his sister—that flesh and blood could have such different attachments!—but he found his way to the master bedroom. He was not gentle, he did not hide his intentions, he went straight to his sister, looked at her, sleeping on her side, her hands under her cheek pushing the flesh up to her eyes, her mouth open, her hair in a net, the smell of her eau de cologne. Her husband Hackse Sieseby had his back turned to her. Benedikt put his hand on her shoulder. She opened her eyes, dangerous holes in the darkness, and he said, 'I cannot sleep.' He became aware of his brother-in-law, up on one elbow glaring at him. She turned to her husband, and looked for a sign from him.

Finally her husband sighed. He threw back the blankets, and said, 'Come in, then,' allowing him to crawl like a small child between them. Once there, his sister turned away from him. He lay on his back between them till loneliness, still unappeased, made him double up, pull his legs up to his chin. Something like sobs wracked him briefly, although he did not cry, no, his eyes were dry, he suffered a kind of mental nausea, his desire to get rid of the awful truth: that he was so unhappy.

It was Hackse who turned to him, muttered, 'There there,' took the long thin man into his arms, and rocked him to sleep.

CHAPTER 30

*Singing pain: Benedikt returns to Berlin and tries to
forget his loss by finding another child*

Upon his return to Berlin the next afternoon he found that
the city now consisted of children. He had parked the car
in front of his apartment building, but the idea of returning
empty-handed, alone, so troubled him, that he had turned away
from the front door. He began to walk, taking the familiar path
to the train station, finding that this thoroughfare was occupied
entirely by carriages and strollers, by toddlers guided by hands
overhead, by tired, complaining children forced on wearying
treks to dull, overcrowded shops, children who wore their personalities like bright, crazy clothes, recognizable from a distance.
They took up more space than their bodies allotted, and their
babble, breathless and incomprehensible to him, now drowned
out all other sounds.

High above them, Benedikt heard the adults cajoling, demanding, instructing. The word 'hysterical' rustled in their
mouths, again and again. He and the children did not bother
trying to understand what was meant. After a while the word
took on other contours, became 'historical'; the adults were talking about walls and a football match won a month earlier. With
this one football match in which they had conquered Europe and
parts of Africa and Latin America, they had buried the past, as if
it were a witch that had oppressed them. The present was carrying them towards a future where the witch would never set foot.
The children neither knew about the past nor cared about it.

They found the present such a slow vehicle they could not see it move.

Benedikt soon completed his accustomed circuit but he pressed on, discovering streets he had never seen before. Occasionally, children joined him. The population had changed. These children were older: they trudged with heavy schoolbags locked to their backs that seemed to subdue them. But even so, they came in variations. There were docile children in that age before puberty, when strange ideas of heroism turn them for a short time into well-intentioned beings, older ones, whose faces were complicated maps of their feelings.

He found himself at his own door. He went in. In the entrance he met the five-year-old son of the concierge. He found himself at a loss for communication. The child's young mother had parked him inside the lobby while she foraged for cigarettes. Benedikt wanted the child to accompany him upstairs, go inside with him: it would help. Although—he looked closely—the boy had a pasty simpleton's face, not like Valerie's. This impression would change, he argued with himself, if he had some time with the child. 'Shall I show you some number games?' he asked.

The boy pretended not to hear Benedikt's invitation.

'Come upstairs with me for a minute,' said Benedikt. 'I can show you amazing things.' He took a coin from his pocket and pressed it into the child's rubbery palm. The mailman's shadow appeared, huge on the far side of the glass door. Then he burst in on them, noisy as always. The child looked at him fearfully and his fist tightened on the coin.

The mailman looked at him with mock anger and cried, 'Tonight you go to bed with no shoes on!'

Dismay hung with all its weight on the corners of the child's mouth, and his scream carried one block of the mailman's beat, summoning 'Mami.' Benedikt flinched hearing that word, 'Mami,' he found the word unbearably stupid, laughable; his feelings about the word were red-hot.

She appeared, prompt as a bottled genie, laden with newspaper, cigarettes. 'The lines at the store are getting longer every day,' she said to Benedikt and the mailman. 'Now where did you get that!' She yanked at the boy's hand. She stopped, her hand raised to slap him, and the boy flinched as she snapped, 'So you've been stealing again!'

Benedikt returned to the street. At the corner park, the smaller children pretended they didn't understand his invitation. They shook their heads, looked in another direction, waiting for him to leave.

On the U-Bahn they turned their eyes away bashfully from his stare. At the playground, they ran off or pointed at him, whispering to each other—a pervert. One of them ran home to tell her mother. Another took his telephone money from his special purse to call the police from a pay phone.

He found a gypsy sitting on the pavement rocking a little boy. She was crooning, stretching her hand out to the public in a melodramatic gesture.

An elderly German woman stopped, nudged the gypsy's lap with her heavy black orthopaedic shoe, and began berating the beggar in fury, her Saxon accent strange to most who stopped to listen. The crowd grew. The elderly woman's rhetoric had the jagged edges of incomplete sentences: 'Lazy, ruined your own land, and then come here, locusts, pick everything clean, leave the bare branches for those who planted the fruit trees . . .'

He wondered what Valerie would do if he were this child. And Marja? He imagined Marja laughing and suggesting to the beggar that she should study the classified ads for a dying German looking for a child to adopt. Benedikt found the way his brain kept referring to Marja exhausting.

He carried on, following a current of pedestrians to a fairground. He mingled with a crowd of children who were too old to enjoy the rides without expressing irony or embarrassment. He invited them for a round on the roller coaster. Well, if it was for nothing—they accepted. He bought eight tickets and sat in the middle, surrounded by elongated versions of Valerie, with the same high voices and quick movements. Up at the top, poised to shoot downwards, they squealed like the smallest children. Nausea, like his body's own gravity, pulled all his senses to the middle. He controlled himself till he reached the ground. The children were frightened: a man who excused himself, vomited to the side, wiped his mouth with a handkerchief, and then asked them if they had ever thought about the universe. They refused another round.

He did not realize that he had been walking for five hours without a rest. But no, he did not want to go home empty-handed. He went to a McDonald's and ordered a Coke and fries, sat down carelessly at the nearest table.

The conversation behind him comforted him merely by being close by. 'Jesus, sit with Angel,' a stern voice admonished in English.

'I'd rather kill her!' cried Jesus, a squeaky little boy's voice.

'Celeste, you can share with Joseph and Désirée,' the matron carried on.

'You're too noisy, children!' she cried later. 'You could wake the dead!'

The children were quiet. They looked around, feeling guilty; the tall thin German man at the next table was slumped forwards, his head on his arms, his mouth fallen open, sleeping.

Later, when he woke up and looked around, Benedikt saw the children in the adults. The next table was occupied by little girls of perhaps seventy years who giggled and frolicked with their ice cream. They clamoured together, anxious about insults, talked about their acquisitions, about their neighbours, until a violent argument broke out about the behaviour of one girl who was not present, being in the hospital having her hip repaired. They criticized and scolded each other and as they left they called to each other, 'Until tomorrow, then!'

He sipped his Coke, glancing at a newspaper someone had abandoned at his table, and in the face of the fat politician who claimed to have united Germany, Benedikt recognized the child and forgave him. After a cleaner ran his broom aggressively under Benedikt's feet, he reluctantly left the temporary home McDonald's had provided. He walked behind two little boys, one thin, the other fat, and he overheard them talking and learned that the thin one was rich and the fat one poor. They were cousins. The poor one had come over from the eastern rural part of the country: he had never seen the likes of West Berlin, and waddling along, he exuded intimidation and reserve. And now, said the thin boy, who had a sportive stride, comes the best part. And they disappeared into a sex shop together.

The crowd of black marketeers in front of the central train station was almost impassable. He slowed down, grateful for their company, but his legs were dangerously unstable by now. Fatigue had become his companion. Fatigue brought him home, led him up the stairs, opened the door.

The windows had been shut through the hot months, and the air seemed stiff with dust. The turtle lay in its dried-out moat, its head stretched out on a surprisingly long neck. It had not decomposed but was desiccated, like a laboratory specimen. He left it there. As he lay down on his bed in his clothes for the second night in a row, he smelled something strange close to him. It was a rancid odour that surprised him. He realized it came from his clothes, from his body. But he did not object. The smell was personal.

He felt an awareness of his own perimeters, and of his body passing through time like a boat cutting through water. Somehow the mass of this substance, time, against the smallness of his own existence gave him a sense of his own inconsequence, which some would call loneliness.

CHAPTER 31

An aria: with great expressiveness, including a pinch of irony:
Benedikt searches his body for the source of emotions

I am, for all practical purposes, entirely alone.' From the sofa,
Benedikt addressed a photograph of his grandmother, the dead
turtle, the orchard of dust in his room. 'This is what happens to
someone who lives without any requirements. I hadn't had a
pang of anything in years. Not even hunger. Never gave it a
chance to develop. Sated it. Sated desire, boredom, affection. It's
incredibly comfortable. Like morphine. But if something happens
. . . if someone suddenly appeals to you . . . the discomfort is
awesome. You need help. You behave badly. The others run off,
spraying tears and hurling moral obstacles. You ignore these
things. You have an appointment to keep with fate.

'You arrive. It's the dawn of a new day, as it were. But: no one
there. Not even a letter. What I would do for a letter, the pencil
still lying next to it, warm from her hand, "We don't want you."
At least I'd have the pencil and the words. Is this really the end of
the story?

'I don't know. Some dramas refuse every ending one offers
them.'

Benedikt was lying down, his clothes piled on the floor like
faecal matter deposited by a giant creature on the run. The sun
made a huge yellow puddle on the floor; he had opened the
curtains and the windows. The Trabants were gone, but so was
Club Madamn—it had been bought by a wealthy religious order
based in Cleveland, who opened offices in 'moral crisis areas,' in

order to influence the population. They had kept the bar tables
and served free tea and cookies there, for tired shoppers to rest
their feet while listening to taped sermons and religious music.
On this particular morning the boys' choir from Cleveland was
rehearsing with their choir director. The director liked to say
that children needed nine months to learn a piece—they hatched
it the way their mothers had hatched them. They were learning
the Easter mass now, but the choir director was well pleased
feeling that this piece suited the locale, any time of the church
calendar. Benedikt heard them fussing around, heavy American
accents distorting the text, 'Wiewohl du warst verachtet . . .'

On the back of the couch, against the wall, he had propped
the stamp-sized photograph of his grandmother that he had
inexplicably found in his wallet—had Dolly placed it there, or
Marja? It was the very last photograph taken of her, about
twenty years earlier, when a journey to a funeral in France
seemed imminent and she needed to have her passport renewed.
She ordered the photographer to her bed. The passport required
three-quarters profile but she had refused to turn her head on
the pillow, so the passport was never made, she did not attend
the funeral, but the picture remained, showing her the way she
wanted herself seen by others, from the neck upwards, face fully
there, in full command of her features, in full control of the
photographer and of the hapless viewer of the photograph.

Benedikt took the picture from the couch, held it right up to
his nose, looked it in the eyes, pinching it between his fingers so
that it would pay attention, and begged, 'Dear Grandmother.
Now's your chance to do something for me.' She stared back,
unblinking, uninterested in any changes.

'Grandmother,' he whispered, 'don't let me suffer! Take away
this pain. It was better without it. I should never have met her.
The boy is not even half the problem. Believe me, this pain is
spectacular. Perhaps you don't know these calamitous feelings.'

The Countess did not reply and he felt rebuked, lying there
fully naked in front of her.

'*All Sünd hast du getragen sonst müssten wir verzagen* . . .' sang the boys, giving the text the lilt of a pop song.

He returned the photograph to its place against the wall and sighed, 'If you won't help me, then I will have to help myself.'

He concentrated. 'They've got to be here somewhere. Where do my feelings come from? I want them removed. I have emptied all my pockets and not found them in there. So I have undressed. Somewhere in here! But where? Oh, my toes, do you shelter this unpleasantness, perhaps?'

He was lying flat on his back, his legs draped over the end of the couch. Now his foot, addressed, mysteriously responded. Impaled on the ankle, it suddenly rose into the air, hung there, and he could berate it.

'The big toenail. The enemy? Yellow, corrugated, serrated edges. From wearing handsome shoes. Never put in any complaints about pain. And pleasure?' By bending his knee, he brought his toe within reach of his fingertips. He patted the big toenail. 'No. Therefore a serious candidate for the container of all emotions, as it feels no sensations itself. Coldness and sentimentality go together. But somehow I doubt it.'

He inspected the rest of his toes. 'Warped, all of you. I never noticed before. Tucked up against each other. Huddling in order of size. Perhaps it is the foot that dictates social order, the strongest ones first. That is the law of the foot. The individual toe does not stand out unless you cause him pain.' He flicked his fingers, smacking them, 'Relatively insensitive.' He twisted his foot in the sunlight that came crashing in through the wide open window, over his desk, along the floor, lighting up the wall, so that his raised leg cast a shadow of a leg above the sofa.

'As a shadow, the shape is easier to decipher.' He was put out. 'That's age for you. Your body looks better as a shadow, an outline.' He continued his investigation. 'The ankles?

'The ankles direct the pressure from above downwards, so that one can kick and crush things. So in a sense they give stage directions for all relationships. And the calves? They do not respond to emotions, only to exertion. Emotions are involuntary reflexes.

'What about the skin? Bit of rash on the calves. Rather pretty if you don't know what it is, circular pink spots, with subtle surface ripples. Pores are much uglier.' He lowered his leg carefully. 'Could skin at least be the holder of vanity?

'No. Feelings come from somewhere inside, aroused by something outside.

'It is Marja's surface that I miss. Tight black silk on her head, the skin on her face also very tight, I hadn't noticed how perfect it was. But even those things that weren't perfect at all, the funny way she walked, the way she smoked, I see her inhaling, blowing out the little poisonous cloud, the way she spoke, her accent, it became dear to me, I would like to see it again, hear it, smell it again, more than anything else.

'By simply existing, Marja inflicted a continuous, self-renewing pain that doesn't leave a trace. The perfect torture: she left.

'Marja, come back!!' He touched his patella with his fingertip. 'The kneecap jumps beneath one's hand, but not far. A passive piece that merely registers emotions, in their essential form: it either bears them or it does not bear them, giving up, collapsing. Therefore it cannot be in charge of them. It doesn't even have the healthy malice of the paid servant. All those rumours that the knee contains feelings: unfounded.

'Sometimes I think I am talking like Einstein.'

He looked sideways at his grandmother. 'I guess you wouldn't applaud that, Grandmother. But perhaps you would, too, who knows? Marja was actually your idea. But I have to keep going now.' His finger continued along his left thigh. 'Find the feelings. Tear them out. I'm getting closer now. Warmer.

'Because at the top, right here, a bit of pink and grey and purple flesh, that seems to have extra portions of skin. This lies there, charming, wrinkled, babyish, by all the usual standards: ugly.' He tugged at it, a gesture so familiar he barely knew he was doing it. His tone became annoyed now, sarcastic. 'This piece of anatomy responds passively to the touch, more so than the patella—it behaves about as autonomously as a lock of hair. There was a time when it led its own life, to my annoyance. Even small and passive, it possessed great powers of sensation. That's the trouble.

'That's the trouble. Now I've got it.'

He put on a lecturing, professorial tone.

'The antidote to the feeling of love no doubt lies in the sexual organ. As long as it produced tactile sensations then it negated feelings. My emotions were safe. Absorbed. I can't think of any other explanation: impotence makes one incredibly susceptible to feeling. No wonder so many murderers are said to be impotent. They can't bear the wash of feeling. If my potency were restored, I would feel less. But it's the medicine that made me impotent.

'I welcomed my impotency at first, seeing it as a newfound control of the situation. Now I know how dangerous it is.' He teased himself, but without eliciting any reaction.

'When I close my eyes I can remember Schmidt's willingness to partake of it—he did so with the passion of the zealot. It was an image I disdained. Now I understand Schmidt was just trying to ward off pain, ward off feelings when they slice into the mind. I believe he has no feelings for me at all, either. Somehow that makes me feel close to him again, my friend.'

He entertained his abdomen, a soft, slender area, with a white-and-blond fuzz. 'The torso is an interpreter. It does not invent. And, like all interpreters, it is far too busy to harbour feelings.

'The navel? Is the scar of an old dependency.

'Hands, arms, shoulders—appendages, tools, not containers. I'm getting warmer and warmer. Soon I'll have it.

'My chest. I have never actually looked at my chest before. It did not ask for attention. It is impotent in the man. It cannot give. That makes it a prime candidate.'

He put his hands over his heart, the old dramatic gesture. 'Women can use their breasts. That's why they have no feelings.

'There is a silent noise in my chest. A fearful racket. That sends vibrations into my head. It is getting louder by the minute.'

'*Sehet ihn,*' sang the American children. '*Erbarme dich, o Jesu . . .*'

He stroked his breasts, and found they were highly sensitive—he had never noticed. His fingers went faster and faster over the surface until the nipples became hard. And indeed, the sensation of pain that he could not localize or define, an absence that was crushing, seemed to emanate from his chest, as if he had lost something that he wanted to hold there, to nurture. 'But for heaven's sake, I'm not like a mother who has misplaced her infant.'

And this feeling of loss kept intensifying, carried on waves of impressions that he had not cherished, so that they first acquired their value as memories. These recollections began to speed up, like charged atoms full of mysterious energy, like tarot cards flying through the air, recollections of the figures he had known and loved without knowing it, his grandmother, his sister, various aunts and uncles, maids, cooks and chauffeurs, Valerie, and finally Marja, slipping through rooms, laughing, sleeping, hurrying up, slowing down, existing.

The boys downstairs were beginning at the beginning again: '*O Lamm Gottes, unschuldig . . .*'

A rush of sensitivity to memory, which some would call sorrow, overwhelmed him. His eyes began to burn, his chest began to heave, the corners of his mouth dropped, his forehead creased, and seas of sadness that had been frozen in his eyes suddenly melted, rose, and poured over his face.

CHAPTER 32

*At the tempo fate designates: Benedikt, his friends, and his acquaintances
prove once more that if novelty repeats itself again and again, turning
over like the ingredients of a soup cooking in a pot, then the soup in
the pot must be oblivion, and this proves that novelty is oblivion*

O n the first of September, five people died in Germany of
salmonella poisoning after eating uncooked eggs imported
from Poland. These deaths had a curious history:

Herr Weltecke had fallen on hard times after his business
partner in the restaurant turned himself in for tax fraud. Herr
Weltecke was helping out wherever he could in the restaurant in
order to keep the costs down. The day the lawyer told him that
in fact the restaurant no longer belonged to him but to the state,
so huge were the back payments, Herr Weltecke began spitting
in the soup.

He did not just spit. He blew his nose in it; he had a summer
cold with profuse mucus. He wrote an open letter to his customers which he faxed to the magazines his wife read. It was enti-
tled: 'Confessions of a Restaurant Owner':

> There was spit in your soup. The reader who finds
> this disgusting should stay clear of restaurants for the
> rest of his life. This is nothing compared to what the
> more horny or hard-boiled, not to mention women,
> are capable of. If you are opposed to your dachshund
> licking excrement on the street, well, you are not
> getting anything different in a restaurant.

He was bent on wiping out the restaurant industry single-handedly, taking them all down with him. He signed with the name of his establishment.

Herr Weltecke went about his routine. He did the shopping for his family, bought all sorts of fancy vegetables and a lovely cut of veal. As he was kissing Frau Weltecke goodbye deep into her fat cheek, one hand was fumbling in his pocket to make sure he had the receipt. On his way to work, he stopped at the busy Polish black market and bought eggs, vegetables, and cheap meat, including a slab of ancient veal from a dealer, and he brought this and the shop receipt to the restaurant and began to prepare. He only had a few portions of *Kaltschale* left from the day before. He considered and decided not to make more; it was nearly winter. He spat into everything but the *Kaltschale*, a cold summer soup made of milk and raw egg yolk with icebergs of egg white on top. He intended to eat that himself. The *Kaltschale* was a bit thin. He beat a few egg yolks into it. He could not see or smell that two eggs were contaminated with bacteria.

In southern Germany, the first of September was a cool, dry day. Bertha woke up in a perfectly good mood. The night before she had engaged in a slight nonverbal tiff with Cook about hanging up her clothes in the Countess's dressing room: Cook had come in without knocking, opened the dressing-room door without asking, and glared at Bertha's uniforms hanging there in the apparently eternal cloud of the Countess's old perfume. Bertha planned her revenge. She would correct Cook's housekeeping. She did not feel like getting dressed yet. Instead, she pulled on one of the Countess's robes as a kind of bathrobe. It was too long for her, but nevertheless, clad like that, she tramped into the hall and looked for something to improve. She spotted the tray on the hall table. The Countess's best porcelain, along with the schnitzel platter, was arranged on it. Cook had cleaned out the cabinet where the old china was kept and had set the contents down on the table. She had not put the things back, having had migraine for two days.

'Well, well,' chafed Bertha, 'I'll have to see to it, or it won't get done at all.'

She picked up the tray. The movement of hoisting her arms jarred loose several key pins holding her robe up. Nevertheless, by shuffling, she managed to keep it from catching on her plush bedroom slippers. She began the precarious crossing of the long room. She was halfway across when an edge of the robe tucked beneath her foot, pulling her up short at the front, making her topple, beneath the ancestors! The tray travelled forwards, like a well-directed machine, losing velocity and altitude by gradual harmonious intervals. Bertha herself landed on all fours, watched it whizz away in the slow-motion horror created just for her. The tray approached the stone floor. It touched down, slid along, emitting a metallic shriek, and finally crashed into the wall. The plates lifted up, the platter too. They travelled upwards and then downwards, cracking apart on impact, into fragments, chips, seg-ments—one piece landed on the piano, making it groan. The schnitzel platter bounced along, ringing.

Dust drifted over the destruction. Bertha lay there observing this. She knew what it meant. She didn't panic. She registered, first things first, that her body felt all right. Secondly, that no one had heard. She scrambled to her feet. She ran for her fake alligator bag.

Schmidt was still in bed. He had slept until eleven because it was Saturday and he didn't have to teach. His wife had taken the children to the market to buy fresh vegetables. She didn't believe in buying vegetables from stores. Without the children, the apartment felt abandoned. Once again his mouth felt uncomfort-able, his tongue furry. It must be the heat. Although it had cooled down, pockets of heat remained in the bedroom, in the sheets. It was a relief to get up. He headed for the bathroom. Schmidt, his shaving utensils on the sink in front of him like a surgeon's, faced himself in the mirror and saw that his skin was slightly reddened. He ran his fingertips over it, annoyed at this ugliness. He turned his head and noticed lumps beneath his ears.

His fingers found them soft, the size of the chestnuts his children had brought him yesterday. They seemed to float beneath the skin, he could push them around, and they didn't hurt. How peculiar. He stretched out his tongue. It had a thin layer of white cream on it. His heart began tolling in his chest; he listened like a deaf man. Even as it continued, he carried on with his life. He picked up the shaving cream and lathered his face, with the old-fashioned utensils his wife favoured, and shaved, his fingers shaking with the vibration of the inner gong. He shaved from his ears downwards, taking special care with his upper lip, his chin, with its Cary Grant cranny.

Then he rang Isabella and told her he would be there straight away.

Benedikt was sitting in the middle of the sofa, his hands folded in his lap. The apartment was a mess. He had not thrown the dead turtle away, and he still hadn't changed his clothes; he had nothing to wear, anyway. His own strong smell had seeped into his apartment, which in turn had added its scent to his clothes and hair. He had grown used to it. Then the phone rang.

This ringing affected him viscerally. His heart jumped into a higher frequency of tempo. He was terrified. At the atomic level, the molecular turnover was speeded up, cells being cranked out at a faster rate—skin, hair grew in response to the ring. He pushed himself up on his legs and balanced on them across the room, reaching the telephone. In his imagination all the possibilities took place at once, overlapped. It was the Swiss police, his sister, having found out what he had done, Marja somehow forgiving him, calling from the village to ask his help (he would give it!), the boy (impossible); he lifted the receiver to his ear.

It was Hackse. 'There you are!' he called. 'We have to talk. A religious group has offered five million for the castle. An old people's home is just the thing. The mayor is very pleased, I've already talked to him. There's no institution for old people in Biederstein. The buyer's a Frau Schunter. She's not from a straight religion, it's something Indian, they wear orange, I forget the name. They apparently have a lot of older members.'

Benedikt pouted, 'I don't want an old people's home in there. I want to live there. If not, then I'd like a school there.'

'A school!' cried Hackse. 'An expensive boarding school! A great idea. But I think it's too complicated. Anyway, they sent someone to look at it yesterday, I forgot to tell you last night, and this morning they made an offer it would be ridiculous to turn down. I've already signed a preliminary contract.'

'But the von Biesterfelds are still living there.'

'Frau Schunter told me the whole place is empty. They went back this morning and the front door was open, and no one was home at all. The gardener came at some point and said he had no idea where anyone was. He was looking for the pig. The pig had broken out of the pen. And then Frau Biesterfeld, the cook, showed up in a taxi and said as far as she was concerned, the place should be bombed to smithereens, she just wanted to get some of her personal possessions out first. Don't know what got into her.'

When Hackse hung up the phone, he turned to Dolly and said, 'He's home. He sounds miserable. He'll be grateful to us. But I didn't say anything because it's better if it comes as a surprise.'

The von Biesterfelds had left the night before, in order to pick up Isabella. Cook had shown Chauffeur his perfectly packed suitcase, remarked, 'If you want to throw me away again like an old shoe, you can. But for the meantime, I'm here, doing everything for you.' She would have organized and overseen his breathing function for him if she could. Chauffeur had been too excited to notice her. He had driven with extraordinary speed and dexterity despite the swarm of East German cars that stuffed up the lanes. His long white hands lay lightly on the steering wheel or cupped the gear stick; now and again a difficult manoeuvre required him to grasp the steering wheel, and then the veins in his hands and forearms bulged, rivers of masculinity up his strong arms, and his profile, with the big skull and the rapier nose, offset the hunch of his shoulders, so that Gerda sitting beside him had wept with happiness and admiration.

Alfred von Biesterfeld had decided, telling himself it was a whim, to stay in a pension one street away from the seamstress's atelier. When they had unpacked their bags he suggested to Gerda that she go to a museum while he went to look for Dolly's daughter. Gerda acquiesced, crying a little more that he was being so kind to her. She braided her hair and tied it up in a bun, the way Seamstress wore it in a photo he kept secretly in his wallet. On her way to the subway, she had spotted the seamstress from behind. She was unlocking the door to her atelier. Cook had not gone to the museum. She had gone directly to the airport and had flown to Stuttgart and then taken a taxi all the way home. She had packed her bags. Once, she said to her brother, is enough. He was looking for a new housekeeper anyway. 'I cook everything but schnitzels,' said Gerda. 'And don't ever mention the name Alfred to me and then we'll get along fine.'

The chauffeur had waited until he figured she must be half-way to the museum. Then he had hurried out. He passed the seamstress's atelier, reminding himself that this was quite by accident. He went in, of course. He was extremely agitated. He hadn't seen her in months. She was sitting behind her sewing machine, a small young woman with a blond braid, simple earrings, long simple dress, and a plain face that did not call special attention to itself but once noticed made an impression of friendliness. When she saw him, she smiled bashfully.

Seamstress had a simple heart that loved easily. She viewed life as a fair, with rides and spook houses and games of chance and skill, and she was determined to have a good time. She was married now, to a young, pleasant, suitable man, but she was shocked and glad to see the hunchbacked nobleman, Baron von Biesterfeld. She noted at once his return to shortness, the tight jackets that emphasized his hunch and made it difficult for him to look up to her.

In truth, his face wore fury, because as soon as he saw her, he began recalling all her insults, her intransigence about marrying him. When she saw his dismal expression she laughed and delighted in him for being exactly what he was, a hunchbacked nobleman who could drive. She felt a pleasure at his existence some would call love. She stood up from her sewing machine, put her hands down on his shoulders, and kissed his sallow cheek. There was nothing calculated about it, she did not wonder how he would react, she simply acted: familiarity is one of the hardest habits to break.

He was pleased, pulling away from her with bitter pride. 'I'm a faithful husband,' he said.

She frowned and took a step back, regretting her tender impulse. 'Actually, I'm married now too, I had a big wedding, I thought you heard.'

He was so shocked by this news, as well as by the evidence that she was perfectly happy without him and probably sleeping soundly at night, that his strong hands began to shake, and he pitched his words directly into the old hurtful conversation, which time could not interrupt. 'I am very contented,' he said. 'Very. You can't imagine. Gerda looks after me. I can devote myself to cars. It is a wonderful life now. Gerda loves cars, too. She has such understanding. She has been writing poems. I will send you one. About how we are chained together in eternal love, beautiful words.' When he spoke the name Gerda his mouth felt unwell, as if it were having one of her headaches. And having the girl so near again, remembering the feel of her in his arms, her vitality, her enthusiasm for happiness, her wholehearted love of the primitive activity, sewing, he had felt his misery suddenly rise in him, come retching out of his mouth, how strange and wrong and lonely he felt with Gerda, and he had cried out, 'I'm not happy with her, mind you. But she's happy with me, talks about it nonstop, so what can I do? I was happy with you. But you spoiled everything.'

She had defended herself against the net of old reproaches he could throw over her with just a few words. 'Well, I couldn't help it,' and then his thin lips curled into a smile, he had leaned forwards and looked at her with teasing intensity. She had not drawn away, being afraid to hurt him and respecting what she assumed were his honourable intentions. His ugliness had always seemed proof to her of the goodness of his character. He had taken her silence as confirmation of his powers over her, and relaxed. Finally, he forgot that he was a von Biesterfeld, that she had offended him. He felt instead that she still belonged to him, that he was a normal Man with a normal Woman, just like in the movies. He remembered the out-and-out happiness he had felt with her, and he reached for her, pulled her over to her couch.

She had hoped this would placate him, but afterwards, she knew it had not. Although she'd done her best to please him, which included a show of being pleased herself, he soon remembered: that he hated her. He was still lying with her when his desire to hurt her had inflated again to its original size.

He said, 'I have to go and pick up one of the family girls now and take her home. The city's unhealthy for young women. Although sometimes I think Gerda would be happier in the big city. She would be very happy here, I know. With so much culture. You don't profit from that at all, because it's not important to you. You have no understanding of culture. Or of cuisine. Painting means the colour on the house walls to you. Gerda is so refined.' And once he had set his anger alight it began to burn, and he danced around it with savage joy. Years of contempt for himself, for his deformity, for the humiliation—fully deserved, he feared—of the younger woman's not wanting him, made him murderous.

'You'd sleep with anyone, wouldn't you?' he had said to the seamstress.

After Benedikt hung up the phone he sat on the sofa for a very long time without moving. Now the house was being sold. He had given his word. He imagined the new owners going in and out, calling it their own. He felt a pang of possessiveness. 'It's mine,' he mumbled, amazed at the intensity of this conviction. A queer noise interrupted his reverie.

He listened for a long time, without being able to identify

the sound. After a while, it turned into a pounding at his door. It had been the doorbell.

He was perplexed. Finally it occurred to him: someone was at the door. He obeyed. He opened the door, turning his body to the side automatically. Marja stood there.

She had an expensive suitcase at her side. And Valerie.

His relief took a long time to disengage itself from his despair. Like the very first time they had stood at his door, he did not let them in, until she prompted him.

'We have come back,' she said, 'although you didn't ask.'

And then he stepped aside and waved them in, a carnival taking place in his brain: delight that she was there, terror that she might leave again, charged hope that she was glad to see him, fear that she might rebuke him, that the boy might be cruel. It occurred to him that he should fill the refrigerator with delicacies—Coke and sweets—that this would hold them there. He pleaded, 'You remember where your room is. I'm just going out for a minute. I'll be back shortly.'

He had not eaten anything in two days, and as he reached the store he felt weak with hunger. The food on the shelves seemed ready to topple over on him. Everywhere the threat: cans with glistening sharp edges, two-litre milk bottles that sapped the strength forever from hands attempting to lift them, sausages squirming in their skins, ready to slide down his throat and suffocate him. He managed to acquire bread and milk by rolling them over into his cart. It required great strength to budge it. Nevertheless he kept adding supplies, deliberating over what his family would like—cake and canned ravioli, white bread, Coke, and a box of chocolates. He returned to the street with four plastic bags. As he passed the restaurant where he had eaten with Dr Anhalt, he stopped, considered, and went in.

Schmidt had successfully executed his visit with Isabella: driven rather than hampered by his fear of illness, he managed to affirm his own vitality. He had made love to Isabella the way it's done in the animal kingdom, without complications or tenderness.

Pride in this success made him forget the peculiar feel of his tongue and his glands; he lay with her afterwards in her cheap pension room, enjoying his pride. He was not afraid that she might notice something, realizing instinctively that she would not mind in any case. No, she would be more than happy to put fate in his hands—the more he marked her life, the better.

'I have to go home now,' he said, adding carelessly, 'or I'd have some explaining to do. I don't want to upset my poor wife.'

'No, that would be wrong,' said Isabella, but she wanted him to stay and curled up next to him.

The perfection of her long young body began to annoy him. He was hungry. 'I haven't even eaten breakfast,' he said.

Nor had she, but she said nothing, she was quivering with his sudden annoyance. They dressed hurriedly, and while he stole past the front desk, she passed regally, proud to be with this man. She could not have said why, but it seemed to her the essence of her love that she was willing to humiliate herself for him.

He was worried and irritated that she was accompanying him and when they reached the street he turned to her, gave her a formal peck on the cheek, and said, 'Goodbye.' He looked her in the eyes and added, 'You're wonderful.' He turned away quickly, decisively. She had to go see Dr Anhalt, anyway. Walking home, he envied her that.

At home, he embraced his wife before she had a chance to ask him where he had been and said, 'Let's go for lunch—somewhere really nice.'

In the course of the next two hours, a collection of acquaintances arrived at Herr Weltecke's resturant, as did the same journalist who had interviewed Isabella the day before; that morning he had received the restaurant owner's confession from his editor, along with the assignment to interview the man. And all the diners sat, one after the other, at the very same table, in the very same chairs, without ever seeing each other, and all chose from a menu that included a potentially last supper: the infected *Kaltschale*.

The first to arrive was Isabella. Dr Anhalt had reserved his regular table for the two of them, in a corner, where the other customers did not disturb one. She took a seat and waited. He did not come. She studied the menu without much interest. A soup would be enough.

Soon afterwards, Dr Graf came in. He was shown to the same table in the corner, because his blue jeans would not disturb the public there. He was feeling better, somehow. He was looking forward to the autumn and everyone coming to their senses, including himself. The German Immigration Agency had turned down his application for citizenship, although he had been living there since 1942. The rejection was based on a letter offending Germany's honour that Dr Graf had written to the Agency in 1949; a photocopy of the letter was enclosed. Dr Graf had immediately applied for Hungarian citizenship. Hungary had turned him down too, because he'd been living in Germany since he was fifteen. So stateless it was. It came as a relief, not having to change anything. Isabella's visit had made an impression on him, though. But he wasn't sure what it meant. He was looking forward to seeing her again. He was curious. He looked at the menu. *Kaltschale?*

Then the Schmidts arrived. The family was shown to the same table in the corner because there the children would not disturb the serious diners. Schmidt wanted the *Kaltschale*, but Frau Schmidt said the summer was over now, and cold soups seemed somehow in poor taste.

Benedikt came in, dragging his plastic bags. The smell of unwashed clothes made his neighbours look up suddenly. He appeared dignified, though—the silvery curls on his head made them suspect the smell was somehow a mistake. In fact his face was relaxed, pleased—not the usual expression of someone obviously shopping for a lot of people. He was shown to that same corner table, where other customers wouldn't trip over his bags.

The fortune-teller arrived. She had steered clear of the restaurant since the last time she was there, when she was hustled out after tipping over a table. She did better in the East, where drink was cheaper. But she had come downtown to visit her son, who ran a travel agency. He always gave her a wad of notes just to leave again. He was her next stop. First she needed to use the bathroom. It was at the back of the restaurant. She cased the place on her way there, looking for someone who might want his fortune told.

The photographer who accompanied the journalist was highly amused at this company, all sitting at the same table and never knowing it. He took photos of the coincidence. The photos would unite the wedding guests one more time. The guests could not see each other. They had spun by, without a glimpse, being separated from each other by minutes rather than metres. This proves, he thought, that time is a much more effective barrier than space. Except for us photographers.

Dr Anhalt never did show up at the restaurant. He had tried sending his wife away to visit another relative. She had been reluctant, remembering his shenanigans the last time she had left. But on Saturday she went shopping. He raided the new bottle of tranquillizers. He swallowed forty tablets, with one glass of chilled white wine. He didn't believe in exact repetitions; he left out the part with the note this time. Instead, he took a taxi to the emergency room of the hospital.

He walked in and said, 'I have just swallowed forty ten-milligram tablets of phenobarbital. I am very depressed.'

The attending physician smelled the wine on his breath. He took blood. There were only trace amounts of drug. The physician, studying the patient's records, spotted the recent suicide attempt and the subsequent stay on the psychiatric ward. The patient was lucid, he could walk around the examination room, although he had alcohol on his breath, and insisted that the physician have a good look at his rather dirty tie, which he claimed had belonged to Einstein.

'I took forty tablets!' he kept saying.

The doctor deliberated and decided the patient was just

drunk, there was no use pumping his stomach for alcohol, but he wasn't playing around, he was definitely suicidal; if kept on this ward, he might run off into the night and take more pills.

The doctor had him transferred to the locked ward over at Psychiatry. Dr Anhalt went into a coma there an hour later, when the rest of the phenobarbital worked its way from his stomach into his bloodstream. The attending physician would be charged with professional negligence. Dr Anhalt spared himself some unpleasantness. For one, his panic would have ruined his appetite and chances are he would have had the *Kaltschale* for lunch, which was every bit as toxic as the tranquillizer.

Barring this, he would have found himself in the soup a year later, when those he had informed on informed on him. With a different system in force, he would have lost his job, been socially ostracized, perhaps sent to jail. So, instead, he left his friends alone in the restaurant, deliberating over what to eat, unaware of any danger in their decision.

Dr Anhalt's presence was not missed by Benedikt, who ordered a veal soup, revelled in the taste, in the texture, in the act of gulping and slurping. He wiped out the bowl with a piece of white bread, marvelled at the soft soggy contours of bread in his mouth, dropping the spoon with a clatter back into the soup bowl when he was finished, and sighed with satisfaction. On the way home he stopped at the department store nearby, cut his way through the crowd by swinging his heavy plastic bags into the backs of people's legs, and bought a supply of cheap underwear and shirts and some gaudy pyjamas from a sale counter. He had enjoyed the soup so much that he looked forward to eating again at home.

Dr Anhalt was missed by Isabella, who felt offended, and suddenly, as if this final small embarrassment made her aware of the cost of her adventure, she had a violent seizure of regret. She decided to go home to her parents as quickly as possible. She left the restaurant without paying for her soda water. When she reached the pension she found Chauffeur waiting in the lobby. He had already carried her bags to his Mercedes. She embraced

him ardently, cried, 'Oh I am so glad to see you!' and they both
felt this was a lucky day.

Dr Anhalt was also missed by Dr Graf, who figured the head
of the Institute had invited Isabella to another restaurant that
served veal soup. He sat for a while at the corner table which
Isabella had just vacated. He meditated. He suddenly understood
what her visit had meant to him: it was the first time in more
than a decade that anyone had come to his apartment. It had
been possible. Dr Graf felt grateful to Dr Waller; he had given
him an idea. Dr Graf was beginning to live again. He would stay
on the lookout now for human contact. He would strike up conversations with colleagues at the Institute, he would get to know
his neighbours; perhaps he would even take out an ad in the
classifieds. Why not? Well, why not? He left the restaurant without ordering, narrowly missing the Schmidts as they came in.

The Schmidts had not expected Dr Anhalt and they did not
recognize his usual table. They started arguing about the menu
with the informed hatred common to marital quarrels and civil
wars. Schmidt was dying to have the *Kaltschale*, if only to re-
establish his right to an aesthetic opinion. He remembered
domineering Benedikt Waller, the lessons on the wrongness of
condensed milk in coffee, on the rightness of saying 'croissant'
instead of '*Hörnchen*.' He stopped arguing with his wife. His ugly
rage at Benedikt Waller aged suddenly, metamorphosed into intense affection and longing for his old friend. All the slights
added up to nothing and disappeared. He felt he had wronged
him and could think of nothing else, certainly not the soup question.

'Have your way,' he muttered to his wife. 'I'll have a salad.'

She was shocked by her sudden victory; her husband had
tears in his eyes. The children began to cry, because there were
no *pommes frites* on the menu. They were given *pommes frites* anyway
and were soon hurling *pommes frites* at each other.

The owner of the restaurant, Herr Weltecke, eventually
struck Dr Anhalt's name from the list of reservations. He was
sorry Dr Anhalt had not come, because he had hoped to confide

in him, his loyal client. He had been wondering whether old customers like Anhalt might pitch in to save the establishment. But then Herr Weltecke forgot his woes. The reporter flattered him with his attention and he enjoyed posing for the photographer at the stove with a sad expression he did not feel as long as he was being photographed. When the photographer announced that he had the pictures he needed, and the reporter put his pad away, Herr Weltecke became sad; he was going to miss their company. He wished they would stay.

'Now we'll all eat something,' he said grandly. 'You are my guests. Let's finish the *Kaltschale* together. It is clean, if you know what I mean.' They sat down together at the corner table.

'It's extraordinary!' exclaimed the reporter. He took another portion.

'There's still a little left,' said Herr Weltecke. He hated waste. 'I'll give it to that nuisance with the proviso that she leave afterwards.' He grabbed the fortune-teller as she was just leaving the ladies' room, and when she whined, 'I'm thirsty,' he replied, 'Come on, old girl. Today you have a treat.'

When Benedikt returned he found that his family had made themselves at home. Marja had vacuumed and dusted and made up the beds with the verve of an ordinary housewife; she had even thrown the deceased turtle in the garbage, its plastic housing after it. Now she was unpacking her suitcase in the guest room, hanging up several new suits in the classic style his sister wore. The boy had a new wardrobe of clothes from his cousin. After losing Benedikt on the mountainside, Marja had profited from her son's petty thievery; he had a pocket full of Swiss francs which they used to call Dolly Sieseby to ask her for help. Dolly had hopped into the car and gone to collect them, bullying her way back over the German border without their passports. She had kept them for a day and then packed them off to Berlin. The clothes and the cases were the Countess's donation, as had been the airfare to Berlin, along with a tablet of Valium for Marja, who was terrified of flying. Dr Graf had picked them up. He had volunteered, feeling grudging sympathy for Marja. The boy had grown up in those two days. He had had his hair cut short, and he had seen karate videos at his aunt's house. He looked at the man coming in the guest-room door who called himself his father and he knew better.

'Papa,' he said in his bitingly clear German, 'is coming to rescue us.'

Marja pushed Valerie aside to silence him, and took one of the grocery bags out of Benedikt's hands, and carried this into the tiny kitchen. He followed her there, and they unpacked the bags together, taking care not to bump into each other or even come accidentally into contact. Yet she was friendly, and she made faces of pleasure at each item as it was pulled from the bag, as if it were a present.

When they were finished she said, 'I'll cook. You go and rest.'

He lay down on his bed and dozed until she fetched him. She had opened a can of ravioli, spread bread with butter, and set the table with a bottle of Coke. All three ate with gusto, and between mouthfuls they exchanged civilities.

'It's cooler today,' said Marja.

'Yes, it's September,' said Benedikt.

'In two months it will be autumn,' said Valerie.

'Before then,' said Benedikt.

They washed up the plates together. Marja handed Valerie a dishtowel and told him to help. Valerie refused, held his hands behind his back, harvested a rich Russian scolding, and finally accepted a towel and a plate. He dabbed at the plate for a long time, finally waving it with ostentatious carelessness around the narrow kichen as if to air-dry it, until Marja snatched it from him. He threw the dishtowel on the floor and addressed it, '*Nein nein nein.*'

'He's tired,' Marja said. 'Come to bed.'

When Benedikt had finished drying the dishes he retired to the sofa. From there, he could hear Marja and Valerie bickering in the guest room, a familiar duet. It did not last long. He heard Marja's voice, speaking softly, with the slow cadence of a story told to bore a child to sleep. She did not appear again, and after a while he heard nothing. He figured she had gone to sleep as well. It was late, after all. The day had been an abstraction, the name of a number preserved on millions of documents, statistics, and papers that did not register the events extraordinary to Benedikt Waller. He dozed on the sofa.

He woke up a few hours later when a soft knocking began somewhere, becoming more insistent. Marja had interpreted it before him. She came running out of her room with Valerie following, and while he was still slowly standing up, she opened the door. A large unshaven young man stood there, his tall haggard body vibrating like a plucked string. His red eyes seemed unable to focus, blinking vaguely at Marja, then at Benedikt coming up from behind, finally at Valerie, who ducked behind his mother and peered out from behind the pink bathrobe. The man's gaze kept slipping off in all directions but at last it settled on Marja's face, staying there, gaining in intensity, until she took a step forwards, Valerie clinging and dragging at her, and gave him a peck on each cheek. When she stepped away again, the man's eyes were spilling tears. He wiped them off with a raw hand and turned to Benedikt, ducked his head, saying, 'Golub, Salmon.'

Marja fetched two extra chairs from the other rooms, set them around the living-room table, and Benedikt sat on the sofa with her, while Salmon Golub and Valerie perched on the chairs opposite them. The conversation was in Russian —it seemed to consist of each partner posing and answering questions. At the beginning Marja translated—Salmon was working on a construction site; he was sharing a room with another construction worker from Leningrad, a geologist, it was quite interesting, he knew everything about the composition of the earth in Berlin; he had received a letter from Marja that she had written a few days after he had moved out, telling him that she was going to go and live with a German, enclosing Benedikt's ad and forbidding him to contact her there; a few afternoons ago, he had suddenly been overwhelmed by her presence; he had thought about her all day long, his longing had become like an earthquake shaking and cracking up his brain. Benedikt would have expressed it differently, but he understood exactly what Salmon Golub was talking about.

After Golub had finally persuaded a German colleague to help him find out the telephone number, the number itself had persuaded him to come as quickly as he could, a beautiful number—the date of their marriage—he had not dared to call. Marja translated all this with a shrug of her shoulders, to convey her view that this was nonsense, and then Salmon Golub reached into his fake-leather jacket and pulled out Benedikt's large-print ad and dropped it on the table in front of them. It lay there, a reminder that Benedikt had not known Marja for long. Thereafter, she stopped including Benedikt in the conversation. At one point the Russian man laughed in a low guttural voice, he spoke rapidly and at length, until she started to laugh, too, and could not stop. When she had recovered, she had tears in her eyes and looked very sad.

Any drama inherent in this meeeting was swallowed by a strange atmosphere of propriety. No one knew how to behave; the rules were mysterious; all were dependent in different ways on one another. And then the night asserted itself. Valerie was kissed and petted and ordered to go back to sleep. It happened quickly. The Russian man went with the Russian child and the Russian woman into the guest room and they closed the door behind them.

Benedikt sat on the sofa and absorbed what had happened. And before long, he heard the regular movement of the bed, the thumping on the mattress, softly at first, then more insistent, and he knew that Salmon Golub was making love to his wife, Marja.

Much later, the door to the bedroom opened. Benedikt sat on the sofa and kept his face turned towards the tree. He heard the soft fall of footsteps but did not turn his head to look. Time passed. He became aware of a presence in the room with him.

Valerie moved with the pretty but uncertain step of a child just woken up, came into the entrance hall, and peered at Benedikt on the sofa. When he did not turn to him, Valerie went closer and, after Benedikt still did not respond to the sound of his footsteps, he went straight up to him.

'I'm hungry,' he said.

At this time, the newspapers with their records of the changes in the day were being bound and stacked, sorted and carried to the trucks that would distribute them to every corner of Germany, to the plateau of opinion in the countryside, to the sleek convictions in the cities, and the dark mutinous disappointment in the East. The news that Benedikt Waller's love was not a true love at all would spend a few hours on this earth and then disappear in the dustbin. And the papers predicted: cold today and seasonably cloudy. Yes, the newspapers were right. A cold cloud came in through the open door of Benedikt's balcony, washed over Benedikt's empty desk, and warming itself on the rug, did not proceed to the sofa or to the hall where the boy stood waiting for Benedikt to help him.

Benedikt got up from the sofa, unwinding his long legs, and he said, 'Let's go into the kitchen, and we'll see what we have.' The first-person plural seemed to him of unstable beauty, and all the more precious for it.

The boy followed him into the kitchen. Benedikt found a box of chocolates that Marja had put in the refrigerator. He walked away, opening it, the boy following him back into the living room. Benedikt proffered a chocolate but instead of taking it in his fingers, Valerie opened his mouth, and Benedikt pushed it in, the way he had seen his grandmother do. The boy's blue eyes squinted without the spectacles, tracking the sweet, sure that it was meant for him, pleased. Benedikt teased Valerie, walking backwards away from him; the child smiled and followed, his mouth wide open, until Benedikt had popped another piece in.

'Shall I tell you a story?' he asked. The child nodded.

Benedikt went over to the Christmas tree and turned on the lights. They sat down next to each other on the sofa, leaning way back. The child's legs did not entirely fit on the cushion—his lower legs dangled over the edge.

'Once upon a time,' began Benedikt, 'there was a king who had everything except his health.' He looked down at Valerie, who was staring at the Christmas tree, his eyes reflecting the flickering lights. Benedikt went on, 'And he was really very ill. So he sought in his kingdom for a wise man who could make him feel better again. The wise man came and said, "You need to find the coat of a happy man. If you put that coat on, you will be healthy again."'

The child yawned, and Benedikt looked down at him. Without thinking, he turned towards the boy, slipped his hands under the boy's arms, and lifted him up on his lap. Valerie did not protest. His eyes were half closed. He adjusted his legs, leaned his head against Benedikt's shoulder. The hair smelt like animal fur. His body weighed very little but left the impression of solidity. Benedikt couldn't remember how the story went. He stopped.

The boy kicked his feet and mumbled, 'More!'

He started up again, in a murmur, that soon became a whisper.

'Yes, yes, have patience. It's another story. Once upon a time there was a man who wanted to understand life. And he thought: In order to understand life, you have to understand emptiness—nothingness. So he sat beneath an apple tree, and he emptied his

brain of everything he had ever known. And suddenly blossoms began to drift through the air down on him.

'And the tree spoke, "That was a marvellous truth about emptiness!"

'And of course the man protested, "I didn't say a word about emptiness!"

'But the tree said, "You didn't speak about emptiness, and I didn't hear emptiness. That is the emptiness that's behind life." And the blossoms fell harder and harder till they covered the man up.'

Towards the end of the night, when the body temperature sinks to its lowest point, when most births and most deaths occur, Marja woke up and felt at once that Valerie was gone. She untangled herself from her husband's arms and went out. She found Valerie nestled in Benedikt's lap on the sofa, Benedikt's gaunt head thrown back, propped against the wall, their faces illuminated and darkened by turn in the twinkling lights of the Christmas tree, like so many days and nights passing very quickly. She regarded them for a while. Then she kissed her son on the temple, where the skin is pale, and the veins show, and he is most vulnerable. She hesitated, and then she kissed Benedikt there too.